"There is more to magical tattoos than just show," I said loudly, letting the glowing ball rise slowly over the designs inked in my palms, then jabbing it so it exploded in a thousand fiery sparks that jetted out among the crowd of vampires and shifters, pushing them back a full yard from the edge of the pit. "And more than just function. True magic is beauty incarnate: let me show you."

I swayed my nearly naked body, drawing mana through the vines on my arms, concentrating it into my upraised left wrist so the tattooed gems gleamed, the flowers bloomed, and the butterfly flapped its wings and raised off my wrist into life.

I whispered, "*Fly*," and the butterfly flew on a wind of sparkles and sunshine.

The weretiger squealed and held up her hand, and trailers of magic bounced off her harmlessly. The butterfly settled on her hand, fluttering, and she stared at it with wide eyes, and something closer to delight than fear. It flickered, once more, then lay its wings down and merged with her hand.

"You get one tattoo for free," I said. "More will cost you."

And then I was swarmed with a hundred werewolves, tigers, and stags, pressing around me, all asking what I could do for them—or just trying to get close enough to rub up against my bare, magically inked, skin.

SKINDANCER
THE MAGIC BEGINS

FROST
MOON

ANTHONY
FRANCIS

BELL BRIDGE BOOKS

This is a work of fiction. Names, characters, places and incidents are either the products of the author's imagination or are used fictitiously. Any resemblance to actual persons (living or dead,) events or locations is entirely coincidental.

Bell Bridge Books
PO BOX 30921
Memphis, TN 38130
ISBN: 978-0-9843256-8-9

Bell Bridge Books is an Imprint of BelleBooks, Inc.

Copyright © 2010 by Anthony Francis

Printed and bound in the United States of America.

All rights reserved. No part of this book may be reproduced in any form or by any electronic or mechanical means, including information storage and retrieval systems, without permission in writing from the publisher, except by a reviewer, who may quote brief passages in a review.

We at BelleBooks enjoy hearing from readers. You can contact us at the address above or at BelleBooks@BelleBooks.com

Visit our websites – www.BelleBooks.com and www.BellBridgeBooks.com.

10 9 8 7 6 5 4 3 2

Cover design: Debra Dixon
Interior design: Hank Smith
Photo credits: woman - © Stanislav Perov | Dreamstime.com
                  Landscape © Michel Mota Da Cruz | Dreamstime.com
                  dragon © Jaguarwoman Designs

:Lw:01:

Dedication

To Isaac, who inspired me to write
To Richard, who taught me to think
To Sandi, who reminds me to dream

1. DAKOTA FROST

I first started wearing a Mohawk to repel low-lifes—barflies, vampires, Republicans, and so on—but when I found my true profession my hairstyle turned into an ad. People's eyes are drawn by it—no longer a true Mohawk, but a big, unruly *deathhawk*—a stripe of feathered black, purple and white streaks climbing down the center of my head—but their gazes linger on the tattoos, which start as tribal vines in the shaved spaces on either side of the 'hawk, and then cascade down my throat to my shoulders, flowering into roses and jewels and butterflies.

Their colors are so vivid, their details so sharp many people mistake them for body paint, or assume that they can't have been done in the States. *Yes, they're real; no, they're not Japanese—they're all, with a few exceptions, done by my own hand, right here in Atlanta at the Rogue Unicorn in Little Five Points. Drop by—I'll ink you. Ask for Dakota Frost.*

To attract the more . . . perceptive . . . eye, I started wearing a sleeveless, ankle-length leather coat-vest that shows off the intricate designs on my arms, and a cutoff top and low-rider jeans that show off a tribal yin-yang symbol on my midriff. Tying it all together is the black tail of something big, curling up the left side of my neck, looping around the yin-yang, and arcing through the leaves on my right shoulder. Most people think it's the tail of a dragon, and they wouldn't be wrong; in case anyone misses the point, I even have the design sewn into the back of a few of my vests.

Those who live on the edge might notice a little more detail: magical runes woven into the tribal designs, working charms woven into the flowers, and, if you look real close at the tail of the dragon, the slow movement of a symbolic familiar. *Yes, it did move; and yes, that's real magic. Drop by the Rogue Unicorn—you're still asking for the one-and-only Dakota Frost, the best magical tattooist in the Southeast.*

The *downside* to being a walking ad, of course, is that some of the folks you want to attract start to see *you* as a scary low-life. We all know that vampires can turn out to be quite decent folk, but so can clean-cut young Republicans looking for their first tattoo to impress their tree-hugger girlfriends. As for barflies, well, they're still barflies; but unfortunately I find the more tats I show the greater the chance that the cops will throw *me* into the back of the van, too, if a bar fight breaks out.

So I couldn't help being nervous as two officers marched me into City Hall East.

City Hall East is in the old Sears building on Ponce de Leon, a great brick fortress squeezed between the empty parking lot that used to serve the Masquerade dance club and the full one that serves the Borders bookstore. Once it buzzed with activity, but now, in 2006, it's like a tomb, soon to be demolished and turned into yet another mixed-use development as part of the new Belt Line project. Even the snack shop has closed. This is the last year of the grand old building's spooky incarnation as a kind of lonely government outpost. All that's left here are a few Atlanta Police Department offices, more offices for the Feds, and some for permits and land planning.

And *lots* of police officers, more than I expected for that time of night, most of them scowling. Lots of them, muttering: *Look at her? What's she in for? Is she a stripper? If she's under arrest, why isn't she cuffed?* The two officers escorting me—one black, one white, both wearing identical buzz cuts—had no answers, for them, or for me. Just: *The police need to see you, Miss Frost. No, you're not under arrest, but it is urgent. Please come with us.*

Our footsteps echoed hollowly as we walked through a canyon of white tile and glass walls towards the metal detectors. There had briefly been a gallery and shops on this floor, but now empty offices surrounded us like cages, only a few showing signs of life.

We paused before the metal detectors, where a fat female officer sat, right hand pumping on her mouse in what could only be Minesweeper. "Anything to declare, Miss Frost?" she asked.

"Frost?" Beyond the barrier, a sharply dressed, Kojak-bald black plainclothes officer perked up at the sound of my name: Andre Rand, my dad's best friend. "Dakota Frost?"

"No, I've nothing to declare," I said, trying to ignore him as he stalked briskly towards me. The woman waved me in, and I swept through the metal detector just in time for him to corner me. I sighed, folded my arms, and stared down at the black man. He was tall, but I was taller. Wonderful. He'd known I was coming—and probably engineered this whole thing.

"Dakota," he said, voice forced cheeriness, sparkling eyes genuine. He was twice my age—I'd bounced on his knee when he and my father had been partners—but he was still a fashion plate, if you go in for the whole GQ look. "Your dad will be glad to hear you're doing well—"

"Hey, Rand," I said, smiling, shaking my head—half at his infectious grin and half at whatever he was planning. "Let's get this over with. Where is he, and when did he get in? You know, I do have a cell phone. He could call me. There's no need for the goon squad—"

Rand's face fell. "I—your dad's not here, Dakota. We needed to see you."

"We?" I asked.

Rand's face went stony, blank. "Homicide, Dakota. Homicide needs to see you."

We got in the elevator and Rand punched the sixth floor, motioning to me to join him in the back. The officers—big men, almost my height—stepped in front of me, making me feel even more like a prisoner . . . or perhaps someone being guarded? But the guard theory evaporated when a sandy-haired older man slipped past the officers and joined us in the back of the elevator, leering at me and nodding to Rand.

"Hey, you old cockroach," he said. After a moment his eyes slid to me, my tattooed arms, and my bare midriff, then forward to the officers. "Forgot to pay your fees?" he leered.

"What the fuck?" I asked.

"Miss Frost isn't here for floor five, Jack," Rand said. "She's working with me."

"Well lucky you," the man said, slapping his shoulder. He caught my pissed-off, puzzled look and shrugged, with the conspiratorial leer suppressed but still trying to peek out. "Floor five is where you get your stripper license."

"And fuck you too," I said.

"We don't license for that," Rand said, deadpan.

"I'm just saying, girl, you could do the job if you wanted."

"Which one?" one of the officers said, and the other one chuckled.

"Floor five is *also* where you get your license to do magical tattoos," I snapped, "which always *sounds* funny until you wake up with a working asshole tattooed on your forehead."

Suddenly the cab got quiet. The two officers stiffened up, and Rand jammed his hands into his pockets and leaned against the back wall of the cab. He was trying to look pissed, but he looked so hot he came off more as a brooding GQ model.

But the sandy-haired Jack was staring at the officers, suddenly serious. "Cut the boys a little slack," he warned me. "Things are crazy. You don't want to go to jail tonight, do you?"

"Kind of feels like it," I said.

"Nobody's going to jail tonight, unless it's you, *Jack*," Rand said.

"Already been," Jack replied, not the least bit perturbed. "Second time this week—"

"Oh, no," Rand said. "Don't tell me your boys messed up bookings—"

"Nope," Jack said, grinning, "one of *your* boys tripped a power cord. *Again*."

"Jeezus," I said, abruptly hot under the collar. One of the only college jobs I'd enjoyed had been lab tech, and I couldn't *stand* people who fucked up my computers. "You should set up a webcam to find out who's doing it."

Jack blinked at me. Then smiled and said, "Not a bad idea, for a girl."

And *just* when I was starting to warm up to him. "Blow me, you old cockroach."

The doors opened, and Jack just grinned. "Not a bad idea either." Jack strolled out to the right and began beeping a door's keypad, and we followed.

Once again our footsteps echoed hollowly down a long, narrow corridor. On the left were conference rooms and APD offices, but on the right was a long wall of tinted glass with a Fed-smelling seal engraved on it. Behind one window I saw a figure standing; as I drew closer I saw dark sunglasses and a devilish goatee. Sunglasses, at night. *Come on.*

We paused before another keycoded door, and I became acutely aware that the man behind the glass was checking me out, staring at me, sipping his government coffee. Finally, I looked over and saw a trim form inside a crisp black suit. He was looking straight back at me, raising his cup towards me in salute, his smile not a leer but . . . appreciation?

Jack opened the door with a *beep beep beep*, strolled in and disappeared into a warren of ratty old cubicles. We followed him through, and the door closed behind us. I looked back at the big, knobbly lock. I was sure you could get out without the code, but . . . it still slowly swung shut with a solid *click*, and I felt trapped.

In moments I was in a plain white "evidence" room, looking down on a salt-and-pepper haired, Greek-looking officer improbably named Vincent Balducci, seated at a large table in front of a large manila folder. There was a side door to the right, and a huge mirror dominated the rest of the wall. If you squinted you could just see the blinking light of a camera, or maybe a video recorder, and I felt the invisible presence of a dark figure somewhere behind the glass. Maybe I was imagining it, but, come on, I've seen this movie before.

"Taller than I expected, Miss Frost," Balducci said, not moving to greet me as I sat down. My long leather vestcoat *shhhed* against the tile as I settled into the chair, but after that, the only noise was the hum of the air conditioning.

Rand was seated at the edge of the table, naturally, easily, like an Armani model dressed on a police officer's salary, but losing none of the class. Finally he seemed to lose patience with Balducci and said, "Show her."

"This is pointless," Balducci said. "She can't tell us anything that—"

"Chickening out?" Abruptly Rand flipped the manila folder open and turned it towards me, then stood and staring at the glass. "What can you tell us about this?"

Curious, I stared at the picture: it was a bad photocopy of a circular design, some kind of braided wreath with a chain and a snake eating its own tail. Big black blotches covered the upper quarter of the design, but after a moment I puzzled out what I was looking at. "This is flash," I said. At Balducci's puzzled look, I explained: "A tattoo design, or a part of one."

Balducci nodded dismissively. "Told you," he said to Rand.

"And?" Rand asked.

"And . . . you need to tone the contrast down on your copier?" I said. It was half blotted out . . . but then I realized it wasn't a photocopy, but some kind of printout of an image, posterized to the point that it was almost illegible, with large-brush black blotches of a digital pen redacting some of the details. But it still had that distinctive natural look that meant it had started life as a photograph, not a drawing.

"This isn't flash," I said. "It's an actual tattoo."

"Told *you*," Rand said.

As my eyes studied it I became suspicious. The reproduction was terrible, but something about the wreath and chain had the flavor of a magical glyph. What if it *was* magical? These mundanes would have no way of knowing. But how could I tell from this printout? "Do you have a better picture? No—a *different* picture?"

Balducci sighed, and slipped another piece of paper out of the folder. A similar shot, similarly degraded, but . . . I put the two next to each other and planted my hands on the table, staring down upon them. After a moment I saw it: the head of a snake in the design was three links past the belt of the chain in one, and five in the next. It was moving.

"This is magical," I said. "This tattoo is moving. It's a magical mark."

"*Told* you," Rand said triumphantly.

"Holy—" Balducci breathed. I looked up, and saw him not looking at the flash, but at my hands. "Hers are doing it too. I swear the fucking butterfly *flapped*."

"What, did you think they only moved *after*?" Rand asked.

"What do you mean, after?" I asked. No one said anything, and my stomach suddenly clenched up. "What do you mean, *after*? You don't mean, like, after death—"

"I can't discuss the details of an ongoing investigation," Balducci said.

"Why did we bring her here if not to discuss it?" Rand said.

"It was *your* idea," Balducci said. "She's your old partner's daughter—"

The side door opened.

The dark-suited Fed I had seen in the hall walked out. His crisp goatee and short wavy hair made him look more like an evil Johnny Depp than a laid-back agent Mulder. One hand was in his pocket, the other still holding the cup of coffee. In his dextrous fingers, the Styrofoam cup looked like alabaster.

"Show her," he said, with unassuming authority. "Or quit wasting our time."

Balducci looked up, at a loss. "You've got 'it,'" he said.

The Fed just looked at me, mouth quirking into a smile, at which point Balducci touched his head in a "senior moment" gesture, then hit the intercom. "Rogers," he said. "You got 'it'? Yeah. Bring 'it.'"

After a moment, a tall, drawn man stepped out of a back door I hadn't noticed, gingerly holding a large, white plastic envelope with the same Fed logo on it. The cadaverous man paused in the white light of the doorway for a moment, eyes twitching as he saw me—not unfriendly, but . . . in pity? Then I noticed a long plastic tray in the man's other hand, and saw the padded envelope bulging with something.

I suddenly didn't want to see 'it.'

The Fed touched his left ear for a moment, then turned to go. "Aren't you going to stay?" I asked nervously. I wasn't quite sure why I was asking *him* for reassurance, but there it was.

He paused. "I've seen 'it,'" he said, and stepped into the blackness.

The tray clattered against the table, shockingly close to my hands, and Balducci and I both leaned back a little. The evidence technician, if that's what cadaver man was, put on a pair of blue gloves before opening the envelope and withdrawing a smaller, plastic-wrapped object. "Even though it is wrapped," he said, putting it in the tray, "it would help if you do not touch 'it.'"

My skin grew cold.

'It' was a ripped piece of human skin pinned to a stained wood board.

2. GOD'S FINEST CANVAS

I stared in horror at the scrap of human skin, stretched across the board like so much canvas. The braided wreath curved across the flesh, marred by a few small cuts that had been blacked out on the print copy. On most sides the skin curved over the board, but at the upper left, the skin was torn away, revealing both the bloodstained wood and a set of torn holes in the skin that indicated it had been stapled underneath, like a leather seat cushion.

Without another nod to Balducci, Rand took over, channeling Joe Friday.

"Do you know what this is?"

"It's a tattoo," I said, unable to take my eyes off it.

"Do you know what it means?"

"It's a . . . magical ward."

"To protect against evil spirits?"

"No, it's . . . like a capacitor. It collects, or deflects, magical power," I said. "Which depends on the intent of the wearer."

"Do you know who inked this?"

I'd have to look closer at the design to tell that. I really didn't want to do that. I looked up at Rand, eyes pleading. His face had gone cold, a bit stony; not unfriendly, but all cop. I leaned forward, looked through the clear plastic bag, at the wreath, the inking. The board exposed through the rip was smoothly polished and finely worked, despite the bloodstains. Suddenly I knew.

"Yes, I know the artist," I said. "Not, I mean, personally. It's Richard Sumner."

"Do you know where he is?"

"Buried in Cincinnati," I said. "Sumner was famous, but he died in . . . 2005, I think?"

"Hell," Balducci said. "*That* rules out a suspect—"

"Do you know who this was inked on?" Rand asked.

"No," I said, closing my eyes at last. That piece of skin had come from a living human person. I'd *really* been trying not to think of that. My mind cast around for *anything* else. "Sumner did thousands of people. You could email the *Lancing Dragon* in Cincinnati, though. Sumner took extensive pictures. They're stored there."

Rand smiled. "We'll do that." His smile faded. "Do you know of anyone who had a grudge against Sumner, or against any of his subjects?"

"No," I said. "I mean, I don't know anyone who has a grudge against *anyone*—"

"Really?" Rand said. "What about against other tattoo artists? Especially magical ones?"

"According to our newsletter," I said sarcastically, " 'there are over two hundred licensed magical tattoo artists in the United States,' so it's a pretty big list—"

"Could we get a copy of that newsletter?" Rand asked.

I thought about it for a moment. "Yes."

"Is there anything you would like to add?" Rand said.

"Yes," I said, nodding at the skin-covered board. "I would like to add a *what the fuck is that thing?*"

"Tell her about the box," Balducci said.

"What about the box?" I said, eyes drawn back to the thing on the table.

"We had a witness," cadaver man said. "He didn't live long enough to tell us much, but he mentioned . . . a box. A box covered in scraps of tattooed skin—"

"Don't tell me more about the box," I said, getting up. "Oh, God, it's a fucking *lid*—"

"Dakota," Rand said, motioning to cadaver man. "You don't need to stay any longer, Dakota, though our friend the Fed there may have more questions for you later—"

"Why did you bring me here?" I said, watching cadaver man slip . . . *it* . . . back into its opaque envelope. "Is this some kind of cruel joke, some kind of arrangement with my dad to get me to come home—"

"Dakota," Rand said. "I didn't lie. We *did* need to see you, and not just for your expertise—"

"Rand," Balducci warned. "She's just a civilian. And just a kid—"

"She's got to know," Rand said, staring up at me with the same sad eyes I remembered looking up to as a child. "Dakota, this just fell in our lap, but our 'friends' tell us they have had a dozen killings over the past five years where magical tattoos were taken, almost always on or near the full moon, moving from state to state each time. This last one was in Birmingham, and our 'friends' tell us all the signs point to an attack here in Georgia . . . soon."

"And the full moon is next weekend," I said. "Just after Halloween."

"So you see, Dakota, I needed to talk to you," Rand said. "We don't think you're a specific target but . . . Kotie, stay safe. Your Dad and I are very worried about you."

My childhood nickname rang in my ears as I watched cadaver man carry 'it' back through the door of white light.

"That makes three of us," I said.

I said my goodbyes to Rand and then got the hell out, escorted by the black-and white twin officers who'd picked me up. Tweedle-White and Tweedle-Black turned out to be Horscht and Gibbs, old buddies of Rand's, who were doing him a favor by scooping me.

Gibbs was a sexy beast, like a younger version of Rand himself, but after staying for the show with the lid, Horscht turned from stony Aryan Nazi to protective den mother. After some arguing, they agreed to take me back to Mary's to pick up my Vespa. But as we started to pull out of City Hall East's garage the colorful lights across the street gave me a better idea.

"Wait," I said. "Drop me at the Borders."

"Are you sure?" Horscht said. "It's a long way to East Atlanta."

"It's . . . nine fifty-five," I said. "I can take care of myself in a brightly lit commercial fortress, and call on a fare-slave to cab me back to Mary's for my Vespa. I never leave before midnight, anyway."

"But after seeing that—"

"The full moon is like, ten days away," I said, with false bravado. "I'm not worried."

"The lady can take care of herself," Gibbs said, smiling. "Anything else we can do?"

"Sure thing," I said. "Next time you give me a ride, I want to do it in cuffs."

Horscht was befuddled, but Gibbs whistled low. "Sure thing, girl."

"But if she hasn't done anything wrong—"

"Damn, Horscht, you never got a Sunday morning call?" Gibbs said, punching my raised fist gently. "I'll explain it to you later. You're all right, girl. Later."

I started sniffing around the bookstore for something on Richard Sumners. It was hopeless—I hate bookstores and this one was a brightly lit warren. I ferreted around their computer kiosk for a minute, browsing for any of the books I knew: *The Craft of Ink*—no. *Flash, Ink, Flash*—out of print. Anything by Richard Sumners—yes! One, titled *Richard Sumners*, three in store, shelved improbably in *Art & Architecture | Photography | Photography Monographs*, where I had absolutely no luck. Finally I collared a pimply-faced teen manning the Customer Service kiosk, whose end-of-day funk brightened considerably as soon as he saw my breasts.

"Oh, yes, *that*," he said, staring straight at the bulge in my top. In fairness, my breasts were about level with his head, and he seemed scared to make eye contact. "Right over here."

In Bargain Books: *Richard Sumners* by TASCHEN – $7.99. Right between *Sicily in Pictures* and *More Amazing Kittens!* I wanted to pop a blood vessel, but just stood there, seeing Sumners's life work end up in a bargain rack. Finally I picked it up, thick little brick, thumbing its thin but curiously heavy pages.

"At least it's selling," I said.

"Anything else?" he asked, eyeing my breasts again.

"You got an almanac for 2005?" I asked, but he shook his head.

As I turned to go, finally his eyes darted upward. "*That*," he said, "is one cool-ass shirt."

I looked down. Edgar Allen Poe stared upside-down at me between the lapels of my coat-vest. I'd sewn glitter and sequins onto the shirt to jazz it up, and his sparkling eyes had ridden up over the ridge of my breasts. "Thanks," I said, but by that point the kid had fled.

I grabbed a maple mocha and camped out in the café. There in the *ghetto library*, as we affectionately called it, I started flipping through this glossy tombstone to Richard Sumners's work, looking for clues to who might have worn the tattoo.

Richard's magical inking began before I was born, back in the 60's, but the wreathed snake had a modern flair to its design. I started to see some of the distinctive elements that made up the tattoo crop up in THE EARLY NINETIES section, but it wasn't until EVE OF THE MILLENNIUM that I hit paydirt.

At first I thought I had it: a man covering his eye with a tattooed hand bearing a mark nearly identical to the one on the lid. But it was too small, and I remembered Sumner didn't design his own flash: he had graphomancers do that for him, just like I did, which meant he ended up reusing the same design. Sure enough, there were three other people with similar tattoos, ending with a full-page shot of a young woman with the mark just above her breasts.

The tat was close—really close: the same size, on a flat piece of skin, sans belly button or the curve of a shoulder that would have shown up as a wrinkle on the lid. I stared at her – she had sharp, punkish hair like I did, and a sexy, come-hither smile. Automatically, I checked out the curves of her breasts, pressed beneath one delicate hand—they were full and luscious and looked quite lickable. Then my eyes drifted up to the tat, and I felt queasy. Had I just seen this woman in the flesh—flesh torn from her chest and stapled to a board like a seat cushion?

There was no way to know. I'd give the book to Rand at the first opportunity and hope he could find out. But then I started thinking: Sumners was tattooed himself, and some of those tats had to be marks of great magical power.

I flipped to the bio, trying to find out a clue about how he died, but it was no help. It had been printed in 2003, and the most interesting piece of information was that Sumners had 'recently had his hands insured with Lloyd's of London for over a million dollars.' Useless.

I'd originally gotten the book to try to find out who had worn that tattoo. But now here was a new question: did Sumners die near a full moon?

And then a creepy voice breathed in my ear: "Give me some skin, Dakota."

∽——

3. ENTER THE RAT

"Jeez!" I cried, recoiling from the foul-smelling breath behind the voice, splattering my mocha across the table. "Spleen, don't do that!"

Life had cursed Diego "Spleen" Spillane to look like a rat—long, pointed nose, thick, scattered, grey-brown hair, and one yellowed, fake eye. Generally he played above type. Today he was full of himself, and apparently couldn't resist working it.

"Come on," he said, curling his head around my shoulder, breath foul. "Be a sport."

And then I saw his hand hovering over the table, held out for five. "Garlic," I snapped, grabbing his hand and pulling him round to deposit him in the opposite seat, nearly losing the rest of my mocha when I brushed it again. "Don't be such a fucking sneak—"

"Cops give you crap?" he said, grinning.

"No—how did you know—wait, how *the fuck* did you find me?"

"Mary's," he said. "I showed up just in time to see ya snatched. You weren't in cuffs—"

"I tried," I said, but Spleen didn't take the bait.

"—so I figured you were all right, but I tailed them anyway, figuring—"

"What do you have for me that couldn't wait?" I leaned back and looked at the ceiling. "I keep telling you, no one needs an emergency tattoo—"

"Ah," Spleen said, suddenly knowing. "But this time you're wrong." He got up and held his hand out to me. "Let me take you on a little trip."

I got up from the table. "This is a bad idea." I started to leave the mocha and the book. Then I stopped, and looked down at the book, stained on one corner where I'd splattered it. The ghetto library had given me what I wanted; but I wasn't a college dropout anymore. In a good year I made over fifty thousand dollars tattooing. And besides, it was a clearance book, probably about to go out of print; I'd be a butt if I pointed Rand or the Fed to it and it turned up gone.

"Just let me pay for this," I said.

"Need it for *reee*-search," Spleen said, "or just wanking?"

I glared at him. "What do I 'wank,' Spleen?"

"Anything that moves," he responded.

"*You're* moving," I pointed out.

"Touchy," he said, though it sounded like he meant *touché.* "Let's tango."

We tore south on Moreland at what felt like two hundred miles an hour in Spleen's battered old Festiva, though we couldn't really have been doing over forty. He'd bought the car off of me, well-used, five years ago and had not treated it well. The engine squealed like a worn-out carnival ride. At one point we hit a tiny bump and my hair scrunched against the roof.

"Spleen!" I said. "Thought of new shocks?"

"Shocks?" he said. "Just another mechanic's scam—"

We bumped on, getting a brief panorama of downtown Atlanta as we crested Freedom Parkway. I stared over at the glittering spires, glowing with fairybook promise denied to those of us who lived across the canyon of the Downtown Connector. Somewhere in there was the real Five Points, financial heart of Atlanta, but the view was quickly cut off by the King Center. We kept going, and I kept staring to the right, as if by keeping my eyes turned away, to the city, to the King Center, to John Hope Elementary, oh hey, look, there's Javaology—that I would not notice when we crossed Auburn Avenue.

"Thinking about her?" Spleen said, suddenly serious.

"No," I said. "We split two years ago, Spleen—"

"Never too late to catch up on old times," he responded, livening up a bit. "I could whip it back around, take a little detour down Auburn to Old Wheat—"

"You do, I get out and roll."

"This is the vampire district," he reminded me. "Nasty to have a scrape—"

"I don't care. And I thought you said this was an emergency?"

"I'm not saying we should stop, just, it's not out of our way—"

"If you really cared about making time you'd have taken Glenn Iris—" and I suddenly drew a breath. Glenn Iris turned into Randolph—

"That would have taken you right past her front door, dipshit." Spleen said, scowling again. "Give me a little credit. I was just needling you."

True to his word, he kept driving, taking us onward, south of Auburn, south of Decatur and the tracks, growing perilously close to the foggy, haunted tombs of Oakland Cemetery—Margaret Mitchell, Bobby Jones, Reb and Union soldiers from the Battle of Atlanta—before finally hooking round the Mill Lofts back up north into Cabbagetown.

"I thought you said we were going to the Krog Street Tunnel—"

"Not Krog Street, babe," Spleen said. "Just Krog. The Krog Tunnel—"

"Oh, hell," I muttered. "The Underground."

To most locals, "the Underground" means "Underground Atlanta"—a subterranean tourist trap downtown near Five Points, reclaimed from turn-of-the-last-century storefronts that had been covered over by modern streets and buildings, rediscovered in the 60's. An ordinary historian might know that *before* then, "the Underground" referred to the Atlanta sewer system. But ask an *Edgeworlder* . . . and they'll tell you that the *real* Underground is a series of tunnels beneath Atlanta, covered over by the Confederates just prior to the burning of the city, and forgotten to the wider world since the Civil War.

Spleen parked on a side street off Wylie and led me through someone's back yard downstairs to an ancient, crumbled well, half hidden in the curve of the slope by a newer upper room held up by rusted pipes. Scattered around were magical tags—wards and wayfinders scribbled on walls with chalk or spray paint. The magical Edgeworld was alive, here.

Something fragile crunched under my boots when I stepped back to let Spleen lift the grating, and I scowled. I didn't want to look down to see whether they were crack bottles or blood vials. I'd thought this area was coming back—I often ate a block or two away at the Carroll Street Café—but it's amazing what even an Edgeworlder like me can miss.

We climbed down a rusted steel ladder about one floor before stepping off into a damp tunnel. The air was foul, and the floor was piled with garbage. I heard the rustle of something moving and, in the distance, the clink of a bottle falling to the stones. Spleen looked off sharply into the darker part of the tunnel, eyes narrow; I saw nothing, not even a rat, but after a brief moment Spleen saluted the darkness, then turned his back on it and marched on.

The garbage trailed off quickly as the tunnel brightened. This part looked new, with utilitarian lights that were part of the actual sewer system, but with tags hidden in corners and on sills that marked this as the border of the Underground. We went north for maybe a quarter mile until we could hear the squeal of a train overhead, and then Spleen pried open a dingy, metal door and gestured down a dirt-encrusted, well-warded stairwell.

"After you, my dear," he said.

"Fuck that," I said.

"I'm just messin with ya," he said, and led the way down.

Here, there was no light other than a dim, yellow, fluorescent wand he carried as he stumbled down worn steps. The stairwell switchbacked through a grim, cinderblock shaft—one flight, two flights, three flights, four: by my count, three stories beneath the streets, maybe more. The door doubled back the way we came, revealing a wider, vaulted tunnel, paralleling the one above us, filled with still, black water. A rowboat floated in the bile, waiting.

"You have to be kidding," I said, as Spleen got in the boat.

"The old Confederate runoff tunnel," he said, looking down into the water. "Or maybe a secret train tunnel that got flooded. Everyone who knows . . . is *looong* dead."

"Let's get this over with," I said, getting in behind him grumpily.

"Ready? Ready. Ready!" Spleen said, pushing off and clambering forward to grab the oars. "You sit yourself back and enjoy the ride."

"Whatever you say, Spleen," I sighed.

The bastard grinned, and then started singing.

"We're off to see the werewolf," he warbled terribly, and my blood grew cold. "The wonderful werewolf of Krog. He is the were the wonderful were—"

"The full moon is like, ten days away," I muttered. "No, I'm not *at all* worried."

4. ENTER THE WOLF

At night you can't see the color of my tattoos—unless I want you to. The darkness robs the blue from the scales of the dragon, the red from the feathers of the eagle, and the gold from the wings of the butterfly, leaving a black pattern of tribal runes like columns of hieroglyphics.

They're mesmerizing—at least I *hoped* that's why the werewolf stared at me so intently with his gleaming eyes. Oh, he looked human, even handsome, crouched on the dock under the yellowed lantern light, but his white incisors were a bit too sharp, his brown beard a little too scraggly, and something hungry lurked behind the lashes of his green eyes.

I stared back, frozen. Deep in a maze of tunnels marked with magical signs I couldn't decipher, surrounded by blocks of stone that rose above us like a dungeon, trapped in a rocking boat too precarious to even stand, here I sat with the bare flesh of my arms exposed to a werewolf staring at me like dinner. Charming.

The tension grew thick enough to scare me out of my wits before the werewolf said, in a deep, rumbling voice that chilled me to my bones, "Such exquisite color. Such attention to detail. I could gaze on them all night, and not ask the question—can you do *this?*"

The werewolf flicked an old photograph at me, but I was too stunned to catch it.

"Don't lose it," Spleen cried, reaching out impulsively and damn near falling out of the boat, and both the werewolf and I reached to steady him.

Our hands touched—the werewolf's was shockingly warm—and we both jerked away. Spleen leaned back up, one hand drenched

where he'd pitched forward, but the other—and the photograph—
still held high and dry.

"Idiot," Spleen snarled at me, shaking stinking drainwater off his
hand. "Why do you think I brought you down here? So he could eat
you?"

"No," I said, staring at the werewolf a bit sheepishly. We were
both holding our hands carefully, mirroring each other, and I'd
caught a lively spark in his eyes that seemed to promise that he was
interested in more than dinner. "That wasn't what I was worried
about."

"What then?" he asked, handing me the photograph.

I ignored him, holding the photograph gingerly, trying to parse
it. It depicted a . . . stone carving of a wolf—a wolf in chains, which
looped around it in an elaborate design.

"A control charm?" I guessed.

"I'm told you are the best," the werewolf said. "Seeing your
work—" he stared hungrily, no, appreciatively, at my arms—"I'd
trust no one else. Can you ink the image on me?"

I pocketed it. "Of course, but I have to get this vetted by a local
witch. I don't ink marks I haven't done before without a second
opinion—you never know what lurks in the magic."

The wolf pursed his lips. He had nice lips. *Very* nice lips, and a
strong jaw beneath the scraggle. I notice these things.

"Of . . . course," the werewolf said. "But this cannot take too
long—"

"She *can* do it," Spleen said, jerking forward slightly. "Believe
me. Dakota, give him the show. He needs to know what he's
buying—"

"No need," the wolf said, eyes fixed on me. "I can see the magic
in her marks."

I held his gaze, then cracked my neck a little and prepared to
breathe a word. It didn't really matter *what* word; an old-school
magician or one of my Wiccan friends would no doubt have a whole
vocabulary of nonsense for every different occasion. But the specific
word didn't matter: with magical tattoos, all that mattered was the
intent of the wearer.

"*Show him*," I said, and the tiniest magical tremor rippled through
my body, the barest fraction of power, gleaming down my tats,
spreading through the vines, illuminating the scales, the feathers, the
wings in a sparkling array like a cloud of fairy dust marching down

my skin. I even made the wings of the butterfly on my left wrist lift up and flutter in the air. The big bad werewolf's eyes lit up like a little child, dancing over my form, drinking in the magic, edges crinkling up in a smile.

"All but these are mine," I said, holding up my right forearm as the last glimmers of magic sparkled away, "and the man who did my inking arm works with me in the Rogue."

The wolf leaned back, impressed. "I would say I am now convinced, but I was before."

I glared at Spleen. "You could have brought him to the Rogue—"

"NO," the wolf said. "It's not safe—"

"This," I said, "is the twenty-first century. In Atlanta. In *Little Five Points*. Trust me, no one is going to hassle a werewolf. Heck, no one will even notice you."

"I didn't mean it wasn't safe for me," the werewolf said, still staring at me with those hungry eyes. His eyes no longer lingered on my tattoos, but roved all over me, like I was a particularly delicious banquet. Then he caught himself and looked away, shaking his head, face twitching in a pained grimace—I was a banquet he was forbidden to touch.

He was embarrassed. I felt sad for him, forced to hide in these tunnels, afraid of himself, holding on to what little scraps of dignity he could, like his battered suit. Even looking away, his chin was held up with pride, as of he were trying to be more than the monster most people would choose to see.

Not that a twinge of fear wasn't still nagging me: here I was, facing a real Edgeworlder, ripe with danger, popping his cork monthly, all too interested in my tattoos. I couldn't help but think of that skin-covered lid in the evidence tray. But I sensed no malice in this werewolf—in this *man*, this dangerously scruffy but still charming man with gleaming green eyes. And behind the hunger and the pain in those eyes I saw sadness . . . and interest?

"What's your name?" I asked.

The green eyes looked away. "Uh . . . Wulf."

A lie. Charming. Unoriginal. But not unexpected. He *was* hiding in the basement of the Edgeworld; no big surprise that he felt like he needed to hide even his name. I didn't know what drove him to that—but I did know I didn't like how guilty that lie made him feel.

"Well, 'Wulf,'" I said, cracking my best smile, "I'll get right on it."

Wulf glanced back to see acceptance, not judgment, on my face. He smiled back, an odd, shy grin, and I brushed back one of the feathers of my deathhawk, where it had curled about my neck. Then Wulf leaned back again, all the way on his heels, putting his hands easily on his knees. "This," he said, addressing Spleen, "has been an unexpected pleasure."

And then he looked straight at me, eyes hungry with something new. "I look forward to seeing more of you, Dakota Frost."

Without another word he rose and left, climbing stone stairs up into the blackness of the vault. Even as Spleen turned the boat around, my eyes still lingered, watching Wulf go.

By the time we got back to Mary's in East Atlanta it was damn near 1 a.m., and my evening was a lost cause. The tiny dance floor was empty, the VJ was putting up his discs, and even the bar was starting to thin out. I was so stressed I debated downing a Jager, but it was just too late and I had to drive.

The streets glistened blackly as I steered the Vespa back to Candler Park, and hidden shapes flitted among the bony fingers of the trees. The moon had long since set, but I could feel it out there, looming, itching for fullness, an hour closer to midnight each day.

When I parked my Vespa underneath the stairs and lurched up to my flat, I could feel a presence behind me, every step of the way. Wulf, stalking me? The yowling of my cats and the mechanics of setting down some canned food on the kitchen floor did nothing to dispel my mood.

In the end I lay in bed, alone, staring at the ceiling.

Someone out there wanted the skin off my back.

And I just might be doing a tattoo for him.

5. TRUST BUT VERIFY

In the morning light I felt better. The timing of Wulf's request was creepy, coming right on the heels of Rand's warning, but I didn't think a tattoo killer stalking a victim would arrange a meeting with a witness present. In fact, I had no reason to believe that the killer was after me personally, other than Rand's mothering; if he'd had even a whiff of evidence that I was the target, Rand would have put me in overprotective custody faster than I could blink.

My clients were another thing: scattered all over Georgia, with some of the best magical tattoos in the Southeast on their bodies, and without relatives on the police force who cared enough to track them down and warn them. I needed to figure out how to get the word to them—in my discreet line of work, clients didn't often share their email addresses or cell numbers—but there was some time before the full moon. First things first—Spleen.

The little rat had extracted a thousand promises from me to meet him "the very next day," to go over the contract for Wulf's tattoo, and I'd agreed—though he'd have gotten the same effect just by showing up for my shift at the Rogue Unicorn.

One of the glories of being a tattoo artist, other than having God's finest canvas at your disposal, is that I rarely need to get up before ten. Like most high-end shops, the Rogue doesn't open its doors to the public until noon, though I and the other artists are usually there by eleven for consultations and prepwork.

So despite yesterday's excitement I was able to sleep in, stroll to the Flying Biscuit cafe—after the breakfast crowds had died down, but before the towering, eponymous biscuits had lost their fresh-baked, morning fluffiness—and *still* putter in by ten-thirty to meet Spleen.

As I buzzed off of McLendon onto Moreland, I smiled. Little Five Points is the true heart of Atlanta. Forget the bigger Five Points, forget Buckhead, forget Midtown—it's only in Little Five Points, in that vortex of alternative culture whirling through the colorful pile of eclectic shops at the crux of Euclid, Moreland and McLendon, that Atlanta truly lets itself be Atlanta.

The main square is a parade of dudes hanging out with yuppies, homeless people harassing executives, hot young gay men and cute old lesbian couples, consignment shops for New Age crystals and recycled old duds, bookstores and bondage shops, teahouses and tattoo parlors, protesters crying, "No blood for oil!" and vendors crying, "Get some hot pizza!"

Glorious.

If you look closer, you can see more—pale, gothy boys whose high collars hide the bites on their necks, tough butch chicks trying to disguise that bit of wolf in their eyes, and New-Agey grandmothers pretending not to be as hale and hearty as their potions made them. Plus a whole carnival of firedancers and piercers, taggers and tattooers brimming over with magic and trying to hide nothing at all. In the Southeast, Little Five Points was the center of the Edgeworld, a brand new subculture rejecting the secrecy of magical tradition and defying centuries of religious oppression, dragging magic kicking and screaming into the light.

Even *more* glorious.

The Rogue Unicorn wasn't the largest tattoo shop in Little Five Points, but it was the best—and one of only two licensed to ink magic. Catty-corner from the giant skull that marked the Vortex Bar and Grill, the Rogue occupied most of the top of a converted Victorian whose sprawling bottom floor housed the quite decent *Make a Wish* clothing shop.

The sign for the Rogue was easy to find—a brushed metal unicorn, rampant, that we'd gotten in a deal with the city a few years back when they were trying to push a new artist—but getting into the shop itself was quite the trick: you had to park in the back, climb rickety wooden stairs, and worm round the balcony to the Herbalist's Attic. But—for the view alone—the trees, Little Five, the skull of the Vortex—it was worth it.

And I had the *best* view. My office was small, but streetside, with a broad front window whose dark-slatted blinds were always cracked to give me the aforementioned view of L5P. A glass, L-shaped desk held my computer, scanner and papers. A narrow bookshelf put all my books and tapes within easy reach from the desk . . . or from the sturdy marble workspace of the butcher's block, whose locked glass cabinet held my precious magical supplies.

I started the scan and leaned back in my chair, regarding Spleen, who'd arrived right on time. He bounced back and forth in the little space like an animated garden gnome, rattling the cabinet periodically. "Wulf's one of my best clients," he said. "I swear it, if you could just do this for me—"

"Hey. I said I'd do it." I shagged my hands through my hair, trying to shake my deathhawk back to life after being pinned under my helmet. "So stop trying to persuade me, or I might change my mind." The scanner whirred to life, and I kicked up my feet, staring out over Little Five. Something was wrong. Spleen was nervous, damp, almost sweaty. Damp and sweaty weren't new, but—"Should I change my mind?"

"N-no," Spleen said. Another lie. Not that he never did it, but— even more charming. At my scowl he turned away, stammering; but it was too late; I had him.

"What is it, Spleen?" I asked.

"Crap, Frost," he said. "What can I say? The design is fucking Nazi."

6. THE ACCURSED FLASH

"It's *what?*" I said, falling forward in my chair to look as the scanner finished its pass and the image popped up on the screen. The contrast was all fucked, but a moment's tweaking in Photoshop brought the contrast back up, along with all the nice German letters and genuine swastika printed on the bottom of the singed photo.

"It's Nazi, Frost," he said. "I don't mean neo-Nazi or skinhead or anything. It's a genuine fucking World War Two buzz-bombs-and-lost-arks Nazi tattoo design."

"Holy . . . crap," I said, staring at the image on the screen. Then, gingerly, I raised the scanner cover, hoping nothing would leap out and bite me. The photograph was very old, yellowing, and quite singed. Half the wording was gone, but a rescan at 600 dpi and a bit of fiddling would recover it. No amount of fiddling would bring back my forgotten high school language classes . . . but with what was left, I recognized the words as unmistakably German.

"Look, look, look," he said, wheedling. "Wulf's one of my best clients—"

"For how long?" I asked.

"The last six weeks—"

"Hell," I said, disgusted. "What have you gotten me into?"

"He says he needs the discipline, or he's going to lose it at the next full—"

"Next Sunday, I know," I said, staring at the tattoo, at the German words I could no longer read. "I don't know how I feel about inking some Nazi . . . occultism. If I was Jewish I'd probably throw this in your face."

"I wanted to chuck it at first," Spleen said, a bit bashfully. "But Wulf says he looked for *years* and couldn't find a better design. And he paid me a *lot* of money—"

"Slide," I said, standing, and Spleen moved so I could unlock the cabinet that held my supplies. I pulled out a long, plain wooden case and opened it slowly. The inside was divided into two long compartments, one holding a glass tube containing a fragment of a long spiral horn, and the other holding ten compartments for tattoo needles, six of them empty.

I held up the fragment and examined it. "Enough for the needles, I think—"

"Is that—" Spleen breathed, eyes gleaming, reaching out for the horn.

"Yes," I snapped, "mitts off. It's naturally shed, vestal gathered. I need needles made from untainted horn to ink a white charm—this *is* a white charm, isn't it?"

"A . . . Nazi . . . white charm?" Spleen asked, perplexed.

"The Nazis had candy and ice cream, didn't they?"

"Well . . ."

"Just because Hitler painted pictures of Baby Jesus, Jesus's image didn't suddenly 'go bad,'" I said, checking the bottles of ink. Newtseye green, nightshade black—I'd need a replacement for my cinnabar red; a recent FDA study had linked it to melanomas, even when inked with the healing power of free-range horn. I stood there a moment, spinning the newtseye in my hand, watching it glimmer, when I started to get a sinking feeling that I was getting ahead of myself. The design was made by Nazis. There were no obvious swastikas or more subtle black magic marks on it, but really, I knew nothing about this tattoo . . . or its future wearer.

"Look, Spleen, I only ink white or grey."

"That looks green," he said, somehow playing dumb and wheedling at the same time.

"You know what I mean," I snapped. "What do you know about this tat, other than what he told you?"

Spleen looked at me helplessly.

"What about Wulf? Other than the obvious?" Nothing. "Who recommended him to you?"

"I, uh . . ."

"So he found you, is that it?" I kneaded my brow. "So you know zip—"

"He seemed genuine," Spleen repeated. "And he paid a *lot* of money—"

"How much?" I held up my hand. "How much is *my* cut?"

"I ... dunno?" Spleen said. "I mean, how much would *you* charge—"

"Stop being a dick," I said. "And don't lie. I'll have him under my needle for ..." I squinted at the screen " ... three or four hours. I guarantee you, he'll spill the details."

"Seventy-five hundred," Spleen said.

A thousand for the needles, five hundred for the ink and powders. Another five hundred for graphomancy and license fees on a "new" design. Take out the Rogue's twenty percent cut ... and I could stand to land close to forty-five hundred dollars—putting me halfway to a new Vectrix electric motorbike to replace my old Vespa.

"I'll d—" I began, and stopped. Before the money made me stupid.

I have rules. I don't do black ink. I don't do religious marks. And I sure don't do bad charms. And I knew zip about this tat. For all I knew it was originally an evil Norse mark designed to curse a werewolf with terrible pain every full moon, but after the Nazis fiddled with it . . . the tat might be just as likely to set him on fire. "I'll . . . consider it. My statement to Wulf stands—I need to get this flash vetted by a witch before I ink it."

"Do we *reeeally* need to deal with that?" Spleen said. "I mean, the fees—"

"When's the last time you changed the oil on your car?"

"*You* last changed the oil on that car," Spleen said. "I *save* the money—"

"Spleen!" I said—then stopped and kneaded my brow. "Look, I know you don't think your engine's going to catch on fire, so why spend the money—"

"Exactly," Spleen said with triumph. "Ex-ZACTLY—"

"—but if this sets him on fire in my chair, we won't *get* any money. He won't pay up."

"He's got the money, he's got it," Spleen said, waving me off. "I got a retainer, yes I did, five *thousand* when he came to town, so don't josh old Spleen . . . " But then he saw my face. "Wait, you're . . . serious? Set him on *fire*? Tattoos can do that?"

I squeezed one hand tight, letting power flow into the yin-yang in my palm, then thrust it under his face, letting the mana out explosively into a tiny ball of lightning. Spleen leapt back and yelped, eyes wide in terror, and I blew him a big kiss, sending the little crackling ball of light towards him. It bounced around him like a kitten, and he stumbled back, batting frantically at it with a folder until it disappeared into a cloud of sparks and color.

"Jeez, jeez, *JEEzus*," Spleen said. "Don't do that—"

"This is a fifty-year-old Nazi tattoo, Spleen," I said, taking the folder from him. "For all we know it was designed to make a werewolf explode on contact with moonlight as a kind of living magic *bomb*. So no, I'm not going to ink it until someone can vet it."

"Well, tell that *someone*," Spleen said, shuddering, "'Hello, spooky-eyes.' For me. "

"Spleen!" I said. "Be nice. What if Jinx heard you?"

"*You* call her that," he protested.

"*I've* known her forever," I replied. "Now shoo. I have to make some calls."

And I needed to make them quickly. If Wulf's problem was as bad as it sounded, and the tat was as good as he claimed, we needed to move right away. First I called Jinx, who agreed to meet me on my break that afternoon. Then I buzzed our receptionist and asked her to pull the licensing paperwork for some new magical flash.

"Sure," Annesthesia said, sounding irritated. "Spleen left like fifteen minutes ago—why aren't you ready yet?"

"Ready for . . . what?"

"Don't you check your emails? You have two clients waiting for a consult—"

"I've been with a client," I snapped, "and I don't check emails until—"

"Hell freezes over," Annesthesia replied. "I'm sending them back now—"

"Wait," I said, but the line clicked dead. *Really.* The waiting room was thirty feet away. She could have knocked or something. But Annesthesia is pretty, coquettish, and beautifully tattooed. Other than me, she's our best advertisement—no, honestly, for straight guys, she *is* our best ad, since I can scare the little dears—so I put up with her.

I opened the door to the hall, hoping to intercept the visitors and draw them off to our "conference" room before they could see the mess which was my office, but stepped back in shock at the sight of a small but wiry old man with a flaring beard and hair. He was standing so close to the door it seemed like he'd materialized. Behind him, a dark-suited young man with blond hair smiled down at him, eyes lighting when he looked up and saw me.

The kindly old man stepped forward, and my jaw dropped in more shock. "Hello," he said with a wicked, cheerful grin, devilish black eyebrows serving only to accent his twinkling blue eyes. "I'm Chris Valentine, and this is my colleague, Alex Nicholson—"

"Christopher Valentine," I breathed. "The Mysterious Mirabilus!"

∽——

7. THE VALENTINE CHALLENGE

The Mysterious Mirabilus smiled, and gave a slight bow. "The one and only."

Christopher Valentine, AKA "The Mysterious Mirabilus," was the world's most famous magician—and debunker. Technically he was what real practitioners called an illusionist—someone who simulated magic through nonmagical means—but this Einstein-haired "illusionist" could do *without* magic things that most experienced sorcerers couldn't do *with* magic. I mean, showy, big league stuff like walking on water, parting a small lake, and, most famously, appearing in two places at once, a trick he'd demonstrated on TV's famous talk show way back when, *The Night Shift with Jack Carterson.*

I'd caught that one live. As a child, before I was old enough to know stage magic from real Magick, the Mysterious Mirabilus had been my hero, and I'd stayed up countless nights to catch his appearances performing his latest trick. By the time I grew older and had turned to real magic, the Miraculus Mirabilus had come out as Christopher Heywood Valentine, stage magician, and had turned his considerable talents to debunking what he considered "the flim-flammery of our age." He traveled the country, issuing the Valentine Challenge to all magicians: to do a magic trick he couldn't replicate under controlled conditions.

I know, I know, you're thinking, charmingly naïve—no real practitioner would advertise themselves, and the rest are all charlatans, so why did I still idolize this guy? But like many other Edgeworlders, I find myself sifting through endless tomes of New

Age fuffery looking for something real. Valentine's probing books and debunking tours helped me winnow through the crap to get to the occasional nugget of gold.

And so—"I have all your books," I blurted. Like a schoolgirl. How embarrassing.

But the Mysterious Mirabilus looked at me with sharp new interest. "How interesting," he said, sitting in the client's chair opposite me as I sat down at my desk. "That strikes me as very unusual. Given your profession."

I grinned. "And why can't a tattoo artist read Christopher Valentine?"

"I meant, as a professed magician," Valentine said, all serious, dark pointy eyebrows beetling into a serious look of concern. He was much more interesting in person: on camera he looked all pale and WASPy, but with him sitting in my client's chair I could see a slight Middle Eastern slant to his features and a subtle, swarthy tint to his skin that would have made it a wonderful canvas to ink on. "After all, I have spent the last few years of my life—"

"—exposing all the junk in the so-called 'magickal' world," I replied, "freeing the rest of us practitioners to focus on the good stuff?"

Valentine and Nicholson looked at each other.

At this point I really noticed his colleague, Alex Nicholson: young, not too tall, tanned, with firm angular features that hinted at little or no body fat beneath his trim suit and turtleneck. Subtle, colored streaks wove through his wavy blond hair and the trimmed tuft on his chin. A single blue captive-bead ring hung in one ear. Like a slightly edgy Ken doll. Yummy.

"A skeptical witch," Valentine said at last. "How about that."

"Technically I'm not a witch or warlock," I said. "I don't have a magical bloodline—I do technical magic, with potions and tools and leylines, which makes me a magician—"

"I thought *I* was the magician," Valentine said.

"A practitioner would call you a *illusionist*," I replied, "though I prefer the term *wizard*. As in Mister Wizard? Because what a stage magician can do with science is far more than conjuring. But . . . I somehow don't get the feeling you came here to quiz me about what I call you, because it might be different when you're not around. How can I help you?"

"Well, then," Valentine said, rubbing his hands together. "I hoped you might help me with, as you put it, 'helping people focus on the good stuff.' I've heard you claim to be able to create 'magic' tattoos—"

"I 'claim' nothing. My work speaks for itself," I responded, shrugging my shoulders so the vines and snakes rippled down my bare arms. Nicholson was trying not to look, but it wasn't working; I was trying not to smile, which wasn't working either. "I am an expert artist, and if you have a tat in mind, I can ink it, whether the design be mundane, magical, even spiritual."

"Weeell, then," Valentine said. "Perhaps you could help us. I and my lovely assistant—"

"He is that," I said. Nicholson suddenly looked down, embarrassed, which made him doubly cute, and Valentine blinked a couple of times before continuing.

"Ahem. I and my assistant would like you to participate in a little test. We would like you to draw a magical tattoo—and then I, who happen to be trained in the tattoo arts myself, will attempt to replicate it, to our mutual satisfaction."

"Are you issuing me the Valentine Challenge?" I said, now openly grinning.

Valentine bowed. "That I am."

I leaned back in my chair. Fuck the Vectrix—this was a brand new Prius, with a house and garage to put it in. "A million bucks. Mmmm. I do so hate to take your money. BUT—I don't ink as a performance, or for tricks. Tattooing is an invasive procedure that violates the body. It needs a sterile environment—and an encircled one, if magic is involved. And it's a permanent mark on the human body; I don't ink as a stunt—"

Valentine had listened with mild interest, then with a triumphant smile. "So you won't do it?" he asked, grinning at Nicholson.

"I didn't say that," I said, looking straight at Nicholson. "Does your lovely assistant actually want me to make a permanent mark on his body?"

Nicholson looked up, caught my gaze, and looked away again, embarrassed. It was so cute! "Actually, yes," he said, flushing, looking up at me at last, his eyes catching on mine with a bit of electric desire. "On my wrist."

He held up his left hand, pushing his watch down to expose his wrist. "A hider," I said, reaching for the Big Blue Binder. "I have a good selection of magical flash for the wrist—"

"Actually," Valentine said, smiling, "we had a specific design in mind."

"Oh...kay," I said. "But if you want a magical tattoo—"

Nicholson pulled out an envelope, "I hoped you could do this."

Oh...kay. This was a bad scene. I took the envelope gingerly, while Valentine and Nicholson looked on—Valentine gleefully, Nicholson bashfully, a bit skeptically. I opened it up and unfolded a bad photocopy of an ornate bit of flash, a Victorian-inspired design with constellations and Roman numerals and circular filigree that was the magical equivalent of gears. It took me a moment to realize what it was—a clock.

"I'm not going to do *this*," I said, tossing the paper down.

"I knew it," Valentine said, slapping Nicholson's shoulder. "You owe me—"

Nicholson batted him away. "Why not?" he said, almost hurt.

"It's a *watch*," I said. "This is a permanent mark and you want me to do a *watch*?"

"Why not?" Valentine said, grinning even more broadly. I was starting to dislike the man, and this after such a good start. "Won't it keep time—"

"Obviously not," I said, pointing at the zodiacal marks. "It's calibrated to the stars, to a *sidereal* day, not a solar day, so it will lose time—a whole day, as the Earth goes around the sun. Didn't you take astronomy in school? And what if he moved? It would be off by however many time zones were involved!"

Valentine's jaw remained open. Nicholson remained undeterred.

"It has 'knobs' so you can reset it," he said, pointing.

I stared at the design for a moment. "It . . . does," I said. The more I looked, the more masterful the design appeared. "That's . . . good. To use the knobs, I'll need to tattoo contact points on the fingers of . . . oh. That's these associated disc designs here?"

Nicholson leaned forward. "Uh, yes. So they are."

"Who did this?" I looked back and forth at Nicholson and Valentine, who looked back and forth at each other. "This is expert work, but *I* certainly didn't do it, nor did anyone I know of in the Southeast. Where did you get it?"

"I have my sources," Valentine said, leaning back in his chair.

"Weeeell," I said, miming his earlier intonation. "I can't just ink this as is—"

"I told you so—sorry, am I jumping the gun?"

"Don't be a dick, old man," I snapped. "I take my profession as seriously as you do, and I am not going to put a permanent magical mark on the human body without two things: first, you have to get me some virgin flash—meaning *unfolded*, without lines that obscure the design. And no low-quality photocopies, either. I need something as close to the original as possible or a high-resolution digital image, TIFF preferred."

"A . . . 'tiff'?" asked Valentine, looking at Nicholson.

"It's a . . . graphics format," Nicholson said. "Like a JPEG. Not a problem."

Valentine shrugged, nodded. "Sounds fair," he said. "We can do that."

"Second, I need to get it vetted by a local witch," I raised my hand before Valentine could say anything. "I'm not weaseling. I can ink a known design, but for something this complicated . . . I need a second eye, someone trained in graphomancy. Normally that would cost some coin, but I can get a witch to do it for free. If—and *only if*—she approves, I'll do your tattoo, and I guarantee it will do what she'll say it will do. But I make no guarantees about what Mister Valentine can pull off, no matter how skilled a tattooist he is. And if he can replicate my work—" I cracked my neck, then cracked a smile. "Hey, more power to him."

After that, I fixed my smile and stared straight at Valentine. He stared back at me for a moment, then looked at Nicholson. "Sounds fair, Alex?"

"Sounds fair," Nicholson said. "Can you get her some better flash?"

"Today, preferably," I said. "I have an appointment with my witch this afternoon—"

Valentine jiggled in his pocket and pulled out an USB drive on his keychain. He scowled at it for a moment, then seemed to think better of it. "I have a picture on here, but it's really no better than the photocopy. Can I email you when I get back to my hotel?"

"Sure—it' s just *dakota at rogue unicorn dot net*, no dash."

"Will that take large files?"

"Yes, it just goes to my gmail account," I said.

"A skeptical witch with a gmail account who wants TIFF files," Valentine said, jamming his hands back into his pockets. "What is the world coming to?"

"I'm not a witch," I replied. "I'm just a tattoo artist."

Valentine was as good as his word—I had the file before my break. I printed out a copy of his "watch" and Wulf's suspected Nazi flash on the 11x17 printer to speed things up, and dumped his files and my scans on a USB key to meet Jinx. I'm nothing if not prepared.

A distant noise of a leaf blower greeted me as I stepped back to our reception area, and I grinned at Kring/L, a big, beefy bald man with a walrus moustache, going over flash with a young couple over the distant noise of the leaf blower. Unlike me, he did jinxes—lover's names—so he got work I generally didn't; but he still felt the same way I did about them, and was trying to sell the kids on matching designs rather than something they'd regret in six weeks.

"You think all the leaves would have fallen by now," he said, looking up at me, cocking his head back at the muted whine from the parking lot. He was a great artist, and yet didn't sport a single tattoo. "I thought they did this on Wednesdays."

"That's the beauty of global warming for you," I said. "Blow the leaves around enough with a gas mower, and you get to watch them fall later every year."

He cocked his head at the two kids—they were actually pretty cleancut, kind of preppy, and had stiffened at my crack. I took the hint and shut up. I slipped out the door, then stomped in my big old boots back to the balcony at the end of the stairs. I was willing to bet I'd see a huge-ass SUV in the parking lot—no, two. Why should I expect that they'd ridden together?

My jaw dropped. A black helicopter sat in the back parking lot of the Rogue Unicorn, its blades spinning down slowly from a light whine to near-complete silence.

The leafblower had wings.

8. SECRET AGENT MAN

In shock, I descended the stairs, watching the set of counter-rotating, oddly spaced blades slowly come to a stop. The helicopter was simultaneously sweeping and angular, landing gear curving back from its nose in a horseshoe, tail swooping up like a fin, making it look like a giant metal Shamu carved from matte black panels that ate up all the light.

Then I noticed the same Fed logo I'd seen at City Hall, black on black, embossed on the helicopter's side in a slightly shiny effect similar to what you get if you push the levels too far on Photoshop . . . and leaning against the 'copter, next to the logo, was the same dark-suited Fed.

"Miss Frost?" the Fed said, detaching himself from the 'copter. People in movies duck when stepping under a chopper's blades, but he just strolled forward, letting the wind tousle his wavy brown hair. "Special Agent Philip Davidson. We met at Atlanta Homicide, but didn't really get a chance to speak. I was told you would be expecting me?"

He extended his hand, and I stared down at it, not sure what I was seeing was real. His suit was tailored from a fabric whose sheen somehow matched the 'copter's hide, and his well-trimmed goatee still reminded me of Johnny Depp or maybe Spock's evil twin. His sunglasses were straight out of the Matrix, and I swear if he'd had a tie with a horizontal tie tack I'd have started calling him "Agent Smith." But he exuded a gentle sincerity, staring up at me with an easy directness I rarely saw in shorter men. His surprisingly delicate hands were warm, his handshake firm.

"In not so many words, but yes," I said. "Rand said something about it."

"I would have made an appointment," he said, in a voice as warm and firm as his hands, "but since we were in the neighborhood I thought I'd drop by and hope you were on your break."

Abruptly the twin sets of counter-rotating blades whined and folded up, closing like two Chinese fans and tucking themselves back over the body of the craft until it was narrow and compact enough to fit in the width of a single parking space.

"You decided to drop by in *that?*" I asked. "*Really?*"

"Budget cuts," he said, spreading his hands—as if budget cuts explained anything. "Ever since we lost one in Iraq it's been harder and harder to justify spending money on Shadowhawks, so the brass took them public and is playing up their silent-running so we can market them to local law enforcement. One of its features is the ability to land quietly in a restricted space—so I told the pilot to land here, kill two birds with one stone."

Suddenly I could see an APD officer inside the copter talking to the pilot—no one I knew through Rand, but clearly high ranking and *highly* interested.

I laughed out loud. "Secret-*agent*-man, now copter-*salesman*-man—"

"It wasn't my idea," he said, mouth quirking up in an embarrassed smile that made him seem even less 'agent' and even more 'human'. "They're fun, but personally, I drive a Prius."

"Riiight," I said. "Well, as it so happens I've made an appointment for my break, but I don't want you to have wasted all the gas on this trip. What can I do for you?"

"Based on your comments last night, I believe you can help our investigation into the murder. I had *hoped* to ask you a whole series of questions," he said, calmly staring up at me, radiating disapproval without dropping into an accusatory tone. "Is this appointment of yours something that can't wait?"

"Yes, it's urgent, and a friend is doing me a favor," I said. Suddenly, inspiration struck me. "Hang on. You don't happen to have a picture of the victim's tattoo on you?"

"Why?" I expected him to say 'yes' or 'no' or play neutral, but he had a cheerful directness that was hard not to like, and when he pursed his lips thoughtfully I felt like I could stare at his lips all day. Then they moved. "It is evidence, you know."

"I'm seeing a graphomancer," I said. "Maybe she could shed some light on it—more information about what the mark does, or who did the design."

He leaned back, thinking, and, damnit, I started to think the smile was just from looking at me. "I thought you said Sumner did it?"

"Sumner didn't do his own designs," I said. "He used graphomancers. Even *I* use graphomancers—"

"So you're better than Sumner?"

My face flushed. "I'm not saying that, it's just . . . my training is—"

"That's all right," he said, smiling. "Look. I didn't mean to hold you up. I'll get straight to why I'm here. I want your client list." He must have seen my jaw tighten, so he raised his hand. "Now, don't get antsy. I won't force you to turn it over—"

"You're right about that," I snapped. "In Georgia tattooing is practically a medical procedure—that list is private, and sensitive. I could lose my license if I gave it to you without a warrant, and I really doubt you can get a warrant."

"Really?" Philip said, raising an eyebrow. "You don't think *I* could get a warrant?"

"*Maybe*," I said, "if you were investigating a crime, and not trying to prevent one. Unless I or one of my clients were suspects in the prior killings. *Are* we suspects?"

"Well, no, but given the circumstances there are other legal avenues I could—" Philip began, then stopped. "Look, I'm not trying to be a dick here. I know how the Edgeworld works—I don't want to come down heavy and scare off the very people I want to protect. But I would like to talk to you about setting up a procedure to warn your client base. They could be targets . . . if you are as good as you look."

His eyes were drifting over the tattoos on my arms, but his mouth quirked up a bit as he said it, and I gaped. I could swear the cheeky little gnome was hitting on me! OK, perhaps "gnome" was too strong: that was just an automatic reaction to an advance from anyone in a suit. Strip him out of the suit, on the other hand . . . he'd be buffer than Alex Nicholson. Oh my. Either way, I was too dumbfounded to speak, so he continued.

"Think it over," he said, all serious. "I know you think I'm spooky-black-helicopter man, but I'm really a nice guy who doesn't want to see you or any of your clients hurt. Please think about how we might warn them—perhaps you could contact them, let us know who's willing to talk to us?" He held up his hands. "No innuendo here—seriously. Twelve people have been killed. I don't want to see that number hit thirteen. You should think about it."

"I'll . . . ask. No promises."

"Okay. For now. And about the tat we showed you," he said, "we don't normally let evidence into the wild. You never know what may tip off a suspect, or spawn a copycat. Perhaps your witch would come to the offices and view the piece there?"

"No," I said. "For this witch, you bring things to her—she's got an elaborate computer setup to analyze images. Makes her fees high, but it's worth it." I stared at him. "Twelve people murdered? You should think about it."

"I'll ask," he said. "No promises."

"Fair enough," I said, turning to my Vespa to ferret out the Sumner book from my saddlebags. "And now I have a present for you, Special Agent Davidson."

"Oh, you shouldn't have," he said, throwing up his hands in mock astonishment. Then he saw the book's title and the few bookmarks I'd put in it, and his face went solemn. "Scratch that—you should have."

I told him about my theories—the potential victims in the book, the good chance that someone else might have the tat, the likelihood that a graphomancer had inked it sometime around the turn of the millennium, and even my fears about Sumner's death itself.

"So much fucking time lost," he said, staring at the book in his hand. "We should have been looking for graphomancers from the very beginning—"

"You didn't have a name until yesterday," I said, hoping it would reassure him.

"We had hints," he snapped. "We're supposed to be the ones that follow up on them. We're the ones who're supposed to catch the bad guys based on a torn receipt and a funny smell. At the first clue the tattoos were magical we should have been talking to magical inkers and graphomancers and the whole lot." He was silent for a moment, glaring off into the distance. "We—*they*—those *dolts* at the *Bureau*—treated it like a normal serial killer case for two years. Two whole years! And when *they* finally get wise, *we* have to pick up the crap—"

"I'm sure you did your best," I said.

"Not likely," he snorted. "We could have found out at least half of what you've told me without knowing Sumner's name. Five minutes listening to you and I feel like I'm caught with my pants down—"

"Well...not yet you're not," I said.

"Don't you start," he said, eyes back on me with that same appreciative look he'd had scoping out my tattoos. "Scratch that—do."

Oh, Lord. Me and my smart mouth—I hadn't meant to open that can of worms. I already had a werewolf as a secret admirer; I didn't need another suitor. I held up my hands, which made his eyes light on the yin-yang and magic circle tattoos on my palms. "Agent Davidson," I began. "I'll do what I can to help you find the killer—"

And then a horrible thought struck me. All the other tattoos, presumably, had been ripped from someone's body. But this time, we had the tattoo, not the victim—

"What?" he said sharply. "What else have you thought of?"

"You . . . you don't have a body for the last one, do you?" I said. Davidson scowled, hand clenching on the book, and my stomach churned. "I mean . . . at least I *hope* the victim was dead when they . . . when they took the tattoo..."

There was an ugly pause. He just looked at me. Oh, God.

"I'll talk to my clients, and to the witch," I said.

"I'll talk to my agents, get them on this," he said, holding up the book. "And talk to Nighy about releasing images of the lid, maybe even some of the other tattoos—"

"One more thing," I said. It had been bugging me the whole time, but still I hesitated a moment; this would reopen that can of worms. But that held me back only a moment.

I reached out and took his glasses off carefully. He twitched, just a little, and I guessed it was more from our eight-inch height difference than the invasion of his space. I waggled the glasses. "I could see the smile in your eyes even through these. You have *wonderful* eyes." I slid the glasses into his pocket. "You shouldn't hide them, Special Agent Davidson."

He smiled at me, the same warm, quirky smile he'd given me back at Homicide, given me a few minutes ago, now enhanced by warm, blue-grey eyes.

"It's Philip, Miss Frost."

"Dakota," I said, turning and walking away.

I'd just met one of the fabled "black-helicopter men," of conspiracy theories and New World Order fame, and he was darned cute.

Talk about having men falling out of the sky...

———

9. ELEGANT GOTHIC LOLITA

The Starbucks in Little Five Points is on Moreland, at its farthest northern edge, as if the raw power of LFP's eclectic vortex had repelled the chain's sterile corporate heart and this was as close as it could come. Me, I come for the dark roast—at least Starbucks claims it's made from sustainable beans.

My young witch pored over a book, murmuring, dressed in head to toe in frilly black—ornate petticoat and satin dress, Victorian corset and ruffled jacket, black bonnet and folded-back veil, all outlined here and there in shocking white lace. *Elegant Gothic Lolita*, the style was called, though you rarely saw it outside of a science fiction convention.

Yet here Skye "Jinx" Anderson sat, decked out in the middle of the Starbucks, oblivious to the stares of the college boys at the next table as she moved one hand over a spiral-bound book, still murmuring. Whenever she took a sip, raising her coffee to her lips with a delicate hand wrapped in a fingerless black lace glove and jingling charm bracelets, the boys drew in a breath; when she set the cup back down with deliberate grace, they all seemed to sag.

I knew the drill by this point—Jinx already knew I was here, but didn't care to be interrupted. So I waited in line and got some coffee, creamed it, and joined her.

Jinx looked up at me over her black disc sunglasses, and now *I* drew in a breath. I never failed to be shocked by her eyes: blue, gleaming, the iris inlaid with a milky white ring, like a snowflake embedded into the surface of blue marble. She caught me looking and pushed her glasses up with one delicate gloved hand, at which point I could see the glowing nub of a Bluetooth mike poking out of the lace mesh and curls of dyed, blue-black hair. Beside her book, there was a cute little laptop with raised spider decals. She'd been dictating notes.

"Hi, Jinx."

"Dakota," she said, smiling, drawing her fingers over one last line of Braille before closing the book. "It's been too long. You're normally not so shocked."

"Actually, I always am, spooky-eyes," I replied. She scowled, and I said, "You'd prefer 'Little Miss Anderson'?"

"NO!" she said, throwing her hands to her cheeks in mock horror. "Shame on you for dredging up high school memories, Miss Frost!"

"Don't you start," I said. "I've heard that far too much over the past few days—"

"So," she said primly, leaning her elbows on the table, folding one hand over the other, and propping her chin atop them, "Let's see this tattoo you've got for me."

"Actually," I said, pulling out the envelope, "I have two today, and maybe one later—"

"Oh, goody," she said, clapping her hands together.

"Don't get too excited, I may be taking one of them on spec."

"Anything for you, Dakota." She leaned her head against her hands. "What are they?"

"The one I called you about is a werewolf control charm. Spleen—"

"Feh," Jinx said. "He smells."

"Spleen hooked me up with a were who wants more control over his beast." I grew uncomfortable, but Jinx kept 'staring' at me from behind her black glasses. "I think it may be a Nazi design, or something they collected. Frankly it scares me. I'm not comfortable inking it without knowing what it does."

"As you should be," she said. "And the rest?"

"A magical wristwatch."

"Oh, my," Jinx said, making *gimme, gimme* motions with her fingers.

"This one is a . . . stunt," I said, holding off. "I don't know if I'll get paid, but I'll cut you in for ten percent if I win the contest."

"Dakota," she said reprovingly. "Anything for you. But really! A contest. That's so unlike you. What's my cut going to be?"

"One hundred thousand dollars," I said.

"Mmm...hmm," she said. I couldn't tell whether she believed me. Or maybe she missed the 'thousand' part? "Well, anything for you, Dakota. Let's see what you've got."

I slid the flash out of the envelope and arrayed it on the table. She stared down at it for a moment, then let her fingers run over it, looking off into the distance, murmuring. Then she pushed her glasses down and picked the flash up, holding it close to her spooky geode eyes, staring first at the detailed joins of the clock, then at the edge of the wolfsbane charm.

I felt so sad. Growing up, Jinx had always had the best vision of any of my childhood friends; now she could see little more than a murky blur. It was painful watching her rock her head back and forth, trying to eke some sense of the figures through the ruin of her eyes. Finally she put the flash down on the table, drummed her fingers, and nodded.

"It will take me a day or so to 'look' them over," she said.

"I figured," I said, pulling out a USB key. "I have some files if you want the originals—TIFF, JPEG, PNG, and for the clock, even something called SVG—"

"Scalable Vector Graphics," she said, suddenly breathless, upraising a gloved hand into which I dropped the key. "Excellent. That will save me a step."

"I don't have the other one. We're trying to get a picture now—"

"Do you know the general kind of inking it's going to be?"

"It's . . ." I stopped, deciding how much to tell her. This was police business, nasty stuff, and I knew how she felt about the police—heck, I felt the same way. But this was *Jinx*, after all. What could I hide from her? "I'm not inking it. Someone ripped a tattoo off one of Richard Sumner's clients."

"A copyright infringement case?" she said, shocked. "Dakota—"

"No," I said, very flatly.

Jinx's face drained. "Oh, Dakota," she said, horrified. "You mean literally. Oh, *Dakota!* What have you gotten yourself into? How did you ever come across such a thing—"

"Andre Rand," I said. "He wanted to warn me. Somebody's targeting people with magical tattoos." Her hands went to her mouth. "I'm, uh, trying to help them—"

"Well, *duh*," she said. "Quit dancing around it, I can smell your reluctance from here."

I didn't say anything. I *was* a bit embarrassed. Jinx hated the police, for reasons she never disclosed. In fact she'd nearly cut me out when she found out my dad was a cop, and even now she barely tolerated him—though on that score I knew how she felt.

"Well," I said, "It's just, I didn't think you'd like me working with them—"

"'Them,'" she said. "Say it. 'The police'—and 'the Feds,' I'll bet. You're helping the police, and you're worried about what I'll think."

"Yeah," I said.

"Well, stop worrying, Dakota." She sat up straighter. "Someone may be stalking you, and has already killed somebody else. Of *course* you're helping the police. You have nothing to be ashamed of. I know you better than to think you'd engage in a modern witch hunt."

I let out a breath, relieved. "So, if we could get them to release the pics, you'll help?"

"Dakota," she said reprovingly. "Oh Dakota. Of course. Anything for you."

Her phone beeped, and Jinx sighed. "I have class," she said primly, closing her little laptop, slipping it and the spiral-bound Braille book into a brown leather satchel, and then withdrawing a spirit cane.

"I know," I replied.

"Walk me to the bus stop?" Jinx said, standing, all black ruffles and white lace, unfolding the springloaded white cane to its six foot length sharply, *tik-tik-tik-tik-CRACK*.

"Certainly," I said, stepping to the door and opening it. She walked forward towards my voice, sweeping the cane back and forth, *click-clack*, acutely aware of her effect on the boys at the side table as she swept past them. She took my extended arm naturally as she stepped through the door, and we walked out into the warm Atlanta sun. "Just like old times."

"More than you know," she said. "I think I can evaluate the clockwork flash, but as for the control charm . . . we'll want to call in an were-expert."

"Let me guess," I said. "Not a wereologist, but an actual were."

"Right, first time," Jinx said. "Goes by 'the Marquis.' We're texting all the time, but he's a real Edgeworlder. No email, no fixed address—you'll have to take the flash to him physically, in person, at the local werehouse—"

"Which warehouse?"

"*Were*-house," Jinx said, pronouncing the first syllable distinctly. I still heard little or no difference, other than she was leaning on the *were*, but I got the gist.

"Fine, fine," I said. "I actually like werewolves, or were-whatevers—"

"You've never been to an actual werehouse, though," she said. "They're homes for werekin who can't 'pass'. I've only been once, and I had the distinct sensation that I was tolerated only because I'm blind. Humans just aren't wanted there, so you'll have to be escorted in."

"*Won*derful," I said.

"Oh, it gets better," Jinx said. Now *she* was dancing around something, which wasn't like her. "There's a new wrinkle, so…"

"So what? What's the wrinkle?"

"The werewolf clan has contracted with some . . . low-lifes . . . for protection."

"Oh hell," I said. "Vampires. No, let me guess—*rogue* vampires. I'm going to need an escort to deal with my escorts!"

"It's not that bad," she said. "They're a vampire gang, yes, but they do abide by the protocols. So you can get protection from them . . . but, it's just . . . as a Little Fiver . . ."

"Oh, hell," I repeated. "I have to ask for help from my ex-girlfriend."

10. THE JUNIOR VAN HELSING DETECTIVE AGENCY

If you follow Auburn Avenue east from Boulevard to Randolph Street, just where Auburn splits back off from Old Wheat, there's a small, unassuming box of a building sitting at the narrowest of the five corners of the intersection. It's shy on windows and has broad double doors pointing straight at the street, giving it a small-church feel; and indeed it was once a church, now deconsecrated. And inside, in the karmic convergence of holy ground built on a ley-line crossing near a five-pointed intersection (found by our very own Jinx), lived the vampire queen of Little Five Points.

My ex-girlfriend, Savannah Winters.

Back when I had my Festiva, you parked on Old Wheat; Auburn had some kind of city right of way and you'd quickly get towed. With the Vespa I expected to be able to putter right up and park on the sidewalk, but when I arrived, there was a new wrought-iron fence up around the whole main building. Finally I parked behind a small connected Victorian building that had once been the church school, next to a couple of unfamiliar cars. *Had she moved?*

But the church buildings had been reworked too, now with a semi-formal entrance and several carved wooden signs, like a doctor's office:

L5P VAMPIRE CONSULATE
DARKROSE ENTERPRISES
JVH DETECTIVE AGENCY

I scowled. Apparently Savannah was setting up her own little business empire trading on her vampirism. I wondered if she was *ever* going to get her Ph.D—not likely, at this rate.

Once she'd dreamed of becoming the world's very first vampire vampirologist, becoming a vampire herself to try to "study the vampire world from within." I told her not to do it, the 'vampire world' would eat her alive. She went and got herself turned anyway. We split.

I'm not bitter.

As I predicted, the vampire world consumed more and more of her time and life, pushing everything else out. The careful planning she put into her change made her into an extremely powerful—and sought after—vampire. Soon, Savannah Winters became the head vampire of the Little Five Points district, helped by a little bit of vampire nepotism from the vampire who made her.

She'd called to tell me she was now the *Lady* Saffron. I'd hung up.

It was the last time we'd spoken.

Now here I was, staring at the signs, nerving myself up for this. Finally I rang the doorbell and was buzzed in.

Inside, the remodeled building felt even more like a doctor's office. It was a small but brightly lit room, in earthtones, with padded chairs, magazines on coffee tables, and even a couple of potted plants. A reception desk served as gateway for three doors going left, back and right. Except for the blonde girl behind the desk, the room was empty—things had to be slow at nine-thirty on a Friday night. Then the phone rang, and I realized that it was only a couple hours past sunset. Vampire business might just be starting to heat up.

"Hello, Junior Van Helsing Detective Agency," said the girl into her headset. Surely she couldn't be in college. She had to be a high schooler . . . or a *something*. "I'll put you through to Detective Nagli." She pressed a button, then looked up at me. "How can I help you?"

"I'm here to see 'the Lady Saffron,'" I said, pronouncing her vampire name carefully, trying to hide my resentment. "Is she still—"

"Ah, Vampire Consulate business," the girl said, oddly embarrassed. "You're, um, you're in the right place, but . . . I'm sorry, can you wait maybe an . . . hour?" She cringed at my glare, and said hastily, "The Lady Saffron is here, but she's . . . ah . . . entertaining the Lady Darkrose right now. They won't receive visitors for at least an hour—"

Huh. She'd gone and shacked up with someone else—another vamp from the sound of it—and built up a whole entourage. I don't know why it pissed me off, but it did.

"She'll receive me," I said. "I'm an old friend of 'Saffron'—"

"Are you now?" said another voice. A young, young man, wearing a suit with all of the grace of a bum, had come to slouch in the side door. Just beyond him was a hard-looking man with a dark beard, openly staring at me with an unfriendly scowl. The boy's gaze had no such hostility, but still pinned me with a calculating eye. "If you're an old friend, surely you know Saffron doesn't like to be disturbed when entertaining Darkrose."

"Or maybe I don't," I said. "I don't know who this Darkrose is."

"An old friend of Saffron who doesn't know who Darkrose is?" The boy raised a manila folder to his lips. "An old friend . . . or an estranged friend, perhaps?"

"Both," I said. "Now take me to see Saffron. I'm headed to a werehouse, and I need to ask for her protection—"

"Ah," the boy said. "Makes sense now. Show her in."

"*You* do it," the girl said. "They're in there with Doug—"

"*You're* the secretary," the boy replied.

"*You're* the idiot who wants to interrupt her after she gave orders not to be disturbed—"

"You're forgetting they're *vampires*," the hard-faced man said, with a sudden, bitter laugh. He had an odd accent, not English but maybe somewhere from the ruins of the empire. "They'll love the chance to show off their little court."

The boy and the secretary looked at him, then each other. "Vickman's right," she said.

"Fine," the boy said, handing the envelope to Vickman. He whipped out his phone and tapped off a few quick instant messages, then snapped it closed and said, "Come on, old friend of Saffron, and let's see how you handle *this*."

He opened the door to the left into a small hallway that led to a conference room, dimly lit, with a wetbar and overstuffed couches opposite a conference table. The hum of a refrigerator came from a set of built-in cabinets behind the bar, and I swallowed. What kind of drinks would a vampire serve at a bar? The boy stepped between the table and wetbar to an elaborate, heavy wooden door, and pressed a button on an intercom.

"Just who the hell are you?" I asked.

"I work for the Junior Van Helsing Detective Agency," he said. "We have an . . . arrangement with the Consulate to handle their reception in exchange for the office space."

He pressed the button again. After a moment, a woman answered in a strong but oddly clipped variant of an English accent, like Vickman's. I didn't recognize the voice.

"Yes, what is it?"

"I have a . . . supplicant for the Lady Saffron," the boy said, looking at me.

"I'm not a 'supplicant,'" I snapped. "I'm an old friend—"

"I understand," the voice replied. "Show her in."

"Thanks," the boy said. "After you, my dear—"

"For the second time in as many days," I said, "Fuck that."

The boy shrugged, smiling. "Have it your way, Miss Frost."

"I never told you my name," I said.

He tapped his head. "Quick." Then he shrugged, as if he hated calling attention to his smarts. "Also notice 'detective' in Junior Van Helsing *Detective* Agency?"

"You're a real little dick, you know that?"

He looked back in shock, saw me smiling, and then got it. "Have it your way, Miss Frost," he said, and opened the door.

The interior of the church had been redone since I'd last seen it. The altar and pews had been long gone when Savannah had converted it to a living space, but now her futon, beanbag and Target end tables were gone too, replaced by a large L-shaped sofa and elegant coffee table, which faced a widescreen TV sitting on a circular platform. Sweeps of fabric hung from the ceiling, pouring down like tapestries on the walls where her posters had once hung. Small statues stood on pedestals beneath the stained glass windows; an elaborately dressed maid was dusting one bust carefully. And at the end of the room, on the raised dais that had once held the altar, an unfamiliar black female vampire sat on a throne, staring at me with cold blue eyes.

The door closed behind me, and I stepped forward. The vampire was stunning: tall, strong, body wrapped in a tight leather corset-like bodice that accented her bust. Crossed legs seemed poured into boots that came all the way up to her bare thighs—just Savannah's type. Beside her, a masked man knelt, his young muscular chest harnessed in crisscrossed straps of leather, and wearing cheekchiller chaps that exposed his backside. I arched an eyebrow: the boy was wearing a collar and leash, and the leather mask was in the shape of a dog's face. *Also* Savannah's type.

I was confused. The black vampire on the throne was not Savannah . . . but this scene was all *too* Savannah. The colors of the fabric sweeping the ceiling were those Savannah liked. I remembered shopping for couches with her and looking at this specific one. Even the statues on the pedestals looked familiar—Savannah had once kept them in her storage unit. The entire scene was something she might have designed, down to the leashed dog.

"Who are you," the vampire said, "and what made you brave disturbing—"

"And who the fuck are *you?*" I asked. "And where's the Lady Saffron? I need to—"

The vampire inclined her head, and the maid turned to look at me.

I blinked in shock.

The maid was Savannah.

11. The Vampire Queen of Little Five Points

Savannah Winters was dressed head to toe in black and white. A black, corset-like mask covered her delicate oval face from neck to nose. Her glorious flaming red hair swung free beneath a frilled maid's cap. And she wore a matching black satin French maid's dress, whose elaborate white lacings barely seemed to hold in her curvy form. The uniform was a hell of an outfit; Jinx would have *died* for it, if only she could have seen it; on the other hand, Jinx and Savannah still talked, so maybe they shopped at the same store.

But the outfit was more than pretty. The mask had no opening for her mouth. Restrictive leather mittens came up to her elbows. And barely visible beneath the ruffles of her dress were a pair of thigh bands: steel, black-rimmed, and connected by a short chain that rattled with each step. Thigh-high black boots with locked buckles finished the outfit. The boots ended in platforms so totteringly high that I felt like I'd fall over just looking at her.

"Savannah," I said. "What the hell's happened to you?"

At that Savannah glared at me from beneath her maid's bonnet and tossed her antique featherduster down. She stomped loudly over towards the center of the room, rattling with each step, and stopped straight in front of me. Even with her platforms, I still towered over her, which ruined whatever effect she'd been aiming for.

She glared up at me, silent beneath her mask; then imperiously— and it's quite a trick to do that wearing a fetish maid's outfit—she held up her two black-mitted hands like a surgeon. Without a word "the Lady Darkrose" and the dog-boy got up. Darkrose's boots clacked against the floor; the dog-boy was silent except for the rattling of his leash chain. They stepped to either side of Savannah and quickly unlaced the white lacings on her mitts; then, when she snapped her freed fingers, the dog-boy began unlacing the mask from the back. Within a few moments, he was peeling it off Savannah, and I could briefly see her long, sharp canines release the chewed black ballgag, glistening with saliva, that had kept her silent.

That didn't last for long.

"*Ptheh*," Savannah said, wiping her mouth. "Why the hell are you here, Dakota? And it's the Lady Saffron now. Our receptionist *should* have explained that we were busy—"

"Whatever happened to you as 'the vampire queen of Little Five Points'?" I asked.

"I still am," Savannah said, sulkily, turning away, eyes flicking sideways to the black dominatrix figure before strolling back to the throne, the chain between her thighs continuing to rattle with each step. "This is the Lady Darkrose, who came here from Africa to contest the appointment of such a junior vampire to this post—"

"So you folded?" I said. "You let her move in and take over—"

"Move in, yes, but take over, no. I am still the *Lady* Saffron," Savannah said, seating herself in the throne straightly, stiffly, as if she was afraid she'd sit on a tack. "And this is my domain. Make no mistake—*I* am queen of the vampires in the Little Five Points district."

She snapped her fingers, and both the Lady Darkrose and the dog-boy knelt by the side of her 'throne' and stared at the floor. I stared at Darkrose; the black dominatrix' face was controlled—no, composed. Her eyes flicked up at me, and I arched an eyebrow, as if to say, *is this for real?* Darkrose briefly nodded; then looked back down. I saw no resentment . . . in fact, she seemed completely comfortable in her role.

"Then what the hell is this show?" I asked.

"I am the queen of the vampires in Little Five Points," she said, "and if I want to be the *bondage* queen in my own court, then I shall have it."

I touched my hand to my forehead. "Darkrose is your domme," I said.

"That she is," 'Saffron' said, smiling down at her. "*And* my second in command."

"Both roles I am happy to play, my Lady Saffron," Darkrose said, staring at the floor, still perfectly composed. Clearly she had some BDSM training beyond just picking out her wardrobe, as she was as comfortable kneeling on the floor as she had been on the throne.

"Sorry," I said at last. I felt so stupid. They'd warned me to expect a show in the outer office, and I still came in here and took everything so damn seriously. "I am such an *idiot.*"

"That you are," Savannah said, still smiling.

"Who's the lucky dog?" I asked.

"Ah, Doug," she said, patting his head. "Friend of a friend. I'm training Doug for a show. But you know all about training, don't you, Dakota?"

I said nothing.

There was a long pause, and Savannah just seemed to look at me, drinking me in. Finally, she leaned forward in her chair, clanking a bit as she did so, still smiling with the slightest wince. "Now. Tell me why you're here."

"I need some help," I admitted. "I'm doing a new kind of magical tattoo—"

"I cannot believe you still do that . . . Satanist stuff," Savannah said.

Oh, Lord, not this again. "*Excuse* me, the lesbian bondage queen is going to lecture me about Satanic?"

"There's nothing Satanic about bondage—"

"There's nothing *wrong* with bondage," I said, "but when you play the Satanist card you also get fifty million Bible passages asking God to deliver people from—wait for it—bondage."

"Please," Savannah snapped, "The terms aren't analogous and you know it. Magical tattooing, on the other hand, is derived in an unbroken chain from ancient religious ritual bloodletting—"

"Excuse me, *vampire* bondage queen?"

"I'm primarily a vegetarian," Savannah said. "I only drink what I have to survive—"

"Great. But I don't care. I'm not here to debate with you, *Savannah,*" I said.

At the second use of her real name, the tall black vampire and the dog-collared submissive both twitched. Savannah's hands tightened on her throne, and after a moment Darkrose sighed, stood up and walked out. Doug the Dog flinched, but he was leashed to the throne, and Savannah made no move to free him.

At no time did the crosses on the wall even so much as shimmer, not even when Darkrose passed them. Normally when a vampire expressed ill will or anger or even got a little cross—*ha*—in front of a crucifix, it would flare up like magnesium. Even the religious tats on my knuckles tingled sometimes when I faced a pissed-off vampire. But despite Savannah's scowl—I got nothing. No flares, no tingles, no sign she bore me any ill will.

Interesting.

"Your self-control is extraordinary," I said.

"I have help," Savannah replied. "You're not helping, but I have help."

I scowled at her. I knew exactly what she meant—she was saying she was drawing on her Christian faith, on Jesus, to help her handle her hour of trial—me. The whole idea of hearing this from a lesbian vampire in a fetish bondage outfit continued to leave me speechless, and Savannah took the opportunity to deliver a lecture that I'd heard before.

"Dakota. I am a vampire now," she said. "I have entered a whole new world, with rules and customs that have evolved over the centuries to keep us civil. Here, we leave our human names behind to protect our loved ones. In this world, I am the Lady Saffron. You are *not* to use my human name in front of a fellow vampire—"

"And what name do you still write on your scientific papers?" I asked.

After a moment, Savannah replied, "Savannah Winters."

"And what's wrong with that?" I asked. "It's a beautiful name. I loved your name. You could have been Lady Savannah—"

"It was taken," Savannah said, a little piqued. She looked at me, hurt maybe. "You think I didn't *try?*"

"Not very hard." I said. I was starting to wonder what I had seen in her. "Just like you didn't try very hard to stay human after I *begged* you not to become a vampire."

The side door opened, and the Lady Darkrose appeared, having donned a long, shimmering transparent coat and acquired a small, boxy purse.

"Excuse me," she said—speaking directly to *me*, oddly subdued. Then she leaned in to kiss Savannah's cheek, and said softly, "I am stepping out."

"Oh please don't," Savannah said, oddly pleading. "We never have time to play anymore. Dakota and I will be done in a minute—"

"You two will be arguing for an hour," Darkrose said, in her odd accent. "I am just going clubbing. And it is not like I am leaving you to your own devices."

"Aw, c'mon," Savannah said, very quietly.

"You're not leaving us like this, are you?" Doug asked, whining through his mask. His leg shifted, at which point I noticed that the metal codpiece of his shorts was actually a *cage*, hiding nothing—at which point I immediately looked away, turning quite red.

"Please, Brer Rabbit, don't throw me in the briar patch," Darkrose responded, touching Savannah's glorious red hair tenderly. Then, impulsively, she leaned down and kissed her.

Two lesbians kissing for real is nothing like you see in porno. It's nothing showy, no flicking tongues or exaggerated heavy breathing. It's simple and pure and as natural as any man kissing a woman: a moment of attraction, a moment of vulnerability, a moment of pure tenderness as lips press against lips and eyes close with bliss.

I turned away. Savannah had found someone, and I was watching my more than adequate replacement. That stung like a son of a bitch.

I heard the clacking boots again, and shifted to look at Darkrose as she approached. She was tall for a woman, easily six-one counting the boots, which left her over an inch shorter than me not counting *my* boots. And, yes, I am petty enough to like being taller than Girlfriend 2.0.

"A pleasure to meet you at last, Miss Frost," she said. She was having a far better time than I would, coming face to face with a lover's ex-girlfriend; in fact she seemed to be enjoying herself as she looked at the pair sitting on the throne, then back at me. "Have fun."

"So . . ." Savannah said, shifting uncomfortably on the throne and scowling. "Now that you've ruined our Friday evening, could you finish telling me why and then get the hell out?"

"Well, uh," I said, kneading my brow, trying not to look at Doug's crotch. The cage was surprisingly distracting, once you noticed it. "Uh, I'm—"

"Spill it," Savannah said.

"I need to go to a werehouse," I said. "I'm doing a tattoo for a werewolf, and Jinx needs to consult with another werewolf about it before she can clear the design. But there are vampires running protection for the werewolves, so she sent me to you."

"And exactly *why* is your little problem important enough to disrupt *my* play night?"

"My *werewolf* client," I said, "seemed to think it was urgent that he get this *control charm* inked before the next full moon, which is a week from Saturday. Did I mention *werewolf*? Full moon—werewolf. Any more questions?"

"No," Savannah said, shaking her head with a wry smile. "Life sure is complicated."

"Tell me about it," I said.

"Sooo . . ." Savannah said. "This would be the werehouse . . . near the Perimeter, out towards Six Flags?"

"Suuure," I said. "I don't know, Savannah. I don't keep up with all the people who come running to the vampires for protection. Jinx seemed to think you would."

"As it so happens, I do. But . . . should I now add you to that list?" she asked. "Are *you* now running to *me* for protection?"

"If that's what you want to call it," I said. "If that's what it takes to get free passage—"

"Do you want my protection?" she said, firm, almost formal, but still smiling.

"Yes," I said. "I want your protection. So, look, what do we have to do? Do you just call them and put me on a list, or do I need some kind of visa or something?"

"Or something," Savannah said, smiling even more wickedly now. "Doug," she said, crooking her hand. He stood, and I turned my head to inspect the sofa, the widescreen TV. I heard ripping of Velcro, his leash rattle to the floor, and then Savannah's stage whisper:

"Fetch the box with the . . . signs of my house . . . from the dungeon."

Doug disappeared through the same side door that Darkrose had first gone through. I looked at Savannah; something about the way she was smiling was making me very uncomfortable, though the crosses were not shimmering, so she meant me no harm. Suddenly I wondered whether that was a myth; but before I could ask, Doug returned.

He had shed his puppy mitts and was carrying a large plastic box filled with metal bands similar to the ones on Savannah's thighs. Savannah ferreted around in it a bit, and withdrew a metal collar and a golden padlock. She held it in her hands, staring at me; I swallowed.

"Doug," she said. "If you would be so kind, give Dakota the sign of my house."

Doug took the collar and lock and padded towards me, and as he turned I got a good eyeful of the cage on his cock. I winced—now I'd gone and named what it was. I'd really been trying not to think of it. In all fairness, it didn't show as much as I first thought it did: it had thick metal bars and you had to think for a second to realize 'he' was in there. But I still ended up with Savannah's caged submissive standing next to me respectfully holding a collar.

I raised an eyebrow and looked at Savannah. "Is this really necessary?"

"Actually, it is," she said, smiling. "Think of this as your visa."

I sighed. "Fine," I said, turning my back to Doug.

He fumbled with the collar a bit, reaching up. "God, you're tall," he said, voice muffled by the dog's mask but clearly audible.

"You're not gagged in that thing?" I asked.

"I couldn't go 'ruf, ruf' with a gag in my mouth," he said. "Could you kneel or—"

"Give me that," I said, taking the collar. It was curiously heavy in my hands, and I felt all tingly. It was heavy and silvered on the outside, backed with dark rubber on the inside. A dangling ring hung beneath an elaborate engraved *S* on the front, and there was an odd little post-and-hole contraption on the back where it came apart. Now *I* was fumbling with it, and I looked over to see Savannah smiling, amused.

Damnit, I could figure this out. I stretched the collar open, pulled it around my neck, and closed it. I felt Doug's fingers reach up, slipping my hair from beneath it, and then pulling the edges together until the post slipped through the hole with a clack; then he pushed something heavy onto the back of the collar . . . and locked it with a sharp CLICK.

Doug returned to kneel at her side, and I turned to face her, adjusting the collar. It felt oddly . . . right about my neck, neither too tight nor too loose. I started to wonder if she'd had the collar made for me, and had kept it, waiting, all this time since we split. I caught her wicked grin, and became convinced that she had.

"This collar is the sign of my house," she said, reaching down to tug at Doug's collar, which I now noticed was identical to my own. "A sign to any vampire that sees you that you are mine, that you are not to be touched—"

"Wonderful," I said. "Is there anything else, or can I go now?"

"Oh, there's just one more thing," Savannah said. She leaned forward in her chair, looking at me with hungry, hungry eyes, and I swallowed. Surely . . . surely she didn't think . . . I was going to actually give her blood?

"Now, Dakota," Savannah said, licking her lips. "Strip."

~~

12. PROTECTING DAKOTA

"Excuzme, *what* did you say?" I said, tugging at the steel collar.

"I said, *strip*," Savannah said. "What are you worried about? It's not like you're in any *danger*," she said, lifting her skirt to reveal a set of metal 'panties'—a chastity belt, connected by glittering chains to her thigh bands. "You've already seen Doug's safe, so relax. So, Dakota, strip—" and for the *briefest* moment I actually considered doing it "—and pleasure yourself."

"*What?*" I said. Had she actually said that *with company?* "No way! I mean, good grief, what is *wrong* with you, Savannah? You two are horny, strapped in and can't play with each other, so you decide to play with me, is that it?" I adjusted the collar. Again. "Look, I don't care what you and Doug do when Darkrose leaves the two of you alone. Just don't involve me."

Savannah and Doug looked at each other in shock, then started laughing. "You think I—I mean, with him—" Savannah laughed. "Dakota, *you're* the one who likes boys."

"And I'm *not* about to come between two lovers, much less two *vampires*," Doug said. "I'm just here for the training, at the request of Sir Charles—"

"Sir Charles?" A whole forgotten world re-opened in my mind— a road not taken, or at least not traveled in a long while. Sir Charles had been a kindly old Santa Claus looking fellow who was just as comfortable chatting your ear off for hours on end as he was with whipping you until you cried and felt warm and goosy inside. It had been Sir Charles who had introduced Savannah to bondage and puppy play. The last I'd seen him, at least a couple of years ago, he was looking about a hundred and quite unwell. "How is he? Did he ever . . ."

Savannah lowered her head. "Well . . . no. He's still on the heart transplant list. He's not doing so bad beyond that, better than before, but he's definitely still on the list."

"I'm sorry to hear that but . . . look, I'm on a mission, Savannah," I said, tugging at the ring on the collar. "I don't have time for games. Let's just stipulate that you've made me remember that you're hot, that you've put me in my place, and move the fuck on—"

"But," Doug said, confused, "if she won't give blood . . . and she won't, um, you know, how are we going to get a sample?"

My jaw dropped. "How are you going to get a *what*, Pup?"

"A *bodily fluid* sample," Savannah said, and all I could do was stare at her while she tripped over her words in the rush to explain. "It's not just part of the ritual. We need them to tell if any vampire has drained you—"

"Can I spit on you? Will that do?" I said. "Hold out your hand—"

"No," she said, in all seriousness. "We need a sample more . . . charged with your aura. And since I know you'd rather die than give me blood—"

"*Savannah!* This is the *twenty-first fucking century!*" I said. "If you *really* need samples you can get a finger stick or some swabs from any medical supply house. Between all your bondage games and this 'Vampire Consulate' crap you've probably got one on speed dial!"

"Yeah" she said. "Actually . . . yeah. It's not the usual form of the ritual but . . . Doug, you think he would go for that?"

"I think he almost certainly would," Doug said. "After all, it is your court."

"*Who* would go for what?" I asked, suspicious. "Anyway, you've had your little fun. Now take this thing off and—"

"We can't," Savannah said. "Darkrose has the keys."

My eyes bugged. My fingers reached up and felt the lock: it was solidly closed.

"You have got to be shitting me," I said. "Take this fucking thing off!"

"We . . . we can't," she said, suddenly apologetic. "We used the same lock that she puts on Doug and me, and only she has the key—"

"You idiots," I snarled. "What if there was a fire?"

"She never chains us *to* anything with those," Doug said. "The leash is just a snap—"

"Get this fucking thing off me or I swear I will go down to Home Depot and buy a pair of metal clippers and snip the fucking thing off—"

"A little late for that," Doug said. "You know, the twenty-four hour Home Depot dialed their hours back, so—"

"I know lots of *welders*, not to mention professionals specializing in body modification," I said. "Somebody's got *something* that will get this off—"

"Dakota! Dakota!" Savannah said, holding up her hands. "I'm so sorry. All right? Given our history, I didn't think it would bother you so much."

"We split because you started drinking blood which you did because—wait for it—*you never think!*" I shouted. "If I didn't know better, I'd swear you were a guy always thinking with his *dick*—"

"Hey," Doug said.

"Shut up, Pup," Savannah and I said in unison.

Savannah studied me in the silence that fell. "Darkrose will be back in a couple of hours. We'll take that lock off and give you a new one with the key, but . . . you need the collar. I wasn't joking when I said it was the symbol of my house—if you don't have it I can't guarantee that other vampires won't bite first—"

"You have to be kidding. You *have* to be *kidding!*"

Doug shook his head. "She's not. Even I've been harassed by vampires, and they only quit after I showed them the collar—"

"Did you have to give a 'sample'?" I asked.

Doug looked away, embarrassed. "Yes. I don't give blood either."

The intercom buzzed, and I jumped.

"Yes, what is it?" Savannah said.

"Lord Delancaster is here," a man said, and I drew a breath. Delancaster was the vampire who made Savannah into Saffron. "He says you called upon him, Lady Saffron."

"Tell him our crosses are uncovered, so we shall join him in the vestibule."

"As you wish, Lady Saffron." The intercom went dead.

Wonderful. The vampire who made Saffron. I'd never met him. Sight unseen, I despised him. And didn't intend to hang around and do a polite little meet and greet now. "Alright," I said. "Thank you, 'Lady Saffron,' for this damn visa, and for the lovely little show that left it locked around my neck. *You* go meet with your master, *I'll* go meet with the werewolves, and we can talk about getting this off me when I get back—"

I turned to go, but Savannah raised her hand. "Wait, you can't leave. We're not done. Don't you want my protection?"

I let out my breath. "At this point, no, not really. It's not like every vampire you meet is a serial killer . . . but . . . damnit, I do still worry about the pesky few. *You* know this gang, you tell me—do I *need* your protection?"

Savannah sagged in her chair. "It's on the west side," she said, scanning the floor as she considered. "Yes, you do need it. I'm sorry. I'm sad to say, if you really want to be safe, you even need it in the vampire district, if people knew you were my ex—"

"Damn blood junkies," I said.

"We're trying to do better," she said, leaning forward, almost pleading. "We really are. Lord Delancaster approves of our efforts. You'll like him—"

"*Not* likely," I said, "and in any case I'm not planning to stay and get chummy—"

"But you *have* to," she said. "He's the Lord of Georgia. He has to confirm my protection. You need his 'ban'. The sample is for him—that's why I summoned him."

My jaw tightened. I counted to ten and reminded myself that if a vampire worried about where I was going, I needed protection. And this was from Savannah, who probably really did have my best interests at heart. Son of a bitch. "Of *course* I have to meet him. How stupid of me not to have realized. The hits just keep on coming," I said. "Let's get this over with."

"Please don't make a scene," Savannah said. She got up and snapped for Doug to follow her. He started to crawl, and she muttered something, so he got onto his feet, which had the side effect of exposing his little cage again. Oy. The hits really *did* keep on coming.

Lord Reynold James Delancaster waited in the vestibule, the perfect parody of a modern vampire. His long silvery hair poured back over the soft brown cape and coat he had apparently stolen from Sherlock Holmes; one hand checked a pocketwatch, which he deposited back into the pocket of a brocaded vest; the other hand rested on the top of a jewel-headed cane.

Before she'd turned, Savannah had told me breathlessly that he'd been the model for Louis in *Interview with the Vampire*. Personally, *I* think he was just hamming it up, and it made him look like a bad copy of Lucius Malfoy.

"You called," he said, his deep voice sounding more like Lurch from the Addams Family than the whine of everyone's favorite angst-ridden gothy vampire. "I trust it was urgent."

Delancaster lived in the Little Five Points District—not far from me in Candler Park, actually—but not as Savannah's subject; as her ruler. Officially his full title was Lord of the Vampires for Georgia, making Savannah kind of like a mayor in the world of vampire politics.

"Lord Delancaster," Savannah said, smiling, bowing deferentially to the vampire. I wondered how smart giving her a court was: 'Saffron' was *extremely* powerful for a such young vampire, and history was filled with empires toppled because the heirs were eager to inherit. Vampire nepotism might make it just as hard to hold onto power.

But, watching her bowing . . . I remembered this was Savannah. For all of her supposed power, she was still a wet-behind-the-ears twenty-seven-year-old with a submissive streak. She was obviously treating this like some kind of grand game where she was the star player, and by letting her ham it up Delancaster had no doubt wrapped her round his finger.

Savannah was up and talking again. "Thank you for coming on such short notice."

"That is . . . quite the outfit. Going out for Halloween?" Lord Delancaster asked, kissing her hand. As he did so, he caught sight of Doug's cage and flinched. "Oh my. Hello, Douglas. I take it you are *not* going out tonight."

"Hello, RJ," Doug responded, nodding briefly. "Not like this, no."

"Well, my Lady Saffron," the Lord Delancaster said, with a forced smile. "Your court is always a show."

"Tell me about it," I muttered. "The sight of a three hundred year old vampire flinching *alone* was worth the price of admission."

"Be nice," Savannah said icily. "I'm sorry, my Lord Delancaster. My *supplicant* here interrupted the Lady Darkrose and me during our play."

Lord Delancaster looked at me.

I've heard you're not supposed to look vampires in the eyes, but I've never had any patience for that, so I just stared straight back at him. His eyes were fine amber; they would probably glow gold if he exerted his power, giving me a chance to flinch if I needed to; but apparently he had far too much control for that. "You must be Miss Frost," he said. "The young lady who almost kept my Lady Saffron from me."

"The one and only," I said, tilting my head. I had a whole *list* of other things I had always wanted to say to the bloodsucker who stole Savannah from me, but I gritted my teeth and kept it to, "Best magical tattooist in the Southeast."

But Delancaster caught some of what I had *not* said from the look in my eyes. "You have a fire in you," he said. "I can see why she nearly turned down my offer of eternal life—"

"You don't have that to offer," Savannah said coldly.

"Bodily immortality, if you prefer," the Lord Delancaster said, bowing. "Or agelessness. I meant no offense to your religious beliefs—"

"Fine, fine, fine," I said, before he could get Savannah started on that again. "We're all one big happy vampire family, respecting each other's beliefs, and even managing to pretend Doug's whing-whang isn't hanging out. All that still leaves me wearing this stupid collar *just* so I don't have to worry about *other* vampires gnawing on me while I go consult with a graphomancer they're guarding. So whatever you're here to do, let's do it, so I can get on with it. I am on the clock."

Lord Delancaster looked at me, face oddly blank. "Very well," he said, his mask of humanity seeming to filter away, leaving something cold, ancient and impersonal. "Please tell me this one is willing to give blood—"

"No, and no on other bodily fluids," I snapped.

He looked at Savannah, humanity flooding back into his features. "Then how is this going to work—"

"We're going to use a finger stick," she said, stepping behind the wet bar.

"Of course," Lord Delancaster said, tapping his fingers to his forehead. "This *is* the twenty-first century. But that will only grant a partial protection. I will still need to taste—"

"No," I repeated.

"Your *aura*," he said pointedly. "Your aura will do—"

"And what precisely is the purpose of this?" I asked. "Why isn't the collar enough protection? Can't you just use your vampire telepathy to put out the word—"

"Vampire . . . telepathy?" Lord Delancaster said, puzzled.

"You can't fool me," I said. "She summoned you without ever leaving her chair."

"*I* called him from the bedroom," Doug said. "He has a cell phone."

"To answer your question, my Lady Frost," Lord Delancaster said, "While many of us in the vampire community desire to be a part of the normal human world, others do not. When you asked for our protection, you called on much older rituals. In the olden days, if you had asked for our protection, I would have drunk your blood, tasted your flesh and bathed in your aura, and then, if you were attacked, even if the body were well hidden, I and the other close members of my court could sense your blood in his veins and scent out whether he'd despoiled you."

"So drink my blood and you're a walking vampire crime lab," I said. "Neat. Let's call CBS and see if they're interested in doing *CSI: Vampire Atlanta*."

"I like that," Lord Delancaster said. "That's more appropriate than you know. With the finger stick, I no longer need to drink your blood, and with modern rape kits, we were already considering phasing out the tasting part of the ritual. But there was another purpose to the tasting; the fluids your body produces are charged with your life force and transmit the essence of your aura. A drop of blood from a wound won't do it. If I cannot bite you or taste you, I will still need to feel your aura."

"What's that going to involve?" I asked, trying to keep contact with his tiger eyes and glancing away, nervous. Savannah came out from behind the wetbar with a small medical kit. She sat herself down on a barstool and patted for me to join her. As I did so, Lord Delancaster came to stand behind me, placing his hands gently on my shoulders. I looked sideways at them, swallowing: his fingernails were long and sharp, like claws.

Savannah pulled out a small orange piece of plastic and grabbed my hand. Actually she didn't grab it, she just took it gently. But her grip was like steel, completely unyielding, and I bucked uselessly. "Hey, wait—"

"I don't want to lick a slide," Delancaster said.

"Doug, fetch us a spoon," Savannah said, matter-of-fact, holding the orange thing over my finger and preparing to jab. I tried to twist away, but her grip tightened. "Hold still."

"You're hurting me," I said. "And not the right, it's my tattooing hand."

"My Lady Savannah," Lord Delancaster breathed, voice so close to my ear that I felt my heart flutter. "Be nice."

Savannah glared at me, then her eyes flicked aside to Lord Delancaster. Finally she let go my hand. "I'm sorry. But if you want our protection we do need to do this."

Lord Delancaster's breath was warm and alive in my ear, and I could feel his power prickling over my skin. "O-okay," I said, holding out my left hand.

Savannah took it, pricked my forefinger quickly, and squeezed slightly. A dark, red drop of blood welled up, and her lips parted with a small sigh like a little orgasm. Mesmerized, she took the spoon from Doug like a sleepwalker, squeezing my finger gently to release the flow of blood. She looked up at me, squirming on the seat, eyes filled with as much lust for my blood as she had ever had for my naked body—and then Lord Delancaster's lips brushed my throat.

"I will not break the skin," he said, breath spreading across my neck, deep voice thrilling through me down to my very toes. "I promise."

"O-okay," I repeated dreamily, leaning back against his hard body, slipping my thumb into the buckle of my belt, letting my fingers play over the buttons of my pants as Savannah drained more blood into the spoon. Now I wished I had taken her up on her offer to strip; this was so intimate, so erotic that all my clothing, my armor seemed . . . inappropriate.

His lips parted, and I felt the side of his fangs pressed against my jugular, just above the collar. My blood pounded in my ears, thrummed though my neck, and I felt a warm, distant drumbeat echoing across the magical ink woven through my tattoos—Lord Delancaster's heart. The drumbeat grew louder and louder, and I squirmed on the seat, sinking back against him, curling my toes. A new drumbeat joined the jungle rhythm, one I instinctively recognized as Savannah's; and I opened my eyes to see Savannah's slender extended arm, and Lord Delancaster draw his lips aside from my neck to drink the blood from her proffered spoon.

The silvery spoon drew back from his lips, and Delancaster closed his eyes in bliss. Apparently chocolate ice cream had nothing on blood. Then Delancaster leaned away. "I have her pulse," he said. "Yes, I have it."

I looked down sharply, clearing my head. Savannah, looking as sad as a cat whose food bowl had been swiped away, held a white cotton ball over my finger, and was unsuccessfully trying to unwrap a Band-Aid with her other hand. "Doug, a hand here."

"Whoa," I said. My forehead was feverish, and I felt sweaty.

"I have tasted your aura, drunk your blood, felt the beat of your heart," Lord Delancaster said, stepping back to the center of the room. "If any vampire I meet has drunk your blood, or taken your life, I will know it. In honesty, I will very likely know if they were to spoil you. I will make this known that you have the protection of the House of Saffron, but the ban of the Lord of Georgia as well."

"Swell," I said, a bit woozy. I shook my head, and the room swam. "Swell."

"Before I return to my Halloween party," Lord Delancaster said, stepping back to retrieve his cane, "is there anything else you want to protect?"

"Isn't my blood, my life and my sex enough?" I asked. I took a deep breath, tried to get a grip on myself. He hadn't even broken the skin, and I'd damn near had an orgasm—no *wonder* mortals got so easily seduced by vampires. "Seems, ah, seems pretty comprehensive—"

"What if they decided to take their anger out on one of your friends?" he said, and I swallowed, pulling at the collar. "Or did something as childish as trashing your car? I'm sorry, but immature vampires can be petty . . . and creative. We do need to be specific."

"A young witch recommended this to me," I said. The sudden surge of adrenaline was doing a better job of clearing my head than my own efforts had. "Skye 'Jinx' Anderson. And I drive a POS Vespa, but I don't want that trashed either."

"I don't know all modern car makes," he said. "Is POS the model number or—"

"Piece of Shit," I said, "and it's a scooter, license plate MAGTAT."

"I saw it," he said, closing his eyes briefly, as if recalling and re-memorizing every detail. "Is there anything else you'd like to protect?"

Abruptly I flashed on Richard Sumners—he'd insured his hands for a million dollars. What the hell? It couldn't hurt. "Just my hands. I'm a tattoo artist."

"Your life, blood, and sex; your friend, scooter, and hands," he said, reciting the odd list in complete seriousness. "I think that is as extensive, and as specific, as we can make the ban; but it will have to do."

"Thanks," I said.

He took my hand, raised it, and kissed it chastely. "Remember, this protection only lasts in the inner city. Outside the Perimeter, the vampires can no longer protect you.. So please, do not forget: if you travel outside the circle of I-285, you should stick to the safe places that humans instinctively gather in—or else you will run into creatures far more dangerous than either vampires or werewolves."

My lip pursed up. "Thank you, Lord Delancaster."

I still couldn't wrap my head around the *vampires* being Atlanta's force of supernatural law and order.

13. THE WEREHOUSE

The werehouse stood at the edge of the Chattahoochee, a bombed-out vestige of ironworks damaged beyond hope of repair on the river's slimy banks. The entrance was an unlikely path struggling down an embankment of a bridge crossing, a trail so trampled that the earth opened up in a jagged wound of red clay. Trash was piled everywhere, cigarette butts, beer bottles, ants swarming over mustard packets spilling out of a discarded Chick-fil-A bag. I gagged. I couldn't stand the smell. I couldn't imagine how the weres did either.

No doubt it was a steal on the rent.

The moon was swelling close to whole—what did that make it? New? *Gibbous*?—and I heard a soft thump as the vamp guard I'd been told to expect jumped down behind me.

"Ah-ah-ah," a soft, velvety voice said, almost near enough to taste. You could almost hear him wagging his finger. "You don't want to go down that path at this hour, mortal."

I turned, and the vampire cringed at the blaze of my cross.

"Jeez!" he said, half choking on the word.

"Sorry," I said, slipping the cross back under my shirt. I squared off with the vampire, hands jammed into the buttery leather of my trench vest, letting my tattoos gleam in the silver of the streetlight. "You must be Insomnia?" I said, hoping I got his name right.

I was wrong.

The little vampire punk quit cringing and glared, drawing himself to his full height, pale, made-up face falling as he realized I still towered a half a head over him, even counting his ridiculous teased hair that made him look like an albino member of the Flock of Seagulls. His face fell even further as he realized I was not the least bit intimidated.

How could I be? A vampire in makeup, designed to make him look more like a vampire? *Total poseur.* He looked like he shopped at Hot Topic—not that I don't—and had even gotten mud on the hems of his bondage pants, the ones with the cheap plastic handcuffs and glittering chains that are supposed to look all Goth and edgy. And *this* was supposed to be a *guard?*

"I," he said pretentiously, fake accent and all, "am the Vampire Transomnia."

"Dakota Frost," I replied, and the rest of him deflated. "I was sent by Jinx to see the Marquis, and I travel under the protection of the Lady Saffron, Queen of Little Five Points." I tugged at the metal collar once or twice to make sure he saw it.

The little vampire glowered at me—ok, perhaps not little, most likely average height for a guy—and I hopped down from the slight ridge to land in the clearing next to him, hoping that reducing the height difference would set him at ease. It didn't help. The proximity apparently made me even more threatening. His lips parted in a slow sigh, tips of his canines pointed past human, eyes glinting in his pale pudgy face like black olives shoved into the surface of a puff pastry.

"*Saffron* protects you?" he said, hot breath curling on the air, a dull red glow building in his eyes. I suddenly realized I was within arms' reach of a vampire—a scrawny, poseur, threatened, insulting vampire who wanted a pissing match. "You could have done better than to ally yourself with that . . . maid."

His lip curled further, and the bit of dried blood at the root of his fangs erased any illusions as to whether he'd been the one to eat the fast food from the sack tossed on the ground. Christ, he'd fed, not minutes ago, and not from the drive-thru window. He'd been sloppy about it. I hoped to God it had been a rat, but . . .

I swallowed and slowly took my hands out of my pockets— empty. Showing him I wasn't carrying a stake or something.

"I didn't have a choice," I said. "I live in her district."

"No, you *had* a choice," he said, his lip twisting up into a mocking sneer. "Not to come here. Now that you have . . . you have to pay the toll."

I raised my hands. "I'll use a different entrance—"

"Too late," he said, grin widening, both fangs now exposed. "You're already under the bridge, and *I'm* the troll."

Shit, so much for Saffron's *protection*. "Hey, I just want to speak to the Marquis," I said, raising my hands higher. "And I'm glad to go through you to do it."

I said it so placatingly that he actually blinked as he processed it. In that split second I flipped my hands, and when his lids opened he got an eyeful of the crosses, stars and sickles upon each knuckle. They blazed with power, resonating with the vampire's own projected aura of hostility, and when he flinched, my right fist popped out and landed the holy symbols on his face in a twisting one-inch punch.

All the mana stored in my tattoos and all the hate feeding back through the holy symbols released with a flash and a solid, satisfying BANG, and the vampire flew back into the mud and slid halfway down the riverbank.

"I protect Saffron as much as she protects me," I said, strolling over to where the vampire lay, planting my fist in my other hand to let the charms charge up against the yin-yang in my palm. "Now would you, pretty please with sugar on it, take me to see the Marquis?"

The vampire was blinking, twitching, and I started to worry I'd hit him too hard. Then his eyes focused on me, and I felt the holy symbols on my knuckles start to tingle in a hot wave of hate. I settled back, feeling adrenaline flood me. He wasn't supposed to get back up—what the hell was I going to do if he rushed me with vampire speed? "You're dead," he snarled, fangs fully exposed. "You are so *dead*, bitch!"

He reached toward a bush to pull himself back up—but before he could, the bush put out a strong male hand to steady the vampire. "Enough, Trans," said a deep voice, and the bush unfolded, branches morphing into the proud antlers of a deer's head that flowed into the shoulders of a ruddy Native American warrior—a werestag, in half-human form.

"Homina," I breathed.

"Lord Buckhead," Transomnia stammered. "I—I didn't see you—"

"You were not meant to," the werestag said. "I was watching your watching."

Lord Buckhead carried a staff topped with the skull and antlers of a deer, adorned with eagle's feathers, but beyond that wore only a loincloth, buckskins, and an ornately woven chestpiece of beads bumping against his broad chest. His bare feet were almost as ruddy as the clay, but left only the slightest impressions as he effortlessly helped the smaller man up the bank and set him down beside me. I paid the vampire no mind. The werestag was almost seven feet tall—without the antlers—and despite the oddly solemn expression of his deer's head, there was a lively, reactive intelligence behind his eyes that I never saw in any beast.

"Luh-Lord *Buckhead*," I stammered. For years I'd heard Edgeworld stories that 'the lord of Buckhead' was real, and not just a character cooked up by the marketing team of Atlanta's party district, but now when he stood before me all I could think was how *nice* it was to stare *up* at a guy, even if he had a deer's head. "The Lord of the Wild Hunt?"

"The one and only," he said.

I became convinced I'd *seen* him before—and after a second, I realized exactly where. "That—that statue of you in downtown Buckhead . . . is for *real?*"

"The human sculptor Fleming used me as his model," he said, extending his hand. "I can take you to the Marquis. Trans, you will accompany us."

"I'm not supposed to leave my post," he said, staring at the ground.

"Your post is well-covered by my hunt," Lord Buckhead said. The little vampire looked around suddenly, but nothing was visible. "It is your orders that I want to clarify."

"Yes, sir," Transomnia said, hunched over.

We wove through the weeds along a path that was little more than a crease in the grass. Lord Buckhead seemed to move without a trace, and I suspected the rest of the werehouse's population also didn't leave the mess left by humans or vampires.

Lord Buckhead stopped by a weathered POSTED – NO TRESPASSING sign and lifted a heavy section of chain-link fence for us to step under. As I did so I saw a trio of magical runes and Edgeworld tags listing this as a were-lair, a no-man's land, and a safe house. An odd combination, but it made sense. *All who are not werekin are not welcome.*

The werehouse was a long, low brick building with cracked walls and rusted cranes that resembled a derelict battleship more than the fortress I'd expected. A few spotlights on the roof and at the edge of the weed-grown parking structure made pools of light, but beyond that I could only make out outlines. My tattoos tingled with a whisper of power, and I felt as if the place was crawling with movement I could not see. Figures seemed to lurk at the edge of the lot, behind the windows, on the battlements, but I could never draw a bead on a one. I could hear the din of a party, or a barfight, raucous cries of humans mixed in with rougher cries of something else. And then, shockingly close, a howl.

I looked up to see a dark form howling at the moon from the tip of a crane: he looked . . . bipedal, but when he quit howling and looked down at me, his eyes glowed a brilliant violet, and when he ran off he ran too low, too hunched and too fast for any man.

"Keep moving," Transomnia said, bumping me roughly with his shoulder as he passed. "Let's get this over with."

He stopped at the base of a loading dock, staring up at a huge freight door, and two shadows detached themselves from either side to glare down at us with cold, blue eyes. This time, I didn't risk looking the vampires in the eyes; I'd never been hypnotized by one before, but my experience with the quite friendly Lord Delancaster had put the fear of God in me—something these guys probably lacked.

"Brought us a snack, Trans?" one of them said, hopping down from the dock to land at our feet. He was scrawny, but confident, letting his long trenchcoat drape along his thin form with an ease that Transomnia lacked. Like the poseur vampire, his frosted locks were upswept, and keys dangled from a glittering chain at his belt; but somehow he made it look right. The other vampire's teased locks were brown but he had a similar trench, similar chain, and equal grasp of style. The first vampire was all business, but the brown-haired hanger-back made an odd hand signal that Transomnia shot back at him.

Gang signs. Jinx wasn't kidding—a real vampire gang.

"You are a pretty one," the vampire said. "What's your name, morsel?"

I glared at him. I couldn't make out anything about his face other than his glowing blue eyes, but I glared anyway, screwing up my forehead as if I could force myself to maintain my concentration in the face of any psychic assault that he might mount—ridiculous, of course, as my psychic training was about zip. But I could feel my tattoos start to burn as he began to project his aura, and I looked away, jamming my tingling hands in my pockets. I didn't want a repeat of my insult to Trans, not in the middle of three vampires.

I heard a sudden exhale behind me that ruffled the hair of my 'hawk.

"My Lord," the vampire guard said, beginning a bow. Then he caught sight of the collar around my neck, and I saw his eyes widen—and the blue glow fade.

"My apologies, *Emissary*," he said, with some respect. "What news do you bring from Lady Saffron's court?"

"I am here under her protection, but on my own behalf," I said, looking up to meet his now more-human eyes. They were blue, a clear blue that stood out even in what little light we had from the few spotlights, and his face was fine, even handsome, when he wasn't putting out his scary vampire mojo. "My name is Dakota Frost. I'm here to consult with the Marquis at the behest of Jinx. I'm told he's expecting me."

The vampire stared at me, then inclined his head and spoke to his brownhaired fellow guard. "Should I know any of those names?"

"Well, the *Marquis* for starters," Transomnia interjected sarcastically.

"And why did you abandon your post?" the vampire said sharply, and Transomnia stared at the pavement. "And why did the Lord Buckhead see fit to escort you back here, bloodied and covered in mud?"

"These two fought," Lord Buckhead said, and I suddenly became embarrassed. "He barred her way . . . and she objected. Forcefully."

"My, my," the brownhaired vampire guard said, leaning close in to me. "*You* objected . . . and brought our 'mighty' Trans low?"

"I could have taken her," Transomnia said.

"Knowing she was under the protection of the Daywalker?" the blond guard said. "You're lucky Lord Buckhead intervened. You're *already* on your third warning; had you done anything rash, we would have given her your head on a platter."

"But I—"

"Enough! This is a good gig, and we don't need you screwing it up. Revy! Take his post. Scare away the curious and the riffraff—especially the prostitutes. But if you get anyone persistent, do what Transomnia was ordered to have done—call the guardhouse for an escort."

"Yes, Calaphase," the guard said—and quicker than a blink, leapt off. I whirled, but by the time I had turned, all I could see was the fence shaking. He was gone. I looked back to find Calaphase towering over Transomnia. "Our guests should not find it necessary," he growled, "to have Lord Buckhead watching over them."

"How are you really different?" I asked. "*You* were going to nosh on me."

Calaphase stared at me briefly, calculatingly. "My apologies," he said, not sounding apologetic at all. "I was . . . playing the role I thought you expected. Not all fear us as you do. You have the scent of blood and vampires on you so . . . I thought you were a *willing* morsel."

"We just did this stupid ceremony not an hour ago," I said, tugging at the collar's ring. "Besides, Sav—the Lady Saffron is my ex. Every time I see her, she gets clingy."

"You weren't in her court before?" he said. "You took her collar just to come here?"

"Just because I was afraid of you, yes," I said. "Or more to the point, both Jinx and Saffron thought that I needed her protection, and the ban of Lord Delancaster, to come here."

Calaphase glared down at Transomnia. "You have not helped our reputation."

"Except our reputation as scary motherfuckers," Transomnia said.

"Not even that," Calaphase said, "Apparently, she won Round One."

He extended an arm towards a set of stairs, and I climbed the stairs up the loading dock. Transomnia, Lord Buckhead, and Calaphase leapt up on to the dock nimbly, as if they'd just climbed a single step. Calaphase looked at me, then Transomnia, shaking his head; then with one hand he pulled the huge freight door open to reveal a carnival of light and sound.

"Come with us, Lady Frost, and the Oakdale Vampire Clan shall apologize to you for our rudeness before the Bear King."

"And then," Transomnia said, unsmiling, "we shall see what he will make of you."

14. THE MARQUIS

Drums beat, strong and primal. Fire blazed from burning barrels. And on the broad floor of what had been a warehouse, a crowd of nearly-human shapes cheered on as a huge wolf the size of a tiger faced off with a stag the size of a Buick.

I started to think that maybe this job wasn't worth it.

Ragged young boys ran the outer perimeter of the werehouse, human in form but snapping and snarling at each other with the voices of dogs. Wolves padded back and forth around the largest and scruffiest single group of men; both wolves and men stared at me with hungry eyes. There were other groups—tall, proud men I took to be werestags, another group crowded around a werebear, and many others. Or perhaps there was no relation between their human forms and their beasts—I had not seen any of them change yet.

To the snarling was added whistling. I looked up, and saw an upper set of loft structures, perhaps once offices, that had been converted into living space. Boys and young men, expertly tattooed with wolf's heads and cat's paws, hung from the railing, whistling down at me. I laughed. *Actual wolf whistles and cat calls!* My laughter faded as I saw girls mixed in with the boys, angry, indignant—hitting their men and glaring down at me.

Then an orange-haired girl leapt down from the railing, shoved a knot of boys apart and stalked up to me. She wore a cropped top and vest and short pants that showed off elaborate, tattooed tiger stripes—and it was good work, I mean, *I* was impressed—but the claws erupting from her fingers and the tail curving behind her were quite real.

"You thinks you can just waltz in here and get a taste of our men?" she said, glaring up at me with yellow cat eyes, which made her all the more exotic and beautiful. She held up a long, sharp set of claws. "You thinks you can go through me to do it?"

I leaned in down on her until my face was inches from her exotic, oval face, and her tufted cat ears folded back as her eyes grew wider. I closed mine, and drank in her scent. She was warm and spicy with sweat, with a hint of real perfume that tasted of cinnamon.

"Oooh, you smell *yummy*," I cooed, opening my eyes to see hers terrified. "Why would I want *them* when *you're* throwing yourself at me? Give me a taste, little girl."

Emboldened, I licked her face, and she leapt back with a squeal, hissing at me and swatting like a frightened little cat. It made her all the more cute, like the younger Savannah I remembered, and I watched her back all the way to a clump of the very same boys she'd challenged me over, hissing and swatting at them as they laughed.

I licked my lips. "Definitely cinnamon."

"*Most* interesting," Calaphase said. "Definitely *Saffron's* ex."

Lord Buckhead suddenly strode forward and broke into the ring, pulling the wolf and stag apart like a pair of stuffed toys. The stag snorted and challenged him, but the wolf just whined and tried to get away. Both twisted uselessly at the ends of his straightened arms.

"Enough!" he shouted, his voice ringing out throughout the house. "We are not animals, that we should fight like dogs!"

"But this is a werehouse, Lord Buckhead," snarled a voice that was half laugh and half roar, as Lord Buckhead slowly lowered the combatants to the floor. "This is not a place for decorum. This is a place to celebrate our beasts! And when is more appropriate to celebrate our beasts than Halloween?"

Oh, just wonderful. Halloween was just next Tuesday . . . and this was Friday night. This was *literally* a Halloween party. Every werekin in the Atlanta metro region was probably here tonight, and I'd wandered straight into it.

Lord Buckhead released the fighters, and they slunk away. The stag looked back once or twice, but Lord Buckhead did not acknowledge him. Buckhead just stared up at the end of the hall, to a raised platform, and even though he had a stag's head I could tell he was glaring.

"But what is this?" the voice said, and I swallowed as the crowd parted to reveal the massive shape looming on the platform. "What have you brought before us tonight?"

A huge chair welded from parts of cars made the throne for a massive man-bear easily nine feet tall. The long claws of his "hands" curled over the working headlights of an old Cadillac. The engine and grille had been removed to make room for a huge bench seat groaning beneath the weight of two hairy, brawny legs. The hood had been flipped up into a backrest for his hyperdeveloped chest and shoulders, which were covered in a shaggy mane that would have made a lion proud. And atop his massive neck loomed a head that looked like it could have swallowed me whole, with two glowing green eyes fixed straight upon me.

"My name is *Dakota Frost*," I said, voice ringing out in a silence that was unexpected. "I travel under the protection of the court of the Lady Saffron and the ban of the Lord Delancaster, but I come here to see the Marquis on business of my own."

"I think Lord Buckhead was supposed to introduce you," Calaphase said under his breath—and I noticed he'd moved quite a few steps back, with Transomnia skulking behind him like a wayward child.

"Ooops," I said, turning back to face the Bear King. At least, I assumed it was the Bear King; hopefully there weren't two of these monstrosities floating around.

A wolf lying at the monster's feet snarled something, and the Bear King snarled back so deep it reverberated in my gut. "We have a human in our court," he spat. "If you have not learned to use a human voice in that shape, don't talk to me."

The wolf ran off, snarling and whining, and the Bear King leaned back, seeming to become even larger against his oversized throne. He waved a hand at the throng. "We care not for vampire politics," he said, eyes boring into me. "Tell me, why have you dared to interrupt our Halloween revels, little one?"

"Little," I snapped, stalking forward. The vampires hung back as I walked forward through the predominantly werewolf crowd, climbed the steps of his throne and stopped straight in front of him. The huge beast's jowls were only a few feet from mine.

"Little," I said, projecting my voice, turning around to face the throng. On one level, I was scared out of my wits; on another, the only way I could get through this was to brazen my way through. "I can't tell you how good it is to hear a man call me 'little'!"

The bear leaned closer. "Are you challenging me, little one?"

"Good heavens, no," I said, waving my hand to indicate his legion of followers. "You get plus three, plus three to attack as long as seven or more cards are in play."

The Bear King froze for a moment, befuddled; I guess he didn't play *Magic: The Gathering*. Then he laughed, a long, hearty laugh that sounded jarringly human coming from his monstrous face. "Very well, little one, tell us what was so urgent that it could not wait?"

"I'm doing a tattoo for a werewolf," I said, "and he wants it done before the full moon."

The bear head stared at me, then laughed uproariously, the whole crowd laughing and howling with him. "Oh, I very much doubt that."

"A *werewolf* wants *her* to do a tattoo," a female voice cried, and I saw the girl who had challenged me hanging on to one of her boys and pointing at me. I blew her a kiss, and quicker than a magic trick, she was hiding behind her friends. Satisfied, I refocused on the bear.

"Marquis, this one is no threat to you," the Bear King said. "Approach without fear."

I turned, and saw a man with a raised brown Wolverine haircut and long brocaded coat step cautiously out from one of the doors leading to the warren of side offices and shops. He looked like an extra from the Renaissance Faire who fell off the back of a truck and then got run over by it. He had elaborate pants and a ruffled pirate shirt beneath the brocade, but all were old, dirty, nearly as unkempt as his hair. He approached us with a curiously mincing step and upraised hands held slack, as if he deigned to touch nothing other than his tattooing tools.

He hopped up onto the platform gracefully, and bowed to me. He didn't do the standard double take when he stood and found me still towering over him, which notched him up in my regard; but then he turned to the throng and spoke with evident disdain. "I heard this is the 'artist' who would tattoo a wolf," he said to the crowd, in a high-pitched voice that nonetheless carried. "Show her we need no more inkers!"

A young man leapt forward, baring his chest to show a gleaming tattoo of a wolf, woven with marks for sharp sight. Another leapt forward with tribal signs granting increased hunting powers; the young girl paraded back and forth, and I could see stealth and grace written into her tiger stripes.

It was all excellent work: the outlines were sharp, the shading subtle, the colors vibrant; but I needed to know more, and impulsively I stepped down into the little crowd of exhibitionists, who now numbered five. There were others showing off tattoos behind the front row, but it was all just normal ink or minor marks: these five were the finest the Marquis had to display, and knew it.

I stretched out my hands and felt the power through their marks. The subtle interplay of ink and line necessary to call upon magic were woven through all their signs. I recognized some of the larger signs, but just as many were clearly new, having none of Jinx's mathematical subtlety but instead a raw grip on the rules of power inked with a firm, well-trained hand. The Marquis was not just an inker; he was a backwoods graphomancer, with a fine grasp of the magic of the wolf. No wonder Jinx had recommended him.

"Impressive," I said, loud enough to carry through the throng. I was getting pretty tired of playing this like I was on a stage; I much preferred meeting in a coffeehouse, Jinx-style, to all these theatrics. "I can see why Jinx sent me to you."

"The blind witch is truly gifted," the Marquis called out to the crowd, smiling with a bow as I ascended to the stage. "Even she can see my superior talent."

I smiled at him. He smirked back at me, yellow glowing eyes the only thing wolfish about his weak, effete face. Well, in truth his hair was pretty wolfish too, but that was clearly achieved with just a lack of grooming than any expression of wolf. Or maybe I was rapidly losing my patience and not inclined to give him an inch. So I just stared straight back at him, smiling, until the glow faltered and he looked away.

"So, 'Marquis,'" I said, in a quiet tone designed to be heard only on the stage, withdrawing a picture tube from my vest and unrolling the flash, blown up to 11x17 and cleaned up as much as Photoshop would permit. "Tell me what you make of this?"

He looked at it for a moment, then took it from me with an offended hiss, strolling away. He stared down at it dismissively, then with more and more interest. Finally he turned back to me. "Where," he whined, loud enough to play to his audience, "did you get this?"

"My *client*," I replied. "He thinks it will give him more control over his beast."

"Oh, it will," he laughed, still speaking to the crowd, eyes never leaving the tattoo. "It will . . . it most definitely will."

"'Most definitely will' as in 'will definitely control his beast by interfering with his changes in a bad way,'" I asked, "or 'will definitely give him more self control?'"

He looked at me sharply, eyes flicking back down. "You would not understand."

"Try me."

"It will . . . contain his excess power as the moon approaches," he said, "then release it when he decides to trigger the change."

"See, I understood that just fine," I said. "Was that so hard, Mister Wizard?"

He flapped his hand once or twice to dismiss me, waltzing off. "Enough, girl. You have done your duty. Send this wolf to me, and I will ink him."

Hear that *snap*? The camel's back—right after the last straw.

"Not going to happen," I said, crushing the picture tube in my hand.

"Excuse me?" the Marquis said, slowly turning back to me.

"This is *my* client," I said. "I did not risk life and limb coming here *just* to hand him over to you. I need your advice, for which you'll be well paid. That's it."

Hot breath brushed past my face and feathered my 'hawk, and I looked aside to see the glowing green eyes of the Bear King not two feet from my face.

"The Marquis tattoos all the werekin in my realm," he said, voice crackling like two slabs of granite sliding over each other. "We need no other."

"If he was in your realm, he'd have already come to the Marquis," I said. "He's not. He's a Little Fiver, an Edgeworlder. He's under *Saffron's* protection, and came to *me*—and he's going under *my* needle."

"You *are* challenging me, aren't you, little one?"

I should have been filled with terror. Alright, I *was* filled with terror—despite the fact I've never been afraid of bears, even when I watch some giant Kodiak's crap-inducing roar on the Discovery Channel. For some reason they're not as scary to me as tigers, much less the fake stuff dreamed up by H.R. Giger, that really twists my gut. But here, inches away from the Bear King's bared teeth and red glowing eyes, I was terrified and frightened to the point of useless bravado.

So I squeezed my fist tight, pouring a cascade of *mana* down the vines into my yin-yang, and then shoved my glowing palm at his face.

The Bear King ducked his head back as if stung, snarling, but otherwise frozen, making no move to respond. I could feel his magic, his power sparkling on the edge of my tattoos, and it was far weaker than I expected; surely it took more power than that to change man into beast? The Bear King's eyes tightened in very human rage and his muzzle wrinkled in a very feral snarl, and he began to shake, his claws drawing a squealing whine out of the metal of his throne, tires supporting it squeaking ominously as he shifted his weight. Now I *was* challenging him, on his own throne; but he was afraid of magic; and there was no easy way out for us without one of us showing weakness. He *had* to respond to *this*.

And then it was the Marquis who rescued us, leaping forward to come between me and the Bear King, grasping my hand with one tattooed thumb pressed into my yin-yang to bleed off the power. "And so we have ourselves not just an inker, but one inked! A real magician," he said, crying out to the crowd, holding my hand up high. "Surely she is not afraid to prove herself worthy in front of our King, to prove she has the magic to ink a mark upon a wolf!"

"I accept your challenge," I said loudly, and then more quietly, "Thank you."

The Marquis looked over at me, yellow eyes glinting. "Thank me?" he giggled, sounding less like a half-wolf monster who could tear out my throat than a catty little prima donna . . . who could *still* tear out my throat. "You don't even know what the challenge is, much less how to win it. I'll take your flash and your client, and send you home with your tail between your legs, you tall skinny bitch."

"I don't have a tail," I said.

"You don't now," he said. "But . . . we shall see."

∽———

15. The Duel

We faced off in the pit. Somehow, the vampires were in my corner, though I doubted whether the sulking Transomnia, sitting on the edge of the pit staring at his muddy pants, was actually on my side. Instead it was Calaphase and the recently returned Revy (short for 'Revenance') who had my back, while the young feral tiger girl and the wolf-chested boy tended the ego of the Marquis as he preened opposite us in the ring.

"What's he doing?" I asked, watching Lord Buckhead speaking with the Bear King.

"Apologizing for you," Calaphase said. "And explaining what Trans did that put you in such a foul mood." Trans looked up sharply, then looked away. "We were contracted to keep mortals away so that the weres could let their beasts roam free without fear of discovery and blackmail, not to make it impossible for those with legitimate business to conduct it."

"*This* is the kind of legitimate business you conduct?" I asked, watching a werewolf throw down money in challenge to two stags. "I'd hate to see the customer service department."

Revenance snorted.

The sudden sound of wood striking on concrete caught everyone's attention. Lord Buckhead struck his staff twice more upon the rock, then raised it. "Hear me, Man Herds and Packs of Upper Georgia," he cried. "I am Buckhead, fey Lord of the Hunt, whose magic runs through and binds you all. All who wish to run under my protection abide by my rules."

The great hall remained silent as Buckhead spoke, and I took a moment to look around. The "man herds" and "packs" were rough, surely, but I started to notice designer jeans, Members Only jackets, even glittering watches and cellular phones. With the exception of a few monstrosities like the Bear King and lifer weres like the Marquis and the feral girl, most of the crowd was starting to look . . . normal.

OK, some of them had wolf heads, yes, but otherwise . . . normal.

Suddenly the hidden meaning behind Calaphase's mention of 'blackmail' sank home. Most of this crowd probably weren't wild dogs, running free on the edge: they were old-school magickers, living normal lives, magic carefully hidden under the old rules and ways, coming here in secret to release the curse of their beasts safely.

"These people," I said. "They didn't contract with you to protect their lives . . . but their identities? So that no were-whatevers would be needed to guard the perimeter, where they could be seen and exposed?"

"Smart girl," Calaphase said, "she can color between the lines."

"I feel like a shit now," I said. I'd been so pissed off by the hoops I'd gone through to get through the security of the werehouse, it had never occurred to me that the security was in place for a legitimate reason. "I didn't realize how much everyone here has to lose—"

"Why are *you* apologizing?" Calaphase asked. "Transomnia had no excuse to treat you the way he did, and as for the Marquis . . . well, werekin can be aggressive."

"You mean they're going to try to take a piece out of me?"

"No, I mean a lot of them are successful lawyers and businessmen," he said, breathing in my ear, expanding his aura ever so slightly. "Count the Rolexes. Twenty-eight days out of the month, these cats and dogs are living in the lap of luxury."

"They have even more to lose then," I said, dreamily. He was trying to roll me.

"But they know how to fight to keep it," he responded. "Fortunately . . . *I* can protect you."

The smooth syllables of his voice poured over me like liquid. Or maybe like water over a cat. "Oh, Cally, your warm breath feels so good. And if you could just take a take a bite out of me, right there, I'll be so grateful that I'd punch you *clear* into next week."

He leaned back with a laugh. "Can't blame me for trying."

"Actually I can, and usually will," I said.

"Thank you, Lord Buckhead," the Bear King said. "Little One. You came to us for help, not knowing our rules, and were treated unconscionably. Calaphase, you and your fangs are on your third warning. I expect that those responsible will be . . . punished."

"Yes, my Lord," he said. I heard a sudden movement behind me, but did not bother to look back to see Transomnia's reaction. "I will make an example of him."

"Good," the Bear King snarled. "See that you do. See, Little One, we do have rules. And one of those rules is that no one may ink magic upon a wolf or werekin unless they have proved that they have the skills to do it properly."

He paused, and I realized I was expected to speak. "I understand, and approve."

He nodded gravely. "Then you will accept this trial to prove your skill. If you pass, the Marquis will advise you honestly and fairly. If you fail, you will give this wolf to the Marquis . . . or pass upon doing the tattoo entirely. Do you agree?"

"I agree," I said, then under my breath, "Not like I have a choice."

"You are correct," the Bear King said. "You do not have a choice."

"Never underestimate a werekin's hearing," Calaphase said.

"Help me out here," I said. "What will this trial entail?"

"I have no idea," Calaphase said. "I've never seen a magical tattooists' duel."

"So, girl," the Marquis said, "think you can ink magic? Where's the proof?"

"My work speaks for itself," I said, dropping my coat into Calaphase' hands, better exposing the vines, butterflies and jewels adorning my arms, shoulders and upper back.

"But does it speak loudly enough?" the Marquis cried, doffing *his* coat to expose an elaborately tattooed chest and arms, throwing his arms wide to the wolf boy and tiger girl.

A man and a woman leapt down on either side of the ring. Both were dressed normally, him in jeans and a rough mountaineer's shirt over a white tee, her in fleece and shorts that looked like they'd taken a hell of amount of outdoor running. They prowled up around me, him catlike, her wolflike, inspecting the lines of my tats, eyeballing the colors, lingering over the more prominent designs. He began sniffing my arm, and I scowled; laughing, he backed off.

After a moment inspecting the Marquis and his pets, the referees or judges or whatever they were returned to the center of the ring and conferred. "Her marks are equal," the woman cried.

"You lie," the Marquis cried. "Her flowers are no match for my beasts!"

"Her work is of exceptional quality," the man said.

The Marquis' nostrils flared. "And how could you tell from such little work? It is easy to ink one line. Only a true artist can do so consistently. Is she consistent?"

"Her lines are strong, her shading subtle—" the woman began.

"The Marquis is right," the man interrupted, turning his attention to me, his eyes roaming over my body. "Have you no other samples of your work?"

"I didn't bring pictures," I snapped.

"We would not accept them," he replied. "Have you no other living ink to show?"

"She has no friends here, how would she—" the woman began; then stopped. Now *her* nostrils flared, and she glared at the man in disgust. "You lecherous *bastard*," she said softly.

"If she has no other ink to show, the Marquis' challenge must stand," he said, smiling.

The woman judge turned to me stiffly. "Have you no other—"

"I get the drift," I said, glaring at the Marquis. *Thank God I was wearing a bra.* I gave the woman a nod of understanding. "I assume you will rip out his throat for me later? If I rip it out I think that might be construed as an insult."

"Gladly," she said, and the man laughed.

"Of course I have more ink to show," I cried, throwing up my hands, glaring at the Marquis. I was going to kill him, him and his horny little judge, too. But maybe not the little feral girl, smirking at me; I blew her another kiss, and again she hid, this time behind the Marquis, to the delight of the catcalling crowd. Then slowly, sensually, I pulled off my top.

The wolves whistled and the stags snorted and brayed as I lifted the rim of the black cloth up and over my head, revealing my sports bra. I'd thought about this carefully and made the movements slinky without turning it into a complete striptease: I had no desire to further taunt an entire crowd full of werewolves and end up raped or eaten. But my movements had another effect: they shifted and stretched my skin, making the tattoos shimmer like fire.

Tattoos are just pigment inserted into the second layer of the skin, just below the layer of cells you slough off every time you take a shower. So, for starters, you can do with a tattoo anything you can do with regular ink—tint the skin a shade, draw a pretty picture—or draw a design. Some of the simplest 'magical' tattoos are just benevolent symbols inked with, essentially, an alchemists' version of glow-in-the-dark ink.

But real magical tattoos are filled with the compounds that dispense, control and discharge mana; and with the life force of a living being beating just beneath their surface, magical tattoos are some of the most powerful marks around.

When I dropped the shirt into Calaphase' waiting hand, the vines rippling down my arms were glowing bright and the gems actually starting to glitter. Tattoo magic worked best when exposed to the air, and I was already feeling the burn on my legs where excess mana was bleeding back into my body; so I reached down, lithely, and unzipped first one boot, then the other, making the snakes curling through the vines move and the butterflies shimmer.

There was an art to this, an actual magical skill: the magical tattoo artist I'd apprenticed to called it *skindancing*, and while I didn't know the details of that art, over the years I'd grown quite good at storing and dispensing mana simply by flexing and stretching my skin. Until now, I'd only done it by myself, in front of a mirror; or very occasionally, in front of Savannah.

As for now, I was glad that the ruddy glare of the torches was hiding my flush of embarrassment. Stripping before strangers, even partially, was terrifying.

"Do not let the fear go to your head," Calaphase warned, quietly but urgently. "There are werewolves in the audience; they can smell your adrenaline, hear your heart race."

"Thank you, Calaphase," I said, letting my breath out slowly. Then I turned, and slowly began unbuttoning my pants.

"Whoo!" cried a young wolf, leaning into the pit, surprisingly close. The female werewolf batted at him, but he leaned back and yelled anyway. "Take it all off!"

"I would not want to embarrass the Marquis," I replied, twisting so that the pants slid softly to the floor and the rest of the vines and flowers flickered to life. "Nor would I want to be accused of influencing the judges with too many samples of my canvas!"

The crowd laughed, as I stood there half-naked in front of them in my black bra and panties, turning slowly with a bravado I didn't feel. The male tiger prowled around me and nodded. "It is a *fine* canvas," he said, ignoring the wolf-woman as she struck him. "And an exceptional *body* of work—"

"Those *cannot* be all *her* artistry," the Marquis said, eyes boring into me, nostrils flaring.

"They indeed are," I replied, turning oh so slowly, eyes thanking Calaphase as he dusted off my pants. "I did all but these on my hand and these on my thigh—"

"You lie!" the Marquis hissed, and the crowd grew silent.

"Be careful with your accusations," the male referee said quietly. "She is a guest. She does not know our rules—"

"She lies!" the Marquis said again. "Can you not see it! All of you who have been under my needle know it. She cannot have done her own knees—"

"A shaking leg can be held down," I said. By Kring/L, in fact, and it had taken both of his big, beefy hands to hold just one of my legs still—tattooing your knee *hurts*. "It need not disrupt the hand—"

"She cannot have done the dragon," the Marquis yelled. "It covers her whole body!"

Now my nostrils flared. I prowled across the ring until I stood just in front of the Marquis, then held up my right hand, clamped as if holding the electric needle. Then I slowly bent down, and began to trace the tattoo.

The Dragon's tail starts curling around my left big toe, a black and gold design with blue and green gems that make it sparkle with life. I lifted my foot off the ground, curling my hand around the toe, the ankle, once, twice, three times, the limit of my balance. I then stretched out my leg and touched the ground, drawing my hand up my leg and over the outer curve of my thigh, tickling the Dragon as it marked its circle around the muscles of my belly.

By now it was clear to anyone who could see that I'd drawn that one single design where my own right hand would reach. But the Marquis' eyes tightened skeptically, and truth be told, I had done this bit in a sequence of short strokes, alternately twisting over my shoulder and behind my back in a sequence that had taken five sessions over three days. But the crowd and judges were not likely to listen to any kind of explanation; I needed to make a show.

So I began twisting around slowly, showing off the reach and flexibility of my long arms and supple neck. The movement agitated the Dragon, making his tail flicker and withdraw from my foot. You'll rarely see a skindancer fully covered in tattoos, and not just because we know how to use negative space; it's for the magic. Our tattoos need room to move.

The Dragon moved as I moved, coiling and shifting about my body as I stretched and flexed my skin, drawing his glittering form underneath my hand as easily as I had when he was just an outline. The Marquis was half right: I couldn't have done the Dragon if he was a normal tattoo; but since he was magic, once the major components of the design, the logic of the magic, was in place, I could move him almost anywhere I wanted to fill in the details.

But some points were better for the magic than others, and in case the Marquis was savvy enough to know that, I made one final show. As the Dragon coiled around, I moved my hand into that final difficult arc around my own back, ending up in a twisted but still comfortable inscribing position under my left shoulder blade—right as the head of the Dragon slid precisely beneath what would have been the point of my tattooing gun.

I couldn't quite see whether I'd got it quite right—I had no full length mirror with me this time—but I felt the Dragon rippling under the skin as he moved, and scratched him under the chin with my forefinger. His whole body rippled with pleasure, sending waves of light, movement and color cascading through all the other tattoos over my whole body.

"Challenging a skindancer about where she inked her tattoos is *pointless*, and the Marquis should have known that," I said loudly. I turned to look at him through one half lidded eye, then straightened and walked back to my side of the ring without a backward glance.

"The Dragon is mine," I said. "You cannot top it."

But the Marquis was not deterred. "I concede your skill . . . at dancing, if not inking," he said, to the delight of the crowd. "I cannot compete with it. But magic is more than performance. Real magic has *function*. Show us, Dakota, can your marks do this?"

I turned, and gasped. The golden cat eyes of the feral girl hovered not three feet from me, barely visible within a column of shimmering heatwaves, like a catstriped version of *The Predator* effect. She growled and lunged at me, and I leapt back: only then could I see her outline. I sure as hell didn't know any flash that could do *that*, and had no idea how to top it.

Then the wolf-boy leapt forward, displacing the girl. He snarled at me, eyes glowing; then the eyes of his tattoo began glowing as well. Suddenly his human head shifted in a blink to a wolf's head, snapping at me, howling at the ceiling; and all the wolves whistled and applauded. I could now see that what I had thought were far-seeing signs were actually the marks of a magical capacitor, and guessed that the applause of the crowd was that the tat had made him a quick-change artist. Impressive . . . but I was starting to get an idea.

Now the Marquis stretched his thin chest. Wolf tattoos began to move across his shoulders, and tribal designs on his chest began to shift and interplay. His marks gave off quite a bit of light, and were moving impressively fast—as long as you hadn't noticed the trick. The Marquis was powerful, but he only inked *surface* magic. His tattoos were shimmering back and forth on his chest in a running display that I assumed was some kind of history of the pack, and the wolves were lapping it up; but all I saw was—

"A magical *screensaver*," I cried, clapping slowly and loudly. The Marquis's jaw bulged. "Clearly you are an expert at the two dimensional form. I cannot equal you."

"Well, then—" the Marquis said, confused and suspicious.

I clapped my hands together firmly and rubbed them against each other, Mister Miyagi style. When I pulled them apart, the *mana* I'd built up in *my* magical capacitors on my palms released slowly, into a glowing ball of light.

The crowd grew silent, then drew back as the ball grew larger and larger, from softball to soccer to basketball. The Marquis just stared, eyes wide, clenching his jaw. I was right. He was a backwoods artist; skilled, but without the training or the flash to do real skindancer marks that could affect anything beyond the wearer. If the crowd's reaction was any gauge, none of them had seen this kind of magic either. Now it was clear why the Bear King feared it.

"There is more to magic than just show," I said, letting the floating ball rise slowly over my upraised palm, then jabbing it so it exploded in a thousand fiery sparks that jetted out among the crowd and pushed them back a full yard from the edge of the pit. "And more than just function. True magic is beauty incarnate: let me show you."

Then I swayed my whole body, drawing mana through the vines, concentrating it into my upraised left wrist so the gems gleamed, the flowers bloomed, and the butterfly flapped its wings and raised off my wrist into life.

There was silence around me as the glowing image of the butterfly flapped in the air, as I sheltered it with my hand like a dying flame, feeding all the mana left in my body into it to bring it back to life. Then I raised my hand, whispered, "*Fly*," and blew one more kiss to the feral girl—and the butterfly flew with it, on a wind of sparkles and sunshine.

The girl squealed and held up her hand, and the trailers of magic bounced off her harmlessly. But the butterfly settled on her hand, fluttering, and she stared at it with open, wide eyes, and something closer to delight than fear. It flickered, once more, then lay its wings down and merged with her hand.

"You get one for free," I said. "More will cost you."

She cried out with joy, and the Marquis reached over and grabbed her hand, running his thumb over the design, peering at it with wide and inquisitive eyes. Then he looked sharply over at me, and took a sharp bow.

"How could I not concede to such skill?" he said. "Dakota may ink any of us."

And then I was swarmed with a hundred werewolves, tigers, and stags, pressing around me, all asking what I could do for them—or just trying to get close enough to rub up against my bare skin. The referees and vampires pushed them all back and made a space for me at the edge of the ring, where, exhausted, I quickly began putting back on my clothes.

The Marquis and wolf-boy were staring at the feral girl's tattoo. She was alternately looking at it and looking at *me* with equally wide eyes.

"I'm sorry," I called out to the Marquis.

"I do not feel robbed," he said bitterly. "I just lost."

"I do want your advice on the control-charm tattoo," I said. "I really need your help."

"I think it is safe, but I will . . . review it," he said, looking back at me. "I will report my findings to the blind witch, and charge only my standard fee. But if any other . . . requests . . . come out of your little display, any other ink for one of *my* wolves, you must first show me."

The little putz wanted to see my flash. Fine. Apparently he didn't know the new rules, the Edgeworld rules which recognized our need to collaborate; perhaps it was time to show him.

"Of course you can see my flash," I said, and he looked over sharply. "I can bring you a selection of designs, even show you how to ink some of the more complicated—"

"Why are you placating me?" he snapped, almost taking a chunk out of the air.

"This is the twenty-first century," I reminded him. "And I'm not an old-world, secret-magic practitioner keeping all my best tricks for myself. I'm an Edgeworlder, and we share our gifts with each other and the world."

I stood, letting my coat drape over me. "Besides, I might get another request for a tattoo from a werewolf. You give me good advice on this one, and I'll send more work your way."

The Marquis nodded, pulling on his own coat. Then without another word, he swept off, taking with him wolf-boy and the feral girl, both looking back at me.

I looked up to see Lord Buckhead standing at the edge of the ring, and the Bear King slinking off his stage towards the farther loading docks. "I have smoothed over any remaining difficulties," the werestag said, "but the Bear King does not wish to speak further with you today. We should go, before the crowd becomes . . . boisterous."

"Amen to that," I said, shifting my coat, turning back to Calaphase. "You know what? Thank you, Calaphase. You're quite a decent fellow—"

"For a vampire?" he asked.

"For not leering like all the rest," I said.

"Oh, that. Well, I do like to be a gentleman," he said, and then, leaning close, whispered, "And just between you and me? Half the time—your back was turned."

16. NOT-SO-SECRET ADMIRER

I woke up sweaty, feeling warmth beside me in the bed, where one of my cats had curled up into the curve of my body. The rest of them yowled around me, and I shifted sleepily, trying to push off the heat source—boy, they didn't know their own weight, did they?—and ignore them. But my nose wrinkled: whoo, the stink. Had one of them farted or, worse, sprayed? No; the scent was different, less cat stink than gym sweat . . . with a touch of cinnamon.

I opened my eyes to see the face of the feral girl.

"Aaaaa!" I screamed, jumping and klonking my head on the headboard. She was still there, and I shoved away, falling onto the floor, dragging half the bedcovers with me. I lay there frozen a minute—I couldn't see her; had it been a dream?—and then pulled myself up to see the feral girl still curled up on my bed, looking straight at me.

"I let myself in," she said. "I hopes that's OK."

"How the hell did you manage—" and then I saw overturned glassware in the kitchen: she'd let herself in through a second floor window. "Never mind. How did you find me?"

"I followed you. You gots the world's lamest bike. It was easy to keep up—"

"My precious Vespa is a *scooter*, not a bike," I said, "and she gets like sixty miles to the gallon." My brow furrowed. "You mean followed, like on foot?"

She smiled, her tail flickering up in the air.

"I find myself less and less enamored of were-whatevers," I muttered, cracking my neck where the collar had kinked it in my sleep. I reached up to the desk next to my bed and batted at my computer mouse: after a moment the monitor turned itself back on, and I peered at the system clock. "Jeez! It's like, eight in the morning! Who's up at this ungodly hour?"

"The day is young," she purred, slinking forward to peer down at me on the floor.

I eyed her warily. I didn't like the way this was going. And in the light I could she was a *lot* younger than she'd looked at the werehouse. "What's your name, kid?"

"You called me Cinnamon," she said dreamily. "That will do."

"Look, Cinnamon, the last thing I need is another spice-themed girlfriend, suitor or ex," I said, standing up at last. "You had a name before I smelled your perfume. What was it?"

"They called me Stray," she said. "Or Foundling."

Oh, God. She was serious. That was *horrible*. "I'm so sorry."

"Don't—don't you be sorrying me!" she said, face fierce and tragic all at once. "You didn't talk down at me before!"

"I'm sor—" I stopped, and held up my hands. "I'm sorry you're an orphan and I'm sorry I'm sorry. Get the hell over it."

She started to get mad, then just smiled, a huge sunny smile. "Okay, DaKOta!"

I stared at her suspiciously. "How the hell old are you?"

"Twenty-three," she said proudly.

"And how old are you when you're not trying to buy beer?"

Her face fell. "Nineteen."

"And how old are you when you're not trying to get down my pants?"

Her face fell further. "Seventeen."

"Not likely," I said, looking at her face. Lots of baby fat, few lines even for a street cat. She had a *lot* of tattoos, but—"Not even fifteen. Maybe thirteen—"

"I am *too* fifteen," she said indignantly, then held her hands to her mouth.

"Jeez," I said. "You are not old enough to be alone on the streets—"

"I can take care of myself," she said.

"I don't doubt it," I said. "But *being* able to take care of yourself, and *having* to take care of yourself, are two different things."

"I'm a foundling," she said. "My mother spent most of her time as a beast during her pregnancy so . . . so I wouldn't die when she changed. And after all that time..."

"She couldn't change back," I said. "I'm so sor—so, you know."

"They say my dad went with her so . . ." She stared at her hands, at the tufts of fur between her fingers, then said, "So I don't have any parents. The werehouse is my home, but I gots to take care of myself."

"Look . . . uh, Cinnamon. Why are you here?"

"T-to get down your pants?" she stammered, eyes wide, a little shocked at herself. "I—I—means, I means like you said that you thought that—"

"You haven't thought this through at all, have you?" I said quietly.

I just stood there, in pajama shorts and an old Emory t-shirt, staring down at her with my arms folded. Where I'd changed clothes—except for the damn collar—Cinnamon wore the same ghetto-chic vest and crop top, the same pants: probably the only ones she owned. She was on her own, on the streets at the same age I'd been a choir girl in Stratton Christian Academy, only Cinnamon had more tattoos than *I'd* had at twenty.

Finally she held out her hand, the one bearing the butterfly mark. "No? Then maybe another super tattoo to match this one?"

"I can't do a tattoo on you, Cinnamon. You're a minor."

She actually hissed at me. "*You* gave me this—"

"When I thought you were older," I said. "Technically, transferring a mark by magical means doesn't count, but if I actually inked you—I could lose my license."

"Oh, come on," she said. "You looks so cool, but you're just a big square—"

"You like my apartment?" I interrupted.

She blinked, then looked around, at my posters, my DVDs, my books, my cats, even glancing curiously at my glass computer desk and its Herman Miller chair. "It's a cool pad, I guess. I means, cool for a square. Yeah, I likes it, in a dorky kind of—"

"So do I," I said. "I keep it by keeping my job."

"Oh, come on, who'd know?" she said. "It's so pretty. I want another one—"

"Cinnamon . . . you're thirteen." I said. She started to protest, but I held up my hand. "I got my first tattoo, and started tattooing, when I was *nineteen*. I've been doing it for nine years. I'm five years older than who you were *pretending* to be. You could be my daughter."

"Oh, *could* I?" she said sarcastically. Then her eyes grew distant.

We stared at each other for a moment.

"Oh, hell," I said. "I've gone and picked up another stray."

"I am not 'Stray' anymore," she shouted, standing up on my bed. "I'm Cinnamon!"

The bed squeaked underneath her as she shook with rage, and the noise seemed to catch her attention. Experimentally she threw her weight on it, then started bouncing. I was about to say something . . . and then my cell rang.

The number was unknown, a 770 area code—outside the Perimeter. I let it ring once more, then reluctantly answered it. Maybe it was a client. "Dakota Frost."

"Hello," said a deep voice. "This is Buck."

"Buck?" I said, confused. Then it dawned. "Lord Buckhead!"

"The one and only, but Buck will do," he said. How was he using a phone with a deer's head? Did he have one of those faux old-timey candlestick phones with the mouthpiece on its own cord? "The Bear King just called. He was quite agitated. He seems to think you may have taken something that belongs to the werehouse."

"Let me guess," I said, watching Cinnamon jump up and down on my bed, both feet together. "You're missing a cross between a tiger and a pogo stick?"

"The wonderful thing about Tiggers is, Tiggers are wonderful things," Lord Buckhead said. "But yes, that does sound like their Stray."

She looked over, enraged. "You ratted me! You fink!"

"S-T-R-A-Y seems to want to go by 'Cinnamon' now," I said, turning around, to keep the phone out of reach of her tufted claws. "And I didn't 'take' her. She followed me without my knowledge and broke into my home—"

"That does sound like their missing Tigger," Buckhead said. "Lady Dakota, I do not mean to impose, but would you do me a very great favor?"

"Certainly," I said. "After you interceded on my behalf, I am in your debt—"

"Watch over Cinnamon today."

I froze, staring back at Cinnamon as she stamped her feet and made claws at me to get the phone. "Uh, *suuure*, Lord Buckhead."

"Thank you, Lady Dakota," Lord Buckhead said. "She rarely has opportunities to leave the werehouse. It will do her a lot of good to see the mundane world."

"Buck," I said. "She's . . . not a prisoner there, is she?"

"No, it is not that she is never allowed to be out but . . . it is good for her to be out," he said. "The Bear King means well, but he can be overprotective of his fellow foundlings."

"Oh," I said as the full meaning of "fellow foundlings" blossomed in my consciousness. I assumed that his monstrous bear form had been a deliberate effect, or side effect of his power, or something to do with proximity to the full moon. I looked over at her ears, her tail. "She . . . uh, mentioned she was a foundling."

"Humans have traditionally been harsh towards the werekin, especially those who could not hide their beasts. The Bear King is merely trying to keep them safe. I do not think he realizes that a place safe from human wrath is not necessarily a safe place for a child."

"What aren't you telling me?" I asked.

"Lady Dakota, please. The werehouse is her home, and they care about her," he said. "Take good care of her today, and I'll send Calaphase to fetch her in the evening."

The line went dead.

"What wasn't he telling me?" I asked Cinnamon. She squatted rapidly, batting at one of my cats with an outstretched arm, which batted back at her like her tufted hand was a toy. "Cinnamon, did the . . . did the Marquis take advantage of you?"

"The Marquis? No, he's a faggot," she said, looking away. "But in the werehouse, if you're not 'under' someone, you gets . . . passed around."

My hands clenched on the back of my Herman Miller.

"So yeah, I hangs with him, lets him ink me," she said. "I'm part of the prissy fuck's 'entourage,' and he keeps me safe." She saw me scowling, and shrugged. "He never once touched my stuff, if that's what you're asking."

"Other people did?"

"Only werekin," she said. "And mostly boys, ones I already likes to run with. One creepy old geezer tried hitting on me, but the Bear King gutted him." She grinned abruptly, vicious, feral. "It was *sweeet*. Some of his intestines flew all the way to the rafters. They says he was shitting blood for a week."

I felt better, but only a little.

"Cinnamon, if they're using you . . . I can't let you go back there."

Cinnamon stood slowly, opening her mouth in a feral smile. Fine orange down spread over her face, furring it up like a fast-motion movie you'd see of a growing plant on the Discovery channel. She raised her hands, lengthening them into long, vicious claws.

"You can't stop me," she said, hissing with a full mouth of teeth.

I stared at her, then leaned forward slowly until my head hung over hers and she had to crane back her neck. Her eyes widened as I said slowly, "You scratch me—just *once*—and I'll be able to do *everything* you can do, plus *this*."

And I let the mana in my hands flow out, quickening the butterfly in her hands until it broke free and began flitting around in the air.

"No! No!" she cried, reaching for it, batting it around. "No no no! Please! Please! Give it back! Please give it back."

It settled slowly on my hand, flapping its wings once or twice, the light going out of it as it prepared to merge back with my skin. She cried and held her long claws out over it, cradling it, breathing on it like I had, trying to coax it back to life.

"No no no," she said, as it began to sink back into my hand. "No-one's ever given me anything nice. Don't take it away. Please don't take my butterfly away. Please. *Please*."

I stared down at her, then waved my inking hand over the butterfly, bringing it back to life. "Oh, all right," I said. "Hold up your fist. I want to align it right this time."

In moments the butterfly was back on *her* hand, *me* cradling it, coaxing it into the right alignment to best show off the shape of her hand, even with the claws.

"I'm just a big softie," I said.

"Th-thank you Dakota," she stammered, as the design sunk into the skin. "I—I—mean, *Lady* Dakota, I overheard Lord Buckhead and I didn't mean to disrespect—"

"Oh, don't *you* start," I said. "If *you* call me Dakota, I'll call *you* Cinnamon."

She held up the back of her fist, showing me the tattoo that had once been mine, now brightened by her own super-sunny smile. "Okay, DaKOta!"

I kneaded my brow, falling back into my chair.

I was sure I was going to regret this. But I wasn't at *all* sure what "this" was.

17. JUNKMAN'S DAUGHTER

After much negotiation, I convinced 'Cinnamon' to take a shower—and, with additional effort, convinced her to take it *alone*—and then took her down to the Rogue Unicorn for an impromptu 'Take Your Daughter to Work Day.'

She wanted to run behind me on the Vespa, but after *another* fifteen minutes of wheedling I convinced her that it wouldn't do to be caught running down McLendon at forty-five miles an hour in broad daylight.

"Ow," she said, adjusting her helmet. I hadn't realized how small she was: Savannah's old helmet seemed ridiculously outsized on her head. "Can I ditch this? It's crushing my ears."

"We'll get stopped," I said, and then, being unable to resist, fished for a little information. "You can't, you know, shrink them, like your claws?"

She lifted the brow of the helmet so she could glare at me, then got back on the back of the bike, wrapping her arms around me a bit fearfully. Ok, more than a bit. Actually—

"Can't—breathe—" I gasped. "This isn't going to kill you. I'll go slow—"

"I can takes anything you caaaan—"

And after some to-go from the Flying Biscuit and a short drive, we got to Little Five and climbed the steps up to the Rogue. Cinnamon's helmeted head snapped back and forth so fast I thought it would twist off, and finally I told her that she could take it off.

"My ears," Cinnamon said.

"This is Little Five," I said. "You'll be a hit."

But even Annesthesia was shocked when Cinnamon took off her helmet and then began peering down into it like a fishbowl. I hadn't noticed, but you could see down into her ears, like you would with a real cat: her weretiger features weren't just outer-cosmetic, they'd actually changed the structure of her skull. No wonder she couldn't change. I know I shouldn't have stared, but when she started scratching—

"I do believe you have *ear mites*," I said, laughing.

"If you thinks what the Bear King did to that guy was bad," she growled, "you should sees what happened to the last guy who tried to put *drops* in my ears."

"Who's the Bear King?" Annesthesia asked. "And I love your collar, Dakota! Where'd you—"

"Don't ask, and don't ask," I said. "I don't have the king of Siam and the queen of Sheba waiting on me today, do I?"

"Not yet," she responded.

We made it back to my office and I pulled up the blinds. "Like the view?" I asked.

"Yeah," Cinammon said, staring out over Little Five. "I mean, the place is a dirty dump, but the people—and hey, *hey*, that guy's even a *werekin*—"

"Actually, no," I said, peering out. "He's . . . just a Fiver. But Cinnamon—look around you. This is my office. This is what I do. This is how I pay for my apartment—"

"What, are you trying to *save* me, Dakota?" she jeered, throwing herself down in my chair and spinning around, jarring the computer and watching the screen hum to life. After she spun down, she kind of looked to the side and got sullen. "Ok. I'll gives it a shot."

"A shot?" I asked.

"You wants a new apprentice, or something? Need an 'entourage'—"

"No," I said. I wasn't really comfortable with her going back to the werehouse, but I wasn't prepared to take a weretiger under my wing just yet either. "You don't have to be my apprentice to hang out with me. Think of today as an outing, courtesy of Lord Buckhead—"

My phone rang again, and I picked it up hastily. "Dakota Frost—"

"Hello, Dakota," came a smooth voice. "It's Special Agent Philip Davidson."

"Philip!" I said, feeling a big grin spread over my face.

"Who's that?" Cinnamon said, her big, toothy grin mocking my own. "Your *boooy*friend? Wait a minute—"

"Hush," I said. "Philip, it's good to hear from you. What do you need—"

"I think I may be able to swing approval on getting some images to your graphomancer," he said. "Have you had a chance to talk to your clients—"

Oh, Hell. "No, Philip. I—I haven't even gotten started. I feel like I've let you down, but—" I glared at Cinnamon, and she stuck her tongue out at me "—to be frank I had one hell of an evening working to sort out a complicated tat for a difficult client. And this morning—"

"It hasn't even been twenty-four hours yet," Philip responded. "I didn't expect miracles."

"Hey, if you're going to talk to your *boy*friend," Cinnamon said, "can I go shopping?"

I covered the phone and stared at her. "I'm supposed to keep watch over you."

"What's someone going to do, mug me? Unless they gots silver bullets—"

"Oh, all right. Don't go far," I said, starting to raise the phone. She stared at me expectantly, and it took me a few seconds to get it. "Oh, you have to be kidding!"

"What?" she said innocently.

I opened my wallet. Typical—I only had hundreds, a five and two ones. "Here," I said, giving her a single Benjamin. "Don't go far, or spend it all in one place—"

"Thanks, DaKOta!" she said, snatching the money and darting out.

"Oh, hell," I said watching her go. What was I doing? *Phil!* "Sorry," I said. "I'm babysitting today."

"You? *Baby*sitting?" he said. "I'd pay money to see that—"

"It's quite the show," I responded. "But tell me, if you weren't expecting miracles, what could you expect? I don't actually know how to go about this—"

We talked for a while, both of us slowly realizing just how hard this was going to be—after all, I wasn't the only magical tattooist in the office, and a lot of them would be hesitant to talk to Phil, much less fork over their customer lists. A lot of *serious* tattoo collectors are rebels: someone sporting 'FTW'—Fuck The World—wasn't likely to cooperate with the Feds. After a bit we nailed down some options and I agreed to at least raise the issue with my team.

And since Cinnamon was gone and the day was just starting, it was the perfect time. I went to Reception: there were a fair number of customers looking at flash, but nobody queued for inking, and we already had two other artists in for their shifts. I made the decision.

"Annesthesia," I said. "Call Tess and Banner and put them on conference call, my office. If you don't get them leave messages for them to call me. Kring/L, CJ—come on. Pow-wow."

"Whatever it is, it can wait," Kring/L said, kinking his head at a biker-type dude going through the big blue binder. "This one's serious—"

"It can't wait," I said, walking over to the biker. He had a surprisingly friendly face, small beard and big curly hair giving him a pointy, elfin look. "Hey dude, I'm going to borrow your tattooist. Can you hang for thirty minutes? If you have him ink something, I'll throw in something small for free."

He studied me, eyes sharp under his dark brows. "Which one are you?" he asked, pointing at the tableau of artists and collectors along the wall.

"Frost."

The huge brows went up and he grinned abruptly. "A free Frost bite? Sure thing."

"Frost bite. I like that," I said, grinning, walking back towards Kring/L. "Satisfied?"

"Damn, you're serious," Kring/L said. Then the big, beefy bear-of-a-man started to look scared. "Dakota. What the hell would make you give away a hundred-dollar tat for a freebie?"

"That would be the second hundred I've given away this morning," I said. "Come into my office, and I'll tell you."

Behind closed doors, I told Kring/L and CJ, with Banner and Tess on the speakerphone . . . everything. I mean *everything*.

The lid, the killer, Philip, even Wulf. I even gave the short version of what I'd gone through to get Wulf's Nazi flash checked out, just enough to explain why I was babysitting a mercurial weretiger foundling for the day. But I came back to the killings, and emphasized that every single one of our magical clients could be a target.

"We've got to tell those cats up at Sacred Heart," CJ said. "And Dino's crew."

"No argument," I said.

"How the hell are we going to find all our clients?" Kring/L said.

"Half of them won't want to be found," Banner warned over the speakerphone, "especially our one percenters."

I scowled. '1%' was a tattoo worn as a badge of pride by those that didn't see themselves as one of the 99% of tattoo wearers 'who are law abiding.' I had no patience for '1%' or 'FTW'—both jinxes I wouldn't ink. But most of the rest of the crew would. Still—

"Maybe that's not such a big deal," I tried. "How many of them have magic marks—"

"Most," Banner said.

"They're coming here, Dakota, to the Rogue," Kring/L said. "Often they start with FTW or Lady Luck and then move up to something more dazzling—"

"I know, I *know*," I said. "Maybe we could start with some of our bigger collectors—Bob Sierra, Teresa Regis, Gregory, um, what's his name—"

"Gregor Alan Ivanova," Kring/L said. "Haven't seen him in a while—"

"He moved to Birmingham," Tess's voice said. "I think I have his number—"

"You can't just pass it out," Banner said. "He moved for a reason. He don't want people finding him—"

"The Feds aren't after *him*," I said.

"How do you know that?" Banner said. "How do you know this ain't just a clever ploy to flush one of our clients out? Haven't you watched *Most Wanted*? They send out a thousand 'you have won a prize' letters to fugitives and then arrest the ten dumb saps who show up!"

Kring/L was scowling. "He's got a point. Dakota, how can you trust this Fed guy? How do you know he's not just trying to get a list of the magically inked so he can disappear them?"

I felt my skin growing cold, that old familiar feeling. "He wouldn't do that—"

"Dakota, you're sweet on him. I can see it—"

"I barely know him. But the *Feds* don't do that," I barked.

"They sure do!" Banner said. "You think the 'witness protection program' is to protect the witnesses? It's just to disappear them when big money don't want cases to come to trial—"

"That's just an urban legend—"

"You think you're so smart reading all those damn books," Kring/L said, "and yet still he shows up in a frigging *black helicopter!* Tell me *that's* an urban legend!"

"He had a black helicopter?" Banner said, agitated. "Hell, what if they're tapping the lines? They could have gotten a dozen leads just listening to us—"

"Now listen to *me*," I said. "He was recommended to me by my dad's best buddy, and they had a fucking wooden box lid with a real human tattoo nailed to it. A tat that may have been cut off while the wearer was still alive." The room got quiet, and I continued. "He says he wants to keep that from happening to anybody else, and I believe him, and I want to help." I looked around the room. "What about you guys?"

"Yeah," Kring/L said. CJ and Tess also assented. Only Banner held out.

"All right," he grumbled. "But if half our client list gets disappeared—"

"Look, look," I said. "We do this in stages. We talk to them first privately, in person if you're afraid to do it over the phone. Nobody gets forwarded to the Feds unless they want to talk to them. And if they don't want to go through us, Phil gave me his number—"

"Oh, so he's *Phil* now? Gave you his *number!*" Cinnamon said, bouncing back into my office. She'd swapped her clothes out almost completely for an outfit that was nearly identical— still short pants, crop top and vest, but now all new, the chunky vest orange to match her hair, the top a shimmering black with sparkling diagonal stripes, and the worn shorts swapped out for pale capris that matched the trim on the vest and looked surprisingly good on her tiger-striped skin. "But enough about your square boyfriend. Oh my *God*. There's this store, called the Junkman's Daughter, it's so fabulously cool—"

"That's great," I said. "Thanks guys, Tess, Banner. Let's get started."

"—and this other one, Psycho Sisters, where I gots the coolest shirt and vest—"

"Good luck," Kring/L said, raising his brows at Cinnamon as she bounced around my office like a pinball in a machine. "Can I get you guys anything—coffee, tea, a trank gun—"

Cinnamon hissed at him, baring her claws, and Kring/L hopped out, grinning.

"Hey, DaKOta," she said, words tumbling out like a running stream. "There's this oils shop, or something, round the corner, and so I was thinking when you're on your break maybe you and me could go down there and checks some of it out?"

"Such lung capacity," I said. "But what's stopping you? Are you out of money?"

"No way," she said, spinning around. She had a cute Tigger backpack, held by bungee cords, with some cloth from her old vest and top poking out of the flap. "Thrift stores are your friend. I got this, plus this change of, and still had some change."

"So why do you need me?" I asked.

"Well," she said, swaying back and forth. "You said you were going to take care of me and . . . I didn't want to go out of eyeshot. In case anything happened."

I looked out my window. Every store she had mentioned was within view, if just barely; the oil shop was round the bend. "All right. All right. But my breaks are at one and four today—"

"One!" she said. "That's like over'n hour away. Why do you have to works today anyway? I thought squares got weekends off—"

"They do," I said, grinning, "and that's why *I* work on weekends. Half my business is either scheduled on the weekend or done on the spot by weekend walk-ins. So the shop has one artist here at all times on Saturdays and Sundays—and today's my day."

"Whatever," she said, sitting down hard in my chair.

"Why not go up to Criminal Records and check out the books—"

"What for?" she said. "I can't read for squat."

I drew a breath. I was going to have words with the Bear King, jaws of death or no. Then an idea struck me. I hunted through my desk drawer and found my old CD walkman—I hadn't used it since I got my iPod, but . . . "Then listen to an audiobook."

"A what?" she asked, spinning the chair around, her tail following her in an arc.

"You know my friend Jinx?"

"The blind witch?" she said. "Yeah, the Marquis disses her all the time. Means really he thinks she's sweet—"

"A lot of people do," I said. "You know, she can't read either."

"Oh!" she said, suddenly interested in the CD player, reaching for it the way a cat bats at a ball of string. "So what's this then? A stone-age MP3 player?"

"I have an iPod," I said, "but her CDs will play on this."

We stared at the selection Jinx'd given me, and then I realized how pointless that was and started reading them out. "*Blink* . . . *The Golden Mean* . . . *This is Your Brain on Music* . . ." I shrugged. "I haven't had time to burn them to MP3 so I haven't read any of them—"

"What's this one?" she said, holding up one with a blue dragon on the cover, flipping it over. "She's a pretty pretty—"

"*Eragon*," I said. "You'll like that. It's about a couple of foundlings."

I started to show her how to use it, but then my phone rang again. "Dakota Frost—"

"Sorry to call you so early," Spleen said. He sounded like hell.

"No, no problem," I said, checking the clock. It was eleven-thirty. "It figures that the first person to apologize for disrupting me this ungodly morning is the first person who waited to the point that he doesn't need to apologize anymore. What can I do you for?"

"Give me good news about Wulf's ink," Spleen said, no pleasantries.

"I'm having the flash checked out," I said. Surprisingly, Cinnamon had no trouble getting the CD player running. I showed her which one was the first CD, and she took it delicately and popped it in. "Jinx had to refer me to a specialist—"

"Can't you hurry it along?" he snapped, his voice a little faster, a little higher-pitched than normal. "I still don't see why you can't skip it—"

"Spleen, what's wrong?" I asked. Waiting for a response had worked well on Buck, so I just hung there on the phone and waited for Spleen to spill. Cinnamon brightened as the CD started spinning, and I gave her a thumbs up and watched, amused, as she tried to find a comfortable place to set the headphones over her ears. "I got all day, Spleen."

"He threatened me," he said.

"No!" I said, shocked. "Wulf—"

"No, I mean, not literally, but he was very *threatening*. I felt threatened. He's a fucking menace, is what I'm saying. He cornered me about the ink and when I said I didn't know he snarled and got all wolfy, that he couldn't trust me, that you'd take his flash and scram—"

"Spleen," I said, conflicted. "You tell Wulf I risked my life to check out his tat. I *did*," I said. "Punched out a vampire last night trying to get to a were-expert."

Spleen hung there on the phone. "You're shitting me."

"No, I'm not," I said.

"You stay away from the vamps," Spleen said. "They're sickos—"

"You tried to take me down to see Savannah," I said.

"I was just messin with ya," he protested. "And she's different!"

My nostrils flared. "You have *no* idea. Look, I've scanned in his flash. If he wants the original back, he can have it—tell him to call the Rogue and he can come pick it up."

"No, no, I dunno, Dakota, he's not too big on meeting people in public places. What say I come by there tonight?" he said. "After your shift?"

"You're a prince, Spleen," I said. "But give him my number anyway. I want him to feel free to talk to me."

Cinnamon pulled down her headphones and made a face at me. "Giving him your number? But what would *Phiiilll* say?"

"Hey, Spleen," I said, thinking about something Phil had said about speeding up his investigation. "Can you give us a ride later this evening? There's something I need to do."

18. IN THE EXTRAORDINARY DEPARTMENT

"This is a bad fucking idea," Spleen said, bumping down Lullwater towards Ponce.

"Language, Mister Spleen," Jinx said beside him in the front seat.

I grinned. She rarely turned her head unless she was talking directly to you, so I could just barely see her wrinkle her nose from my perch behind Spleen—but I knew the expression. Cinnamon, beside me, was alternately peering at Jinx wide-eyed, sniffing at Spleen and diving back into her audio book—she'd eventually put the headphones down around her neck, which she said she could hear just fine, even though she had it turned so low I could hear nothing.

"So where are we going?" Cinnamon said. "To see your *boooy*friend?"

"You have a boyfriend now?" Jinx asked.

"Not really," I said. Hey, one could hope, but—"Cinnamon is referring to my contact with the Feds, Philip Davidson. He's working with Andre Rand, trying to get APD Homicide up to speed on the case."

"What fucking—excuse my French, Jinxy, what the F case is this?" Spleen said.

"I can't comment on an ongoing investigation," I said with a smile.

"Then why the F am I here?" he asked.

"Because I can't fit the two of them on the back of my Vespa," I responded. "And I have my reasons for asking you and Cinnamon to come."

"So, Cinnamon," Jinx said. "Like the book?"

"ER-A-GONNNN," the werecat said, grinning. "*ER-A-GONNNN.*"

"I'll take that as a yes," Jinx said, folding her hands atop her laptop bag. "I like hanging out with you, Dakota. I get to meet all the most interesting people."

"Wait until you get a load of this one," I said.

We pulled into City Hall East and parked. Andre Rand was waiting for us at the entrance, but I waved him off and turned to the trio.

"Maybe I should just wait here, you know, like in the car," Spleen said. "I mean, what if they try to disappear you? Maybe someone should just hang back and—"

"We won't need to make a getaway," I said. "And, trust me, you don't want to be a suspicious-looking person sitting in a police parking lot."

"You're saying I'm suspicious looking?" Spleen said, twisting round so his good eye could get a look at me round his long, ratlike nose.

"No, I'm saying that anyone sitting in a police parking lot at seven-thirty at night acting like a getway man is *bound* to look suspicious," I said. "But look, we do need to have a few ground rules going in. Cinnamon, come back from Alagaesia for a minute."

When she stopped the CD, everyone was looking at me.

"First: no-one mentions Wulf, or the Marquis, or any other Edgeworlder," I said. "They're so skittish they won't even meet with *me*, so we're not going to rat them to the Feds."

"We're going to go see the *Feds?*" Spleen said, half sitting up in his seat. "Oh, hell—"

"Spleen," I said. "You haven't done anything wrong. You don't have anything to worry about from these people here."

"So we gots something *else* to worry about?" Cinnamon said, eyeing me warily.

"Second, Cinnamon and Spleen are going to wait with Andre Rand," I said, pointing at him. "He's my dad's old partner, and I trust him. I've told him you're 'edgy' and that if you get scared, or even just uncomfortable, for *any* reason, you're just going to leave—no arguments. He knows to call a cab for me and Jinx."

"We're not scared," Cinnamon said, jutting her jaw.

"Speak for yourself, tiger," Spleen said. "*You* can soak up lead bullets."

"Third . . . I have a little negotiating to do with Philip. And if it goes well…"

"*You* wants to get down his *paants*," Cinnamon said.

"—*if* it goes well, Rand's going to escort you back so Philip can brief you."

"About what?" Spleen said, his one good eye gone surprisingly wide.

"I can't talk about an ongoing investigation," I said, "but maybe Philip can."

After a moment, I nodded roughly, and got out of the car. I guided Jinx, and Spleen shepherded Cinnamon. Andre Rand met us and ushered us in through the metal detectors, with as little verbal comment about our guests as possible. I'd briefed him about Cinnamon—who was now ignoring us all, engrossed again in the audio world of Alagaesia—but still he raised his eyebrows at me.

Rand took us to floor six and beeped us in to the long corridor divided between Atlanta Homicide on the left and "Federal Magic" on the right. Breaking the law with magic turned a local felony into a federal crime—but you needed that local conviction to make it stick, so the magical Feds tended to be friendly with the locals. I'd never heard of the relationship being this tight, but it figures it would be that way in Atlanta, where there was more magic—and misuse—than anywhere else.

Rand stopped at the end of the hall, knocking at the door to the Fed offices, to summon Philip, I assumed. While we waited beside him, I took a good look at the agency's logo, etched into the office's frosted glass wall. The seal bore an eagle carrying a lightning bolt, and around the rim were the words DEPARTMENT OF EXTRAORDINARY INVESTIGATIONS. I found myself wishing I could see inside, see where Philip worked—and looked back, surprised to see Rand holding the door open to the Federal offices. Grinning, I led Jinx inside.

The DEI reception room was small but surprisingly stylish, with fresh-off-the-stands issues of hip magazines neatly arranged on a granite-topped end-table sitting between two comfy chairs. An array of paranormal-themed posters curled around the walls, including an honest-to-gosh X-Files "I WANT TO BELIEVE" poster next to an official-looking one that said "DEI: A CENTURY AND A HALF OF SERVICE, 1856-2006."

But as we filed in, we weren't looking at the posters. All our eyes were drawn to the granite-topped reception desk—and Philip, resting a hip on it casually, like a shot out of GQ.

"Homina," Cinnamon said.

"I like his cologne," Jinx said, her hand on my wrist giving a brief squeeze.

"Miss Frost, thank you for coming," he said, winking at me. Then his gaze took in Jinx's cane, Cinnamon's headphones, and Spleen's one-good-eye fidgeting, and he actually seemed at a bit of a loss. "So," he began, one hand brushing his dark, evil-Spock beard, "I, uh—"

"Special Agent Philip Davidson," I said, "please meet Skye 'Jinx' Anderson, my graphomancer. She's graciously agreed to come down to get this process started, and my . . . associates were kind enough to give us a ride."

"I'll wait out here, if that's OK. OK? OK," Spleen said, fidgeting harder, looking around the office, trying not to stare at the single heavy black door that went out of reception and into the back. "You know, to watch her." He nodded at Cinnamon, who growled.

"Y'all do that," I said, pecking Rand on the cheek. "I owe you one, 'Uncle Andy.'"

Phil ushered us through yet another big heavy door with a big knobbly lock. "Your cat friend," he said in a low voice. "That's not makeup—"

"Drop it," I said. "She has it hard enough as it is."

Philip conducted us through a clean, well-lit group of offices paralleling Atlanta Homicide, and then through a darkened observation room into the same evidence room where I'd first seen . . . 'it.' The cadaverous man was gone, but wiry-haired old Balducci was there, scowling, leaning back from the evidence tray before him like it might bite him.

"Miss Frost, good to see you again," he said, obviously not pleased to see me again at all. "Agent Davidson, I'm still not sure this is a good idea."

"We need all the help we can get," Philip said. "Miss Anderson, if—"

He paused, and I turned. Jinx was frozen in the door. "Jinx, are you all right?"

She stood for a moment, then took a deep breath. "Yes, yes, I'm fine," she said, slowly stepping forward into the room. "So. It is here."

"Yes," I said.

"Well," she said. "Show me."

Balducci raised his eyebrows but said nothing as I pulled out a chair for her and guided her into it. I started to reach for the tray, but Jinx held up her hand.

"I can tell where it is," she said, a bit sharp. "Could I have a little room?"

Balducci's chair squeaked back as he popped to his feet, and suddenly he, Philip and I were in three corners of the room, all far from Jinx. I looked over at Balducci, then Phil. They were just as uncomfortable and sickened by the lid as I was.

Then Jinx reached for the lid—and *screamed.*

19. HOT ELECTRIC SHOCK

I felt a hot electric shock ripple through my tattoos and fell back against the wall. Jinx jerked her hand back, tumbling out of her chair, knocking it sideways onto the floor—and screaming, screaming the whole time in repeated, high pitched, full-voiced wails.

Balducci clutched himself, reaching for his heart. After a shocked moment, both Phil and I stepped forward just as Jinx's screams subsided.

"Jinx," I said, reaching for her. "Are you—"

"Don't touch me!" she snapped, holding out her hand, and I recoiled from the blind glare burning out from those spooky geode eyes. "Don't help me."

We stood back as she collected herself and straightened her glasses. She groped blindly for the chair, found it, and righted it. With one hand she lifted herself up and brushed herself off, still keeping that fixed-head stare that was so very Jinx. After a moment she bent, collected her cane, and sat down primly at the table, folding her hands in her lap before sighing.

"My, my," she said. "Quite a shocker you have there. May I continue?"

"Uh…" Balducci said, staring at Phil, who nodded. "Yeah."

She reached out a hand abruptly and put her whole palm across the lid, screaming instantly like she was pressing her hand on a hot stove. Her other hand tightened on her cane, and she twisted in her seat and screwed her face up until she stopped screaming.

"*Not* the first clear images I wanted to see after twenty years of darkness," she said, voice ragged and angry and very *un*-Jinx. "*Not* what I wanted to see *at all*."

"What did you see?" Phil said.

"Impressions, really," Jinx said. "A woman, mid-twenties, blond, naked. A sort of circular tattoo. Cut from her flesh with an *athame*, a ritual magic dagger—"

I looked at Balducci, who was holding his hand over his mouth cautiously, skeptically, following every word. Up till now Jinx had not told us anything she couldn't have gotten from me, a cold-reading trick typical of most of the charlatans claiming to be psychics. I couldn't blame him for being skeptical—

"And then—dear goddess!—he poured *salt* on the wound—"

She shoved the lid away, and Phil and Balducci looked at each other and raised their eyebrows. "The psychic record ends there. I'm pretty sure the salt was to sever any remaining magical connection to the living host." She lowered her head. "I can't say for certain, but I got a *very* strong impression that dagger wanted to end the ritual in her heart."

"That's . . . consistent," Philip said.

"That's fucking *amazing* is what it is," Balducci said.

"Language, Officer Balducci," Jinx said calmly. "I'm afraid that touching the lid is quite . . . aversive . . . to a sensitive such as myself. With your permission, I'd like to encircle it before I begin my examination. It might serve to dampen some of the 'vibes.'"

"That . . . that wasn't the examination?" Balducci said.

"No," she said. "That was a side effect."

"Miss Anderson is a graphomancer," Philip said. "She's here to analyze the tattoo and give us her thoughts on why the killer may have wanted it."

Jinx had pulled out what looked like a small makeup case from her shoulder bag and was feeling the table. "May I draw on this?" she asked, retrieving a piece of chalk from the case.

Balduci let out his breath. "Sure. Why the hell not?"

"Language, Officer Balducci," Jinx said, drawing a wide circle around the evidence tray. "I'm only doing this because I'm trying to help."

"Uh, Philip," I said. "There was that matter of my . . . other associates—"

"Davidson," Balducci warned. "I appreciate you bringing APD in on this, but you're—*we're* letting out a *lot* of information about this case to a *lot* of people—"

"Current thinking," Philip said, ushering me towards the observation room to talk but speaking to Balducci, "is that if you have a known victim category, you alert them. That it's better to prevent more crimes than to nail the perpetrator."

Balducci threw up his hands.

Philip joined me in the observation room, and the door closed with a sudden *click*.

There, alone together in the near darkness, I forgot what we were going to talk about. We stared at each other for a moment, his grey eyes glinting with reflected light from the window on room beyond, his strong physique outlined by the soft glow of the monitors. I drew a breath, and his eyes lit up and sparkled at me, hungry and alive.

We closed the gap. His hand touched my waist, my hand touched his cheek, my head bent down, our lips almost touched—and then, just as abruptly, we pulled apart.

"Whoa," Phillip said, reddening. "I'm, uh, sorry, Miss Frost—"

"Me too," I echoed, feeling my face flush with embarrassment as well. "I—"

"I *assure* you I didn't call you in here for that," Philip said, stiffening.

"I didn't mind," I blurted out, then raised my hands as he raised his eyebrow. "Wait, I didn't mean it like that. I assure *you*, I stopped moving that fast back in college. I meant, I don't interpret this as any kind of harassment, Special Agent Philip Davidson."

"That's a relief," he said, staring at the hand that had touched my waist like it was a foreign thing. Then his mouth quirked up in a wry smile. "Inappropriate touching!"

I choked off a laugh. "Maybe inappropriate," I said, "but . . . still, I didn't mind."

Philip glanced up at me, and his smile warmed. "Even more of a relief."

Suddenly a bright wave of color splashed into the observation room. "Whoa," Philip said again, hopping back from the window as Jinx whirled her cane above her head with an odd, doublehanded motion, drawing a bright circle of light in the air like a giant halo. After a moment, the rainbow faded, an echo glittering across an elaborate magic circle she'd inscribed over the table. Despite myself, I leaned toward the window and looked at it: effective, but exhaustingly filigreed. I'd swear half of it wasn't necessary, done just for tradition—or because Jinx wanted to be 'extra special safe.' Trust a Wiccan to overthink everything.

Frost Moon

"She's the real deal," Philip said beside me, staring through the glass.

"Yes," I said. "Did you really doubt—"

"After all the shit I've seen?" Philip said, shaking his head. "But not doubting something and seeing it in the flesh are two different things."

Which reminded me of our little plan. "Speaking of seeing it in the flesh…let's get the others in here so that Cinnamon can get a look at the lid."

"Are you sure we want to do this?" he said, not directly meeting my eye, scratching behind his neck. "Your friend, she's a were, but she's young. And magically tattooed. And, I repeat, a *were*. If I had my druthers she wouldn't be out in the open like this at all—"

"And what's the alternative? Send her back to the werehouse?"

"We have safe houses," Philip said thoughtfully. "Keep her safe from prying eyes—"

I let out a breath and glared at him. Maybe Banner was right. Philip was a spook with his very own black helicopter. What was he doing to me, making me lose my judgment like this? "You just met her and you're already thinking of disappearing her?"

"I didn't say that," Philip said. "Just . . . I hate to see people get hurt."

"Me too," I said. "But you don't know these people. They'll barely listen to me. They sure won't listen to *you*. We need a big splashy show that will make the threat clear."

"Well, this will do it," Philip said, nodding toward the box lid. "What's wrong?"

"What's Balducci saying?" I asked. Balducci was now reading from a document while Jinx worked, and she was responding—almost like he was interrogating her.

I threw the door open.

"And your employment?" Balducci was asking, taking notes on a form.

"I'm a teaching assistant at Emory University's Harris School of Magic," she said, leaning over the lid without touching it, glasses off, spooky geode eyes flickering back and forth over the tattoo. "I also do contract programming for Wolfram Research."

"What's with the fifth degree?" I asked. "Jinx is *not* a suspect—"

"Background check," Balducci said, not looking up. "We gotta check her out before we release any evidence to her. It's a requirement."

"It's all right, Dakota," she said, leaning her right eye close and waving her head back and forth. "You two have fun in there?"

I reddened. "We, uh—"

"We were . . . negotiating," Philip said.

"Mmm, hmm," Jinx said, sitting back down. "Officer Balducci, I can roughly tell that this is a 'vessel,' a kind of magical capacitor but . . . I'm basically blind. It's like looking at it through shower glass. To really give you answers, I need to scan it and run it through my software."

Balducci flipped through the form briefly. "It'll take a couple of days to get approval for that."

"We are under some time pressure," Phil said. "Any initial thoughts you may have can help. Couldn't we scan it into one of the DEI computers so Jinx can 'look' at it there?"

"Not unless you've got *Mathematica* with the Emacspeak extensions installed," Jinx said smugly. "And I very much doubt you have someone who could install that, much less—"

Balducci leaned back thoughtfully and then picked up the phone. "I.T? This is Balducci. Tell me, you still got Jack Conway still working back there?"

"Jack the jerk? *Wonderful,*" I said, letting out my breath. "I'll go get Cinnamon,"

"I'll escort you," Philip said, leaning away from the wall.

And so Philip and I fetched Cinnamon, Spleen and Rand and brought them up to the observation room. We stood there behind the mirrored glass, watching the sandy-haired asshole I'd met in the elevator on my last visit helping Jinx set up a scanner and some other equipment.

"I won't lie to you," I said, putting my hands on Cinnamon's shoulders. "This is nasty."

"You gots nothing to scare me," she said, half petulant, half eager. "I sees plenty of guts at the werehouse—and they crawls back to their owners. Can you tops that?"

"In gore, no," I said. "In horror . . . yes."

Cinnamon fell quiet. "Then why be showing it to me?"

"I need you to take a message to the Marquis," I said, and she tensed. "And I need him to understand how important it is. He won't trust me, but—"

"Oh, good luck getting him to listen to *me*," she said, ears twitching. Phil's nostrils twitched as well, looking at her, as if somehow her presence in his observation room was violating some commandment. But he said nothing, and eventually Cinnamon sighed. "Alright, I'll do it. I can handle anything you squares shows me."

Philip opened the door.

"No, I need version 6.1 of the Emacspeak *extensions*," Jack was muttering into his cell phone, tapping a key on his giant slab of a laptop. "Put it in the 'cygwin/opt' folder. You know, if you had a *real* computer, girlie, we'd already have this done."

"Don't listen to the bad man, dear," Jinx said, stroking her laptop, then pulling out a USB key and lifting it for Jack to take. "I think this key is yours. Hello, Dakota."

"Oh, hey, chickie," Jack said, taking the key and plugging it into his laptop. They'd set up a scanner and were clearly about to start work on the lid; best get this over with before they got started. "Thanks for that tip on the webcam—"

"If we could interrupt for a minute," I said, standing behind Cinnamon, my hands on her shoulders for support. "I'd like to show our guests what we're dealing with."

Jack's face grew grim, stony, and without a word he moved aside, exposing the evidence tray. Cinnamon whirled, burying her head against my chest, but turned enough just so she could keep one eye fixed on it, as if it might leap up and bite her. Clearly her time at the werehouse hadn't left her as hard boiled as she had pretended, and somehow that made me feel better.

"What's in the tray?" Spleen asked, hiding behind the safety of the mirrored glass. His voice cracked a little. "What's in the fucking tray?"

"If this is too much you don't have to—" I began, squeezing her shoulders.

"No. No, I can do this," Cinnamon said, turning back slowly.

She stepped forward, and I walked behind her, not crowding her, but just letting my arms rest on her shoulders and stepping only when she stepped. Finally we stood over the evidence tray, looking down at the wooden lid. It was even more pathetic, now looking at that piece of a person wrapped round the board like a seatcover.

"That—that's *horrible*," Cinnamon said. "Why are you showing me this?"

"Someone ripped this off a person while they were alive," I said, and Cinnamon swallowed. "They've done it before. They take tattoos—magical tattoos—and only on the full moon. And we think he's here, now, in Atlanta."

Cinnamon took a deep breath, then shuddered. "That smell—"

"So you, and me, and the Marquis, and all our clients—we're all targets," I said. "That's why I wanted you to see it, and Jinx to inspect it thoroughly. I want you to warn him, and then he can call Jinx to confirm that what we're saying is true."

"But then you'll wants the Marquis to talk to your *boooy*friend," Cinnamon mocked, but her heart clearly wasn't in it. "But he won't even talk to *you*. He doesn't deal well with the outside."

"He doesn't have to," Philip said. "I've worked the Edgeworld for years. All he needs to do is keep his people safe, and feed us any leads he gets through Dakota or Jinx."

"Will you tell him?" I asked. "Will you tell him to watch out, to keep his people safe?"

"But, but what can we do?" Cinnamon stammered. "The wearer of that . . . she, she, she was a *were*, a were*cat*, I can smell it!" Balducci raised an eyebrow, staring at Philip, then me. "If, if they could take her out—under the *moon*—"

"We are not going to let that happen," Phil said, stepping forward to touch her shoulder. "I'm tracking this man, but my first priority is stopping him from taking anyone else."

"Don't worry Cinnamon," I said, patting the head of a werecat who could rip my throat out as easily as she could sneeze. "*I* won't let anyone hurt you."

20. OFF THE BEATEN TRACK

"Calaphase?" Savannah asked incredulously, smile growing so wide you could see her fangs. "You meant *Caiaphas*."

"I know, I *know*," Calaphase said, leaning back in his chair with a similarly toothy grin. "But what am I, a Bible scholar? I thought I'd made it up."

It had taken over an hour for Jinx to walk Jack the Jackass through what he'd need to do to scan the . . . evidence . . . into formats she could use, once APD and the DEI got permission to release the files to her. By the time they were done, it was after nine—making options for the handoff of our werecat cargo quite limited. Finally I'd settled on Manuel's Tavern, a grand old liberal pub northwest of Little Five just past the Freedom Parkway, and had coerced Savannah and her crew to show up to provide us protection in case things turned nasty.

But instead of a vampire/werewolf showdown, we were all now gathered round one of the Tavern's huge circular wooden tables, sharing beers and trading stories in the huge raftered tavern, like King Arthur's knights on their day off.

Spleen had left us to go take the Nazi flash back to Wulf, so Calaphase and Revenance were the sole representatives of the werehouse, styling in cool, long-tailed biker jackets that quickly helped them scoop up two would-be paramours for the night from the bar. Savannah and Darkrose sat next to them with easy familiarity, in matching biker jackets and turtlenecks that screamed "lesbian couple." Next to them sat Doug, who was surprisingly cleancut without his puppy mask, with dark wavy hair and piercing eyes that he simply couldn't take off of Jinx, who sat next to him, smiling, staring straight ahead but occasionally leaning towards him to whisper confidentially. Cinnamon sat between Jinx and me . . . which, not coincidentally, put me and Savannah about as far apart across the table as we could get.

"I don't get it," Cinnamon said. "Who's Caiaphas? And why's a vampire lord in the Bible?" Savannah spit up her Bloody Mary and Cinnamon hissed at her. "Don't you be funning me—"

"Went up my nose," Savannah said.

"Caiaphas wasn't a vampire. He was the high priest who tried Jesus," I said. I got some surprised looks and shrugged. "Bible Bowl, eighth grade champion. Why ever did you pick—"

"I have *no* idea," Calaphase said, smiling at the girl leaning on his shoulder. "Like I said, thought I'd made it up. I only found out months later when a new recruit—"

"Present." Revenance raised his hand.

"—asked, 'Aren't you spelling *Caiaphas* wrong?'"

"To which Cal says, 'Don't worry, it's *easy* to get a screen name for a misspelling!'"

Calaphase shrugged. "Started a tradition—now the whole clan does that with our vampire names—"

"Wait, wait," I said. "Don't tell me the big bad vampire biker gang picks their names based on how easy it is to get a Gmail account?"

"But it *is* easier if it's a made-up word," Calaphase protested. "Consider it an intelligence test. Who's going to take seriously a vampire named BloodSucker17?"

"Or AtlantaNosferatu2," Savannah said, grinning.

"What?" Darkrose said, putting her drink down. "Oi! That's *my* screen name—"

"Can I get you guys anything else?" the waitress said. Annie was a blackhaired punkish girl who kept checking out my tats—and from the way she also kept checking out Revenance and Doug, it was safe to assume I had a potential customer and not a suitor on my hands.

"I'll have a Guinness," Jinx said. A boy at the table beside us looked over when she said that, raising a Guinness of his own. His eye fell on me, on my tats, and he smiled; I responded with a polite bob of my Sprite, but filed him away in the "suitor" category. He was with a group, and turned back to his conversations.

"I'll have one too," Cinnamon said, grinning wickedly.

"And I'll see your ID's," Annie said. Clearly she'd been around the waitress block enough to spot a fake ID, because she tossed

Cinnamon's back without a word—but then she handed Jinx's ID back too. "I don't think so."

"Hey," Cinnamon said.

"Gee, *thanks*," Jinx said in shock.

"Don't be surprised," I told Jinx. "In that getup you look about twelve. Annie, I met orange-hair yesterday," I said, pointing at the outraged little werecat, "but *her* I've known since grade school. Jinx is twenty-six."

"I can vouch for that," Savannah said. "I've known her since kindergarten."

The waitress frowned. "All right, but I'd better not see you slipping that kitten a sip. Honey, can I get you another Sprite?"

"Fine," Cinnamon said, slumping over the table. "Rub it in—"

I leaned back in my chair, laughing, and bumped into Guinness-boy behind me. His eyes caught mine and lit up briefly, but he rolled back into his story without missing a beat—something about how a spilled Guinness had led to a bar flight in Colorado and a bit of kung-fu fighting.

"So," Jinx said, drawing my attention back to our own table just as she was putting her Guinness down, "on the note of old friends getting together . . . it's really good to see you two together again." Both Savannah and I spluttered, and Jinx raised her gloved hand. "I meant, at the same time."

I stared at the table, at the Sprite, then slowly looked up at Savannah, who was doing the same hunched, guilty thing. "Yeah," I said.

"Me too," Savannah said.

"So . . . can we stop the 'friends having to choose sides thing' . . . Dakota?"

I looked sharply at Jinx. I wanted to say something. But she was right. "Sure," I said.

"Well, if this is about to become domestic," Calaphase said, scooting back his chair.

"Wait. There is one more thing."

"Shoot," Calaphase said.

"I have a message for the Marquis," I said, putting my hand on Cinnamon's shoulder. "I've given it to Cinnamon but . . . I'd like you to make sure that he and the Bear King get it."

Calaphase scowled. "Ladies," he said, cocking his head at his and Revenance's new squeezes. "Could you excuse us for a minute?"

"Oh, hon, do you have to?" the girl on his arm said.

"I'm 'fraid I do, Cheri," Calaphase said. "Wait by the bar, if you would."

After the girls walked away, I said: "Tell them what you saw, Cinnamon."

She stared at her Sprite. "A fucking wooden lid with somebody's tattooed skin nailed to it."

"Holy crap," Revenance said. I didn't think a vampire could get any paler, but somehow he managed it. "How did—"

"The Feds say there's a serial killer skinning the tattooed," I said. "I believe them."

"*Jesus*," Savannah said, crossing herself, making the other vampires flinch.

I had forgotten Savannah didn't know, but I just plowed ahead. "After our little tussle I don't think the Marquis will listen to *me* about anything but . . . now Cinnamon has seen it, too. I need you to make sure they don't bust her chops for this. That they take her seriously."

Calaphase nodded. "Yeah. I mean—yeah. I can do that."

"If they give you any crap," I said, "the Marquis can call Jinx for confirmation—she's 'seen' it too, and I don't think she's on his shit list, so he'll trust her. Besides, giving Cinnamon a message to take back may take some heat off her for her little walkabout."

"That's . . . that's a really good idea," Revenance said thoughtfully.

"Well, Lady Frost," Calaphase said. "You're just full of surprises."

"It's just Dakota," I said. "And just . . . keep her safe."

Cinnamon, still hunched over her Sprite, looked sidelong at me.

We closed up and I cornered the waitress: Annie was indeed checking out my tats, and promised to come by the Rogue Unicorn at the first opportunity. While we talked, I noticed Guinness-boy noticing us; cute, nice skin, but *definitely* suitor, not customer. His eyes caught mine again, and I smiled briefly, but then slipped out before he could nerve himself up.

When I strolled out of the massive, raftered dining area into the bar, I found the vampires had rejoined their companions. Calaphase was dismissing his evening companion with a chaste kiss, but Revenance was still working on his, trying to convince her to take a ride.

"See the short, redheaded biker chick?" Revenance was saying. "She's the Queen of the Vampires in this district . . . and a Daywalker. She can guarantee you'll be safe with me. If you ride off with me on my bike and disappear, she'll blame me—then come open my coffin sometime right around noon."

Savannah stared at him in shock. "Yeah . . . yeah, I would," she said slowly. "And give you a big old garlic enema."

"Ouch!" Calaphase said. "Stings just thinking about—"

"Oi," Darkrose said, wincing. "Less graphic, please."

"I—I don't know," the girl said nervously, excited and afraid at the same time, staring up at him with huge, enraptured eyes. "Maybe next time—"

"But how would I find you?" Revenance said, staring down at her, the slightest glow glimmering in his eyes. "Maybe I could get your numb—"

"Maybe we could all get together next week?" I suggested, and Revenance scowled at me. "Same time, next Saturday?"

"I'd like that," Jinx said.

"Me too," Savannah said.

"We will be in Africa," Darkrose reminded her.

"Maybe the week after, then?" I said, unwilling to let it go.

"That would be better for me," the girl said.

Savannah looked at Darkrose. "I—I suppose—"

"That sounds like a *great* idea," Calaphase said, putting his hand heavily on Revenance's shoulder. "Listen to the Lady, she knows stews taste best when they've had time to simmer." Calaphase smiled at his own potential—victim? girlfriend? I didn't know the rules anymore—evenly, without a hint of a leer; and she just smiled back at him.

"All right, all right, you win," Revenance sighed, kissing his starry-eyed but relieved companion on the hand. "In two weeks, my sweet."

"It's settled, then," Calaphase said. "Dakota, if the Bear King allows it, we'll drop Cinnamon off a week from Friday at your place and pick her up here, same time."

"Sure," I said, forced-cheerful, trying not to let my voice crack as I put my hand on Cinnamon's shoulder. I hadn't bargained on that at all, but—"I'd be happy to watch over her again."

"Don't try to sound *too* excited," Cinnamon said.

"Need a ride back to your place?" Savannah asked as we stepped outside. "It's not so out of the way if we're running Jinx back by Emory—"

"No," I responded hastily. "My bike is a couple of blocks away in LFP, and it's a nice night. I think I'll walk it—"

"*You* have a *bike?*" Calaphase asked, staring at my long leather vest, which nearly trailed the floor. "How can you *ride* in that thing?"

"I tuck it," I admitted. "Last thing I want is to get sucked into the wheel of a Vespa—"

"A Vespa!" Calaphase said. "I thought you said you had a *bike*—"

"Hey, you," I said, my face reddening a little. Technically it was a *scooter* and not a bike, but—"It gets sixty miles to the gallon—"

"Can see why you tuck it though," Revenance said, hopping on his bike. "It's not just hazardous. Death by Vespa would be downright embarrassing."

"Death by Vespa!" Calaphase laughed, hopping on his bike. "Take care, Frost."

"Yeah, Frost," Cinnamon said, wrapping her hands around Calaphase nervously.

"No helmet?" I asked. "Is that safe—"

Cinnamon rolled her eyes. "Unless the streets are paved with silver—"

"I get it, I get it," I said, laughing. Then I looked from her to Savannah, who was standing by Darkrose, arm round her waist, not looking directly at me. "See y'all in two weeks."

"Yeah," Savannah said, looking up suddenly. "See you then."

And with that my ex-girlfriend and her vampire lover departed, blind witch and her newfound seeing-eye Doug in tow. Moments later the werecat and her vampire companions rode off on their Harleys, leaving me alone in the parking lot three blocks from my Vespa for no good reason other than my damn stubbornness.

I'm such an idiot.

I strolled past the edge of the bar and thought about running into Videodrome, but it was late and there wasn't anything I was really buzzed to watch, so I turned onto Highland and headed home.

"Garlic enema," I muttered to myself, snorting. I had to admit it, I missed Savannah. She could be a riot when she wanted to. And so, surprisingly, could Revenance. "Death by Vespa," I said, chuckling. I needed to get home before I pissed myself—

"Hey Dakota!" someone screamed. "Catch!"

I looked up, and a dark figure hurled a white barrel straight at my head.

21. Playing Catch

I raised my hands to defend myself, but I was too slow: with a tremendous *CRACK* the barrel broke against my face, knocking me backwards and splashing me with white, sticky goop. The impact lifted my feet off the ground, and I was momentarily airborne; then my back slammed into the sidewalk and all the air left my lungs with a *WHOOF*, leaving me in a red haze, choking for oxygen through a mouthful of sludge.

I coughed and spat and scraped the stinging muck from my eyes, lying back, wheezing for breath. The hull and contents of a splintered five-gallon paint barrel lay splattered around me. Dully I saw marks on the side of the barrel where it had been scored with a razor, and realized it had been *meant* to burst. Meant to splatter paint—all over me. I held my shaking hands up: the religious symbols and the yin yangs were covered in a thick layer of white paint. In terror I looked up at my assailant.

Transomnia stood over me, eyes twin red coals.

"Let's see you use your marks now," he said, and kicked me in the ribs.

I cried out. My body thudded backward against the wall of a nearby car, but before I could get up or roll away he kicked me again—and again, and again. In the ribs, in the face, cracking against the side of my knee. Not savagely, not with vampire strength, but deliberately, methodically, so the pain built, as I scraped and skidded across the pavement and he casually, oh so casually, savaged me.

"Can't kill you—" *CRACK* "—can't drain you—" CRACK "—can't even *rape* you—" CRACK! "—but I can make you pay for humiliating me."

I started to say something. I don't know what it was. He kicked me in the teeth, and when my hand instinctively went to my face he seized it with immense strength and pinned it to his knee, prying my fingers apart and then crushing the little fingers and thumb underneath his viselike hand so my index and middle fingers waved helplessly in the air.

Then he pulled a pair of pruning clippers from his long black coat.

"Oh, God—"

Transomnia backhanded me casually with the hand holding the clippers, gashing my forehead. "I want some souvenirs," he said, grabbing my fingers within the V of the clippers and squeezing down so hard I squealed in pain and twisted my head into the pavement, bawling.

"Look at me," he said. I twisted my head away, and his grip tightened, making my trapped knuckles pop. Then he squeezed again, and I felt the clippers draw blood. "Look at me. Do it, or lose them."

I looked up, saw my fingers in the curved beak of the pruner, and his unsmiling face. His makeup was gone, making him look older, leaner, meaner. I looked into his cold red eyes—and knew he could do *anything*.

"That's right," he said, releasing his grip on my hand but keeping my fingers trapped between the blade and hook of the pruner. "According to this little thing—" and he grabbed my protective collar so hard I began choking "—I supposedly 'can't' even maim you. But I *can*. I can walk away from here with ALL your fingers and leave you with stumps. I'll put them in the blender when I get home, one by one, and think of your stumps. You'll never tattoo again."

He released my neck, and I croaked: "Duh-don't take my haands—"

He backhanded me, hard, and I felt a tooth loosen in a warm, metallic flow of blood. "Don't speak to me. Don't ever presume to speak to me again. Got that, bitch?"

I nodded, slumped on the pavement, staring at his boots.

He twisted my hand back and forth a bit, squeezing experimentally. I cringed. Finally he said, "You're not worth it," and released me—kicking me, vampire hard, in the gut.

My dinner spewed out onto the sidewalk. I alternately coughed and gasped for breath. Finally I just lay there at Transomnia's feet, dry heaving staring at my bloody, twisted hand.

Distantly I heard voices, running, shouting—and the savage barking of a dog.

"'Oh, look, the cavalry!'" Transomnia mocked, pocketing the clippers, looking off in the distance. "But if I'd meant to maim you for life, you'd be lying there wearing a bloody pair of meat flippers now. And I can have you again, anytime I want, and nobody can stop me—not that dandy or his maid or her Queen of de Nile. You're my bitch, anytime I want—bitch. And next time I *will* get creative. So never cross me again. Ever. *Ev*-er."

I let out a low moan. But I nodded.

The barking dog was almost upon us now, but I never saw it arrive: the last things I remember were Transomnia casually kicking the side of my face, a spray of blood, and one of my teeth skittering out across the pavement.

22. ROADKILL

The fingers of my right hand were bandaged—*all* of them, one two three four five.

Thank God.

I lay back in a fuzzy haze. Bright lights shone in my face. A man was asking me to count. I looked aside, and a doctor was talking to a nurse. I asked, "What?"

They looked at each other. "She won't remember any of this."

Now my knee was itching something fierce. I picked up my hand again, staring at the bandaged fingers. I seemed to see Andre Rand through them, hunched over the edge of the bed, praying, but when my hand fell to the bed, I saw Special Agent Philip Davidson.

"What?" I said again, looking around. It was a hospital room. Emory Hospital.

Philip sat up abruptly. "You're awake before me," he said, blinking sleep from his eyes. "Good. That's promising."

He'd been sitting backwards in an armless hospital-issue guest chair, hunched over the backrest, staring at my knee. I reached down, cautiously, with my bandaged hand—it hurt, but I could move it—and pulled the sheets aside to reveal a white bandage on my right knee.

"What?" I asked again, then marshaled myself. "What the hell?"

"That's my Dakota," Savannah said.

I gasped. Savannah stood there in the sunbeams in a red leather dress—*the* red leather dress, the one I liked, simple and asymmetrical, peaking high over her right breast and sweeping down over the curve of her left. The bottom hem was cut at a similar angle, exposing her right thigh and sweeping down, mirroring the angle of the sunlight shining down on the bare flesh of her delicate bare calf and ankle.

"Savannah," I said, caught with sudden horror. "The sun—"

"S'alright," she said, smiling, adjusting her bomber goggles. "I'm a daywalker. Besides, the glass soaks up a lot of the UV." She held up a light monitor she carried around her neck—and if I knew Savannah and the red dress, the monitor and the goggles were the only other things on her curvy body. "As long as I keep an eye on the levels, I'm safe."

"You look . . . spectacular," I said.

"*You* look like crap," she responded. "Just this shy of Roadkill."

'Roadkill' had been my costume at the last Halloween we'd spent together—layered makeup and printed tire tracks that had actually made Savannah nauseous—and now that she'd pointed it out I winced, feeling what must be stitches on my forehead and some crusty crap on my cheek. In fact, aches and pains were popping up *all* over my body, there was a gap where two of my back left molars should have been, and my left eye didn't want to open all the way. No wonder I reminded her of 'Roadkill.'

"So this *really* is your girlfriend?" Philip said, a half smile on his face.

"Ex-girlfriend," Savannah and I said simultaneously.

"Your ex here used a little social engineering to waltz straight through our police barricade."

"I didn't lie," Savannah said, scowling but embarrassed. "I said I was here *as* her girlfriend. There's no statute of limitations on girlfriendiness, is there?"

"*I'm* not going to give you shit," Philip said, chuckling, smiling at me. "I completely understand your desire to be beside Dakota—"

"Not for the reasons you think," Savannah said coldly. "She was under my protection. Kotie, I'm so sorry—"

"Don't blame yourselves. *I* fucked up," I said. I felt *so* ashamed. "I provoked him. It's all my fault—"

"Do not talk like that," Philip said calmly. "No one had the right to do this to you."

I shook my head. "I-I know that," I said, struggling for words. "I'd like to kick the little fucker's teeth in. It's just—earlier, at the werehouse—"

At which I trailed off. Davidson was a Fed, an X-Files-grade Fed with his own spooky black helicopter, and here I was spilling the guts on an Edgeworld werehouse. What was *wrong* with me—did they have me on some kind of painkillers?

"Werehouse?" Davidson said, arching an eyebrow. I kept looking out the window, and he asked, "What aren't you telling me?"

"Kotie," Savannah said. "Talk to us. What happened at the werehouse?"

I glared at her, but she was just scowling, red bangs and goggles hiding her eyes. But if she didn't seem worried talking to Davidson.

"Transomnia was on guard," I said, looking at Davidson briefly before staring back at Savannah. "He called you a dirty name, and I . . . I punched him in the face, knocked him down in front of Lord Buckhead. During the attack on me he said he was . . . punishing me."

"You *decked* a *vampire*?" Davidson said, astonished.

"Transomnia," Savannah said icily. "I'll remember that."

"Now, now," Davidson cautioned. "Don't go trying to be a vigilante—"

"I'll do as I please," Savannah replied. "I *am* a daywalker."

Davidson scowled. "Daywalker or no, you don't know what you're getting into—"

"If you two are going to fight, could you do it outside?" I said.

Davidson raised his hands, and Savannah looked away, embarrassed.

"Look, I know you just came to," Davidson said. "But I want to warn you. Doctors are going to appear and hover over you. The police will want to take a statement. We've got a police detail on you—all off-duty volunteers right now —"

"*Volunteer?*" Savannah asked, putting a hand on her hip. "She just had an attempt on her life, and you have to use volunteers?"

"Welcome to policing," Philip said. "Many storm the gates, but few man the walls. We're lucky Dakota has family on the force; it was easy to find volunteers—"

As if on cue the door opened, held by Horscht, one of the officers who had picked me up earlier. He winked at me, then stepped back to admit a group of doctors and nurses. There was an older man who looked like he might be in charge, but he deferred to an impossibly young doctor with a broad smile and parted black hair.

Davidson and Savannah stepped back to give the doctors room, but the youngish man looked at them sharply. "We need to speak to Miss Frost about her medical condition," he said, clearly about to give my visitors their walking papers. "Are you with the family?"

"I'm here as her girlfriend," Savannah said.

"I'm here on behalf of her father," Davidson said, "and the police detail is my doing. If I'm not here, someone from the detail needs to be with her at all times."

The doctor twitched a little, and I said, "Let them stay. I'm half out of it anyway. Someone with memory needs to be here."

The doctor laughed. "Very well. Do you prefer Dakota or Miss Frost?"

"Dakota," I said.

"Dakota, your leg has some of the most wonderful tattoos I've ever seen," he said, smiling, sitting in the chair that Davidson had just been in, patting the bed in a friendly way that made me feel like he was touching my leg, without ever actually touching it. "I saw them when I was patching up your knee this morning. I've never seen colors so alive, so vibrant. Maybe I caught a whiff of the anesthetic, but it almost looked like one of them moved out of the way while I was working."

"That would be the dragon," I said. "He's pretty mobile."

The doctor raised an eyebrow, and looked briefly back at Savannah and Davidson.

"Miss Frost is a magical tattooist," Davidson said. "Her tattoos *do* move."

"Well, I'll be," the doctor said, turning back to me. "Dakota, my name is Doctor Blake. I'm an orthopedic surgeon. Doctor Hampton called me in to work on your knee because it was torn up inside. You may not remember everything that happened—"

"A vampire beat the shit out of me and kicked me in my knee when I was down."

He smiled, a wry, boy-I'd-like-to-get-that-fucker smile if I've ever seen one. "Well, Dakota, when he did that he tore the ligament on the inside of your knee—what we call your MCL. It was on the edge of what we call a grade four tear, with some collateral damage, so I had to go in to your leg, do some minor arthroscopy—but it looks good. If we can keep you off the leg for a few days, we can have you up on crutches within a week. We've got to watch it, of course, but with some rest, ice, and therapy, I think you'll regain full use of your knee."

"Oh fuck," I said. "How the hell am I going to pay for all this?"

"Don't you have healthcare at the tattoo parlor?" Davidson said.

I lifted my head to look at him. "Are you kidding?"

"Don't worry about it," Savannah said. "You were under our protection. The Consulate will pay for everything."

"The 'Consulate?'" the doctor asked.

"The Vampire Consulate of Little Five Points," Savannah said. "That collar of hers is a sign of our protection." Her voice grew icy. "It *should* have been enough of a warning."

"Well, I'll be," Doctor Blake said, smile a little more forced. "When she said vampire I thought she was just being metaphorical."

"Doc," I said. "About my hand—"

"Well, you had a *lot* of bruises and scrapes, which is common when some son-of-a-bitch kicks you when you're down. And I won't lie to you—you're going to get some ugly looking facial swelling over the next few days. You'll get even prettier than you are now."

"Hard to believe," Savannah said. I laughed, halfheartedly.

"But, on your hand, there were . . . cuts," he said. "Do you remember what happened—"

I looked up, saw my fingers in the curved beak of the pruner, and his unsmiling face. "I can walk away from here with ALL your fingers and leave you with stumps. I'll put them in the blender when I get home, one by one, and think of your stumps. You'll never tattoo again."

"He—he had some *pruning shears*," I said, eyes tearing up, unable to catch my breath, feeling my heart race and a charge of adrenaline tingle up my spine and churn my gut. "He got my *fingers* in them. He got my fingers and he *squeezed*—"

"Lord have mercy," Savannah said.

"He said he could take them any time," I said. I didn't bother to hide the tears leaking out of my eyes. "My fingers. *All* of them. That he'd leave me with *meat flippers* if I crossed him. That I'd never tattoo again—"

"The police will take a statement later, I think," Davidson said, in his supremely calm voice, stepping forward to put his hand on the bed in a way that made me feel like he'd put his arm around my shoulders. "You don't need to go into all the details now—"

"That's right, Dakota," the doctor said, reaching out to touch my bandaged hand. "I've heard enough. Your hand is fine. You *will* tattoo again. And you have good friends. They're good people. I don't think they'll let anyone hurt you again."

He squeezed my hand very gently, emphasizing it, as if to let me know everything would be all right. I winced a little, but I could feel my hand was still whole. The doc was all right. He was all right. But the effort to smile made my head hurt, and I reached up to rub my temple.

My Mohawk was gone.

My forehead, cheek and temple were bandages, scrapes and bruises, but beyond that there was no 'hawk, just a ragged brush of hair. I tore my bandaged hand out of his grip and raised it to my head, groaning, afraid to touch it. It was almost completely shaved in front, and behind that only tufts of hair were left, like someone had weedwhacked the front of my head. Only the hair at the back of my head had been wholly spared. "Awwwww—"

"You were like that when I saw you," Doctor Blake said, embarrassed. "But I think they did that in the emergency room when they were treating you. They needed to clean your wounds, but your head and face were covered with some kind of paint —"

With a tremendous CRACK *the world went black, leaving me choking for oxygen through a sludge of white sticky goop. A splintered five-gallon paint barrel lay splattered around me, and my hands were covered in a thick layer of white paint. "Let's see you use your marks now," Transomnia said, eyes twin red coals.*

"Oh, *God*," I said, hands cradling my bruised, plucked head, hovering over it, afraid to leave it, afraid to touch it. "That bastard got me good, he got me good—"

Savannah came to my side, patting my hand, saying something soft and bracing.

"Leave me alone." I said, eyes squeezed shut. God, what a horrible way to find out how vain I really was. Someone's hand touched my shoulder, and I shook them off. "I don't want anyone to see me like this. Just—please. Leave me alone."

Philip said a few quiet words, and I let my face fall into my hands. After some time the door closed, and when I looked up, I was alone.

I fell back against the bed. I stared at the ceiling. And then, I cried.

23. NEVER AGAIN

*"If I wanted to maim you for life, you'd be lying there wearing a bloody pair of meat flippers. And I can have you again. You're my bitch, anytime I want—bitch. And next time I **will** get creative. So never cross me again. Ever. **Ev-er.**"*

I lay there in the hospital bed, drifting in and out.

At first all I could think of was how close to death I'd come. Not just with Transomnia—with all the monsters I had just insulted, taunted or spurned. The Bear King. The Marquis. The 'Lady' Saffron. Even little Cinnamon could have torn my throat out.

What was scarier is that any one of them could have done far worse—made me a werewolf, or vampire, or God forbid, a vampire's slave. Transomnia had proved that my tattoos and all the power I drew from them would not stop a determined opponent. I shuddered. He'd let me off relatively easily, when he could have raped and drained me and made me his mindless thrall. Compared to what he *could* have done, he'd been a cream puff.

And nothing he *had* done required any vampire powers. Sure, tossing the paint bucket had been quite a feat, but any big bruiser could have done it. But a big bruiser with a tire iron would have just left me dead or close to it. What was really scary about Transomnia was not his powers, or his strength, but his mind. His . . . creativity.

And then my fingers started tingling and I started thinking about his threat to creatively amputate them. At first it made me even more scared. *I didn't dare cross him.* Then it made me mad. *How dare **he** cross* ***me?*** And then I got scared again. The loop continued until I drifted off into a haze of anger and fear, hearing Transomnia's warning,

"Never cross me again, *ev*-er," play over and over in my mind like a broken record—until my mind itself put a stop to it.

"*Never* again," I said firmly, sitting up in the bed. "*Ev*-er."

Davidson was sitting in his usual seat, and lifted up. "*That* sounded promising."

"What day is it?" I asked.

"Monday," Davidson replied. "Around noon. Savannah's crashed in the waiting area."

"Of course," I said. "Even she can't burn the candle at both ends forever."

"I thought vampires 'died' during the day," Davidson said, holding his fingers up in scare quotes. "I never met a real daywalker before."

"Fishing for information from the vampire's girlfriend?" I asked. "Wrong pond. We split after she started drinking blood."

"I was just asking," Davidson said. "We don't get a lot of vampires in the black helicopter division."

"What does your division handle then? Aliens?"

"*Maybe*," Davidson said. "Fishing for information from the man in black?"

"Touché," I said.

"No, it's not a problem, I've got my flashy thing right here," he said, fishing in his coat pocket. "I can tell you anything you want and then just erase—oh, drat. Left my flashy thing in my other coat."

"You can flash me anytime," I said halfheartedly.

He laughed. "Sounds like our Dakota. You up for a few visitors?"

"Visitors?" I said, suddenly horrified, hands going to my head. Under my fingers my face felt worse than yesterday, and I was pained to feel the tender bald spot which had been the start of my deathhawk, much less the ragged tufts on my crown where they'd run out of paint-encrusted hair to whack off. Oh, no. Oh, *hell*, no. "You can't let anyone in here with me looking like this!"

"Dakota," Davidson said gently. "We haven't been letting them in here at all. Until you woke up we didn't know *anything* about your assailant other than 'a guy in a black coat.' Now we know his name and that he's a vampire, but you were too distraught to give a statement. Not even Miss Winters knows what this Transomnia looks like, though she is checking. So for all I know he's waiting to take another crack at you, sitting in that crowd—"

"Crowd?" I asked. "What crowd?"

"There are a lot of people here to see you, Dakota. A *lot* of people. You need to see them sometime," Davidson said, in that oh-so-calm voice that let you know he'd back your play, but you'd be disappointed in yourself for not stepping up.

Finally I gave in. "Oh, all right. But not in here. Clean me up and take me to them."

"I don't think—" Davidson said, looking back at the hall. "You've just had knee surgery. You shouldn't be walking—"

"Get me a fucking wheelchair, then," I said. "Just don't let anybody in here, not with me laying in bed looking like a . . . like a damn victim."

Davidson abruptly turned and stepped out the door. After a minute he returned, stepped into the bathroom for a hot wet towel, and sat down next to me. His expression was tender as he patted down my forehead; his hands were delicate and dextrous. I closed my eyes as the cloth wiped my cheeks, smiling once when his thumb brushed a bit of grit from beneath my eye. When I opened my eyes Philip was holding up a comb.

"Mind if I use mine?" he asked. "I'm clean."

"I don't have enough hair left to give a shit," I said softly.

"You still look beautiful," Philip said, running the comb over the crown of my head.

"Liar," I replied, as he straightened out the remainder of my hawk.

"But I do it so well," he responded. My hair no longer fell in my eyes, so I'd ignored it; but when he was done, the hair that was left climbed straight back, and I felt much better.

"Philip," I said. "I . . . I want to learn to defend myself."

"Defend yourself?" Philip asked. "But you—"

"It's just bravado," I admitted, near tears. "I play it big and bad . . . but it's all talk. Just talk. I need to learn to back it up—"

"Whoa, whoa," Philip said. "What exactly are we talking about? You mean, as in, to fight? To fire a gun?"

"I mean, whatever it takes," I said. "Just this . . . never again. I mean, ev-er."

"Dakota," Philip said. He sounded worried. "Even trained agents get mugged. Me-heap-bad-man-in-black tried to fight off a mugger and got pistol-whipped, lost the briefcase I was supposed to be protecting and ended up in the hospital, just like you."

I stared at him. I knew what he was getting at—with all his training, with all his equipment, he'd still got caught off guard and ended up in the hospital, just like me. Even if I'd had training, there always was a chance that Transomnia could still have caught me off guard—and so no amount of training would guarantee that this wouldn't happen again.

Philip had a point. It was a good point, but I didn't want to get it, refused to follow it through. In the end, it didn't matter. I couldn't go through this again, not without knowing I'd done everything I could to keep myself safe.

"I-don't-care," I said deliberately. "I want to learn to defend myself."

"Alright, Dakota, I'll help you," he said, though I wasn't sure what *he* meant by 'help' was what I wanted. "Now let's go see your friends."

Philip did a little 'social engineering' to get the chair—it was amazing. If you listened to what he said, he never exactly told the nurse that the doctor had ordered a wheelchair so I could leave my room, but he certainly left that impression and within minutes he was wheeling me out into the hall. Outside my room, I saw Vickman, the hard-faced man from the Vampire Consulate, speaking quietly with a policeman; when he saw me he raised an eyebrow.

"Is the waiting area clean?" Philip asked.

"Yes," Vickman said. "We're checking out everyone who goes in there."

"Great. Thanks for your help, Mister. . . ."

"Just 'Vickman,'" he replied, his eyes curiously flat as he looked at me. "The Consulate is just following up on its responsibilities."

As we drew closer to the waiting area, I started to hear voices. Then I started to smile.

"I can just hear her now," someone was saying. "*What the fucking-fuck de fuckedy fuck do you fucking think you are fucking doing?*"

I put my head in my hand, embarrassed. That sounded like me, all right. When did an ex-Bible Bowl girl end up with the mouth of a sailor? Then I raised my head as Philip wheeled me into a corner waiting room, seeing the raft of friends waiting for me.

Savannah was still crashed on a sofa, blissfully asleep, head and hands leaning on the lap of an older, priestly gentleman in a beige coat, black shirt and white collar. In a pair of chairs next to them, Andre Rand talked with a wiry, bright-eyed young man with wavy hair and a lumberjack shirt that barely contained his barrel chest. Catty-corner to them sat Doug and Jinx, clasping hands, him rapt, her staring straight ahead as she explained something animatedly.

"... fungal corneal opacity," Jinx was saying. "It's like . . . take a piece of construction paper and punch two eyeholes in it with a pencil. Off-center is better to get the full effect. Then tape a piece of wax paper to the back and hold that over your face, so all you see are two blurry dots with some diffuse light leaking in from the sides— Dakota! Is that you?"

"Yeah, she's here," Doug said, squeezing her hand. "I'm sorry for you—"

"I survive," Jinx said, patting his hand with her free one. "But does she?"

"I survive," I croaked, voice unexpectedly weak. "Ahem. I'm all right. I'm all right."

"Oh, Dakota," Jinx said. "I'm so pleased. We were all so worried. So worried."

"Well, speak of the devil," Rand said, looking up at me. He had been the one I'd heard miming me in the hall, and the athletic young man he was talking to was starting to look oddly familiar. "Welcome back from the dead."

"I didn't actually die," I said. "But it sure did feel like it."

"I'm so sorry I couldn't get to you sooner," the young man said, eyes bright on me, and then he made the same sliding motion with his hand I'd seen back . . . back at Manuel's Tavern! The Guinness dude. "That bastard sure could run."

"You were the cavalry," I said, remembering the shouting voices. "Thanks."

"I wish I could take all the credit," he said. "As soon as I saw him standing over you, I yelled for help and started running—but then this huge dog leapt out of the bushes and chased him off before I could even get to you guys. Crazy. The thing looked big as a wolf."

My eyes widened and I wasn't sure I liked the direction my mind was talking. Could that have been . . . Wulf? "Well, however it went down, thank you," I said. "Who knows what he could have done if he'd had more time?"

His nostrils flared, and he shook his head. He had a strong jaw and cleancut features, and now that I'd been wheeled a bit closer I could see that while he wasn't weightlifter bulky, his whole body seemed to bulge underneath his clothes wherever they touched him.

"I gotta level with you," he said, embarrassed. "I ran after you to ask for your number."

"Dakota Frost," I said, extending my hand. "And it's 404—"

"You don't have to do that," he said, shaking it. His grip was gentle, but beneath the surface I could feel muscles like marble. "Darren Briggs."

"I think I do have to. It's a rescue rule or something," I said. "At least come by the Rogue Unicorn when I'm back tattooing—I'll give you a free Frost bite."

"Oh, you're *that* Dakota," he said, impressed.

"Best magical tattooist in the Southeast," I responded.

The older, priestly man, in whose lap Savannah still lay, looked up sharply when I said that, and I realized he probably had the same feelings about magical tattooing Savannah did. "Sorry," I said. "Didn't mean to offend you with that 'Satanist crap.'"

He looked surprised. "Offended? No," He looked over my shoulder. "Agent Davidson, could you work your magic and get us a blanket? The sun's creeping up on her."

"No problem, Canon Grace," Phil said. "Back in a minute, Dakota."

As Philip left, the priest looked back at me, smiling. "What Satanist crap?"

"The tattoos," I looked at the ground guiltily. "Savannah calls them Satanist—"

His eyes widened, and he seemed to take me in anew, looking over my tattoos. "I don't think Satan ever made a flower, or a jewel, or anything for that matter. Savannah really said that?" He sighed, patting her head. "I need to have a talk with her. I have two tattoos."

"*You* have tattoos?" I said, surprised.

"On my shoulder," he admitted, taking a blanket from Phil. "One says *Leviticus 19:28*, back from when I was a biker fresh out of Special Forces, and the second one says *John 3:16*, which I got when I went into seminary."

"Cute," I laughed. The quote from Leviticus prohibited tattoos; the John one promised salvation through faith, not works. The second sort of canceled the first, but—"I wouldn't have done either of them. I don't do religious marks."

Canon Grace's eyes narrowed at my hands, and I stared down at the symbology of the world's major religions tattooed across my knuckles. "Well, not on anyone else, at any rate."

"And why is that?" he asked, mildly surprised.

"They're forbidden by traditional Christianity, and sacred in other traditions," I said. "I can take responsibility for inking myself, but I'm not a priest and I don't *do* sacred. I don't believe all that mumbo-jumbo, even if crosses do make vampires break out in hives."

"That's just a psychic/psychological effect," Canon Grace said, patting Savannah's head. "Our little Christian bloodsucker here proves that."

I stared down at her, then up at him. "I can't believe you can condone that—"

"It would not be my choice of diet, but I think Savannah's proved you can make the lifestyle into something morally neutral, if not even admirable," the priest said. "And contrary to what some people say, God doesn't take sides. Even when he directed the Hebrews to take the Holy Land, he told Joshua son of Nun—"

"He came neither for them nor their enemies," I said, waving my hand. "Yeah, yeah—Stratton Christian Academy, Bible Bowl, eighth grade champ."

"Good," the priest said, laughing. "My point is, God cares about what you do, why you do it and most importantly what—who—you believe in , not whether you've traded sunlight and liquid food for longer life. How is condemning vampires really any different from saying someone's going to hell for eating food and punishing their bodies on a treadmill?"

"I can see why Savannah likes you," I said, and I wasn't sure it was a compliment.

"I didn't start out like this," he said, patting her head. "Back when she first turned I told her *you're going to haaail*, but since then, 'by their fruits shall ye know them'—"

There were voices in the hall, and I craned my neck slowly. Alex Nicholson entered, followed by Christopher Valentine.

"No, I'm not being rude," he snapped back at Alex. "I'm tired of all the tricks these goddam charlatans play. I want to see for myself—"

Then his eyes took me in and widened in shock. "Jesus Christ."

"Language, Mister Valentine," Jinx said reprovingly.

"Thought I was faking it to get out of the challenge, didn't you?" I said, and embarrassment spread over his sharp features. More than one target of the Valentine Challenge had become conveniently unable to continue. I held up my bandaged hand and wriggled the fingers. "You don't get off that easy. We're still on."

The shock and embarrassment in his face spread into a wide, delighted grin. "Hear that?" he said, elbowing Alex. "I look forward to it, Miss Frost."

And then Savannah awoke, stretching like a cat. "Oh, Dakota," she said, smiling sleepily, "it's so good to see you awake."

And then she yawned, showing her shocking canines.

Vampire fangs are huge, sharp and pointed like a cat's, larger than you'd expect; even the lateral incisors have a bit of an edge to them. Brand new vampires often have dental problems, but that's OK; Savannah tells me the self-healing nature of their bodies helps the mouth adapt over time. Honestly, the sight of her vamp teeth never bothered me before, but now—

I twitched, flashing on *Transomnia's* canines, on his face, on his cold, red eyes. On all the things he did to me—and threatened to do. It was too much. I twitched and looked away. There was a tremendous pressure on my bladder, and I squeezed my legs together.

Her yawn ended, and she caught me looking away. "What's the matter—" and then she got it, all of a sudden, closing her mouth and throwing her hand over it. She stared at me in horror for one brief moment, realizing that I couldn't separate *her* from *them*, that I hated and feared what she was—and that her becoming a vampire had left real, deep wounds between us she had never fully acknowledged. Then she got up and ran away.

I felt an aching in my chest. I had *loved* Savannah. I had thought of her as my *wife*. But now she was a vampire, and a part of me was glad she was running away—and the rest of me was just a big old bundle of guilt and pain.

Then Jinx grabbed my hand and squeezed it for support, and in the sudden silence I realized everyone was staring at me. Realized everyone could see I'd been knocked off my personal pedestal of invincibility. Realized everyone—wait for it—*pitied* me.

I tore my hand out of Jinx's and twisted up to look at Phil. "I can't go on like this. I can't let myself become a victim. I have to—I *have to*—learn to defend myself."

Phil scowled. Rand nodded. And Darren rode to the rescue. "That's easy enough. You've got some recovery time ahead of you, but you're a big, confident woman. There are things we can do right now to make you safer."

Philip caught his breath, and did I hear a touch of *jealousy* in his voice? "Now, look, Darren, we appreciate what you did—"

"No, I want to hear this," I said, focusing on Darren. All I wanted to do was hit something, and *hard*, and maybe *this* guy could help me. "In the restaurant I overheard you talking about a fight in Colorado. How you took a guy out with one kick. If you weren't shooting off your mouth to impress me, I want to learn to do that—"

"You'd be better off learning how to deal with your anger," the priest said.

"I suppose *you're* going to tell me to turn the other cheek," I said hotly.

Canon Grace stared at me sadly. "I suppose I am."

"You should listen to him," Darren said, so cheerily that at first I thought he was joking. "It's totally good advice." At the cold glare of the priest he raised his hands and said, "No, I'm completely serious—controlling your anger is a good place to start. The best fights are ones that never happen. Once I was on the beach sunbathing, and some jerk threw water in my face to try to pick a fight."

He slid out of his chair smoothly, a well oiled machine, dropping into a low, coiled stance with one arm shot forward like a blade and the other fist raised behind him in the air.

"So I dropped into jodan, it's your basic low stance, and just sat there. The guy stood there in front of his buddies, cussing, calling me a coward—and then walked off, thinking he'd showed me. If I'd tussled with him, I would have ended up hurting three people—or getting hurt by three people. Instead, we had a perfect outcome—we both walked away winners."

He seemed to notice he was in a 'low stance' and uncoiled, windmilling his hands so he went back to a normal standing position with seemingly no effort.

"I tell my students to turn the other cheek because that shit works," he said. "It keeps you out of trouble. Everything else I or these guys can teach you is all about how to deal with trouble if you've failed to keep out of it. First rule of martial arts—if there's trouble, don't be there."

"Don't be there," I said. "Easier said than done."

He nodded. "But you can learn to look out for trouble, with a little practice. In the meantime, listen to your friends," he said, indicating Philip, Rand, the priest, all with a simple gesture. "They're looking out for *you*. You're not going to go give up tattooing and go become a cop just to get back at this guy, are you?"

"No," I laughed. "Don't think so—"

"Lord knows we need the help," Philip said, a little forced, but holding the green monster of jealousy at bay. "Darren, I think I misjudged you earlier. Where do you teach?"

"I teach the Emory University Taido karate club," he said, "and also I teach some of the children's classes at the main Taido school in Norcross."

"You're a . . . kid's karate teacher?" Rand said, arching an eyebrow.

"I also do some mixed martial arts," he said, shrugging.

"Well, soon as I get out of here," I said. "I want you to show me how to mix it up."

"No promises, other than hard work won't bring miracles," he said.

I looked at Jinx. "Speaking of miracles . . . tell Savannah to come back," I said. There was a horrible pang in my heart when I said it; I hadn't meant for it to come out that way, or maybe I did, because the words kept on spilling out and I couldn't stop them. "I want to say I'm sorry."

"You don't have anything to be sorry about," Doug said. "She bolted to protect you."

"She didn't have to," I said. But I flashed again on her yawn. Her fangs. Those terrible fangs. Her eyes. Transomnia's cold eyes. My fingers in his pruners. His foot in my gut. Sudden pressure grew in my abdomen, and I hunched over, trembling. I wanted to say something else, but I couldn't. I just couldn't.

"Maybe . . . maybe she did," Jinx said at last.

"I think," Phil said softly, "Miss Frost has had enough excitement for the day."

24. WITH FRIENDS LIKE THESE . . .

Intense pain spiked through my hands. I opened my eyes to a darkened hospital room. A black figure with ominous red eyes stood at the end of my bed. He held up something shiny and dripping, like a little sausage. I held up my trembling hands: the first two fingers of each hand were gone, leaving raw stumps. As I watched, the other fingers fell away, one by one, leaving me with two bloody flippers instead of hands. And Transomnia laughed.

I screamed and sat up bolt upright, fingers tearing at the sheets of the hospital bed. It was midday; I had dozed off and fell straight into the same damn nightmare. My fingers throbbed painfully, but they were there. Thank God, they were all there. I rubbed the two fingers of my right hand with the thumb and fingers of my left until the tingling went away.

"I have *got* to get the fuck out of here," I said.

And at that moment Philip strolled in the door, carrying flowers and a wry smile that both indicated he was up to something.

"Up for a tour of the campus?" he asked.

"Up for *anything*," I said, "that gets me outside."

Philip worked his magic on the hospital staff again and got them to cough up a wheelchair. Within minutes he was wheeling me out in the crisp October air, wrapped in his overcoat and feeling sunny.

"They say you're going home Tuesday morning," Philip said. "I'm actually surprised they've kept you this long, if you're well enough for a tour of the grounds."

"It's the knee," I said. "I think if it was just the cuts and bruises they would have sent me home already, but the doc's keeping my knee under close observation."

We curved round the grassy hollow in front of Emory Hospital, turning just short of the buzzing traffic on Clifton Road that cut the hospital and school in half. I looked up through the trees, at the sky: through the peeling red and orange leaves, a contrail slipped lazily by, the body of the jet that made it gleaming in the afternoon sun.

Through it all, Philip kept dropping little hints—notes of caution for dealing with Edgeworld clients, innocent-sounding little questions about the tattoos that I'd been working on, and so on. Finally I could stand it no more.

"All right," I said. "You know something. I've felt the question hanging over me for the whole ride: 'So, Miss Frost, knowing I'm hunting a killer that strikes the tattooed on the full moon, when were you planning on telling me you were doing a tattoo for a werewolf?'"

Philip laughed. "Okay. We can start there."

"I met with him just after Rand released me from Atlanta Homicide—"

"That was the urgent tattoo you blew me off for the next day," Philip said.

"One of them, yes," I said. "He wants me to ink a control charm, claims he wants more control over his beast—"

"Making him a perfect target," Philip said.

I hunched over in the chair, feeling defensive. 'Wulf' was a hardcore Edgeworlder, but I'd gotten a good vibe off him. He was sweet, in a rough, direct way, and would have been more handsome—though lost some of his wildness—if he cleaned up that scruffy—

My eyes widened. What I'd taken to be a homeless man, shambling along with a group of students suddenly broke free and began walking towards us with strong, purposeful strides. As he crossed the street, his face turned straight to me and I found myself staring straight into the firm jaw and direct gaze of Wulf.

"Speak of the devil," I said.

"Hmmm?" Philip said. Then he caught sight of Wulf barreling down on us and brought the wheelchair to a halt calmly, without a word. He started to step forward, but I reached up and grabbed his hand.

"It's all right," I said. "This is Wulf. He's a friend—I think."

Wulf stopped straight in front of us. He was bigger and tougher than I remembered, but had considerably cleaned up. His wild mane of brownish-blond hair was swept back, his beard trimmed, his face washed. Even his worn beige suit had been laundered to the point you could tell it had once been finery. It stood out sharply against a torn but clean t-shirt, whose rips exposed hints of the tanned skin and rough fur of his muscular chest. He stood over me, staring, soaking my injuries in, pale yellow eyes growing more and more wolflike with rage until they were practically glowing.

"Damnit, I was too slow!" he said, voice crackling with anger. His eyes flicked briefly up at Philip, then dismissed him and fell back on me. I tore my eyes away from the rips in his shirt, from the glimpse of the fine concentric lines of some long-faded tattoo, and met his gaze. He studied me for a moment, then snarled. "I'm so sorry. I wish I'd ripped his throat out."

"Wulf," I said, throat constricting in fear. "Were you stalk—following me?"

His eyes widened. "*No,*" he said, kneeling before me, reaching to touch my hand. "No. When I collected my design from Spleen, he said you wanted me to feel free to contact you—"

"I *did,*" I said, and Wulf flinched a little. "And still do, Wulf."

"Thank you, Dakota. He said he'd just met you at Manuel's, so I . . . uh . . . ran down there," Wulf said, with a little smile that sounded like he meant that *literally.* "When I arrived I heard shouting in the parking lot, caught the end of the attack—"

And then his hand met mine, and he looked down in shock to see the bandages.

"Oh, no," he said, jerking back. "Oh, God, no. Please don't tell me—"

"It's all right," I said, as he stared at my hand. "Just cuts and scrapes. I—I'll be fine. Don't worry. I'll still be able to do your tattoo."

Wulf looked up sharply. "Even after all you've been through?"

I drew a breath at the longing and fear mixed with his concern. Up close, he was suddenly more human than he'd been since I met him, all my attention was on the pain in his eyes. Somewhere deep inside, this wolf of a man was a scared, hurt puppy, running from everyone. Ok, maybe a two-hundred-fifteen-pound werewolf was technically not a puppy—but he was hurt, all the same.

"Of course," I said, reaching out to touch his hand. I was still surprised by its warmth, even through the bandages. "Takes more than a sicko to stop me."

"Who was he?" Wulf said. "He was fast—I lost him. Didn't smell like a were—"

"A vampire," I said, and Wulf nodded in recognition. "The other vampires are working with the police to handle it. He's a lot more dangerous than he looks—don't tackle him."

"I don't plan to," Wulf said. "I'd step up to defend you from an attack, but I won't go hunting someone down for revenge. I can't afford to tangle with the police."

He stood abruptly, tense and jumpy, clenching and unclenching his fists, bare feet padding almost silently on the sidewalk.

"I shouldn't even be out here—the moon will be rising shortly." He looked at his watch—and even *I* could tell it was a nice watch—and cursed. "I can't trust myself to be out among people, this close to the time."

"Dakota tells me the tattoo you want her to ink is a control charm," Philip said, oh so reasonably. "Won't that help?"

Wulf suddenly stopped and stared at him, nostrils flaring, feet planted, indignant and inquisitive all at once. "Might keep me from making trouble," he said, but his eyes had grown more wary—and more yellow, almost to the point of glowing. "But it would do nothing to keep my enemies from making trouble for me."

"Enemies?" I asked. "You have enemies?"

"Everywhere," Wulf said, staring back at the hospital. "Always making problems for me, wherever I go—even here. I washed up before I came, even got this old thing drycleaned, and still they wouldn't let me see you—"

"Sorry," Philip said. "The guards on her floor have a list of names. I'll put you on it."

Wulf's eyes tightened more, glaring at Philip. "I never got to her floor," he said. "Security guards turned me away at the front door. They were ready for me. They had complaints about an obnoxious homeless man fitting my description—"

"How the heck could you know that?" I asked.

"I heard the man behind the front desk talking to the guards as they ushered me out. Never underestimate a werewolf's hearing," Wulf said. "And . . . I think someone is stirring up more trouble for me."

I had started to put Wulf's picture next to 'paranoid' in the dictionary, but damned if two police officers didn't come out of the hospital entrance, look around, fix on us, and quickly start heading in our direction.

"Harassment for being obnoxious, even for being homeless, is natural," Wulf said, clenching his fists, "but persecution for nothing—*that* is the work of my enemies."

"O-okay," I said. "Philip, can you call them off—"

"They're not on your detail, and they don't look like they'll listen," Philip said. Abruptly he took off his sunglasses and extended them to Wulf. "Take these."

Wulf's eyes narrowed suspiciously. "Why would you give me your—"

"Your eyes are starting to show, my friend," Philip said.

Wulf took the glasses slowly, staring at them. They were thick and heavy, with odd bulges and two earpieces. "These are Oakley Thumps," he said.

"They'll still cover your eyes," Philip countered.

My jaw dropped, and I looked back up at Philip; he looked sincere. I liked him, almost instinctively, but I couldn't figure him out: one minute he was wanting to take Cinnamon off the streets just for being furry, the next he was giving away two-hundred-dollar MP3 sunglasses to a crazy paranoid werewolf. What was up with *that*?

Wulf started to hand them back. "I can't accept—"

"Take them and go," Philip said. "They're almost on us."

Wulf looked over at the cops and snarled; when they saw the expression on his face, they drew their batons and started running towards us, shouting.

"Later," he said. "I will contact you through the Rogue!"

And at that he whirled and ran off. One cop chased after him, while his older, more obese partner stomped up to us, wheezing. "Are you all right? Did he hurt you?"

"No," I snapped. "He's my friend. He came to see me in the hospital."

The cop's eyes widened, and he looked over at the running pair.

Wulf ran straight out into traffic, dodging one car, then another; at the double yellow line he leapt straight up and over a passing semi like an agent out of the Matrix. The other cop stopped midstream, in the midst of squealing tires and blaring horns, as Wulf leapt from streetlight to rooftop and disappeared into a canopy of red October leaves.

"Quite a friend," the first cop said, still gasping for breath.

"You're telling me," I said, reaching up to hold Philip's hand as it squeezed my shoulder. "You're telling me."

25. HORROR AT THE DOGSHOW

Tuesday morning they let me out of the hospital at last, but I was not yet on my own, or even on my own two feet; I was stuck in my wheelchair, at least for a few more days. Philip insisted that I have some protection until I was walking again, and reluctantly I agreed to stay at the Consulate and suffer through Savannah's mothering—a peace-offering, from me to her. She said nothing about my reaction to her fangs, but at twilight she pushed my wheelchair through the Consulate's garden . . . and we talked. Our little conversation wasn't enough to heal any old wounds, but at least it patched them up for a while. Then we talked—*I* talked—about my meltdown, and after listening for a long time, Savannah said some soft but bracing things. They weren't enough to put the attack behind me, but at least I could put it away for a while.

Savannah agreed with Philip that I should do Wulf's tattoo, but she was insistent that I not try it before I was out of the wheelchair. For once, I had no argument; no matter how badly Wulf wanted the tattoo, I wasn't ready to get back in the saddle yet. Besides, the full moon wasn't until Saturday, and I couldn't imagine trying to do a tattoo sitting in a wheelchair.

But then night fell, on Tuesday the thirty-first of October: Halloween. And wheelchair or no wheelchair, escort or no, I was not going to miss the last hurrah of The Masquerade.

The Masquerade was a mammoth dance club and live music venue on the other side of North Avenue from City Hall East. It was huge, divided into three levels—Heaven, a live music venue; Purgatory, a traditional bar; and Hell—a goth/industrial/techno dance club that had taken the title of "my home away from home" after City Hall dialed the nightclub hours back and my first fave, a fetish dance club called The Chamber, folded.

Now the Beltline project was sweeping around Atlanta, eating up a whole ring of the city like the Very Hungry Caterpillar, and turning every low-rent district in its path into mixed-use monoblocs or greenspace. Supposedly the whole district around The Masquerade and City Hall East was next on the list, and this Halloween was The Masquerade's blowout swan song.

Savannah pushed my wheelchair along the sidewalk through a cavalcade of people in Halloween costumes, fetish gear, and combinations of both. There were zombies, vampires and werewolves, or at least people dressed like zombies, vampires, and werewolves. Women dressed as Wednesday Addams and men dressed as The Crow mugged for the cameras. There was even a pair of fetching young lesbian Borg from Star Trek, turning heads in leather, rubber and laser pointers. Savannah herself wasn't in costume per se, but in a long leather coat over a matching leather bikini and thigh-high boots, she turned heads all the same.

As for my costume? Savannah had heartily approved of my desire to get out of the house and get on with my life, but guessing what outfit I'd had in mind, she'd tried to derail my choice several different ways—rescuing a long leather coat and shiny T-shirt from my apartment, getting Lord Delancaster to loan his cape coat so I could be 'Sherlockina', and even hopefully pulling out a whole array of fetish gear, complete with gas mask.

In the end, I did my own costume: I sprayed the remaining tufts of hair so they stood up in spikes, tore and muddied up an old pair pants, and poured on layers of makeup accentuating, rather than hiding the bruises and scrapes. It was hard to get the makeup right around my neck because of the collar, but in the end 'Roadkill' lived again. I did such a good job, I actually felt a little bit guilty as I wheeled myself out of the guest room, but Savannah was so bossy even with me injured and us split that it felt good to have something to needle her with. Sure enough, she took just one look at me before getting nauseous and excusing herself to the bathroom.

Success.

The queue came to a halt as we got closer—the police had stopped the line as it crossed North Angler Street and were letting people across in bursts as the doorkeep let them in. You could see the flaring lights of firedancers reflecting off the surface of the Masquerade's towering, blocky surface, and I whined. A few days ago, when I'd been naïve and healthy, I'd have bulled across the street, counting on the crowd behind me to overwhelm the police while I darted ahead for a better view.

Now I looked at the tired cop standing in the street, holding up his hand to the crowd while he waved traffic by with his little yellow airport light. That man could just as easily been Rand, or Gibbs, or even Philip, a hero who'd stumbled and was now directing traffic. I looked up, at the dark shape of City Hall East not five hundred yards away. Somewhere, up on the sixth floor, men were working late to track someone who was ripping the skin off my clients, and working to find the man who had beaten me.

Somehow, dicking with the police didn't seem funny anymore, and when we trundled across the street, I threw up my hand for five and told the man Happy Halloween. His eyes lit up. "That is a bad ass costume," he said, calling after me. "The bruises look totally real!"

"They are," Savannah hissed back at him.

"Be nice, 'Lady Saffron,'" I said, and she squeezed my shoulder. It was surprisingly difficult to remember she became 'Saffron' in public, but she seemed to really appreciate it.

We came to a stop at the end of the line. The pumping music from inside The Masquerade was louder now, and the flickering fire was brighter. Occasionally, the crowd gasped as a fiery baton flipped end for end high up into the air, but from where I was sitting, I could see *nothing*. I itched to get out of the chair, and Saffron actually put her hand on my shoulder and pushed me back down.

"Be good," she said, breathing into my ear. "Or I'm turning the car around."

My cell rang. "Dakota Frost," I answered. "Best magical tattooist in the Southeast—"

"This is Philip," came his crackling voice.

"Phil!" I cried. "We're missing you—"

"I'm missing you," he said. "I just wanted to tell you—keep yourself safe, call Rand and the boys for backup if needed, but I think you should do Wulf's tattoo."

I couldn't answer for a second. "And just how did you come to that conclusion?" I asked. He didn't answer, and I grew suspicious. "Philip. What did you do?"

"Who, me?" Philip said innocently.

"Philip!" I said.

"Just gave him my Mission-Impossible style glasses with the videocamera turned on," Philip responded. "I got a wolf's-eye view straight back to his lair—"

"You tracked him!" I cried. Damnit, I *knew* he was up to something when he gave away those sunglasses. "He trusted you!"

"What if he was our killer?" Philip said, slipping into his super-calm, super-reasonable voice. "I can't afford to go weak kneed—"

"You son-of-a—"

"Hear me out," Philip said. "First, before the power on the transmitter ran out, we did get to see his lair. No box, no blood, no *nothing* to indicate he's a roaming serial killer—just a homeless werewolf curled up on dirty blankets struggling through pre-lunar shakes. Next time he moves we're going in to check it out, but as far as the eye could see, he's legit."

I was furious, but I could see why he'd done it. "*Fine,*" I said.

"Second . . . I had my men check out the incident at the hospital. Thoroughly. Wulf was telling the truth. Someone gave his description to the front desk and told them to call the police, but according to the security cameras, Wulf was never in there. And—get this, I love it—it wasn't a phone tip. Someone actually walked up to the desk and complained about Wulf in person, but from an angle *just* out of range of the security camera. Either they really got lucky, or they knew *exactly* what they were doing."

I swallowed. "You mean . . . that talk about his enemies . . . he wasn't off his rocker?"

"I'm not qualified to judge his mental state," Philip said, "but as far as there really being someone out to get him . . . he's right on the money. Someone is *definitely* gunning for him, though we have no way of knowing whether it's some organized criminal element or just an irate hospital visitor who took offense to his looks."

"I'm going to want that backup," I said. What the hell was I thinking? Tattoo artists didn't need backup. At least, we weren't supposed to. "I want to help him, but now I'm more worried about whoever has it out for him than I am about any threat from him."

"Me too," Philip said. "I've already spoken to Rand and he can get you some plainsclothes that work the homeless. They won't spook Wulf—"

"If he really is homeless," I interrupted, "where is he getting the money for this?"

There was silence. "That's a good question. Are you sure he *does* have the money?"

"Spleen referred him," I said. "Spleen doesn't work for free. I think he said he got a five thousand dollar retainer when Wulf waltzed into town six weeks ago. That doesn't sound like someone worried about money to me."

"*Homeless* doesn't always mean *penniless*," Philip said. "He knew what Oakley Thumps were. That ratty old suit of his? Started life as a Caraceni. It's Italian, 'bench bespoke'—made to order. New, it was worth almost five thousand dollars."

"What does all this mean?"

There was another silence. "It means Mister Wulf deserves a closer looking into."

"Don't hurt him," I said.

"Dakota!" Philip sounded hurt. "This is *me* we're talking about—"

"Yeah, well, I haven't known you for all that long. I want to believe you. Really, I do." I said. "But I really don't know what you're capable of. If that little stunt with the sunglasses was any indication, you're manipulative."

He paused one more time. "Maybe I am. I'm proud to be a manipulative bastard, Dakota. But I'm still a good guy. I won't hurt him. Remember what I said in the square—"

"You called him a perfect suspect."

"I said perfect *target*," Philip corrected. "Once he gets that tattoo . . . he's going to have the perfect profile to become one of the victims."

"You're going to use him as bait?" I asked, horrified.

"No, Dakota," Philip said. "This is me. There's always a smarter way."

"I'm trusting you on this," I said. "I'm walking a tightrope between human rules and the Edgeworld here. I want to help you stop this killer, but I won't just hand an Edgeworlder to the Feds— no matter how cute the Fed is."

"I'll take that in the spirit it was offered," Philip said. "Call Rand, and ink Wulf before the full moon. I'll keep you posted on anything I find."

He hung up, but I had already unplugged from the conversation, because the crowd had parted—and I could see Alex Nicholson juggling fire.

He had stripped to the waist and daubed faux Native American war paint over his muscled, trim chest. It was a virgin canvas, and I drooled at the thought of being the first to ink him. Or maybe I just drooled. He was whirling a flaming baton back and forth, flipping it through the air with increasing speed.

But then Alex saw me and winked, putting a flourish on his spinning that sent patterns of color through the air. This wasn't just fire dancing—it was fire magic, *real* fire magic. I'd assumed he was a dyed-in-the-wool conjurer, a protégé of Mirabilus, sticking to old-school science tricks, but here he was drawing great flowing circles in the air that left curving trails like we were watching a time lapse photo—except this one was living and real.

The splashes of color played back and forth—and behind Alex I caught sight of Jinx sitting with Doug. He had on what looked like 3D glasses, and they were leaning close, watching the show together with rapt if unfocused attention. Jinx cried with joy every time Alex shifted the color of his fire from red to green to blue and back again.

Alex traded the batons for flaming balls on chains, lighting them off a brazier with a quick snap that had none of the fumbling "dangle the poi over the torch until it catches" typical of inexperienced dancers. Alex knew what he was doing, both physically and magically. He spun the fireballs round him faster and faster, creating a swirling hula hoop of fire that slowly, surely, lifted his feet off the floor.

The crowd went wild when he tucked his feet up in the air and let the fire ring slip under him, and I damn near came out of my seat. And then he brought the two poi together sharply, dispersing the fire in a flare of magic strong enough to give everyone in the crowd good luck for a week, if you believed such a thing. He bowed, smiling, and came over to see me.

"That was amazing," I said. "And not just because you're the Amazing Alexi."

"Why thank you, Dakota," he said, bowing again. His body was covered with sweat, but his eyes were bright and alive and never seemed to break contact with mine.

"But mistake me if I'm wrong, that that more than just firedancing."

"Digging into my secrets?" he said with a wink. "I'll give you a hint. Not all of us are as closed-minded as Mirabilus. Magic is everywhere. You've just got to learn to see it."

"And so, what about your boss's challenge?"

"You're going to kick his ass," Alex said with a grin. "I *want* a working tattooed wristwatch. I wouldn't have volunteered if I thought you couldn't do it."

"Can I hand Dakota over to you, now?" Savannah said. "I think I'm up."

"Up?" I asked, but Savannah ignored me, beckoning to Doug.

"Sure, no problem," Alex said, stepping behind me. "I'd love to watch over her."

Doug brought Jinx over, and she put a hand on the side of my wheelchair. "Like the show?" she said, smiling, a bit giddy. "I know I did."

"Ready?" Savannah said wickedly, holding up a leash.

"As I'll ever be," Doug said, letting out a breath, and pulled off his black trenchcoat. He was wearing the same black leather harness and cheekchillers I'd first seen him in, with a much more politically correct loincloth rather than the cage. He dug into a bag Jinx was carrying, and pulled out his puppy mitts and mask. "Could you?" he asked.

"Of course," Jinx said, helping him fit the mask on, which she did creepily well for someone almost completely blind.

"You're doing that very well for a first timer," I said.

She grinned and canted her head slightly, never stopping the weaving of buckles. "I'm a quick learner," she said, "and it *isn't* the first time."

Savannah clipped the leash to his neck, and he tossed his head, going "ruf, ruf." The sun had set, and I saw Darkrose stalking up, her all in white leather to complement Savannah's black, towing a black puppy servant in white leather matching her own. The two of them lined up next to each other, almost like an honor guard, and then a grizzled older man walked up to me, supported by Vickman, Darkrose's hard-eyed, bearded bodyguard.

"Sir Charles!" I said with delight. "I'm so pleased to see you!"

Sir Charles smiled at me, dressed in a tuxedo with his signature cat-o-nine-tails whip dangling from his belt. "Dakota," he said, releasing Vickman and putting a hand heavily on my chair. "Might you do me the honor of being my shoulder to lean on in tonight's performance?"

"I'd be honored," I said.

And so I got to enter the Masquerade like BDSM royalty, preceded by Savannah and Darkrose, Jinx and Sir Charles on either arm, with Alex pushing from behind as my motor. The crowd cheered, though it probably had a lot more to do with the matching vampires and dog slaves in white and black leather than any accolades for me or Sir Charles.

We went to a special area right at the base of the stage, right beneath the raised bar and tables where Savannah and I had always liked to camp out at so we could see the dance floor. It would have been hard to get a better view.

"So, Sir Charles," I said breathlessly, as Alex led Jinx off, "do you have a wonderful show planned for us this evening?"

He smiled, a little weakly, a little wistfully. "I'm just a guest of honor today," he said. "I don't have the endurance anymore to perform. It's frustrating because it's not my muscles—it's the ticker. I can start swinging, but in less than a minute, I'm out of breath."

"I'm sorry," I said.

"Don't worry," he said. "I can sit in a chair with a phone and my Rolodex and whip up a performance just by calling in a few favors—half the performers in this town owe their start to me, and would jump at the chance to fill my shoes. The Secret Room is on later, and Darkrose and Saffron have something planned. But first, we have a *very* special show."

Savannah and Darkrose rejoined us, taking posts on either side of us with the dogs kneeling at their feet. "Hey, wait a minute," I said. "What, you're going to allow the leather dogs and vampires in and not have them *do* anything?"

"We have an *extensive* dog and pony show later. Right now, we're here to be seen and let the crowd . . . simmer," Savannah said. "Besides, we—actually, *all* the performers—wanted to see *this* show first."

Jinx stepped to the stage, guided by Alex. "And now, dear friends, we are proud to present a very special demonstration of magic," she said, whipping out her spirit cane and extending it to its full length. She drew it in a great circle through the air, creating a pulsing arc of color that shimmered through every shade in the rainbow—very very Jinx! Then she drew the cane up and down, up and down in a mountain shape—and then repeated it, and my mouth opened as I recognized the logo.

"Please welcome—the Mysterious Mirabilus!"

There was a clap of thunder, and all the lights went out. Two hooded figures appeared in the darkness, each carrying a lone torch.

They stepped forward slowly, in unison, approaching two huge braziers on pillars at each end of the stage. Just before lighting them, the figures reached up ostentatiously, and threw aside their hoods.

Each bore the unmistakable features of Christopher Valentine.

"Oh my God," I said, sitting up in my wheelchair. *This* was the Mysterious Mirabilus' most famous trick, and he was doing it here, at the Masquerade, for *us*—and I had the best seat in the house! Just last week I'd seen a trick in a movie where a man 'teleported' to the other side of the stage—but this *wasn't* teleportation, and it *wasn't* a movie. There were two of him—right in front of me! Even from *this* close I couldn't see how it was done. They weren't masks—each commanding face had the same dark eyebrows and the same mischievous eyes. The torrent of white hair even had the same part on the same side, so there was no way the two images could be simple reflections. *How* was he doing it?

Then the figures plunged their torches into the braziers, and a giant flare of light lit up the whole interior of Hell. I looked back, seeing all the astonished faces, then looked forward again to see the robes collapsing to the ground and—just barely glimpse two dark cat-suited figures disappearing behind the stage. But everyone's eyes were on center stage, where a single Mirabilus now stood alone, in a simple tuxedo and a top hat, which he removed and swept across the crowd to release a torrent of flapping birds of fire that darted out across the crowd before dissolving into a thousand colored sparks.

Christopher Valentine was in rare form. Each trick started as something simple—shuffling cards, juggling, pulling a rabbit out of a hat—and then grew more and more spectacular in typical Mirabilus fashion. He made the rabbit and the hat disappear, then kicked off his shoe to reveal bunny slippers, which he turned inside out to reveal the bunny, from which he improbably pulled the hat. While juggling he got a phone call and stepped off to the side of the stage, the balls still tumbling through the air in his absence; on his return he tossed the cell phone into the mix and glared irritated at it when it started ringing again, seemingly unable to stop himself juggling long enough to answer it.

And then a second Mirabilus appeared. The first eyed the phone, and his clone reached in, snatched it and answered it. He began talking animatedly while the juggling Mirabilus glared at him; then a *third* Mirabilus appeared, also yakking on a phone and tossing a deck of cards. Enraged, the original Mirabilus started tossing the balls at his counterparts, who tossed the phones and deck of cards back in a brief display of three-way juggling. Then the clones took the balls and phones and whirled off—while the original caught the deck, broke the wrapper off, and grinned widely to the crowd as he fanned out the cards.

Now the Mirabilus went straight back to the basics. The spotlight zoomed in, and two enormous screens projected a close-up view of his nimble, graceful hands, shuffling the cards with incredible skill. I wondered if the two projectors and the unseen camera had a big hand in the dueling Mirabiluses we had seen earlier, but I couldn't see how and frankly I didn't care: like everyone else I was mesmerized by his supremely deft prestidigitation. Cards blurred through the air, became flowers, then coins; then the coins were between his outstretched fingers, turning to marbles and gems and dice in rapid succession.

And then I looked up at his face. The lights weren't on it, but I could see Christopher was tired and sweating, scowling with the effort. The Mirabilus was getting old, and I felt saddened. Then his eye looked down and caught me, and he winked, throwing his hands up and turning the glittering marbles into ten sparks of fire.

And with that, all too soon, it was over, the Mirabilus bowing to the crowd and its thunderous applause. He motioned for the mike, also flicking his fingers down at me—and as an assistant named Elijah brought him the mike, I was shocked to see Savannah leaning down to release the bumpers on my wheelchair.

"What are you doing?" I asked, as she started to push me forward. "He's not done—"

"Ladies and gentlemen of the Masquerade," Christopher called out to the crowd warmly, waving his arms so no-one would notice he was pausing for breath. "I am the Mysterious Mirabilus, and I hope you have enjoyed my little show tonight."

The crowd went wild—as did I, as Savannah pushed me up next to Darkrose and turned my wheelchair around to face the crowd. "What, what are you doing—"

"And while the date and venue are yet to be decided, I'm proud to announce here on this very stage—my next Valentine Challenge!" he cried. The crowd went a little less wild—apparently the skeptical set didn't make a big showing at goth-fetish-techno dance clubs—but they cheered anyway as he continued: "You've seen me throw down the gauntlet before to psychics and seers and dowsers and all sorts of mystics, and each time I've won—but this time, I may have met my match: Atlanta's own magical tattooist, Dakota Frost!"

My mouth opened—and then Darkrose and Savannah reached down and effortlessly lifted my wheelchair and set me gently down on the stage next to Valentine, who put his warm hand on my shoulder and winked at me.

The crowd gasped—many of them were close enough to realize that many of my bruises and cuts were not just makeup, and many of the rest realized that my Mohawk was gone. But Valentine raised his hand, calming. "Now, Miss Frost has had a rough time of late, having recently come back from the brink of death—" and everyone laughed, a bit nervously "—but she told me she was willing to go ahead with the challenge."

"No-one would blame her if she backed out," he continued, looking straight at me, ignoring the crowd, "after all she's been through."

I reached up and pulled the mike towards me. "Not a chance, old man."

"Hear that? You hear that?" he cried, smiling out at the cheering crowd. "She's a trooper, and I respect that! Ladies and gentlemen, I give you—"

"Dakota Frost!" a man yelled from the upper railing, and there were screams and shouts as I looked up straight into the barrel of a gun. "You'll never ink that Nazi bastard, Frost!"

There was a terrific bang, everything tilted sideways, and my knee exploded in pain as something slammed into me. There were shouts and screams as I fell off the stage, wheelchair and the world tumbling down on me. I lay frozen a moment, gasping, watching the surge of feet recede; but there were no more shots. So I lifted the wheelchair off me with difficulty.

When it fell aside I saw Christopher Valentine sprawled across me, gasping for breath, clutching his left shoulder with his right hand.

And bleeding. Bleeding fast.

26. VALENTINE'S DAY

Christopher Valentine's head lay tilted on the pillow, hair disheveled, an oxygen tube running under his nose. His eyes were closed, slack, and his breathing was labored. His body seemed as thin as sticks under the flimsy hospital gown—except for his left shoulder and upper left chest, all swollen out of shape, and covered in an array of bandages.

I stood there, on crutches, staring down at him. "Is . . . is he going to live?"

"I don't know," Philip said. "I just don't know."

After a long period of waiting, Philip had worked his magic to get me and Alex through the police guard and the hospital staff. It was amazing, like watching a Jedi out of a Star Wars movie pull his mind tricks. But once inside the ICU, I was too afraid to ask any of the staff anything for fear they would ask us to leave, so I just stood there, hunched over the crutches that had replaced my ruined wheelchair, staring down at the old man who had saved my life.

Valentine opened his eyes to slits. "Miss Frost," he said, voice hoarse and ancient, holding nothing of his normal stage presence . . . but still a bit of his devilish humor. "I may need to delay the challenge a bit."

"Whatever you say, old man," I said, with forced bravado. The old geezer had taken a bullet for me. Christopher Valentine took a *bullet*—for *me!* "Whatever you say."

His eyes slipped down to the bandages, and he held up his left hand slowly. He could barely move his stiff, swollen fingers, and the arm somehow looked . . . limp, as if more than the muscles weren't working right. "Good thing I'm a righty, eh?"

"Good thing," I said, choking up. "A good thing."

"Hey," Valentine said. "I've been through worse—no, *really*, through worse."

"Hello again," said a voice behind me, and I whirled guiltily to see Doctor Hampton—the older doctor that had called in the yummy Doctor Blake to operate on my knee. He eyed me curiously. "Should you be walking around?"

"The wheelchair was smashed in the attack," I said. "But I'm using crutches."

"Could I ask you to step out for a moment?" the doc said. "I need to talk to Doctor Valentine about his condition—"

"That's all right," Valentine said. "She's my . . . protégé. Consider her family."

"You're just everyone's family, aren't you?" Doctor Hampton said. He had a smile that didn't seem at all forced—clearly he had been schooling Blake on his bedside manner, or Blake had rubbed off on him. "Doctor Valentine, I'm a bit concerned about your bloodwork. You've got some spikes that can indicate an opportunistic infection—"

"Let me guess," Valentine said. His voice sounded oddly ragged, and he took very deep breaths. "MRSA?"

"What?" I asked. "What's that?"

"Drug-resistant staph," Hampton said. "We don't know that yet, but the micro lab's looking it over now. We might need to move you into a different ward."

"I get it, I get it," he said, waving his hand. "Common in enclosed populations—"

"I'm so sorry," the doctor said.

"Should you be saying that?" Valentine said, a twinkle in his eye. "What if I were likely to sue you for giving me a bug I didn't come in with?"

"Somehow I think that won't happen," Hampton said. "Let's see your hand."

"It's a little stiff," he said, as Hampton felt it gently. "But I have feeling. I told you, not to worry."

"You hear that?" Hampton said, looking at me. "When I heard a sixty-seven year old man had gotten shot I was afraid he wouldn't last the night, and now *he* tells *me* not to worry. You're one hell of a tough old bird, Doctor Valentine."

"You doctors," he said, rolling his eyes. "Always underestimating me."

"I won't underestimate you, old man," I said.

"Sure I'm not faking it?" Valentine said hoarsely. He tried to grin, but coughed and spat up something black. "You—you don't get off that easy."

He sank back into the pillow, and Hampton looked at us visitors disapprovingly. "I think Doctor Valentine has had enough excitement for—"

"Dakota!" Valentine said. His good hand shot out, gripped mine tightly, for a brief moment incredibly strong, then rapidly fading as he sank back into the bed. "You find the guy who did this, hear me?" he said. "Don't take him on yourself, but you help the police find him and you put him away for me. You'll do that as a favor for old Valentine?"

"Cheer up, Chris," I said, squeezing his hand back. "This one's for free."

27. PIOUS

Stumping up and down rickety wooden stairs in crutches is not the smartest way to speed up your rehabilitation, but I was determined to get back into the game as soon as possible. I'd never realized how handicap-unfriendly the Rogue became when the elevator was out, and after finding out, I was loud and vocal to the rest of the staff about it. Of course, I'm sure my sore jaw from my morning's trip to the periodontist—and the bad news that it would take upwards of six months to fix my teeth—had *nothing* to do with my mood.

They let me putter around the office taking care of administrative stuff so I'd feel useful, but in the end, at five o' clock, when one of Savannah's crew was scheduled to pick me up they shooed me out and told me—with odd smirks—to "Go enjoy the rest of the day."

I refused help, and stumped down the stairs expecting to see one of the red Volvos from the Consulate. Instead I found a black Prius in the parking lot, and my mouth fell open. It had two bumper stickers: one said *COEXIST,* written with each letter as a different religious symbol; the other said *Osama Bin Laden Hates This Car.*

I smiled. "Secret *aaaagent* man," I said, and heard a creak behind me.

Philip Davidson leaned back from the wall beneath the stairwell, stepping up beside me in his immaculate black suit—and with new sunglasses in his pocket. The sun struck his face, and for a moment, the warm light on his skin, glowing against his beautiful blue-gray eyes, made him look like a seer of the future—or a GQ Lawrence of Arabia.

Then he squinted and slipped on his black shades. "Ok, I tried," he said. "I just feel naked without them."

"They're very you," I admitted. "I take it you're my escort to meet Spleen and Wulf?"

Philip nodded. "Saffron was concerned they might be spooked by Consulate muscle, but both of them have already met me. Hopefully I'll be a bit less threatening."

"Less spooked by the spook," I said. "Well, we'll give it a shot. Hey, my shift just ended and I'm starving, and we still have a couple of hours before I'm supposed to meet Spleen and Wulf to set up the appointment to do his tattoo. I was hoping to—"

"Catch a little dinner?" he said with a broad grin that warmed me to my toes. He held his hand out to his Prius. "Thought you'd never ask. Your chariot awaits—"

"We need to talk about this one," I said, pointing at a small black square on his car window that said *W – **Still** the President.*

"Well, he *is*," Philip said mildly, stepping up to the car. It unlocked on its own. *Slick.* "But don't worry. Your boys will sweep the House and I'll be crying in *my* beer."

"Yeah, yeah, throw me a bone," I said, as he opened the door for me and took my crutches. "Rent a Prius, talk nice to the liberal, get down her pants—"

"No, I'm serious," he said. He opened the door for me and took my crutches, stowing them in the back seat. "When I was driving down from Virginia, I caught one of my boys duking it out with some host on NPR, man, what a bunch of progressives—" *slam*, he walked around the front of the car, deliberate but eager, *nice* butt, and *open* "—and, then, the host asks about the polls, and my boy loses it."

Philip pressed a big black *POWER* button and the car hummed quietly to life. He looked back, and the car started backing out silently, without the gas engine ever engaging. I was in love. And not just with the car, though his politics I could do without.

"My boy rails on how he's reading all these super secret Republican polls and whatever and when the host starts nailing him on specifics, he gets even *more* flustered and tells him that 'you can come up with whatever math you want, but I'm entitled to THE math.' And I'm hearing this and the whole time thinking—*'Liar!'"*

He said the last word so fiercely I jumped, and at last the gas engine engaged as he turned out onto Moreland and started heading north.

"In my job, I've got to pick out the truth every day—and when I heard my boy claiming we were going to win, all I heard was spinning." He cut left onto Freedom Parkway, the car humming louder. "So I looked at the polls, at *all* of them—"

"And how did you get access to the super secret Republican polls?" I asked.

"Let's just say the NSA has *nothing* on the DEI when it comes to information gathering," Philip said. "They may trawl wide, but we go deep—"

"Special Agent Davidson," I said, mock shocked. "Don't *tell* me you used the vast powers of your office to fact check an NPR story! But do tell me the juicy bits."

"Our remote viewers will do *anything* to settle a bet," he said. "And as for the juicy bits . . . well, let's just say I think you'll be happy come November seventh."

"You don't know *how* I vote," I said. He looked over at me, and we both snorted in laughter. "Hey, where are we going—"

"Does fish sound good?" he said. "Rand had a few recommendations—"

"Yes," I said, feeling my cheek; it felt like I would be able to eat. "I'm *starving*—I haven't had a bite since my trip to the dentist. The meeting with Spleen and Wulf is near Buckhead, and there's this great place, a little pricey, called the Fish Market—"

He looked over at me again in shock. "Well, what do you know," he said with a grin. "That was at the top of my list."

We crested the hill of Freedom Parkway just as the sun was setting, seeing the same panorama of downtown Atlanta I'd seen with Spleen the first night I met Wulf. This time we shot towards the glittering spires and slid into the canyon of the Downtown Connector, heading north into the fairybook playground for adults that was the Buckhead Village.

"There," I said. "Straight onto Buffered Extra-Strength Highway—"

"Buford, eh?" he said, slipping over a lane onto the long frontage road that paralleled the connector. "He said I had to check out the big fish. Is it that good? I'm on a diet—"

"If you can eat the big fish," I said, "*I'll* vote Republican."

The Buckhead 'Village' was technically within the city limits of Atlanta, but had its own distinctive feel: upscale shops at the feet of high-rise offices and condos, high-end yuppie restaurants side-by-side with come-as-you-are bars. As the boxy, brightly lit shape of the Atlanta Fish Market became visible on Pharr Road, I stared straight at Philip to get his reaction.

"Oh. My. God," he said, staring up at the giant, three-story copper fish statue that adorned the front corner of the restaurant, curving towards the sky in all its grand, ostentatious Statue-of-Liberty-colored glory. "He wasn't kidding. That's a Big. F-ing. Fish—"

"Philip, your lane," I said, as he started to drift over the double yellow line.

A valet took the car, and after we got our names on the waitlist, we walked—well, he walked and I hobbled on my crutches—back to the towering fish and stopped on the little bridge that climbed over its tail.

"Holy cow," he said. "It's got that Statue of Liberty color—"

"Ah, Philip," I said, smiling, leaning my crutches and myself on the railing of the bridge. "It's the copper."

He leaned on the rail opposite me, and I stared at him . . . at the cleancut young Republican in his trim suit and devilish goatee, wondering how on earth I had ended up on a date with him and why I was liking it so much.

But there was a lurking weight on my shoulders, now heavier after the attack on Valentine. Whoever had done that had meant to get *me* . . . and in the confusion the police hadn't caught the guy. That had me more worried about Wulf's improbable 'enemies' that Philip had found all so probable . . . and the hanging question about whether Wulf was tied to our tattoo killer.

Another thought struck me about Wulf and Spleen. "You know—" I began.

"I was thinking—" Philip said, almost simultaneously. "Sorry."

"You go," I said.

"Ladies first."

"Fuck that," I said, and when Philip arched his eyebrow I raised my hand in surrender. "Seriously. Spleen is Wulf's point of contact. If we can find out when they talked—"

"We could figure out when Wulf rode into town from Birmingham, maybe eliminate him as a suspect?" Philip said. "That's what I was thinking. But Birmingham's only a few hours away. If he was our serial killer, he could have gone back easily, killed the blonde, and returned here. Or he could have used an accomplice—"

"But Spleen talked to him several times," I said. "If we could nail down a window of when he talked to him, we could either eliminate Wulf as the man on the scene in Birmingham or establish that he was AWOL from Atlanta during the last killing."

Philip shook his head. "Oh, man," he said, with a huge grin. "Have I mentioned how much fun it is to hang out with you, Dakota?"

My phone beeped. I started to ignore it, but Phil scowled. "What if it's—"

"Buckhead?" I said, staring at the number.

"Aren't we in—"

"*Lord* Buckhead," I said, pressing it. "Buck, this is Dakota. What can I do you for—"

"I sensed your presence in my stronghold," Buckhead said. "Come to the Storyteller."

"The . . . Storyteller?" I said. It was a statue—*the* statue of Buckhead, in Buckhead—not more than a block or two away. "But— we have our name in at the Fish Market," I protested.

"Come quickly, Dakota," he said. "Or it will be too late."

"Too late for what? What's happened, Buck?"

"Your friend Spleen," Buck said, "was just attacked by a werewolf."

28. STORYTELLER SQUARE

Phil's Prius screeched through the knotted traffic of Buckhead. Once, crossing these congested streets at speed would have been impossible—but the block party that was Buckhead was dying, the victim of a hostile business alliance and a colluding City Council that had dialed back bar hours all over the city *except* at the city-owned boondoggle, 'Underground' Atlanta. So now the traffic was thinner, and had occasional gaps that Philip squeezed through expertly, greased by the flashing blue light he'd clamped atop his car.

So in moments we pulled up to "Storyteller Square", a tiny little triangular park where Roswell forked off Peachtree Road. At the center of the rings of cobblestones that paved the square, a little crowd was gathered, huddled about the metal statue of the Storyteller and his woodland companions. Phil didn't even bother to get a parking space: he just bumped the Prius up onto the sidewalk, kicked open the door and pulled out his gun.

"What the fuck—"

"Stay in the car, Dakota," he said.

"Fuck that," I said, kicking *my* door open and reaching for the crutches. Then I saw what he saw, and stumbled out of the car without them, limping.

Spleen lay gutted in the center of Storyteller Square, his thin body bleeding out into the concentric cobblestones radiating out from the statue of Buckhead. A ruddy Native American man I instantly recognized as Buck himself squatted over him, cradling his head.

"Black Mayday, Black Mayday," Philip was saying into the air, approaching with his gun out, but pointed to the ground. "D-E-I asset down. Black Mayday, Black Mayday. I need a medevac at the intersection of Roswell and Peachtree, GPS coordinates—"

The crowd parted in alarm, and Philip flipped a badge out of the breast pocket of his immaculate suit. A beefy man stepped forward, nervous, holding a cell phone. "Thank God, Officer," he said, bossy yet uncertain. "This—this man came up holding this other man—"

"Thank you, sir," Philip interrupted, with a quiet voice that just *radiated* authority. "Remain on the scene and we'll take a statement. Right now, my associate is injured—let her lean on your shoulder."

"Sure," the man said, stepping up beside me. "Ma'am?"

"I'm all right," I said, but I reached out for his shoulder anyway.

"Where did you find him?" Philip asked with tightly controlled rage, staring down at Buck, gun still out but carefully pointed away from anyone.

"A place you cannot go," Buck said. He wore the same breeches and loincloth he had before, with keys and a cellphone now on his belt. His human face was rugged but surprisingly young, and his black hair spilled down onto a proud, bare chest covered in only the barest excuse of a vest. "I brought him here—"

"Ruining the crime scene," Philip said. "We want to catch the guy. Right now it looks like *you* did this—"

Buck waved his hand over the long, raw gouges in Spleen's abdomen. "We both know *what* manner of beast did this," he said. "Now the question is, who?"

"I'm cold," Spleen said. His voice was so weak, and my hand tightened on the rough jacket of the man beside me. Philip jerked, then holstered his weapon, took off his thousand-dollar suit jacket and laid it over Spleen's body, patting him gently.

"Medics are on the way," Philip said. "Who did this to—"

Spleen reached up and grabbed Philip behind the ear, pulling his head down towards his ratlike face and yellowed eye. Philip just let him do it, listening as Spleen whispered something. Then Philip turned to me and motioned me down.

"Dakota," he said quietly. "He wants you."

The Good Samaritan helped me bend. I tried to kneel, but couldn't, so and sat awkwardly in the spreading pool of blood. A second coat—ruined.

"I'm here, Diego," I said.

"Kotie," Spleen said in a whisper. "Nobody calls me that no mores."

Suddenly his hand reached out and pulled my head close. "Kotie, Kotie, you hearing me?" he said. His breath was foul, and I had a close up look of his great, yellowed eye. I'd always thought it was a bad glass fake; now I could see it was *real*, and diseased. What had happened to his eye? How long had I known Spleen and had never thought to ask?

"Yeah, I hear you," I said. "Who did this to you?"

"A wolf," Spleen said, drawing a ragged breath. "*Were*wolf. Big fucker—"

"No!" I said. "Not Wulf—"

"Not Wulf," Spleen said, wheezing. "Don't think. Never caught up with him tonight. Wasn't supposed to pick him up for another half hour. Don't think it was Wulf—"

"You don't *think?*" I said, my gut sinking. "You mean, you don't *know?* How could you not know?"

"How the hell *could* I know, Kotie?" Spleen said. "I never asked the bastard to change into a wolf for me. I just took his money."

"But—"

"Don't matter. Whole thing's got too messy. Stay clear of him. Stay clear of this. *Don't let them get you too,*" Spleen said intensely—and then his grip slipped on the back of my neck, his left eye went as dull and expressionless as his right, and he sagged back into Lord Buckhead's arms—still breathing, but not much.

I looked up at Buck. He shook his head sadly and gently lowered Spleen to the pavement. Philip stood, holding his finger to his ear. "How far away is that evac?"

I stared down at Spleen. How long had I known Diego Spillane, and learned nothing about him other than his nickname? How many times had he been there for me and how little had I been there for him? Had I been scared of him all this time just by a little halitosis and a bad eye? Then I saw the antlers of a stag shifting in the shadows, and looked up at Buck.

It had just been a trick of the light as he stood, a moment where the shadow of his statue form overlapped the shadow of his human one. He stood there, tall, proud, and sad. "He is going. I am sorry," he said. "There's nothing more I can do here."

"No, for starters you can tell us what happened," Philip snapped. Sirens and ambulances were sounding in the distance. "You can help us find who did this—"

"I found him like this in a place he should not have been, a place where you may not go," Buckhead said, with folded arms. "I brought him here for help. That is all."

"That is *not* all," Philip said. "This is not a fucking joke, 'Lord Buckhead.'"

"You are not ready to learn all of the secrets of the Edgeworld," Buckhead said.

"I've seen things even *you* wouldn't believe," Philip shot back.

"Guys," I said. "He's . . . he's going."

A long, low sigh escaped Spleen's lips, and his head slowly slumped to the left.

I stared at him a long time, then looked up to find Philip, Buckhead and our Good Samaritan all standing at attention. Then Buckhead sighed. "I am going," he said. "I am sorry. Lady Dakota, I will pass along anything I learn of this crime."

Then he stepped round the statue of the Storyteller, or into it; because when Philip ran around the statue after him, he emerged from the other side alone.

"Holy fucking shit," the Good Samaritan said.

"Damnit," Philip said. "Stupid Edgeworlders. No offense."

"None taken," I said, staring down at Spleen. "I think both sides of the Edge see me as a citizen of the other."

An ambulance screeched up next to Philip's Prius.

"Oh, Phil," I said. "This looks bad for Wulf—"

"Yeah," he said, staring off into the distance. "Spleen was about to meet our werewolf friend, who told us himself he had trouble with control. That gives him means, motive and opportunity—or maybe Wulf's supposed 'enemies' want us to think that. You heard Spleen—he didn't blame Wulf. A defense lawyer would make hay with that."

"But he never saw him as a werewolf," I said. "So . . . it still could have been Wulf."

"So Wulf is a leading *suspect*," Philip said. "I love that word: 'suspect'. I love its precision. Suspect. That's it, until we get more hard evidence, one way or the other."

"But how are we going to do that?" I said. "Spleen was his *contact*. We're never gonna know where Wulf was when—"

"Cell phone records. Irritated hospital staff. Rental car records or *bus terminal* cameras," Philip said. "We'll find out, one way or the other. Eventually, we'll find out—but right now, I have a question for *you*."

Frost Moon

"For *me?*" I asked.

"Did Spleen ever give any hint that Wulf was hostile to him?" Immediately he caught it in my eyes. "What was it?"

"Before I was attacked, Wulf called Spleen, agitated, asking about his tattoo," I said. "Spleen called him 'a goddamn menace.'"

"'Goddamn menace,'" Philip repeated. "Sure sounds like he was threatened by Wulf—"

"But he met Wulf that night," I said. "That's why Wulf was even there to save me—"

"I remember," Philip said. "But something's just not adding up. Spleen wasn't an idiot—he said stay clear of *them*. Plural *them*. But who was the 'them' he was talking about, his attacker and—who? Whoever took a potshot at you? Whoever was messing at Wulf? That vamp? Someone else? There's an awful lot of 'incidents' around you, Wulf and that tattoo."

"You don't think," I said, "all of them are connected?"

"What I think," Philip said quietly as the paramedics came up, "is that we'd better find your 'friend,' Wulf—because if he didn't kill Spleen, he may be next."

29. WORKING IT OUT

I stomped towards Emory's Student Activity and Athletics Center on my crutches. In the back of my mind, I knew time was running out on Wulf's tattoo, but with Spleen gone the whole picture had changed. First, I now had no way of contacting Wulf; second, I now felt very unsafe in his presence—whether from him or from his enemies, I couldn't say. So it was time to visit the only person who seemed like he really wanted to help me kick ass: Darren Briggs.

You need to buy at least a fourteen-day pass to use the Athletics Center, but I had no intention of paying for that until I'd seen the goods. I'm no Philip; I can't pull his Jedi mind tricks to just make anyone do what I want. But I am a six-foot-two, attractive, large-breasted woman, and that—plus a little preparatory research on Google—usually turns the trick.

"Hello," I said, friendly but firm, propping my crutches over the counter of the Center and leaning down on the tousle-haired college boy behind the counter. "Where can I find Darren Briggs? He witnessed an assault on a police asset, and I need to ask him a few questions."

I started to pull out my Stratton Police Department booster card, which my dad got for me years ago when we were still speaking. It's horribly out of date, but it has the Stratton police shield, my Mohawked picture on it and no expiration date, so it can pass as some kind of official ID as long as I'm showing it off to a complete idiot. But this time it didn't turn out to be necessary; the kid got up immediately and walked around the counter.

"No problem, I'll escort you," he said, a bit too eagerly, while glancing at his counter mate. "Wendy, can you—"

"*Fine*," she said, rolling her eyes.

"I take it *you* are the police asset?" he said, eyeing me as he escorted me through the turnstiles and down to the elevator. "And Darren is more than a witness?"

"He was the savior of my ass, is what he was," I admitted.

"The guy is a machine," he said, walking me up to room 211, a large classroom with double doors, beyond which I could hear rhythmic shouting. "I sneak down here to watch his Taido class sometimes—"

He opened the doors to a floor covered in blue mat. In its center was a ring of students in white uniforms, all in a low, wide stance that was practically a squat, punching in unison. Two had black belts and blue jackets—including Darren, who was counting in what sounded like Japanese.

"EEEtch-nee-saan-shee-gOH-rok-sheech-hatch-kyooo-*jyooo!*" he shouted, finishing up with a punch that just seemed to pop from his waist. The whole class stood frozen in that final punch; then Darren's head cocked slightly to the side, as if he saw me. Then he said, "Come back," and the students popped out to a standing ready stance. "*Toe-et-tay,*" he instructed. "Stretch out."

As the class stretched, Darren walked over quickly without running, smiling without grinning. "Dakota Frost," he said. "This is a surprise. Come to check out the class?"

"I have a few questions," I said with a grin. I was surprised how young he looked in his uniform; I hadn't realized a college karate teacher could also be a college student. "I thought this might be a good place to start."

"Sure thing. But I can't let you on the mat," he said, spreading his hands apologetically. "You have to sign a waiver, and Wendy at the front desk would bust my balls if I didn't have one for you. Even then, with you still healing up, I wouldn't let you on the court."

"Aw, come on," I said, miming Savannah. "Surely you could show me a few punches—"

"Rary, Clarence, over here," Darren said, without even looking. Two of the brown belts quit stretching—the woman rolling out of a full split—and came over to join us. "Side stance for punching. Clarence, keep the fist set, but put your feet together, *toe-et-tay* style."

Rary spread her dainty feet shoulder width, right fist out; Clarence put his huge feet together, looking at Darren quizzically before his head snapped forward to attention. After surveying them a moment, Darren said. "Double punch—*go!*"

Both popped out their left fists with a kind of twist, then shot the right one out while the left snapped back. Their karate gis made little whizzing motions when they moved. Darren had them do it a few more times, but I could already see where this was going—Rary was solid as a rock, but with his feet together Clarence was wavering, trying to keep his balance.

"Again—go!" Darren said, slipping his hand into a red padded mitt and stepping straight into Rary's punches. He caught her punches and pushed back hard, but she stood her ground, shoving him back with each blow. "Again—go!" he repeated, stepping in front of Clarence—and this time it was *Clarence* that was shoved back when Darren caught his punch.

"Good, good," Darren said, walking past Clarence to the end of their short little line. "Come back to the same stance." But as soon as Clarence did so, Darren pushed him, hard, and he nearly fell over. He then stepped up quickly to Rary and pushed, and while she got shoved around a bit, she never lost her balance, her legs bouncing around on the mat under her.

"You can't throw a good punch without having a conversation with gravity," Darren said, "and your legs do the talking. If your injured leg was just naturally weak, I'd invite you out here on the mat, help you figure out how your particular body could talk to the ground with the right accent. But since you're healing, all I'd be doing is helping you tear that leg up."

My student escort waved and left us, and I sagged into my crutches. "I know that . . . it's just . . .one of my best buddies got murdered last night," I said, trying to piece together all the things running through my head. "And a client took a bullet for me—"

Darren's eyes bugged. "Just since I saw you?"

I nodded. "It's been a busy week, and I'm feeling more than a little vulnerable."

"Sorry to hear all that, but it's even more reason to take it easy, sit back and watch, and see if this is right for you," Darren said. The other blue-jacketed black belt stepped up behind him, and Darren nodded to him. "I'll be there in a second. We've got a lot on our plate tonight—but stick around, maybe we can help you out during family fun time. All right! Brown belts and higher: over there; everyone else: with me—"

After that it was like watching out-takes of a karate movie. The white belts lined up and did standing punches and kicks; the greens and purples did spinning punches and kicks; the browns and higher did weird, funky kicks that seemed to involve throwing one's head at the ground while simultaneously kicking an opponent in the face. My knee throbbed just looking at them, but they still did it.

That's around the time I realized I wasn't ready for any of this.

Sure, my dad had taught me some self-defense moves, and I took two years of tae kwon do in college. But I was woefully out of shape. I hadn't been to a gym in years, hadn't been running in months. And I certainly couldn't perform any of the basic self-defense moves now, much less stretch my leg so far I could scratch my own damn ear from the topside.

The younger instructor came to join me. "So, are you really joining the class?"

"I'm *not* going to let this stop me," I said, pointing at my knee, "but . . . looking at you guys in action, my knee sure is going to try to hold me back from getting started."

"You *do* need to be healthy to get the most out of this," he said. He hesitated, then continued: "And I don't mean just the knee. You've been banged up, and it will leave you with a victim imprint. You may not feel it right this minute, but a serious assault will leave you with a lot of issues. You should do more than just learn some kicks."

"What? Like get my head examined? Find a victims' counselor to help me work through the issues?" I cracked. He smiled faintly, and I sighed and said: "All right. I get it. You guys are big on mind, body, spirit being one, or whatever. I'll . . . consider it, OK?"

He held up his hands. "All right, no pressure," he said, then rejoined the class.

Then my phone buzzed, a text message from Jinx: «**elegant, this watch**»

With some difficulty, I thumbed back: «**But will it work?**»

Jinx texted back, seemingly instantly, all in lowercase: «**like a charm**»

«**What about Wulf's tattoo?**» I responded. If I ever did get back in touch with him, I wanted to be able to say we could go ahead and get started.

«**marquis still sitting on it**» was the quick response.

«**Keep on him. The full moon is Saturday,**» I replied. For once Jinx didn't reply; I hesitated, then asked: «**Should I take Valentine's challenge?**»

Another instant lowercase ping: «**o, dakota**»

I sighed. Oh, Jinx! I messaged back: «**Translate, O cryptic one.**»

Jinx: «**elegant ink + $1M reward? srsly! take'im on**»

I grinned. Then I looked at my hand. There were two ugly scabbed lines on the undersides of my first two fingers and healing scrapes all over, but it functioned. I would be able to ink just fine. For all Transomnia had done to me—even knocking out two of my back teeth— he'd still obeyed the rules. I was alive, unspoiled—with two good hands.

It was time to get back to work.

Soon, the class finished with an informal bow and Darren came back to check on me. "So . . . did we sell you on maybe trying this out, starting Spring Semester?"

"Oh yeah," I said. "But you know, while I've been watching, I've been thinking. Long term—I never want to feel helpless again, so I'm going to have to make changes in my life. I can't waste time waiting."

Darren sighed. "You aren't listening. You aren't ready to start practicing—"

"Who said anything about *practicing*?" I said, dialing a number on my cell phone. "I need to start *working*. Alex? This is Dakota. Jinx gave me clearance—I'm ready to do your watch tattoo. How soon do you think the old man will be up for it?"

♁——

30. THE WRISTWATCH TATTOO

Valentine filmed his challenges, so an entire crowd was crammed into the Rogue Unicorn's larger tattooing room. Valentine was in a wheelchair, attended by a nervous-looking, nurse-for-hire type. There were two cameramen and a pair of associated busybodies. And, inside the magic circle that prevented stray *mana* from infiltrating the design, were my tools, my chair, Alex and me—and a stool with a box containing extra paraphernalia I would use later.

We had started early Friday morning at the ungodly hour of nine, as I had lied and told them it could take up to six hours—even before I knew an hour would be eaten just getting Valentine's wheelchair up the stairs. When you got over the intricacy of the linework, however, the watch was bone-simple to ink and *I* would be done in three hours, maybe even two.

I'd stayed up late through the night mixing pigments, performing the rituals to purify them, and generally setting up. In that regard, the watch was simple: it used only seven pigments. Some of the magical tattoos I've done have used upwards of fifty.

So . . . pigments are simple, if a bit repetitive. The hardest part? Preparing the needles. Normal tattoos are done with little needles soldered to the end of a bar that goes into the tattooing machine. Magical tattoos require something a bit . . . different. Something that will soak up magic and release it on cue, not *poison* it like iron does. There are crystals that will work and even some new plastic composites from Japan, but the best material is unicorn horn—preferably free-shed, gathered, if not by virgins, by someone wearing blessed rubber gloves. Yes, Virginia, unicorns do exist. But that's a story for another day.

Making the horn into needles takes many of the same tools that a modelmaker needs—magnifying glass and tweezers, files and sandpaper—and I did my needlework myself, which accounted for at least half of the quality of my work. It had taken two and a half hours to chip all the fragments I needed and file them into all the filigreed 'points' needed to ink the design—a one point, a triangular three, a curved five, and even a comblike seven for some of the larger outlines. You can't solder the finished points: you have to glue them into a throwaway prong and clamp them. I tried reusable clamps once and it was a total wash—running them through the autoclave loosened the clamp, so the horn came loose in the client's skin and he nearly ended up with a magical infection. Trust me—you *don't* want one of those.

With the needles in the autoclave, the next step is the flash—printed on transfer paper so it can be copied to the skin. With an ordinary tattoo, a stencil and eyeballing it are enough, but for a magical design, you have to be more careful; Jinx had given me a list of resonant points, and once I began working on Alex's skin I'd be pulling out a ruler and calipers to make sure the design was right. It can be tricky work—skin does shift and stretch, after all—and it would be a bit trickier since the design was reversed.

But now I had my ink and my needles and my flash and my subjects. All was in readiness—all that remained was to make sure that everyone understood this was *my* stage and my chair, and that inking a magic tattoo was *not* a stunt.

"I still don't see why *we* had to come to *you*," Alex said, fidgeting in my tattooing chair. "Why couldn't you have brought your equipment to the hospital?"

"First, I need a sterile environment," I said, wiping down his hand. He jumped a little when I did it: I've had a lot of men in this chair and I know the signs when they're stalling for time. "You understand *sterile*, right? Hospitals are dirty. That's how the old man got a staph infection—"

"Luck of the draw. *All* hospitals," Valentine said from his wheelchair, "put patients at risk for staph infections. They're filled with diseased people in a confined space constantly being exposed to each other's air, blood and fluids. Emory is one of the finest. Cleaner than most."

"See?" Alex said, still squirming a little. "We could have made arrangements—"

"If James Randi can go on national television on a *gurney* when he was on *morphine*," Valentine said, nostrils flaring, "I can survive a few hours in a wheelchair on Tylenol-3."

"So, first, a few ground rules," I said to the lead cameraman. "Hey you, behind the lens."

"*I'm* the director," a second man said imperiously, stepping forward.

"No, *I'm* the director in here," I snapped, holding my eyes on him. "I'm putting a permanent magical mark on a human body, which I take very seriously whether you get it or not. I'll try to make it easy on you to get a good shot, but when I'm working, the camera works around *me* and not the other way around. If I say slide, you slide. Savvy?"

He held up his hands. "We got it."

"Same goes for you, old man," I said to Valentine. "This isn't a stage magic trick you get to expose. You pull some James Randi shit and leap up to start sprinkling Styrofoam chips on me when I'm working, I tattoo you a new working asshole in the middle of your forehead."

Valentine blinked, then his brow furrowed. "Sure, but we'll have to test—"

"The test is that the tattoo will move when it's *done*," I said. "Normal tattoos don't do that, do they? They're just pigment plaques in the dermis. How *could* a tattoo move?"

Valentine's mouth just hung open. "Uh . . . "

"I have never done this particular design before, so as an extra bit of insurance, we're going to do this in two stages," I said. "First, I will ink it on myself and make sure it works—"

"Didn't you have a graphomancer review it?" Valentine asked.

"Did I leap up on stage in the middle of *your* performance at the Masquerade?" I said, smiling at him. "Give me an allowance for theatrics here. To win this challenge, I need to make it *absolutely clear* that the tattoo works by *magic*, and since Alex is not a skindancer, I'm going to tattoo it on myself *first* and show you. Then, and only then, I'll put the design on Alex."

"Then why'd you wipe down my hand?" Alex asked.

"You're pretty, and I wanted to touch your warm skin." I watched him squirm. "Do I need an another excuse? But seriously, don't go rubbing your hand in mud or anything. It was just convenient for me to pre-prep you; the reasons will become clear later."

Valentine leaned forward. "Isn't it unusual for a tattooist to . . . tattoo themselves?"

"Very unusual," I said, "for normal tattoo artists. For magical inkers, it's practically required. Magical marks can go bad, and when they go bad they can actually *kill* you or mess you up for life. In the old days, inkers sometimes did that to each other deliberately, leaving their magical competition jinxed. Historically, there's not a lot of trust between magical inkers."

"Charming," Alex said.

"*That* was the old school, *this* is the new one," I said, pouring encircling mix into my hand. "I do my work with ethical pride, employing expert graphomancers, and with state licenses, at least in Georgia, California and New York. You have nothing to worry about."

"What is that?" Valentine said, staring suspiciously at the sparkling dust.

"A mix of kosher salt, quartz granules, cinnamon and ginger," I said, "with a little plain old glitter thrown in for visibility. Nothing special—unless you happen to believe in magic."

I said a little prayer over my cupped hands. Someone like Jinx would probably go in with a bunch of Wiccan nonsense about protection from this and invocation of that. I don't believe in all of that stuff. There *are* spiritual forces of evil in this world, just waiting to take residence in anything even remotely magical, and the 'circle'— a blessed ring of crystals layered over a flat plane, preferably of living earth but in this case a disc of cut granite set into the floor—did help to keep them out. But you didn't need elaborate rituals: you just needed to look within, to whatever spiritual force you believed in, and call on it, letting your own aura blossom forth and charge the crystals to life.

My prayer finished, I poured the mix into the circle around us, murmuring. As the circle closed, I could feel our auras mingle with the mana built up in the pigments as a tingling rippled through my tattoos, something I'd never felt when I was unmarked. Some lucky people could feel mana anyway—Alex squirmed in his chair, the nurse looked at us eagerly, and the director with antsy concern. Valentine and the cameraman remained unmoved.

"We're now encircled. This ring will help repel any stray magic or 'evil spirits'," I said, putting my hands up in scare quotes. "Or whatever. Regardless, this is a part of the procedure. *No* one crosses this line. *Not for any reason.* Clear?"

When they nodded assent, I began wiping off my left wrist with alcohol, then soap. "Stage two in inking a magical mark is imprinting the design." I picked up the acetate sheet of the flash. A thin stick of blessed pitch rubbed across the design had made it sticky, so all I had to do was press it carefully to my wrist, where Cinnamon's butterfly had once lived, rub it a few times, and then peel it off. "If this was an ordinary tattoo, I could just start inking it. But I'll check the tattoo out against the instructions of the graphomancer to make sure I got the design right."

I pulled out the ruler and calipers and had gotten halfway through the list of resonant points when someone finally noticed the obvious.

"The design is backwards," Alex said.

"You mean, 'mirror reversed,'" I said. The director leaned in with a handheld camera; he was assisting the other cameramen by providing candid shots, and I lifted my hand so both his camera and Alex could see more clearly.

"Yeah," Alex said. "Won't that affect—"

"Yes and no," I said, measuring the distance across the design. "Normally I wouldn't reverse it, but in this case it is necessary."

"But when you start to tattoo it—"

"Do *you* ink magic, Alex?"

"Uh . . . no," he said. "But if this works I'd like to learn."

"Good," I said, grinning, making a small correction according to the instructions in Jinx's list. "But until then you're going to have to take my word that I need to reverse it."

I stuck a palette knife into some Vaseline and rubbed it on my wrist, then rubbed it onto my hands. "This will make the machine work more smoothly," I said. I checked over my pigments, the needles, the design, my skin. I inserted the tube holding the seven needle into the tattoo gun and started the machine. It began buzzing. I was ready. "And now, I begin."

I touched the needle gently to my skin, the first sharp prick erased almost immediately by the thrumming vibration of the needle puncturing my skin, forty times a second. The hot, spreading warmth and vibration were sensual, almost sexy, and the noise faded into the background as I began chatting.

"First I'll do the outline," I said, curling the needle deftly round my hand. "On an ordinary tattoo, I'd do the outline, take a short break, and then fill in the linework. For a magical tat, I'll stop when the major outline is done and check my resonant points. A magical tattoo is like a circuit, though it obeys different rules; you have to get all the components right or it won't work. A stray line or too much pigment would be like a short circuit or a bad resistor—"

"What does it feel like?" Alex asked, leaning down over my hand. He was supposed to provide color commentary while I worked, but inking myself had thrown him.

"Feels hot," I said, grinning, my eyes never leaving my hand. "Nowhere near as hot as your firespinning at the Masquerade, though."

I reached the end of an arc and lifted the needle. Alex's eyes sparkled back at me. "Fire is life," he said, "and I love life. It shows in my spinning."

"In other things, too, I bet," I said, setting the gun in its stand briefly, wiping the blood off my wrist, then picking up the gun and returning my eyes to my work. "I'd have sworn that you weren't just spinning—it looked like fire magic. What would the old man say?"

"He knows what I do," Alex said. "Thinks it can all be done with chemicals. In fact he says he'd have challenged me already, except he's afraid he'd set his hair on fire."

"Ah, no big loss, that?" I said, reaching the end of another arc and winking at Valentine.

"You kids," Valentine said, waving his hand feebly.

"But seriously," Alex said, as I started again. "How does it feel on your skin—"

"Kinda scratchy. It's intense, but a manageable intense. I've had worse paper cuts and less intense orgasms." I finished an arc and looked up at him. "Of course, that depends on who's giving me the orgasm."

Alex leaned back with a slightly nervous laugh.

More quickly than I thought, the five main magical components of the watch were inked. I set the gun down, wiped off the blood again, and checked the measurements with my calipers. For good measure I sensed the mark with my fingers; everything was right on the money.

"Everything looks good," I said, slipping the tube out of the machine and discarding the needle in a magical hazards vat. "That's the major outline of the watch. Now I'm going to fill in the rest of the magical circuit. I have marks to make with three more needles and seven total inks—I'll end up with sixteen different combinations, so this will take a while."

"Isn't seven by three twenty one?" Valentine asked weakly.

"Obviously she won't use *every* combination," Alex said.

"Right enough, and don't be a jerk," I said, grinning. "That's my job."

But Valentine didn't respond, and I looked up to see him leaning back in the wheelchair, eyes closed. I cracked, "Hey old man, aren't you going to even watch me kicking your ass?"

He flapped his hand even more feebly, with a very noticeable tremor. "Wake me when you do something interesting."

The nurse looked at me, anguished, and Alex and I exchanged a nervous glance. Time to get this fucking thing over with.

The rest of the inking went even faster than I expected. I love working my own skin. It's the finest canvas I've ever decorated. It's smooth and soft and holds ink well and heals crisply, with little blurring of the designs. Even better, it's internally smooth—when the designs move, or when I pull little stunts like I did when I transferred my butterfly to Cinnamon, there's no excess pigment left in the skin.

And then, it was over. I wiped my hand clear of blood and stared down at the design, surprised: it was finished—in an hour and forty-five minutes, by the wall clock, and that's with all the inane bantering, plus a few pauses for Alex to talk to the camera.

"That's it," I said.

"That's it?" Alex asked. The director leaned in. Valentine's eyes cracked open.

"Now, it may not work quite right at first," I said. "The skin will be healing and, normally, the tattoo would take up to two weeks to stabilize—"

"Fair . . . fair enough," Valentine said. He sounded about a thousand years old. "You—you told us—to expect as much—"

"Let me finish, you upstaging old coot," I said gently. "It can take two weeks to stabilize, *but* we might see a little movement now."

Valentine's eyes shot open and he lurched forward, staring, and everyone's eyes all zeroed in on the watch or the monitors. The two hands just sat there, frozen at twelve.

Alex stared down at my new tat, a little disappointed. "It's not moving—"

I on the other hand, was looking at my *real* watch, carefully timing it, charging the yin-yang in my palm. "Give it a moment," I said. "It's not noon yet."

My Timex beeped twelve, and I swept my right hand over the watch on my left wrist in a glimmering shower of mana, right in front of Alex and Valentine and the cameras and everybody. And when my hand had fully passed over the design, the second hand on the watch *started moving*, keeping time as perfectly as a star-based clock could get.

"Would you look at *that*," Valentine said, staring alternately at my wrist, then the monitor. "*Would you look at that.*"

"See the motion?" I said, looking at him, at Alex, at the director. "Can you see it moving?"

"Yeah," Alex breathed. "It's really moving. But . . . backwards."

"I know," I said, opening the box on the stool and pulling out the piece of blessed glass that I'd prepared earlier, with the miniature blessed circle inscribed around its perimeter. I scooted the stool closer, like a stand between us, and set the glass upright in the ridge in its box. "But that's expected. Now we're going to transfer the design to your hand."

"Sure," Alex said. "But . . . you used all the needles. And where's the flash—"

"Won't need it," I said, concentrating mana in my inking hand. Then I passed it over the clock and brought it to life.

The clock *glowed*. Everyone could see its light reflecting off the cameras, Alex's face, Valentine's eyes. And then . . . it separated from my hand and floated in the air, coming to rest gently in the center of the magical circle inscribed in the glass.

"Oh. My. Word," Alex breathed.

My hand stung a bit—it would still need a bit of healing, though not as much as if the pigment of tattoo had remained embedded in it—but I had no time to give it more than a quick glance before moving on. It was time to give Alex his tattoo.

"With a stable tattoo, I could have just transferred this through the air," I said. "But with a new tattoo like this one you need a stabilizing plate. Now, hold up your hand."

"What?" Alex said, blinking as I picked up his hand gently and guided it to the back of the glass. "Oh, my, you mean this is it—"

"Yes," I said, positioning his hand carefully. "The design will flow through the glass. That's why I had to ink it mirror-reversed, like a stamp. Here it comes."

Then I guided Alex's wrist in. The tattoo glowed even more brightly, feeling the pull of virgin skin; then it detached from the glass and landed on his wrist, merging with the flesh. In moments the glow faded and the tattoo returned to normal, like it had been inked there—without the long healing period. And, after a moment, the watch hand started up, right on time, ticking out one 'second' for every sidereal second out of each turn of the Earth beneath the stars.

Alex stared down at his wrist, at the magical tattoo that I'd just transferred to him by purely magical means. Then, wordlessly, he proffered it to Valentine, who stared at it, eyes bugged as wide as the lens of the camera recording his reaction.

I leaned back in my chair, folded my arms, ostentatiously displaying my tattooing gun in my right hand. "Let's see you do *that*, Valentine."

31. Time Is Running Out

I swaggered (well, limped) out into Reception, my spirits on top of the world, to find Annesthesia looking straight at the door I'd exited, worried, talking to Kring/L in hushed tones.

"I know, but they're *filming*," she said. "I'm afraid if he calls *again*—"

"Who called?" I asked.

"Excuse me," Alex said, stepping past me to hold the door for Valentine's wheelchair. He sounded worried.

"Is the old man all right? He's not taking this well?" I asked. Valentine slipped past me on the wheelchair, sound asleep, his breathing labored. As she passed, his nurse glared at me.

"If you knew you were going to *crush* him," she said under her breath, "you could have waited until he was *healthy*."

I stared after her wordlessly as she and Alex wheeled Valentine out. When he was gone I said quietly, to no one in particular, "If he was that sick someone should have said—"

"Damn fool," the director said. "It's my fault, pushing him to get a few shots in the can in time for the early promos. If I'd known he was so weak—still, an excellent show, Miss Frost. Assuming Doctor Valentine recovers, if he can top what you did here today, I'll eat my camera."

"They're *my* cameras," the lead cameraman said, dragging out a bag of equipment.

"It's the principle of the thing," the director said, giving him a hand. Then, turning back to me, he added, "We'll be in touch about the followup interview, Miss Frost."

And I was left there, feeling like the world's biggest heel. Somehow the thing that bothered me most was that Alex hadn't even bothered to say goodbye—not even a curt 'Thank you for your time, Miss Frost.' He must be really worried about Valentine, pissed at me for winning so arrogantly—or both.

"Dakota," Kring/L said quietly.

"What?" I said, refocusing on him and Anesthesia. "Who?"

"Someone called Wulf," she said. Her face was terrified. "He was talking about a tattoo, but Dakota, I don't know, this guy sounds pretty fucking *angry*—"

"Did he leave a number?" I said, pulling out my phone and texting Jinx. I felt a sting of embarrassment that I'd done a tattoo for prize money while Wulf was waiting out in the cold, and the excuse of waiting on the Marquis's approval was growing thin.

"No," she said.

"Well, star-sixty-nine the Marquis," I said, thumbing rapidly: **«Good news on Wulf's flash?»**

"We can't do star-sixty-nine on this system," Annesthesia said.

"Wait a minute, I think you can get the call log," Kring/L said, picking up the phone and jabbing at it. "You want the number—"

"No, call him and put him on speaker," I said.

Jinx responded: **«still waiting 4 marquis»**

Damnit, how hard could this be? **«Well, ping him,»** I texted back. **«Wulf is antsy.»**

The phone rang, and rang, and rang. Finally Kring/L picked up the receiver and dropped it to disconnect the call. "Nothing," he said.

"Try again. He may be using a pay phone," I said, thumbing rapidly. **«Tell him it's urgent – Wulf has the shakes.»**

«marquis != speedy gonzalez» Jinx responded.

"For the love," I said. What did '!=' even mean? **«Speak English!»**

The phone began ringing, and ringing, and ringing. Nothing. Just as Kring/L was reaching for the receiver, the line picked up and a haggard voice said cautiously: "Yes?"

"Rogue Unicorn Tattooing Studio," Annesthesia said cheerily. "Please hold for—"

"Dakota Frost," I said, picking up the receiver. "Wulf? Is this Wulf?"

There was only static on the end of the line. Then, a guarded: "Yes."

"You called? Sorry, I was doing a tat—"

"And what of mine?" he snarled.

I swallowed. He was on edge, his voice shaking. "I'm still getting it researched—"

"I am running out of time," he snapped. "I tire of these games, Dakota—"

"Wulf," I said passionately, and it halted him. "I haven't known you for a long time . . . but do you think *I* would game you?"

There was a long pause. "No, Dakota."

"I am checking with the graphomancers *literally* as we speak," I said, texting **«Hurry!»** into my phone. "But I would never do anything to hurt you."

"Then why won't you—"

"You know the tattoo is Nazi, Wulf," I said—and Kring/L's eyes widened.

"I know," he said, voice quiet.

"So I have to know it's safe. I won't risk hurting you." Now *both* Annesthesia and Kring/L raised their eyebrows. "I can't just take it on faith. I *have* to *know* that it won't cause you harm."

"Thank you, Dakota," he said. "I'd never hurt you either—but it's so hard to control myself, so close to the moon. The beast wants out. It wants me to change. It's so old now. So strong. *So* strong. I would never want to release that savage animal on you—"

"Spleen is dead," I said. "Savaged, by an animal."

There was even longer pause. "It wasn't me," he said. "It wasn't me—"

"I didn't say it was," I said. I heard the panic in his voice and wished I couldn't empathize. But I'd felt that panic of everything closing in on me, of helplessness, of realizing I wasn't in control of anything. Still, I pushed him. I had to. "But if not you—"

"My enemies," he snarled over the phone. "Damn them. Damn them!"

"Wulf . . ." I said. "Who? *Who* are your enemies?"

"The Hunters," he said. Even now, even with me believing he didn't kill Spleen, even knowing *Philip* believed that someone really had made trouble for him at the hospital, Wulf still came off like a conspiracy nut, with his assumed name and vaguely ascribed 'enemies.' "They've been looking so long, so long. They're afraid of me. They never attack me directly. They just make it . . . difficult. Or attack my friends. Always my friends. All my friends. So I won't let myself have any friends."

My phone buzzed: **«marquis sez: "safe, u impatient bitch"»**

I sighed in relief. *Finally.* «**Thanks Jinx, and tell him thanks!**»

"I'm your friend, Wulf," I said, as convincingly as I could muster. "I just got word from my graphomancers, *right now*, that the tattoo is safe. And I'm going to do it for you—"

"I can't let you do that," Wulf said. "Not if you're a friend."

"But you said this was important. You need—"

"That was before I knew Spleen had been murdered," Wulf said, and I could hear him pacing. Well, I wasn't sure I could actually hear someone pace, but his agitation came through loud and clear. "I won't let you become a target."

"I'm not an easy target, Wulf," I said, reddening even as I said it. That was an obvious lie, the old bravado talking.

"The evidence says otherwise," Wulf said.

I had nothing to say to that, so after a moment I plowed ahead: "It will take me most of the afternoon to mix the pigments and make the needles. I can do the tattoo late tonight—"

"*Not* at night," Wulf said. "*Not* after moon rise. It isn't safe for you then."

"Tomorrow, then," I said. "Come to the Rogue—"

"I can't be seen in public—"

"*I need a magic circle*, Wulf," I said. "I cannot do it in the open. *Anything* could get in to the marks and you could end up ten times worse off than you are now."

There was a long pause. "I will find you a circle, then, somewhere in the Underground," Wulf said. "And if I cannot find it before nightfall—"

"The full moon is what, two nights away?" I said. "Not 'til Sunday. You have time—"

Wulf laughed. "The moon hits zenith at two minutes to midnight tomorrow, Dakota, and it will be ninety-nine-point-six-percent full," he said bitterly. Then his words began to speed up, tumbling over one another. "Believe me, I know. That sliver of difference between full and *not* won't make a difference. I know the moon. The first moon of November. It's called a 'Frost Moon', did you know that, Dakota Frost? The frost moon of November. The Frost Moon is always *so strong*. So strong. If I cannot find somewhere safe . . . somewhere safe . . . perhaps it is best I wait it out . . . wait out the Frost Moon . . . and hope."

"Wulf—"

His voice tightened up again, and he regained control of himself. "I will contact you tomorrow if I find a circle. Don't try to contact me—I can't use this pay phone again, it may be tapped. Be safe, Dakota."

Click. And with that, he was gone.

With me having no way to reach him, no way to find him. And time rapidly running out.

I felt safe. But for him . . . I felt it was not safe at all.

32. BACK TO AFRICA

"The airport Houlihan's serves the *best* Bloody Marys," Savannah said, pushing her glass towards me. Reluctantly, I took a sip of the blood-red pulp and raised an eyebrow: the drink was strong and refreshingly tangy.

"You're right," I said, passing the glass back to her. "Who knew?"

Houlihan's was in the Hartsfield-Jackson International Airport's atrium, a vast, round, indoor space filled with shops and restaurants. The atrium served as overflow for the staggering mess of the Atlanta security checkpoint, which fed all the passengers of the world's busiest airport through one measly row of metal detectors. The rest of Darkrose and Savannah's crew kept looking at the mammoth knot of passengers nervously, but Savannah was not perturbed; she just took another sip of her drink and leaned back in her chair thoughtfully.

"Surely," she said, "we could leave her *one* guard."

"No," Vickman said, scratching his beard. Darkrose's chief bodyguard always seemed to be scowling—and it was worse than normal today. "We can't. We're going into the lion's den here. We need everyone."

"I don't think you're even *trying* to find a way to protect Dakota," Savannah said, eyes narrowing at him as they might at Darkrose, or Doug. Vickman wasn't fazed.

"I'm not," he said sharply, meeting her eye to eye. "I don't answer to you, Saffron. I answer to Darkrose, and even then only as long as it doesn't interfere with keeping her alive. You may be modern and progressive, but South Africa is very definitely populated with Old World vampires. I need every hand I have to keep you safe, so everyone is going."

Savannah looked at Darkrose, who just shrugged.

"Good bodyguards are hard to find," she said. "I would never argue with a man who would take a bullet for me, much less a human willing to guard my daytime resting place rather than put a stake in me at the first opportunity. Vickman's word stands."

I stared into my own drink. I knew how important this trip was to them. They were going to Johannesburg, where 'Saffron' would formally petition Darkrose's former master to release Darkrose, so she could join Saffron's court. It had taken a year of delicate negotiations and a huge payout by Delancaster to make this trip happen, but the end result would be the end of animosity between vampires on either side of the Atlantic and . . . and the beginning of a new life of happiness for my ex-girlfriend and her lover.

I couldn't begrudge them going. But right at that moment, I was scared shitless *for* Wulf, *by* Wulf, and by whatever other forces lurked out there around him.

"The full moon is just tomorrow night," I pleaded. "Can't you delay the trip for at least forty-eight hours?"

"We could move the meet to the festival," Savannah said thoughtfully. "It's not too late to charter a direct flight to Sunday—"

"Yes, it is," Darkrose snapped. "Delancaster is already in the air."

"We've been planning for Darkrose to go back to the South African Court for *eighteen months* now," Vickman said. "This is a coordinated operation. We can't stop now. We especially can't leave your *master* hanging around in South Africa alone, no matter how good his own bodyguards are."

Savannah scowled, but slowly nodded. Then she looked up at me.

"So…" she asked. "You going to be OK?"

I stared at my coffee glumly. What was the saying? Unexpected danger on my part didn't constitute an emergency on her part? Maybe that was unfair, but until last week Savannah and I hadn't even been speaking, and now here I was asking her to shitcan her trip out of the country, inconvenience her whole entourage, piss off her boss and maybe even screw up her future . . . just because someone was trying to kill me.

But in all honesty, Savannah's protection hadn't helped me much so far, not even when she'd been standing in the same room as the shooter. Even this damn collar was just a warning to whoever decided to break me that Savannah would pick up the pieces—a deterrent, not an actual shield. Even if she stayed, I was still effectively on my own.

"No, I'll be OK," I said, pulling at my collar. The metal was surprisingly unyielding and the rubber on its inside was damp with sweat. I hadn't realized I was that nervous. "Worst comes to worst, I can always call on the Oakdale Clan—"

"Oakdale?" Vickman said. "Wasn't it one of their fangs that took a chunk out of you? Ain't that why you took the collar?"

"You have it backwards," I said. "*They're* OK. In fact they punished Transomnia for hassling me. That's why he was pissed and took out his revenge on me."

"Calaphase is on the lookout for him," Savannah said. "You know? Calaphase turned out all right."

"That he did," Darkrose said.

I stewed. At first I'd been infuriated when I'd been forced to take Savannah's protection, but now the thought of her and her coterie being gone for a week was . . . unsettling. Then a horrible thought hit me. "Wait a minute," I said. "If you're gone next week, how will you *vote?*"

Darkrose looked confused; Vickman's mouth opened. Vote in the ordinary November elections, as if that aspect of the greater world mattered to their kind? But Savannah just shook her head. "Oh, Dakota," she said, eerily like Jinx. "What am I going to do with you?"

Vickman's watch beeped. "It's time," he said, standing. He carried no suitcase, just a small shoulder bag. Then Darkrose's tall-dark-and-handsome human servant stood, managing the carry-ons. Finally the vampires rose: Savannah, in her simple red leather dress, goggles hanging about her throat, and Darkrose, in a heavy layered coat and cloak that was practically a burqua when she pulled the hood up.

"Sorry to see you go," I said, standing awkwardly. I still wasn't used to how eerily coordinated the two of them were. Had Savannah and I been that way, once, or was it a vampire thing? "Surprised you don't have Doug pulling a pack."

"Doug's a human grad student," Savannah said, "not my enthralled servant. He doesn't have time for all this gallivanting."

"And you do?" I asked. "Are you ever going to get your Ph.D in vampirology?"

"Some day," she said. "But not today."

We stood there, staring at each other.

"Oh, quit being a pain in my ass and give me a hug," Savannah said, stepping in and squeezing me about the waist so that all my air left with a whoosh. "Take care, Dakota."

I waved awkwardly and watched them walk off. I expected to see Savannah look back and wave to me, but she was lost, chatting with Darkrose, who gave her a warm hug.

I sighed, stared down at the table, at my rapidly cooling coffee. I swept it up and finished it in one forced gulp, then considered finishing the dregs of Savannah's Bloody Mary. What the hell. I wouldn't be driving for at least half an hour. I picked it up, finished it, staring at the grainy tomato juice draining off the bottom of the glass, then slammed it down and tossed a few more coins on top of the tip we'd left on the table. Then I picked up my cane and started limping back towards the MARTA station at the end of the airport terminal.

On the way, I took stock. Rand was already working the angle on the shooter, but he was only good against mortal threats. If Transomnia attacked again, I was toast, but if I had some warning, I could go to Calaphase for help—that little shit was now a big embarrassment to him. If, at the werehouse, one of the Bear King's kindred got rowdy, I could count on Buck. I might even be able to ask for Buck's help if Wulf turned out to be behind the killings. If not . . . the full moon hit zenith in less than twenty-seven hours, and took to the sky in even less. Even if I could get the tattoo prepared, I had no way of finding him.

The train slid into the station, a long, smooth, well-lit machine, a pinnacle of modern technology. Then my eyes lit up.

There was *someone* who knew where Wulf lived.

"Philip," I said into my cell when he picked up. I sat down in one of the back-to-back seats near the middle of the car, and other passengers filed in, one taking the seat just behind me. "It's Dakota. What's that noise? Sounds like a Starbucks. Can I meet you?"

"Not unless you're willing to ride that Vespa all the way to North Carolina," he said, voice raised slightly to overcome the sound of a blender in the background. "And 'that noise' is a helicopter I couldn't even admit existed until nine months ago."

My skin grew cold. "What's happened?"

"We got a lead, Dakota," he said, sounding not at *all* happy. "A pizza parlor employee was abducted a few hours ago in Charlotte—heavily tattooed, snatched just after moonrise, so . . . we're riding to the rescue."

"You go, Philip," I said softly. "Did the pizza guy have magical tattoos?"

"Oh yeah, and get this—he had one done by Sumner," he said. "Similar to the one you saw. This is *exactly* what we've seen before, from the distance between attacks to the victim type down to the lead time to full moon. It fits the profile *perfectly*."

He didn't say the cliché, but I could hear it in his voice. "Too perfectly?" I asked. "Jeez, Philip, you don't think it's some kind of trap?"

"I *want* to think it's a distraction," Philip said, sounding angry and disgusted. "Damn goose chase, in fact. But there's a life on the line. I can't let another person die because I sat on a lead."

My eyebrows raised. *Another* person? "You do what you have to, Philip," I said. But his reference kept bugging at me, and finally I asked, "Another person . . . do you mean Spleen?"

"What did you call for, Dakota?" Philip asked sharply.

"I need to find Wulf," I said, and I heard him hiss. "I've lost my contact, and he's not answering the number we have on him—"

"Can you give me that number?" Philip said.

"*I* need to find him," I said. "Do you know where he sleeps?"

"Yes, but he's skipped, Dakota," Philip said. "We already tried to pick him up—"

"You tried to pick him up?" That was more of an accusation than a question.

"Dakota!" Philip said. "A werewolf looking for a tattoo turns up right where we expect to find a tattoo killer that strikes on the full moon. Mysterious forces are plotting against him. His tattooist is attacked—*twice!* His handler ends up dead, savaged as if by an animal. Sounds exactly like a 'person of interest' in the full vagueness of that awful phrase. Of course we tried to pick him up. Please, if you give me his number—"

"He *saved my life*," I said. "Or at least, helped save me from someone other than himself. He's not your guy."

"Dakota," Philip said. "This is *me* we're talking about here. You really think I'd accuse him without damn good proof?" I didn't immediately respond, and he said: "Dakota?"

Finally I said, "No."

"All right then," Philip said. "Give me his number and I'll try to—"

"Give *me* his last known location and I'll try to find him," I countered.

Philip paused. "You need to stay out of this," he said. "Stay away from Wulf—"

"It was *you*," I snapped, "that told me I should do his tattoo—"

"That was before Spleen ended up dead," Philip barked back. "Before someone else tried to shoot you at the Masquerade! It isn't safe—"

"It's not safe for *him*," I said. "The full moon is one day away. I have to help him—"

"He's an old wolf," Philip said. "I researched that suit of his. The style's at least thirty years out of date. He survives the full moon twelve times a year. He knows how to do it again. If you really want to help him, you'll lie low until the moon is on the wane and we've nailed this killer, or at least driven him off. Shack up with Saffron if you have to—"

"She's gone," I said, "To Africa."

"Bloody hell," he said. "Bloody fucking hell. I was counting on her! Hell of a time to— damnit, look, call Rand, get into protective custody—"

"Fuck that," I said.

"Dakota!" Philip said. "You've had *four* attacks on you recently—"

"Four?" I said. "Only two, and the one by Transomnia isn't related—"

"Dakota," he said. "Presidents and gangsters have multiple assassins gunning for them, but even *they* don't get four attacks a week this side of Pakistan. Transomnia, the Masquerade shooter, Spleen *and* that business with Wulf, they're *all* connected to you—"

"Business with Wulf?" I said.

"At the hospital," Philip said. "Whoever ratted him to the hospital staff didn't say Wulf was 'bothering them'—they said, *Call the police, that maniac tried to gut me with a knife!*"

"Holy crap," I said. "Why didn't you tell me before?"

"The interviewing officer didn't tell *me*," Philip said. "I just found their exact words going over the transcripts. Whoever said that didn't want him run off—they wanted him arrested, maybe even shot and killed. That's a premeditated attack in my book."

"Jeez," I said. But I didn't want to admit he was right. I was a skeptic. I didn't believe in all that conspiracy crap. "But, still . . . are you sure you're not being too paranoid—"

"With one dead, two hospitalized, and one man terrorized into going on the run?" Philip said. "You can never be too paranoid with that kind of shit piling up in just six days. Never."

I just sat there, stunned. I wanted to deny it, to tell him he was a conspiracy nut, but he was a very genuine man in black with his own shiny black helicopter, and the body count *was* stacking up. His words left me feeling I was sinking into murky water, getting deeper all the time, able to see nothing but churning ripples left by unseen sharks.

"Dakota, we're going to land soon," Philip said, as gently as he could over the whine. "I'll be busy, but . . . I can start the wheels turning, see if we can track Wulf down."

"Okay," I said.

"Will you please give me his number, then?" Philip said.

"Philip," I said, then stopped. "I can't. I can't betray his trust. Not even for you. It's hard to explain what trust means to us down here."

"Look, Dakota," Philip said. "All right. Wulf is a suspect, and I need to question him. I freely admit it. But just *question* him—that's it. I have no intention of running the first guy I've collared to the DA, not with eyewitnesses denying his involvement and mysterious figures trying to manipulate the police. And if he is innocent, then *he is in danger.* He needs to be cleared, he needs protection, and most of all, he needs your tattoo. To do all that, we need to find him. Could you imagine, just for a minute, just for *one* minute, that I'm not trying to notch up a collar here, but that I want to find him because I have his best interests at heart?"

I wavered, then broke down. "All right, Philip," I said. "678—"

"Wait," he said, "let me get a fucking pen—"

"If you hurt him," I said, "or disappear him, you're a dead man."

"Dakota, I meant it. At this point I just want to talk to him, offer him police protection if he will accept it—and either way, tell him to get a good lawyer."

"Police do that?"

"We do what we have to," Philip said. I gave him the number, and then he said: "Look, I'm gone, but if you need us—you have my number, and Rand's. And if it's an emergency, call 'Black Mayday, Black Mayday' on any police channel. Say you are an important asset in a DEI case, and someone in Atlanta will pick it up and respond as soon as they can."

"Take care," I forced myself to say. I was still angry, though I couldn't really say why.

"You too," Philip said. "I . . . well, be safe, Dakota."

And then he hung up.

I stood there staring at the phone glumly. I was angry at Philip for targeting Wulf, but deep down I knew I couldn't blame him. In his place I'd have been forced to do the same thing, no matter how I felt about Wulf.

And I realized that maybe there was more at work than just the issue of trust between Edgeworlders. I did feel something about Wulf, more than just appreciation that he'd saved my ass. Seeing the man struggling with his wolf made me empathize, made me connect to him. Made me wonder what he'd be like if there weren't so many bumps and bruises in his past. He made me care. But so did Philip, the scary man-in-black with the devilish goatee who in one moment seemed as ruthless as Wulf was wounded, and in the next seemed to be bending rules just because I asked him to.

I was very confused.

And then someone whispered in my ear, "Having trouble with your *boooy*friend?"

33. DISTURBINGLY EASY TO FIND

"Aaa!" I cried, half leaping out of my chair and whirling around. Cinnamon sat on the reverse-facing train seat that backed up to mine, leaning her head over the joint headrest until she'd practically rested it on my shoulder—and I hadn't noticed. "How the hell did you—"

"You're like the world's easiest person to track," she said, sniffing curiously, flicking her big ears at me. "At least this time you hopped on a train, so I gots a good run. Chasing you round on that little bike is so *boring*."

She rolled over, propping her arms lazily on the seat, blinking—which gave her a good look at my hair and face. She hissed and recoiled.

"*Thought* I smelled a beating. Who banged ya up?" she snarled. "Who did ya? Was it that little shit they booted out, Trans? Fuck! I'll kill 'im!"

"Leave him alone," I warned. "He's a real psycho—"

"I don't care how nuts he is," she said in a sing song, "I just wanna see his guts—"

"Cinnamon!" I said. "Did you listen in?"

She rolled over again, looking up at me at an angle. "Yah," she said. "I won't lie to ya."

"Then you know I'm in a world of shit," I said. "It isn't safe for you to be around me right now—"

"You just wants to get rid of me," she said, sniffing. "Oh, boo hoo—"

But she really did sound wounded. "I do not—" I began.

"You were happy to ditch me last week," she countered.

"If you're going to cost me a hundred bucks a week—"

"Hey," she said. "I'm no bloodsucker. I still gots half that."

"Cinnamon," I said. "*Go home.* Stay safe until the full moon is—" Then my blood ran cold.

"Cinnamon, aren't you about to change?" My eyes narrowed. She'd actually grown *whiskers*, huge catlike whiskers. I hadn't seen them before. "You are, aren't you?"

"*Maaaay*BE," she said petulantly. "Tomorrow night, day afta. I won't lie to ya—I gotta be back to the 'house by nightfall 'morrow to make lockdown."

"They lock you up?" I said. "That's horrible—"

"It's a service, not a sentence," she said. "This ain't the country. In the city if you can't control your beast, you die. At the 'house, they cages it, calms it down. You can even go on hunts, supervised like, if they gots a strong alpha on deck."

I just stared at her. It was such a different world.

"So anyway . . . I tolds 'em you were s'posed to take me today," she grinned, leaning back over the seat a little more to look me in the eye. "You gonna rat me again, you big were-fink?"

"No," I said, rubbing my brow. "Actually, wasn't I *supposed* to take you today?"

"Next Friday," she said. "But they don'ts needs to know."

"No, the *last* thing I want is to get you in trouble," I said. "But I don'ts supposes—I *don't* suppose there's any chance of you going back for your own safety?"

"With like twenty hours freedom?" she said, rolling her eyes. "You just wants me gone."

"No," I snapped, "But neither do I want you shot."

"But I'm bulletproof," she countered.

"And I'm busy," I replied. "I've got to get ready to do Wulf's tattoo—"

"I wants to see that," she said, turning round in the seat to face me over her folded arms. "I bets you're a hell of a lot nicer on your canvases than the fag. When are you gonna do it?"

"Tomorrow, I hope," I said.

"You gots a *hope?*" she replied. "Why you gots a hope and not a time?"

"I can't find him," I said. "Spleen . . . Spleen is dead, Cinnamon."

"The little weasel?" she said. "No! Was it Trans—"

"He was mauled," I said. "Like by an animal."

Cinnamon sat there frozen. "It wasn't me! I liked the weasel!"

"I didn't think it *was* you," I responded. "I think Philip suspects Wulf."

"Do you?" she said, looking at me coolly. "Just because he's a were?"

I suddenly realized that I had just shifted in the conversation—from her 'in' group to her 'out' group. "No," I said, disgusted. "He had means and opportunity, but where's the motive? Spleen was his contact. And I got him on the phone, so obviously he hasn't already turned."

"Okay then," she said, still wary. "So what's the holdup?"

"He won't return my calls," I said. "He's chickened out, says he wants to 'protect' me."

"Maybe he is," she said. "Maybe he did gut Spleen and wants to keep you out of it—"

"Or maybe he's just a pussy," I said, and her eyebrows shot up. "I get this all the time from people who book an appointment with me. 'I've decided it's too dangerous.' Or, 'It's too expensive.' Or, 'I remembered an appointment.' There's a thousand excuses and only one translation: He may have gotten cold feet. He's scared to sit in my chair."

"Ya thinks?" she said, grinning.

"Either that or he thinks he'll eat me alive," I replied. "Regardless, he called from a payphone and won't pick up when I call back. And my so-called *boooy*friend was no help either—Wulf bailed out of his lair. Neither of us can find him. If he doesn't call me—I'm shit out of luck."

Cinnamon suddenly yawned and stretched, then sat sideways in her seat so her head rested on the glass, feet kicking out over the end of the double bench. She inspected her claws lazily, and said: "If only you knew someone who was, like, the *bestest* at tracking people."

For one brief moment I wondered about the wisdom of involving a minor in this horrible mess—and then I told myself: hey, *At least she's bulletproof.*

"So, Cinnamon," I said, leaning back so my head mirrored hers. "Wanna go for a ride?"

34. LURE OF THE WULF

"This is a bad fucking idea," I said, having severe second thoughts as I pulled at the grimy door to the stairwell leading to the lower levels. "Why'd I let you talk me into this?"

"Don't lie, you were gonna ask," Cinnamon countered. "I just spat it first."

Going back to the Krog tunnel in the darkness had given me the shakes—I kept imagining Transomnia or werewolves or *whatevers* were going to jump out at us at every moment. But Cinnamon just swaggered through, all the way from the well at Wylie down through the sewer tunnels, tail switching, long, clawed hands at the ready. But when I pried open the door to the stairwell, even she quailed.

"Wheeew—stinks, I won't lie to ya," she said, turning her head, though for me the garbage we'd just crawled over coming out of the well had smelled ten times worse. "Rot and rats and weres and . . . vamps and . . . other things." She stared back into the darkness, and then looked at me. Her irises had widened to huge, eerie ovals, making her seem alien—but her voice was still Cinnamon. "Not too late to find out you're a were-chicken, is it?"

"And you?"

"I'm a were*tiger*," she said proudly. "I soaks bullets up like *sugah*. Not scared of *nuthin*. But if *you* chicken out, naturally I'd go with ya—like, to protect you, o'course."

"O'course," I said, turning on my Brinkman five-cell. "Lets—"

She reached out with her impossibly long, clawed fingers and snapped the flashlight off. "Save the bats on your club," she said. "Your eyes will adjust. Just stay behind me, K?"

"K," I said in resignation, following her down into the dark.

In the blackness, the journey down the stairwell was even scarier than it had been with Spleen and his yellow fluorescent. The cinderblock shaft faded into the darkness until it was just a rough presence around us, a grimy touch that occasionally brushed my shoulder as I bumped down the narrow switchbacks.

"For the love, keep quiet," she hissed. "Clumping like a cow."

I pulled out my cell phone and thumbed the screen twice, creating a ghostly nightlight that gave me enough to see the floor. She was right, my eyes were adjusting, but there was just no light at all here for me to pick up. Finally we got to the bottom of the stairs and exited into the wider, vaulted tunnel where Spleen had first taken me to see Wulf.

"*Great*," Cinnamon said sarcastically. "Doesn't think to mention I'll hafta track through *water*. By the way, could you tattoo my name on my pet jellyfish? Thanks."

"Don't think so," I said, shining the light around. "They only have one outer cell layer."

"*Zactly*," she said.

I stared at her. "That's pretty smart for an illiterate uneducated werecat."

"One of the house weres is a librarian," she said. "She's been sneaking me audiobooks."

"Fast," I said.

"Whatever. You looking for *that*?"

She pointed, and I turned to see the boat. "Yes. We'll take it to the landing where I last saw Wulf—and then you take over."

"Okay, DaKOta," she said, in the same singsong voice, but quieter than normal. She kept looking around the tunnel abruptly, twitching her nose and tail, as if she was hearing things. When I asked, she shrugged it off. "Just night noises. *Fuck!* Let's get this over with."

We boarded the boat, and I rowed us awkwardly out into the tunnels. I'd forgotten how much a maze they were. We had to go through at least half a dozen turns, each tunnel getting smaller and narrower and older. Glowing phosphorescent mold curved over the walls, and occasional runes provided weak light, but it was very difficult to see. Every once in a while a surge of air washed back over us, confusing Cinnamon's nose until she admitted she was completely turned around. I was growing more and more confused myself—my memory of the waymarks Spleen had used grew fuzzier until I started to fear we were lost.

"It's the fucking *House of Leaves* down here," I said, flashing my light into the bottom of the boat like Cinnamon taught me, so the beam wouldn't kill our night vision.

"What?" she asked, eyes tracing over the ancient masonry.

"Sorry," I said. "I doubt that one's coming to audiobook."

"Whatever. This shit supposed to be from the Civil War?" Cinnamon said. "No *ways* they built all this just for the fucking Civil War. It was over in, like, five years—"

"Don't know much about history," I said, "but maybe they built it after that."

"Shit this old?" she said. "You *believes* that?"

"I have no fucking idea," I replied. "I just think we're lost—"

And then the tunnel abruptly widened up, into a vast, dungeonlike vault built from huge, rough-hewn blocks of stone. Only now could I see that Cinnamon was right: No way was this Civil War architecture . . . this was something far older, far more primal. When I'd first seen these runes and waymarks I'd meant to read up on them, but life since I'd taken Wulf's assignment had been so insane I'd had no time—so I still couldn't decipher the marks in the rock around us. All I knew was that the ones painted on it were old . . . and the ones scratched into it, older.

"We met here," I said, pointing to the landing upon which Wulf had stood.

"This is a . . . neutral place," Cinnamon said, flicking her ear. "But not a safe one. You be meeting here, not living here. His den will be somewhere else."

I pulled up to the landing and tied the boat off. "Hopefully in walking distance."

The air surged around us, like the tunnels were taking a breath. It was oddly regular, like we were crawling around the throat of some monster, feeling the rhythm of its lungs.

"*Fuck*," Cinnamon said, looking around wildly. "What is *doin'* that? I mean, fuck! Let's get this over with."

Rough stone steps climbed up from the landing, and we followed them to a high ledge overlooking the docking chamber below. A bare stone corridor tracked off in either direction, but Cinnamon dismissed them with a sniff, taking us into narrow slots perpendicular to the ledge. Here the ancient stonework gave way to merely old brick and well-rusted steel; now it *did* feel like we were working our way through the foundation of some Civil War era structure.

"This is it," she said. "Smells like a den."

"Is he here?" I said. "Wolves are territorial, right? I don't want to barge in—"

"Relax," she said, moving forward cautiously. "I wouldn't take ya into a live den. All the smells are old, and I don't hear nothing, so—"

The air shifted again, hot breath drawn in to the throat of the unseen 'monster' behind us.

"Homina," she said, breathing in deeply. "Does he looks as good as he smells?"

"Better," I said, following her as she picked up the pace.

"How come you gets all the good boyfriends?" she complained, worming her way through the narrow tunnel. "You don't even like 'em!"

"I'm an outgoing, attractive woman with a job that lets me meet a lot of people," I said, "and I do too like boys. I just like girls too."

And then the wind shifted, the hot breath of the monster now wafting towards us.

"Fuck," Cinnamon said, whirling. "I was wrong. He's here."

35. Five Shades From Full

Twin golden eyes glowed in the narrow tunnel behind us, twin golden sparks in the black, silhouetted form of a man. In the gloom you could actually see the light from his eyes reflecting off the ancient masonry, twin rows of vertical lines stretching towards us like golden bars.

"You should not have come here, Dakota," Wulf growled.

Cinnamon and I backed up slowly, stepping out into a pathetic, brick-pillared room, wide and low, littered with old rags and Wendy's boxes. Moments later Wulf emerged between us, standing there in his worn Italian suit, just out of arms' reach.

Then he bulled past us, into the room, and began pacing about. We both relaxed.

"Why are you here?" Wulf snarled, glaring at me out of the corner of his eye.

"You left me no other way to contact you," I said.

"I told you to butt out," he snapped. "Who is she?"

"A friend," I said warily. "She's a good tracker."

"I'm Cinnamon," she said cheerily. Then her ears flattened as he glared at her, and she looked down, avoiding his eyes.

"She's not a wolf," he said, glaring at her. "Why did you bring her?"

"I—I didn't know it was a problem," I said. "No one seemed to care, at the werehouse."

"My beast doesn't know jack about the werehouse," Wulf snarled. "Dakota, I told you to stay away, and here you've brought a morsel into my den at my weakest hour!"

"Then let me do your tattoo," I said. "It will give you more control—"

"It's too late for that," he said. "It will take a week for the tattoo to reach full strength—"

"Then let me do it on myself and transfer it to you," I said, holding up my bare left hand. "Remember my butterfly? Cinnamon, show him."

Wulf stared at my bare wrist, then at Cinnamon's tufted hand, where the design he had seen before now lived. I squeezed my hand and waved it over Cinnamon's wrist, and the sparkle of mana dancing down from my fingers made the butterfly come to life and flap once.

"I don't believe it," Wulf said, in a voice that indicated that yes, he *did* believe.

"I've already tested the procedure out with the other tattoo I was doing, which was a much more complicated design," I said. "Come back with us. I've made the needles and mixed the pigments. Come back to my studio and we'll do the tattoo tonight."

"It's too late for that," he repeated, his eyes glowing an even brighter yellow.

"His wolf is angry," Cinnamon said. "Don't be making eye contact—"

"Come on, Wulf, try, you've got to try," I said, looking at the ground. "It's not even eleven, and the moon won't be right overhead until midnight—"

"Dakota, you fool," he roared. "The moon rises an hour earlier every day. Even now it stands over our heads, five shades short of full!"

Suddenly Wulf snarled, a great rumbling crackle that seemed to ripple through the room. His eyes seemed to flare, twin torches. He hunched low, growling, snarling—then in one spasmodic movement pulled off the coat of his suit and hurled it to the ground.

"Don't run," Cinnamon said. "Whatever you do, stand your ground. Don't run."

But I *couldn't* move. I was mesmerized. Wulf was stripping before me. On some distant level I realized that was a threat, but all my eyes saw were the few tufts of grey in the hair on his tanned, ripped chest, the crisscrossing lines of some ancient tattoo or brand rippling down from that chest over his washboard flat stomach, and his buff arms, muscles bulging and shifting like the skin was packed with croquet balls.

But then the croquet balls began to move, the skin to ripple, his features to shimmer. When my eyes drew back to his face, I saw something hungry and alive peeking out behind those golden eyes, something that had always been there but . . . suppressed. But the beast was not suppressed now. It was awake, aware—and coming out.

"What do we do?" I said desperately. "He's just about popped his cork—"

"*You* stays still," Cinnamon said. "Right now his *man* thinks you're his *giiirl*friend—but if you runs, his *wolf* will think you're prey."

"What about you?" I said.

"*I'll* run," Cinnamon said. "I'll lure him—whoa—"

Wulf snarled and pulled his pants down, kicking them away. Tremors ran down his taut legs, part muscle spasms, part something more. Neither Cinnamon nor I could seem to tear our eyes away from him, from the muscular legs, the dark briefs.

"Yes, run, little one," Wulf snarled, dropping to a squat, one hand touching the ground as the other hooked in to his briefs. Fur began rising on his forearms, and he turned his legs to pull the briefs away as the hair of his chest and abdomen thickened into a full pelt. "Run! Take me away from Dakota before I slay her!"

And then he roared, more like a lion than a wolf, black fur erupting from his arms and spine, sharp cracks sounding like gunshots as the bones of his legs stretched and bent. His thighs and calves shortened as his feet lengthened, turning his ankle in to the backwards 'elbow' of a dog's leg. The bones of his face snapped and popped as a muzzle forced its way outward, and there were horrible ripping sounds as he fell to all fours and thrashed, fur and claw and bone erupting everywhere I could see. A rapid-fire succession of pops sounded as his spine bent and cracked upward. He grew larger, more powerful, and I felt wave after wave of mana wash over me, forcing me back against the wall.

"Don't move, for God's sake, don't move!" Cinnamon hissed. She dropped to a crouch at the entrance of the tunnel, fur rippling out over her own face, claws lengthening, snarling at the behemoth wolf that now stood before her. "Here, doggie, doggie, want a little treat?"

The great wolf snarled and leapt forward, and Cinnamon shot back into the tunnel. I twitched—I couldn't help it—and the wolf stopped, one golden eye fixed on me.

I froze, not making eye contact. The wolf padded up to me, growling, sniffing. It was huge, its shoulder coming well over my hip—and was perhaps the most beautiful animal I'd ever seen. Then it whined, a low, plaintive whine, and shook its head back and forth. It looked up at me, and the golden eyes had gone green and human. The wolf whined again, almost pleading—like Wulf was in there, somewhere, desperately trying to snap out of it.

Suddenly a whistling came from up the tunnel. "Hey, doggie doggie," Cinnamon cried. "Like to go chasing a cat?"

The human eyes vanished into a golden glare and the wolf snarled at me. With a supreme effort I remained still as it whipped away, down into the tunnel, howling and giving chase. Crashing sounds, running feet and clicking claws echoed back up the tunnel, and then the horrible scream of a cat in terror.

"Oh, God," I said, "what have I done?"

36. THE WAITING GAME

Terrified, I screwed up my courage and went after them. By the time I entered the tunnel, the running feet, snarling wolf and screeching cat were long gone. I had no idea what I would do when I found them; maybe there was something I could do with my tattoos? Or perhaps I could coax Wulf back to human—perhaps not with Cinnamon there; she was definitely an *agent provocateur*. But I had to try, damn it. I had to try.

Halfway down the tunnel my coat caught on a root projecting from the wall. I reached down to untangle it, but got only more caught up with the bony protrusion. I looked down, and was shocked by a familiar butterfly, flapping its wings against the black shadow of the "root" that had grabbed me. Shadows and mist clinging to the "root" dissipated like ripples on a pond, leaving Cinnamon standing there, her butterfly-tattooed hand holding me back, her other hand held to her lips as she looked down the tunnel, ears alert, eyes speculative.

"So much for the famed wolf sense of smell," she said.

"Damn, the Marquis is good," I said. Seeing her tattoos 'unhide' her really was like watching *The Predator* decloak. "You tell him that, next time you see him, you hear?"

"Sure," she said, still staring down the tunnel, ears twitching. "Okay, we're clear. Let's go see what we can do back at his place."

"Shouldn't we get the hell out of here?" I whispered, as a howl sounded down the tunnel. "Can't he hear us—"

"Nah, he's sweet on you, and his wolf too," Cinnamon said, heading back to the den. "If he was really after us, he'd be here tearin' us up. I just gave him something to chase to get him goin'— now he's gonna to go try to run himself out. We gots maybe an hour, and then the beast will run out of juice and come back here to change. We should be gone."

I nodded, but she didn't catch it, and looked back to glare at me. "I *means* it. We gotta be gone then, girlfriend or no. You didn't tell me he was a transy."

"A transy?" I said, bewildered. "Wulf is a transsexual?"

"No! He pops his cork on transit," she said, waving her long, tufted fingers over her head. "Most weres turns on the rise, but transies can hold off until zenith—when the full moon gets right overhead."

"The transit of the moon," I said, as we stepped back to the den. "Is it true what he said, that the moon rises an hour earlier every day? I'd never heard of that—"

"Cuz you're not a were," Cinnamon said. "More like forty-five minutes, but yeah. Anyways, the older a transy gets, the stronger their beast gets—and it gets liable to loose when the moon's directly at zenith, completely full or no." Cinnamon looked around, then looked at me. "So what's the plan? Leave your new *boooy*friend a *note* with your *number?*"

"He already knows how to contact me," I said, picking up his fine Italian pants. They were worn, but I could feel how fine the fabric was, could imagine how good it once must have looked on his trim form. "I need a way to make him *use* it."

Cinnamon looked at the coat, then began looking around, examining the pillars around us. "Think this is Civil?" she asked. "Maybe a wall-off or something?"

"I dunno," I said, placing his folded pants and briefs back on his mattress, and turning to get his coat. Maybe leaving him a note wasn't a bad idea. I didn't think he'd take me up on it, but at least I could try. "You don't have any paper on you, do you?"

"Screw that," she said, staring at the ceiling, "I gots an idea. Call Calaphase."

"I don't see how he can help," I said, "and there's no way I'll get a signal—"

"This is a basement," she said, pointing up, "not a cave. We ain't that deep."

I raised an eyebrow, but pulled out my phone. One bar—it was worth a shot. So I dialed. A moment later, a low buzzing sounded in the cellar.

I looked up in shock to see Cinnamon pulling a cell phone from her vest. "Nicked it off him just the other day," she said, grinning, opening the phone and miming a deep, gruff voice. "Hello? Oh hel*loooo*, Dakota! This is Wulfy-wulfy. Oh *yeah*, I'd love to go to the tat studio and get down your pants. I mean, get inked."

"Very funny," I said.

"Yeah, yeah," she said, fiddling with the phone. "Ok, your number's in. Gimme that," she said, taking the coat. She slipped the phone into his jacket pocket. "I don't see a change of, so he's gonna slip this back on—either tonight, or tomorrow. You can call him then."

"I got an even better idea," I said, fishing a receipt out of my wallet. "Why don't we leave him a phone *and* a note just in case he's got more clothes?"

After that, we hightailed it. We didn't hear any howling or any running feet, but the tunnels around us were still breathing, and Cinnamon swore she heard *something* moving in the dark that was neither man nor wolf, so we practically ran down to the landing and shoved off. Once in the water we took it more cautiously, until Cinnamon and I were both certain we were not going to get lost in the maze. When the tunnels started to widen out again and things looked more familiar, I poured a little more effort into the oars, trying to put more distance between us and Wulf's den.

Cinnamon leaned back in the bow, staring over her shoulder at the large vaulted tunnel that meant we were almost out of the water. "That went . . . well, I thinks."

"Thank you," I said. "And now I'm gonna be a big square and tell you to go back to the werehouse. It isn't safe."

"Can't I stay the night?" she whined. "I don't wanna run back to the werehouse in the middle of, 'specially not after I said you would take me for the day."

I scowled. "Okay," I said. "But I'll run you back to the werehouse in the morning, OK? Before anyone adds two and two. I really don't think it's a good idea for you to be AWOL. No joke—if you want them to keep letting you come over, you can't go busting their nuts."

"Yeah, yeah," she said. "You just wants to get rid of me—"

"Not yet," I said, staring at her. "You hungry?"

"Yes," she said, grinning. "What you gots for me?"

"What is it, near midnight?" I said. "You want breakfast or dinner?"

"Moon's fat overhead. I wants *meat*," she said, baring her fangs. They seemed longer, somehow. "Don't care what it's called or when it's s'posed to be served."

"You got your fake ID on ya?" I said.

"Like, duh," she said, grinning. "Don't leave home withouts—"

"Then let me show you a little place called the Vortex—"

And so we went to the Vortex Bar and Grill at one in the morning, stepping through the huge skull that made its front door into the pop-culture chaos of its crowded, kitschy interior, where I introduced Cinnamon to the joys of a bacon-and-cheese bison burger with sweet potato fries. She screwed up her nose at all the smokers— the only reason a burger joint had an over-18 policy, thanks to Atlanta's new smoking ban—but chowed down heartily on rare bison while I munched on a Ragin' Greek turkey-burger-in-pita. Pure heaven.

Cinnamon leaned back again, grinning. "Cain't I stay tomorrow? I want to see you needle Wulf. He gots pretty skin."

"Two people tried to take a chunk out of me," I said, "and somebody actually got Spleen. You may be bulletproof and all—"

"No, I gots it," she said, suddenly sober. She leaned forward, looking around as if someone might listen in. "Somebody's really gots it out for him, don't they?"

"I think so," I said. "I really think so."

She glared down at the remnants of her fries. "Fine," she said. "He hates my guts anyway, 'cuz I'm a cat. Stupid rogue wolves."

Cinnamon stayed the night—sleeping on the sofa—and after picking up some Flying Biscuits I rode her back within striking distance of the werehouse and dropped her off. When I got back to the Rogue Unicorn, I found three missed calls and two messages on my phone, all from 'Calaphase.' In the first message, Wulf cussed me out—at least I think that's what he was doing; it was hard to tell over all the snarling. In the second message, he was more . . . apologetic. After I got settled in the office and had Wulf's flash in front of me, I called him.

"Hey, Wulf," I said. "Sorry about last night."

"No." he said, voice rock solid and clear. "I'm sorry— about. . .well, everything. But it means something that you came all the way to my den. Thank *you*, Dakota. I won't forget it. I had given up—"

"So does that mean I'll get you in my chair today?" I said, cutting him off before we got distracted from the tattooing by another journey into touchy feelie territory.

There was a long pause. "Yes," he said at last. "Yes, I will. How long will it take?"

"Two hours," I said. "I know I said I would do it on me and transfer it to you but . . . I'm not going to start it until you get here. I don't want a werewolf sigil on my body any longer than I absolutely have to." Come to think of it, I should call Jinx about it. I made a note to do so.

"The sun transits a bit after noon," he said. "With it right overhead, we'll have almost the whole earth between us and the moon. I should eat at transit, when the beast is weakest, and then let it settle—that usually keeps him fully at bay a few hours longer. I will come by at one—that gives us four whole hours to moonrise."

"That should be more than enough," I said. "Wulf. You'll be here, right? You know how to get here? You need directions?"

"I know where you work," Wulf said. "I will be there."

But when one o'clock rolled by, Wulf didn't show up. I turned away half a dozen potential clients while waiting for him, but he didn't show up at two, or three, or four. I started calling him at two, but he didn't respond to any of my phone calls. Finally, at five o'clock, with the sun hanging low in the sky, I said fuck it and headed over to the Vortex for another burger.

"I'm right across the street," I told Annesthesia. "He comes here, you call me."

But she didn't call. And he didn't call. And he didn't answer his phone. I went back to the Rogue, but Wulf still didn't show up. I called every number I could think of—Wulf's, Philip's, Buck's. Nothing. I even tried to get Jinx to call the Marquis, but we couldn't figure out a way that he *could* have helped me, even if he was so inclined.

At nine the staff started to trickle out, the Rogue closed up, and I was left pacing in my office, staring at Wulf's flash. Worried. I had given up intellectually, but somehow, I couldn't just get up and go.

It was pushing past ten when my phone buzzed, once—a text message. *Finally.* I slipped it out to read: **«come 2 masq lone»**

I didn't recognize the number. *Go to the Masquerade? At this hour? And it was fucking closed!* I thumbed back: **«Not bloody likely.»**

A moment later, the phone buzzed again: **«time runs out»**

I scowled. I did not need this shit at this hour. **«Who the hell is this, Wulf? *You* need to come *here*!»**

«not wulf»

But who then? Maybe . . . I texted: **«Marquis?»**

«fuck that prissy dog»

Well, they *knew* the Marquis. I texted: **«WHO is this?!»**

There was a long pause. And then: **«i owned u»**

"Oh, *God*," I said. It was *Transomnia*. Oh, hell. Oh, *hell*. I looked at the office phone and thought of calling Calaphase, but then the phone buzzed again, with a picture message. I opened it, and damn near dropped the phone in terror. The tiny screen held Cinnamon's terrified face—

And her bloody mouth was sewn shut with silver wire.

37. GET IT OFF ME

I rode to the Masquerade at just under the speed limit, terrified. I didn't want to get pulled over, not now. Transomnia hadn't given me a deadline, but "time runs out" made his intent pretty damn specific.

One block away I parked my Vespa on a cross street, slipped the keys into its key well and walked, taking the long way round so he wouldn't know where I'd parked it. If I rode it straight up, Transomnia could trash my ride and leave me with no route of escape.

I walked, hugging my vest close, glad for the longsleeved turtleneck that kept out the cold. And then I rounded the corner of North Angler Street and saw City Hall East not a thousand yards away. This was pretty fucking bold. He must be sure he had me.

Well, I was here alone, in the middle of the night, limping and crippled by most definitions, with just my cane. I guess he did have reason to be bold.

I turned the corner. Normally on a Saturday night the Masquerade would be bustling, but now the marquee over the ancient, converted mill read: "**THANKS HOTLANTA—17 GREAT YEARS**." I scowled, grasped at my courage, tried to regain my bravado as I limped round the corner and past the ticket gate. I could do this. I *would* do this.

Two thugs flanked the entrance to the club, one a fat, grinning redneck with a walrus moustache and the other a hard, balding man with glinting eyes.

"Lose the cane, bitch," the balding man said crisply.

"I need it to walk," I said, truthfully, clenching my fists on the cane.

"Lose it or the kid dies," he said, drawing a gun—but not pointing it at me. Curious—he could have left it at 'drop it, bitch' punctuated by a gun barrel, but here he was skipping the direct approach and immediately resorting to leverage. *He has orders not to harm me.* I hoped I could chalk that up to a Transomnia's desire not to disrespect Saffron's collar. I really didn't want to entertain the possibility that Transomina had a desire to preserve the canvas for the tattoo killer, who I really hoped was up in North Carolina getting his ass kicked by Philip.

I dropped the cane and kicked it away, holding my hands up and out placatingly.

"I'll do anything you want," I said, pleading. "Just don't hurt Cinnamon."

"Cinnamon?" Walrus said. "Who's that?"

"That stray cat the fang picked up for his boss, idiot," Baldy said.

The fang's *boss. Oh, hell.* Transomnia was not alone.

"Now hands up," Baldy said, stepping forward, and I raised my hands.

"Hands," Walrus said. "What was that bit the fang went on about painting her tattoos to slow her down?"

"Hell if I know, didn't make any sense to me," Baldy said, eyeing my trembling hands with a mixture of contempt and appreciation. "Not that it matters, fight's gone out of this one—does have nice tattoos, though. I said hands up, girly—"

I closed my eyes and raised my hands higher, pretending to whimper. A boss, a vamp, two thugs, maybe even a driver or a back-door man. I felt Walrus and Baldy closing in on me through a ripple in the mana of my tattoos, and cringed, flinched back, with only one thought:

If I was going to beat Trans, I needed to thin out his support mechanism.

As Walrus's paws closed on my hand, I popped out my other hand and nailed Baldy straight in the face, discharging all the mana I'd stored in the vines hidden beneath the right arm of my turtleneck in a sudden magical POP. Darren might have not let me into his classes yet, but I *had* taken tae kwon do in college. I knew from my time on the mat that even people who could see how tall I was never expected that I had the reach I did. Baldy toppled backward, stone cold, and I twisted my elbow round to block Walrus's punch an instant before it hit me.

"Damnit, bitch, you settle down—" he snarled, hand clamping down on my left. He was immensely strong—hey, he was a guy—but I didn't need testosterone to beat him.

"Big beefy guy like you should have a tattoo," I said, clamping my free hand down on his and twisting it round so I could grab it with my trapped one. "Why not try one of mine?"

And then I let all the mana in my left arm surge into the snake tattoo, which reared to life and hissed at Walrus. He screamed and tried to get away, but I held on as the snake slid off my arm and latched on to his.

Walrus stumbled away, tumbling to the ground. "Get it off me!" he screamed, twisting, doing a passable St. Vitus's dance. All he was doing of course was irritating the hell out of it; you could hear the tattoo hissing and sparking as it coiled over his body, looking for a comfortable home. "Get it off me! Get it off me!"

"Ready to give up?" I said, dropping my vest, pulling off my turtleneck and my sweat pants to reveal a sports bra, short pants— and a hundred magical tattoos.

"—get it off me—get it off me—" Walrus screamed, getting up and stumbling away.

"Crap," I said, watching him go. Apparently my snake wasn't coming back. "I'm going to have to tattoo *another* one."

I heard motion inside the Masquerade, and twisted around sinuously, drawing mana from within my body, concentrating it in my hands, and letting it sparkle across every inch of my tattoos. I prayed this would work; I'd never tried it before. It relied on one very simple thing: magical tattoos aren't just designs. Their meaning depends on the intent of their wearer.

The vines on my body leapt out into the air into a beautiful spiral cloud, and I stretched forth my hands and murmured, "*Spirit of fall: peace, and quiet.*" I could have said anything, but somehow, I knew just what I wanted and just what to say. It was perfect—and a thousand falling maple leaves in a hundred different colors seemed to detach from the vines and blew gently into the entrance, a glowing, quiet wind.

I stared in awe at the magic I'd created. I'd never understood the full extent of my power until that moment. The crucible of the last few days had opened me up to profound sensations, and my new role as Cinnamon's protector added a fierce rush of energy to my fear and

. . . and my *rage*. Suddenly, I commanded a universe of raw emotion, all of it bursting from the visions inked on my skin.

Two men ran out in complete silence, their mouths moving without sound. One drew a gun and raised it at me, and I curled the opposite way, murmuring, "*Spirit of home: safe and sound.*" The vines contracted, the remaining leaves curling around me, and the bullet he fired bounced harmlessly, almost soundlessly, away.

One of the men paused, but the shooter kept running straight at me, raising his gun like a club. I cried, "*Spirit of fire: color and light!*" and the head of the dragon reared up, dousing his face with a rainbow of flame. But I could tell I was running out of juice, so as he fell back, I clenched my fists, concentrated on my back, knelt and said, "*Spirit of air: take to flight!*"

A hawk tattooed onto my back detached itself and flew at the final man, who ran away, screams muffled by the silence spell. The shooter was writhing on the ground, his face a flickering mass of tattooed fire, his cries silenced by the gentle fall of glowing maple leaves. He'd live, but would be sore as hell with some pretty hard-core face tattoos. Walrus was similarly gone—but as I turned, Baldy stood back up, blinking.

I decked him flat, and my knee started to throb.

I left the downed guards outside and stepped into the Masquerade. The lights were out, but I could see pretty clearly. The stairs to Heaven were blocked off with boards and the door to Hell was locked, but Purgatory was open. As I moved out of the range of the dissipating silence spell, I started to hear the world around me again. Then a deep, resonant voice spoke, closer than I expected, and I ducked down.

"Show me," the voice commanded.

"Let's save it, at least until the guards bring her in," a petulant, higher-pitched voice responded. "After all, I prefer to work with an audience—"

"Stop balking," the voice said. "Show me what you mean by 'creative.'"

"You don't get it, do you," the petulant voice said. "Sure, you've got the guts to strip off a bit of skin of someone you've killed—"

"I *must* work on the living," the deep voice said. "The magic will not work otherwise—"

They were at the far end, at the little dance area past the DJ stand. I crouched low, trying to worm my way along the right wall to the bar, to get closer. There were piled boxes and glasses at the end of the bar; slowly I raised my head up, to get a better view. There was a rough table, a steaming black kettle, and—

Transomnia, holding the pruners in one hand—and Cinnamon aloft in another.

___

38. GLOVES OF LIQUID FIRE

"Sure, you work on the living, but you never make it last," Transomnia said. He'd upgraded his coat to a long, black Hellraiser affair. In one hand he effortlessly held Cinnamon, whimpering and bleeding, arms bound behind her with silvery barbed wire. In the other, he held the pruners, twitching, snipping the air with them. "You've got guts. But no strategy."

"You're stalling," the other figure said, a shorter, hooded figure in an ornate brocaded robe whose face was completely hidden from view. "You don't have the will to—"

"Maybe you don't know me as well as you think," Transomnia said. "You're an expert at sacrifice, but you don't know the first thing about torture. Punching, slapping, bruising—fine for foreplay. But snipping— you can't take it back."

"We're going to kill them," the robed monk said. "We need hold *nothing* back."

I gathered my power into the yin-yangs. If I could hit him hard enough with a burst of lightning, it might knock Cinnamon from his hands and give me a chance to save her.

"If you're gonna kill them, fine, you can do things you can't take back, but for hostages—you *save* that," Transomnia said. "If you keep the hostages unspoiled, it leaves you free to say: 'That's far enough, Dakota.'"

I froze. The hooded figure looked around sharply, and Transomnia grinned widely, showing his long, sharp teeth as he raised the pruners and pointed straight at me. The hooded figure looked over in shock, but I stayed frozen behind the bar . . . until Transomnia drew the pruners back aside and pointed in front of the two of them in invitation.

"Now, Dakota," Transomnia said, "or I show you both what I mean by 'creative.'"

I stepped out to the end of the bar. Nothing now stood between them and me but the table, and the steaming kettle of black fluid . . . sitting atop a tin of canned heat.

The hooded figure shifted slightly. "Are those the last whispers of a *silence* spell, Miss Frost?" he said, extending his hand in a slow movement through the air. "And fire? *And* a bird-of-prey projectia?" He rubbed his fingers together, as if he could feel the very texture of the mana in the air. "I am impressed. You have exceeded my expectations."

"Well," Transomnia said. "I can't say the same for my rent-a-thugs."

"I *told* you to warn them about her magic," the hooded figure hissed.

"I *did*. Perhaps they didn't believe me, or perhaps they thought she would have more sense than to risk a hostage," Transomnia said, glancing at Cinnamon. She *mmmm'd* and kicked, and Transomnia shook her once, a sharp snap that flicked her head back and forth and made her body go limp. "Did you kill them?"

"No," I said. "They're all still alive. I just ran them off—"

"*Damnit*, if you were going to fight you could have at *least* done us the courtesy of killing them," Transomnia snarled, fangs flashing. "Now *I'll* have to run them to ground. I *hate* tying up loose ends—speaking of which, step up to the table, Dakota."

He pointed to the table with the shears, but I stood frozen.

"Ever smashed a cat's brains out against the wall?" he said, giving Cinnamon another shake. "Like salsa made from steamed cauliflower and cranberry sauce—"

I swallowed. Cinnamon *claimed* she could soak up bullets; but you could *kill* a were by cutting off her head, so there was no way letting him slam her brains out could be good. I stepped forward to the table, scowling. "Hurt her, and I'll—"

"Now, now, Dakota, as a tattooist you know the importance of proper hygiene," he said, pointing at the kettle. "Why don't you wash your hands before we get started? Dunk them deep—we wouldn't want you to miss a spot."

I stared into the huge kettle, swallowing. It was filled with something black, hot and steaming, running down over the edges of the vessel in dripping, frozen streamers. Some kind of disgusting potion? I looked back at him, and he raised the clippers to her ear—then her eye.

"It's only getting hotter," he said. "And my imagination is just running wild—"

I thrust my hands deeply into the kettle.

Like gloves made of liquid fire: I screamed, jerking backward, pulling back hands and forearms dripping with black, scalding pitch. The sticky goop coated my hands like paint, like glue, cooling and drying so fast that half my fingers were already stuck together. With effort I forced my left hand opened, seeing no marks, no skin, only black sticky goo.

"You—you bastard," I said, shaking. "I'll—"

"Do nothing," he said, pocketing the clippers and pulling out a syringe filled with a clear liquid. I cried out and tried to lunge around the table, but he slid it into Cinnamon's arm with practiced ease and emptied it into her bloodstream. "And neither will she. Just a little medicine to help her sleep, and some silver nitrate to help it along—"

"You bastard," I said, shaking.

"So you said," Transomnia said, slapping Cinnamon's head back and forth with his free hand, watching her sag until her head lolled with each blow. "But keep standing right there, or I'll exercise my imagination."

"Why should we need to do that?" the hooded figure said, with a touch of amusement. "Let's get straight to why I came here—to see the goods. Strip, Miss Frost, and let's see what you've got that I can add to my collection."

Oh, God. Exactly as I'd feared: the robed monk was the tattoo killer.

"You're the third person to tell me to strip in as many days," I said, shaking. "Go to hell."

The killer snorted. "Strip, or we start with the stray—"

"No, no, she's right," Transomnia said, tossing Cinnamon aside like an old gym bag. "There's no need for you to do that, Dakota. After all, it's something I'd prefer to do myself."

The table and vat flew aside as Transomnia leapt on me with blinding speed, and then threw a punch straight into my face.

39. ROUND THREE

When I was a child I used to play on an old squad car my dad kept in the back yard. I think he meant to fix it up and get it running again, but my dad was always more interested in police work than puttering, and so the car just sat there and rusted—until the day, when playing atop it with Savannah and Jinx, I tripped over the light bar and fell backwards off the car.

I thudded solidly on my back, vision erupting in a bright flash of light, all the air whooshing out of my lungs at once. I never lost consciousness, but scrambled immediately to my feet, gasping, unable to speak, unable to breathe, while my mother screamed at my father "Get that damn rust-trap out of here!" When I was older I realized I had bruised my diaphragm, but at the time all I could think of was the pain and being unable to breathe.

That's what it felt like when Transomnia threw me through the door into Hell.

There was the same thudding impact, accented by the sound of splintering wood. The same flash of light accented by a tremendous vertigo. And the same whoosh of air out of my lungs, accented by a dizzying pain spreading over my back. I stumbled away from the door, gasping, away from Transomnia, until I hit the rail around the sunken the dance floor and pitched over. I fell flat on my back again, gasping uselessly like a beached fish for air, but no air came.

Transomnia stepped up to the rail and looked down at me, elegant and cruel in his long black coat. "Oh, come now, Dakota," he said, hopping up onto the rail. "After your performance outside I'd hoped you'd have more fight left in you."

I rolled aside as he dropped, stumbling to my feet, stumbling away—but he whipped round me, vampire fast, grabbed my pitch-covered wrist, and pulled it up behind my back.

"Now, now," he breathed into my ear, wrenching my arm painfully, "see how much trouble little girls get into when they don't do as they're told?"

"F-k," I gasped, "F-k hyu."

"Now, now," he said, even more patronizingly. "We both know I'm not supposed to do that—but if I were, I'd need to get rid of this, wouldn't I?"

And he hooked one clawlike finger into the back of my sportsbra.

"*Shine, solar radiance!*" cried a triumphant voice, and white-hot light burned across the dancefloor of Hell. Transomnia cringed and screamed, dropping me, and I fell back to see Jinx, guided by Alex, standing at the entrance of Hell. He carried a sword dipped in fire, and she held her spirit cane raised high in the air, its tip blazing with the brilliance of a miniature sun.

Transomnia scuttled sideways onto the handicapped ramp and sprinted up towards them, ducking low to use its wall as a shield from Jinx's light. Alex whipped his fire sword round and sent a bolt of multicolored flame down the ramp. Transomnia dodged, leaping up into the upper VIP section in a crash of tables and chairs.

Alex advanced towards him, swinging the sword to bathe Transomnia in flames, but the vampire picked a table up like a shield and the wave of flame boiled away into the air. Alex struck again, but Transomnia rushed him through the fire, tackling him with the table and knocking him past Jinx, all the way back down the stairs onto the dance floor.

Jinx stood there frozen, head canted, listening. I croaked and tried to warn her—but Transomnia just grinned back at me, and advanced.

Jinx abruptly swung her cane backwards in a full arc, sweeping into the table with a crack of thunder. The table burst asunder into a thousand splinters and Transomnia flew all the way across the dance floor and to the opposite raised bar, shattering the back glass and slumping behind the counter. Jinx smiled, tilting her head, feeling for me.

"Dakota?" she said, twisting her cane until it brightened like a sun again.

"Beh—*behind you,*" I croaked.

The dark hooded figure I had seen in Purgatory stepped up behind her and stretched forth his hand, and simply said: "*See.*"

Jinx screamed and held her hand in front of her eyes, tossing her cane away as if blinded by its light. She whirled, and the hooded figure stretched out his arm and clotheslined her, and she fell back to the ground in a little heap.

I tried to get to my feet, as the hooded figure stepped to the rail.

"Let's simplify this problem," he said, stretching forth his hand. "*Sleep.*"

40. SACRIFICIAL LAMB

Icy cold water splashed over me, and I screamed, bucking. I was awake, cold, and in pain, hunched over in a kneeling position, my head pressed to a stone surface before me. I tried to sit up, and found my hands bound together with wire, fixed tight to a steel ring set into the stone . My legs pulled apart by something similarly tight and sharp. And as the water ran down over me, I realized in utter terror that but for my steel collar, I was completely naked.

"Oh, God," I said, looking up to see a box covered in tattooed skin.

I was on the main stage of Hell, tied to a flat stone disk. I'd never seen it at the Masquerade before; it was new. Before me, the dark hooded figure stood, vigilant, one hand resting on the box, that horrible box covered with tattoos ripped from their owners. His other hand held a silver knife. Beside him Transomnia stood, glowering, a little worse for wear but angry and alert, holding the pruners.

"Oh, God," I said. I cringed, and my terror intensified as I realized they could *rape* me in this hunched-over position. Then I looked again at the box, and I realized the real reason I was tied like this was probably to harvest the Dragon from my back. "Oh, *God*—"

"Shut up," the hooded figure said.

"Let her whine," Transomnia said. "I figure her friends ain't done—"

"Good," the hooded one said. "I'm counting on it."

Transomnia's eyes narrowed. "Are you now?"

"Yes," the figure boomed. "Though, you'd think they'd've come all at once."

My eyes caught a bit of movement, and—Oh, Lord—over to my right I could see Jinx and Cinnamon, hanging in the air, back to back, bodies making a cruel butterfly as they slumped away from the bloody nest of barbed wire that bound their arms and feet behind them. As they turned midair I saw they hung from a meathook dug into the wire. Saw blood dripping out of the barbs. Saw the drops fall onto Alex Nicholson, similarly trussed on the floor at their feet.

Oh, Lord. What had I gotten them all into? When I'd messaged Jinx, telling her what I was doing and to come get me if I didn't call back in an hour, I'd assumed she would call the cavalry—not come herself and get killed.

"Or that at least *one* of them would have called the police," Transomnia said thoughtfully. His eyes fell on me, and I cringed against the plate. "I was surprised *you* didn't call the police, Dakota. You were a *good* girl—"

I was going to kill him. Somehow, *somehow*, I was going to *kill* him—

"It wouldn't matter if she had," the dark figure laughed. "I told you, I took care of that. I'd know—but more importantly, I can stop it. Even then, I think my pup's raised enough havoc elsewhere to keep the police busy all night."

"Fair enough," Transomnia said. Suddenly he grinned down at me, and pulled a cell phone out of his pocket—*my* cell phone—and began thumbing through the contacts. "Not one call after I called you, Dakota, a *very* good girl. Is he about back?"

"Almost," the dark figure said, and my stomach lurched. I had a very, very good idea of who he meant, and it was tearing me to pieces. "What do you have in mind?"

"To speed things up," Transomnia said, reaching down and jerking my face up so I faced my phone. "Smile for the camera, Dakota," he said.

"Fuck you," I replied.

"I'll pass, thanks," he said, looking back at the dark figure. "I'd be second in line, after all, and I prefer unspoiled meat."

My eyes widened in terror, and Transomnia took the picture.

"Perfect, perfect," he said, smiling as he hit send. "Just the look I want."

He leaned back and showed the picture to the hooded figure, who nodded.

"You have a great eye," the figure said. "As always, you truly are an artist."

"Thank you," Transomnia said, with a small bow. He winked at me as he bent down, and I looked away again. "Don't fret, little one," he said, reaching down to tousle what was left of my hair, making me flinch, and him giggle. "It will all be over in—"

And then what had been the service door of the Masquerade exploded, showering Hell with shards of corrugated metal and sparks.

"Oh, if only help would arrive!" Transomnia said, grinning. "That was fast—"

"At last," the hooded figure said, reaching out and pulling a staff into his hands with nothing more than the force of his will. "*At last.* He's here."

Lord Buckhead stood in the shattered door in his man-stag form, North Avenue behind him. His huge antlers cut through the upper ridge of the doorway like a hot metal knives as he strode under it. The matching antlers on his staff began to crackle with power, and the feathered skull between them glowed with a warm, green light.

His alien eyes swept over Transomnia, over me, and his brow wrinkled with rage. But then he saw the hooded figure beside me, his eyes widened, his forward charge halted, and his deer's mouth opened. "The Archmage."

The figure beside me tensed slightly, drawing in a breath. I expected some kind of banter, some kind of taunt; but the two figures just stared at each other.

Then Buck snorted and he swaggered into the room. I knew that look. I *owned* that look. It was bravado. Half of me felt flooded with relief that even Lord Buckhead resorted to bravado when facing a serial killer—and the rest of me was batshit terrified.

"You should never have come here," Buckhead's deep voice boomed. He extended his arms, and a small army of coyotes, hawks and smaller creatures began slipping through the door behind him. "I do not permit necromantic rites in my domain."

"*You* don't *permit?*" the 'Archmage' asked. Casually he swept his silver dagger across my right forearm, and I cried out in pain. He jammed the bloody blade into a socket in his staff, just beneath its skull and crossbones, and it began to glow a deep, ominous red. "I'd wager you didn't permit skyscrapers in your domain, but humans built them anyway."

"I do not begrudge the humans their hives," Buckhead said.

"Really? How . . . magnanimous of you," the Archmage said, and I could hear a glimmer of genuine appreciation. Then the glimmer turned to sarcasm. "And wise. One should never begrudge the success of those one is too weak to stop."

Buckhead snorted and stepped forward, onto a design I could now see inscribed on the stage of Hell, and I panicked. "Buckhead," I croaked. "It's a *trap*—"

Transomnia rapped me sharply on the head, but the Archmage pushed him aside. "Give me some distance, lad," he muttered. "For this to work it *must* be one on one—"

"Fear not, Dakota," Buckhead said, striding into the hall with his hunt assembling around him. "Obviously it's a trap. I expected this, and will deal with this pathetic wizard."

"Pathetic?" the Archmage said. His voice, which at first had been cautious even when taunting Buckhead, now became openly mocking. "This from you, *Looord* of the *Hunt*, who once had the mammoth at your beck and call, now reduced to coyotes!"

"They serve," Buckhead said.

"*They serve*," the Archmage said, spreading his arms wide as Buckhead advanced upon him. "See how well they serve—facing my animal, the Wolf!"

A low guttural growl rippled through the room, like the tail end of a clap of thunder, and Buckhead and all his hunt paused.

I raised my head.

Wulf prowled into the room—eyes golden, and muzzle stained with blood.

41. HOUR OF THE WULF

"Oh, no," I moaned, as Wulf entered the room, big as a tiger, teeth stained red, snarling, driving Lord Buckhead's hunt backwards slowly. "It's not true. It isn't true—"

"Of course it's true," the Archmage said genially. "Why do you think he was so keen to have you ink a control charm? He tried so hard to maintain control, so hard, but things kept . . . happening. He didn't know—I didn't let him—but *obviously* he needed more control."

The Archmage rapped his staff against the floor, and dozens of concentric lines of light glowed through Wulf's fur.

"It's a controlling charm," I said. "I thought it was a faded tattoo, but it's just a huge magical mark. You used skin-toned ink to hide it—"

"Pretty damn smart, Dakota," Transomnia snarked.

"No wonder you tried to have me killed," I said. "I'd have pulled it off him the moment I got him in my chair—"

"That you would have," the Archmage said. "I have no doubt. You're *very* powerful—"

The wolf now stood abreast of me, snarling, and Lord Buckhead's hunt began to quail. What few animals could survive in the concrete jungle no longer had the fighting spirit of the wild, and they cowered and fled from the snarling monster before them.

Buckhead had no such limitations, and stepped forward. "Alone or with an army," he said, raising his staff, "I will still defeat you."

"Bold words," the Archmage responded. "Wulfgang . . . eviscerate them."

Wulf advanced, snarling, past me. Nothing human remained. I wanted to cry.

"You didn't lie about your name after all, did you?" I said sadly.

Wulf's eyes flickered sideways—and then he looked at me, and whined. His eyes flicked back to Buckhead, who smoothly relaxed and crossed his arms, averting his eyes, motioning his remaining followers to do the same; thus appeased, Wulf turned back to me, eyes dimming from gold to a warm, glowing green . . . not unlike the glow of Buckhead's staff.

For the briefest moment, I saw the real Wulf inside those eyes, and he leaned forward and licked my cheek.

"Oh, hell, you've tamed him," the Archmage said, and I heard the smooth *shing* of metal on metal. "Well, there's more than one way to skin a cat," he said—and plunged his silver dagger into Wulf's neck.

Wulf yelped like a kicked puppy and flinched aside, and the Archmage twisted the dagger out in a spray of blood that went over me, Transomnia, everybody.

"No, no, no—" I cried, but Wulf went down, collapsing to the side, whimpering, as the Archmage jammed his dagger back into his staff, making it blaze with evil red light.

"Fuck, boss," Transomnia said, laughing. "You're cold—"

"He was at the end of his useful life," the Archmage said. "But that stray you picked up is young, strong, smart—and pretty. Perhaps I should make *her* my new slave—"

"*Not* in my domain," Buckhead growled. Electricity danced between the antlers of his staff like blue fire, and he thrust the staff at the Archmage and roared a mystic phrase that crackled with power: "*Ot'iyagleya cicastaka!*"

Lightning leapt from Buckhead's staff, born in blazing fire between its prongs and striking the grille of the Archmage's fasces. Sparks and arcing bolts danced around the chamber, throwing Transomnia to his knees and forcing the Archmage backwards on the dais. But just when it looked like the old wizard was about to crumble, he thrust the staff upwards in the air and roared, "*By Ba'alat of Gebal, fall at the feet of your lord!*"

The Archmage rammed the staff down into a socket in the central design, completing a circuit between the floor and horns of the altar. With a thunderclap his staff released all its mana, burning my skin like fire, knocking Transomnia flat to the floor . . . and piercing Lord Buckhead through the heart.

"NO!" I screamed. But Buck just slumped to the floor, his staff falling to the ground with an impotent, hollow clatter like any old piece of wood.

"Like bugs drawn to the light," the Archmage said, cloak thrown back by the force of the blaze. "All too easy."

Skin crackling with fire, crying with pain and loss, I twisted forward and craned my head up, at last seeing the face of the wizard behind this all.

My heart stopped.

It was Christopher Valentine.

42. UNVEILED, THE ARCHMAGE

"And to think, when I began stamping out rivals, it involved months or years of painstaking work—detecting, divining, even the odious art of *dowsing*," the Mysterious Mirabilus said to the unconscious crowd, spinning the bronze-handled, triangular-bladed silver dagger in his hand with a broad, disarming grin. "But in this 'modern' age all I need do is divine the right city, scan the yellow pages for likely practitioners, lay out a few bodies and—BAM!"

The dagger stabbed home into the altar right in front of my bound hands, and I jerked back. My hands didn't move, and I slouched back against the altar, sheltering my head between my forward-stretched arms, trying anything I could to get away from that knife—perilously aware this thrust my exposed backside into the air.

"All too easy," Mirabilus repeated, hand resting on the dagger. After a moment of silence, I glanced up cautiously and found him staring down at me. Nothing of the kindly old grandfather remained; all that was left beneath his black, pointed eyebrows were two merciless chips of ice. I was too terrified to speak.

Almost.

"Why are you doing this to us?" I whispered.

"I have always been forthcoming about my goal," he said, his genial tone belied by the cruelty in his eyes. " 'The one and only.' I am to become in truth what I claim on the stage—the last of the magicians, the last and greatest mind to look out on the world with the same eyes as those first wizards who began to see the world with greater eyes at the dawn of man."

"For the love of God—"

"Spare me this *idolatry*," Mirabilus said, jerking the dagger loose, spinning the altar so the world whirled around and stopping it short with a cold, clammy hand slapped on my thigh.

"Oh, God," I said, squeezing my knees together, throwing my head between my elbows and pressing myself as close as I could to the cold stone. This . . . *disgusting* old man was going to *rape* me before I died. "Oh, *Jesus*—"

"*Enough*," he said, and the dagger embedded itself again into the altar with a sudden ring, wobbling back and forth, slapping itself against my buttocks a few times before finally coming to rest, not touching me in any way—except I could still feel it there, a ghostly echo of cold silver and the cool smooth bumps of the jeweled guard hovering there, a ghostly threat hovering beyond sight or reach. "Do not speak the name of that Hebrew *fuck* again. I don't want to hear it—especially not from you. Not from a skindancer. We are the priests of Ba'al Shaman, the children of Ba'alat, you and I; keepers of the secret art, masters of the hidden flame—"

"Oh, G-," I began, and choked it off. I didn't want him to start using the dagger now. I didn't want him to start using it at all. There had to be, *had to be* something I could do. And then I realized: what the hell was he doing walking around after taking that bullet?

"Y-you were shot," I stammered. "You faked it. H-how did you—"

"Stalling for time by asking me how I do my tricks? Dakota, Dakota. For shame. You might as well ask how I pulled off the Dueling Mirabiluses," he said. He smiled at me, then began miming sarcastically: " 'Did he use a *double*?' 'Maybe he's *twins*?' 'Or maybe *triplets*?' 'Is it a hidden *projector*?' *Bah!* What an endless parade of fools."

He stepped back, holding his arms wide, and two shimmering copies of himself appeared where he opened his hands. "You know the truth, Dakota. Magic is *real*, and I know how to use it. How did I survive the Masquerade? I was never *on* the stage of the Masquerade—not before tonight. I created those *projectia* without ever leaving my dressing room!"

"But . . . but . . ." I said, now *really* stalling for time. Wait—his image had gone to the hospital. "But the doctors examined you! They did bloodwork, took X-rays—"

"I could say that I'm just that good," Mirabilus said, "but why lie to you, Dakota? You're in the club. I did a simple switcheroo: I let the projectia get shot, then took its place in the ambulance. A pair of stab wounds, a little more magic, and, voilà, a simulated gunshot. Didn't you hear when the X-rays came back? 'Miraculously', the bullet missed bone. It didn't hurt the illusion that those damn clods infected me with a very real bug."

And that was it. I was out of options. I looked around desperately. My friends were laid out around me like ninepins, and Transomnia was at the entrance Buck had blasted, nailing sheets of plywood over it to hide the interior of the Masquerade from the street. Maybe Doug knew where we were, if Jinx had told him—but supposedly he couldn't tell the police without Mirabilus knowing. We were fucked.

"Oh, please feel free to ask me something else," Mirabilus said, checking his watch. "I've lugged this altar across five continents. I've had many, *many* women on its surface. And I know stalling for time. But it's useless. The full moon is *hours* off yet, and I'm not yet peaked enough to sample your goods—"

I cringed on the platform, pressing my forehead to my bound hands. Oh, Jesus. Oh, *Jesus*. The creepy old geezer *was* going to rape me before stripping the skin from my body. I was fucked. Or was about to be. Oh, God—

And I looked aside for any help, saw Jinx and Cinnamon hanging from a hook, saw Alex and Buck laid unmoving—and then I saw that Wulf still breathed.

"Look. I . . . I know you want my tattoos, and maybe Cinnamon's too, if you decide not to turn her," I said. Mirabilus said nothing, so I cautiously continued. "And I know how you feel about the magicians. I won't get in the way of you eliminating your rivals—"

"Won't?" Mirabilus said curiously, putting his hand on my buttocks. "Or can't?"

I cringed again, but continued. "But you don't need to let Wulf die." I cried. "His marks are too old to harvest. He's not a magician at all. He doesn't even know what you've done to him. He served you well, even if he didn't know it. How could he possibly be a threat?"

"Wulfgang? That old Nazi bastard?" Valentine laughed. "He's no threat at all. In fact he was my favorite stalking horse—all I needed to do was plant a suggestion about a 'cure' for his 'curse', and steer him towards my target. Normally he'd dig up one or two practitioners, but this time he struck gold, I have to say. At last, he's helped me draw out my true rival."

I looked over at Buck. *I'd* drawn him into this. "Oh no. Not Buck—"

"Oh, no, not him, my dear. And not Alex or Jinx either. They're all just wankers," Valentine said. "Even Buckhead, prize that he is, is in the end a pathetic old fool, a fading wannabe-god who never learned anything. None of them, not a one, know the Art."

He shrugged off his cloak, exposing a barrel chest covered in intricate tattoos.

"My true rival, my dear, is you."

43. SKINNING THE DANCER

"Tattooing is the only *true* magical art," Mirabilus said, spreading his arms wide, showing off a hundred, a thousand detailed tattoos, each a hyperintricate knot of runes and sigils I would have been proud to have inked—had they not been woven throughout with scars and brands and symbols of pain and death. "Tarot readings, onmyoji mystics, hexes—all nonsense. Ley lines, sacrifices, potions— mere dabbling. Only necromancers come close to the true nature of magic; their every spell is powered by the spilt blood of a living thing. But do they recognize the source of their power? No—they let all that magic bleed out into the air, catching only a whiff to make some dead thing dance like a marionette."

"Only the Art truly understands the true source of all magic: life." He shrugged his shoulders, and his tattoos seemed to glow to life, coming off his body in a haze of psychedelic color. "All the inks and powders and designs and rituals are just a way of focusing the power that is life. Understand that, and you can do anything."

"From the olden days, the Hebrews tried to stamp us out," he said, raising his voice. "They knew what we could do and murdered us, overturned our stones, defiled our altars. We had to go underground, practice our rites in secret—"

"Baal," I said. "You're *literally* a priest of Baal—"

"Close enough," Mirabilus said, bowing slightly. "You know enough to recognize the words, but have forgotten what they mean. Should I . . . introduce you to the rites of Ba'alat Gebal before I take my prize?"

Something about his tone made my skin crawl—*fuck that.* "I *knew* I saw something Middle Eastern in your skin tone," I said. "You're a descendant of priests of Baal who escaped persecution by pretending to be Jews. You threw me off with that '*Christopher Saint Valentine's Day*' stage name, but I'm sure of it now—what did your family do, switch to pretending to be Christian once the Jews were the ones being persecuted?"

Mirabilus was silent for a moment, then laughed bitterly. "Wrong, but close enough—the Inheritance of Byblos *has* taken many guises over the millennia. You know, the rites of Ba'lat would make this easier on you. Call it professional courtesy for a fellow priest—"

"*Fuck that*," I said, this time aloud. "I'm no priest of Baal or of anything else. I don't believe in any of that hocus pocus—but I was brought up a Christian and if I have to choose I'll go out with Jesus. *Fuck Baal.*"

"Now, now," Mirabilus said, "you'll make me change the order—"

"If you were planning to rape me *after* ripping open my back," I said, "I'd prefer you switched the order." Though I couldn't imagine *any* order of those things that I'd prefer.

"I *will* kill you tonight," Mirabilus said icily, pulling out the dagger and drawing it over the skin of his arm without a flinch. The dagger's pommel began to glow red. "I will link my life with yours with the Art of Ink and Life, drain your power and add it to my own. It will be done now as in centuries past by the Children of the Ba'alat of Gebal."

I swallowed, clenching my hands tightly. I could feel the mana building in my hands, but underneath the stinging pitch it had nowhere to go and the skin of my hands got hotter and hotter until it felt like it was burning fire.

"Oh, please, Dakota, build up the mana in the vessels on your hands until they burst," he said, laughing—and something tickled the back of my mind. "It will only make my job easier, the flow faster. I will kill you, tonight, and then Buckhead, and Jinx, and then Alex—a pity for him, he had such potential."

But I was ignoring him now, concentrating. *Build up the mana in the vessels of your hands until they burst.* What was wrong about how he said that?

"Sorry I'm late," Transomnia said, hopping up to the podium nimbly and tossing down a hammer with a kind of glee. "Anything left for me, old man?"

And then it hit me. He'd hadn't said *the vessels **in** your hands,* but **on** *your hands.*

"You can have *all* the blood," Mirabilus said, grinning. "I just want the skin."

Vessel was an old skindancer word for *magical capacitor.* He didn't mean my blood vessels—he was talking about the magical marks on my palms and knuckles. The word was *old,* falling out of use in the 1800's, used now only by faux-ancients like Wiccans . . . and true ancients like Mirabilus. If I was right about his use of such an old word, Mirabilus had extended his life a century or more with his life-draining tricks—and maybe, just maybe, he was like the Marquis, trapped in a prescientific view that saw magical tattoos as mystical lenses, projecting mana from living bodies into the air through their two-dimensional designs.

In that view, my hands were the biggest threat: with their flexible skin, they were my quickest source of power, whereas any other skindancing movement would be slower, giving him more than enough time to stab me in the back. With my hands coated with goo, all that power could do was burn out my skin, like black paper thrown over a light bulb.

But reality was more complicated: the line between air and skin, skin and flesh was blurry; each had its own capacity to carry mana—but a difference of degree, rather than kind. After all, a cell phone is just like a land line—once you realize *the air* can act like a wire.

I could *use* that coating of pitch, project the power of my tattoos inward, make my body like the air, to hold that power and release it. It might damn near kill me—but with the magic hidden away behind my skin, Mirabilus would never see it coming.

I had a chance, if I could only find a distraction.

"Every drop of blood in her body," Transomnia said, breathing heavily. "Oh, yessss, juice of the forbidden fruit. I will enjoy defying the Lady Saffron again."

But . . . he hadn't *defied* Savannah before. He had practically been a rules lawyer, skirting what harm he could do to me without defying her ban. I twisted my neck to look at him, and he raised an eyebrow, eyes trying to communicate . . . something. He *knew* what he was saying was wrong. *What the hell? What was I missing?*

My eyes widened as I remembered it had been awfully easy to get in here—and yet Transomnia knew exactly how to shut me down. He just hadn't told his guards.

"Maybe I'll make Jinx my apertif before I feast on you, Dakota," he hissed, leaning down close, his desperate face in opposition to his words; but when he leaned back where Mirabilus could see him, he was practically leering in hunger. "And Alex will make a nice palate cleanser before I have Buckhead for dessert—"

I writhed and squeezed my hands. The mana built up in them and fed back, burning my skin, sinking into my body, like I'd drunk an entire pot of hot coffee. I could feel the tingling start, rippling down my insides—but held on to the power, held onto it tight.

"*Please* burn out your hands trying to awaken your marks," Mirabilus said, raising his dagger. "I'll drink in your power until not a scrap is left—"

Transomnia stepped up behind Mirabilus for a better view, leaning in, winking at him, leering down at me, making me duck and flinch. Mirabilus glared and Transomnia stepped back, hands raised in mock surrender. But the moment the wizard's face turned away, he caught my eye and raised his finger to his lips . . . and showed me the pruners.

I looked away in terror. What new horror was this? But his face had shifted from eager leering sycophant to . . . something else, just for a second. Mirabilus stepped forward, to the edge of the platform, and placed his clammy geezer hand on my bare backside. I looked back one last time, and saw Transomnia raise the pruners high behind Mirabilus's head.

"Whatever you're going to do, do it now, Dakota," he said.

And rammed the pruners down with vampire speed.

Mirabilus whirled, crying out in pain as the pruners stabbed into his collarbone. Faster than a vampire, stronger than a werewolf, his fist popped out and clocked Transomnia under the chin; Transomnia staggered back, but pulled with his right hand on the pruners, making Mirabilus scream as they ripped free. Mirabilus shook the pain off, shifted his shoulders and chest, and his tattoos blazed to life.

Transomnia tumbled backwards, screaming as Mirabilus poured all his power out into the air. Snakes snapped at him, bees stung him, and spiders whirled around him, twining his legs so he tumbled backwards off the stage. But somehow, despite all the power, all the artistry, even with the magic flying through the air, there was something *off* about Mirabilus' designs . . . something flat, and two dimensional.

Mirabilus *was* an old school magician. He *had* thought
Transomnia had taken my weapons away by coating my 'vessels' with
pitch to keep the magic from leaking out into the air and awakening
my marks. But that theory of magic was over a hundred years out of
date. I, on the other hand, was an Edgeworlder. We experiment, not
inherit; and I knew from the burning in my gut that what we'd
learned was true: as mana was concerned, the flesh of the body was
just another kind of air—except it could hold a thousand times more
mana.

I ignored the sounds of Transomnia's screams, and drew in one
painful breath. Then I let it out slowly, sinuously rippling my back,
pouring every ounce of mana I had into the Dragon.

The pain of so much mana was incredible as it reverberated
through my body and streamed out of my skin. I screamed. I
squeezed my eyes shut as my vision exploded into white light. Then
the light faded, slowly—and suddenly I saw through new eyes.

The world before me was sharp, but its colors distorted, my
point of view rising through a stream of colors and flame.. My new
eyes looked down, and I could see my own trembling body, could
watch as the glittering scales and rippling form of my finest tattoo
glowed, detached from my skin and came to life. I saw through the
eyes of the Dragon, rearing over a shocked Mirabilus in a fully
dimensional tower of color and flame.

"*Spirit of fire,*" I whispered. "*Show him the light!*"

The Dragon unleashed a torrent of fire upon Mirabilus,
blackening and burning his body. His tattoos seared and dissolved,
leaking mana in fitful incoherent sparks, and he fell backward with a
tortured scream. Then the Dragon reared back and pounced upon
him, jaws snapping down upon his neck as its long, segmented tail
detached from me.

My link to the Dragon severed abruptly, and I opened my own
eyes to see its curling form, rippling and alive—and savaging
Mirabilus. With each bite it seemed to grow more real and strong,
until it stopped and looked back at me, fully opaque, all aglow in
glittering coils and sparking blue eyes. Then it raised its wings,
screeched, and shot upwards, exploding through the ceiling of Hell,
disappearing into the darkness.

Valentine twisted, moaned, raised one weak, bloody hand after
the Dragon. Then he collapsed and was still, mana streaming slowly
out of his ruined tattoos like slow rainbow fire.

"Finally," Transomnia said, clambering back up onto the stage, burnt, singed, but still standing. "*Free* of you, you sick fuck."

He stared down at Valentine's body for a long, long time. Then he looked up abruptly at me, and I flinched. I had nothing left. No way to defend myself. If he decided to come after me—and then his hand came out of his pocket, holding the pruners.

"Oh, God," I said, ducking my head back down to the dais. "Oh, *God*—"

"Oh, quit whining," Transomnia said, strolling around me, cutting the wires on my wrists, then pulling me up to a sitting position. "But we're not done."

He strolled off casually, and I just sat there, propping myself up with one hand, covering myself with another, ankles still pulled apart by the wires. He returned with a rag and grabbed my right hand and began wiping it off roughly. I sat there, trembling, letting him do it, until he finally gave up in disgust and released my only slightly less grimy hand.

"That will have to do," he said, opening his shirt. "Now get this fucking thing off me!"

My eyes widened. There was an elaborate knot tattooed on Transomnia's chest—a bat, practically turned inside out inside an elaborate design pulling at it with fishhooks. It was a controlling charm, from the looks of it precisely the same kind inked on Wulf—Transomnia had been just as much a pawn as he had.

I gathered my strength and reached out with my cleaned hand. At first I felt nothing; then I caught the edge of the mana, began flexing my fingers, and drew the magic out into the air. The bat squealed and squeaked as its prison dissolved. The fishhooks of the design came loose and flailed in the air. But I didn't let them get a grip on anything, and soon the whole design dissolved into sparks, leaving nothing but a faint ghost of an impression on his chest.

"*Thank* you," Transomnia said, buttoning his shirt, somehow taller, more businesslike. He popped the wires on my ankles, left, right, and I gratefully pulled my feet together and huddled in a mound on the dais. Transomnia calmly walked away and stood over Valentine's corpse—and began kicking it, grievously, brutally, methodically, each time releasing a flash of magic and color as his body flipped and skittered across the floor.

"No draining. No maiming. No raping. No killing. Those were the *rules!*" Transomnia said, staring down at Valentine's bloodied corpse with pure contempt. He looked straight back at me, and I twitched back a bit, trying to cover myself. "Consider ourselves even."

"Even steven," I said, trembling, naked but for Savannah's collar, sitting here before a vampire who had almost beaten me to death . . . and who had now saved my life. I slipped slowly backwards off the dais, still trembling. I didn't know if my legs would hold me, but somehow they did.

Transomnia smiled evilly, then threw the pruners down, embedding them in the floor between my feet. I flinched, but stayed where I was. Then he turned to go . . . and paused a moment, scowling. Finally he turned back to me. I flinched again, but didn't try to get away—and I stood my ground before him, damn it, I stood.

And then Transomnia took off his coat, and slipped it on my shoulders.

"I hate your guts, bitch," he said, "but you need this more than me."

"Thanks," I said, drawing it about me. "For saving my life."

Transomnia roughly nodded. "I needed your help, too."

"Then why didn't you just *ask?*" I shouted, waving my hand at the carnage around us. I couldn't keep it in anymore. "Why did you put us through all this—"

"Because I *had to,*" Transomnia snarled. "You saw the design. Mirabilus would have known the instant I turned hostile. I had to play my cards *very* carefully—"

"You *let* me beat your guards," I said, in sudden realization. "You told them what to do, but not clearly enough for them to take me seriously."

"That gamble paid off," Transomnia said. "But Mirabilus would have dismissed the rent-a-thugs from the ceremonial chamber anyway—it's better to have no witnesses to the deed, since even Wulf and I couldn't always tie up *every* loose end. It was always going to be just you, me, and Mirabilus—but the history of our little tussles made it *appropriate* to express hostility in his presence." He smiled grimly. "For that . . . I thank you, Dakota."

"Why did you let him tattoo you in the first place? Did you think he could protect you from Saffron?" I asked—and then I stopped, working out the timing in my head. "No . . . not even vampires heal that fast. That had to be an *old* tattoo—"

"So old," Transomnia said, "I barely remember why the deal made sense at the time."

"You're his advance man," I said. "You roll into town, sniff out the lay of the land—"

"And then help him take out his rivals," Transomnia said. His eyes were burning on me, not hate exactly, but . . . rage? "But this time, it was supposed to be different. This time, I was going to find someone to protect me, a vampire whose aura was strong enough to bind myself to, someone whose power could shield me from Mirabilus' control. I found Calaphase of the Oakdale Clan—and then you went and fucked it up. They kicked me out because of you—"

"—and drove you right back into his arms," I said. "I'm sorry. I didn't know—"

"You couldn't have," Transomnia said, still glaring at me. "How could you know all this would happen, just from one little punch? But remember: *you* picked that fight. I was doing my duty, trying to scare you off—but *I never touched you that first night.*"

My eyes widened. His stayed on me, burning with anger and expectation. Surely the vampire who nearly took two of my fingers wasn't waiting for . . . an *apology?*

"I'm sorry," I said at last. "Sorry . . . that I hit you."

"Finally," Transomnia said, leaning back. "And I'm sorry that led to all this—but it is over, and as far as I am concerned, we are *even*— and *done.* I'm not going to come after you, you're not going to come after me—we leave each other the hell alone."

I nodded, blinked, and when my eyes opened, he had disappeared.

I stood there, swaying, drinking it all in. Then I stepped up Valentine's corpse. It was still steaming with wisps of color and fire, but fading fast. I stood there, watching him go, my skin tingling with magic as the last streamers from his tattoos faded into darkness.

"Guess what," I said. "It turns out I can do a trick you can't do, after all."

44. BLACK MAYDAY

Grimacing in pain, I used the clippers to cut Jinx and Cinnamon down and then tried to free them from the silver barbed wire. Jinx was easy, but Cinnamon was damn near hopeless—and the wires on her wrists cut so deep into the flesh I couldn't get the clippers in there without hurting her more, so I just cut the wires between them, leaving her with two bloody silver bracelets. My hands were tingling with pain, but I tried to carefully clip the wires out of her mouth; when I was done her mouth hung slack and I could barely hear her breathing.

I stared at the others. Wulf looked dead, but Jinx was still whole; Alex and Lord Buckhead were pretty trashed, but they were all breathing, if not stirring; they'd hold. I untied them, prayed to God that they'd hold, and carried Cinnamon up out of Hell. At first I was relieved when I saw that the guards I'd incapacitated were gone, but then I realized that meant they were alive and conscious. I didn't wait to find out whether they were running or plotting: I just ran straight out into the street.

Knee and hands throbbing with pain, I hobbled out across North Avenue, leaving the Masquerade behind, alternately heedless of and wincing at the gravel and glass scattered across the pavement. I headed straight for City Hall East, for the police entrance, where cop cars left after refueling in the night. One black-and-white was pulling out of the gate just as I stumbled up, and I ran straight for it. They came to a screeching halt just as I ran out of gas, gasping, depositing Cinnamon on their hood.

"Holy Mary," the driving officer said, only half stepping out of his car, holding a flashlight with one hand and with his other reaching for . . . his sidearm?

"Help, help, we've been attacked," I said, bending involuntarily as my knee began throbbing like mad. "I and my friends have just been attacked in the Masquerade. I need you to call for backup and ambulances—"

"What the hell you think this one's been on?" the second officer said, crawling out of the car. "And look at the state of the other one—"

I realized how I must look—bruised, naked, with a flapping black coat, carrying a bloody young girl outfitted in the most realistic tiger costume they'd ever seen. They thought we were drugged-out prostitutes, and were tuning out everything I was saying, assuming I was babbling. *Fuck them.*

"My name is Dakota Frost," I barked. "I'm an expert witness working with Special Agent Philip Davidson of the DEI and Detective Andre Rand of Atlanta Homicide—"

The first officer was frozen, but the second was holding up her hands and saying, "Now, far out, little lady—"

"I have just been attacked," I said. "I and my friends have been attacked. This girl is dying, and at least four other people are injured in the Masquerade. We need ambulances and backup in case Mirabilus had any other help—"

"Mirabilus?" the female officer said. "Like the Mysterious Mirabilus—"

"What the fuck is wrong with you?" I said, glaring at her.

"Settle down, now," the female officer said. "I now you've been through a lot—"

Damnit, they were thinking that whatever I'd been through was over, but for all I knew the guards were coming back with shotguns to clean up the evidence. I needed help. We needed help. For a moment I thought of lunging for the car's radio and calling for help myself, but my dad was on the force: I knew I'd never make it. Something more subtle was required.

So I did the first thing that came to mind. It's lame, I know, but it works: I swayed.

"Oh God," I said, tottering. Then I leaned heavily on the hood. "Can—can I sit down for a minute?"

"Sure thing, little lady," the female officer said. She stepped to the back passenger door and opened it, and I smiled weakly, leaning on the car with one hand as I walked around it—but as I passed the front passenger door I dove in and shot one long arm in to grab the car's mike.

"Black Mayday, Black Mayday, D-E-I assets down, Black Mayday, Black Mayday—"

"God damn you, you tricky bitch," the female officer said, hauling me out, twisting my arm round and slamming my cheek to the hood of the car. I screamed and bucked at the pain in my hand, but she twisted harder and pushed me down. "Jeez, she's strong," she said, and I winced as a cuff went on one wrist. "Help me—"

I bucked up and clocked the woman in the jaw with the back of my head, and then the other officer surged around the car and pinned me down in. "You shouldn't have done that," he said, grasping my other squirming wrist and cuffing it too. "She's my *partner*—"

"Go easy," I heard the female officer say. "Look at what they've been through. Between the drugs and whatever their pimp did to them she's probably out of her mind—"

And then the most beautiful sound I'd ever heard swept over us, a rising, high-pitched purring like a mechanical cat—or a muffled leafblower, sweeping out of City Hall East and swooping over us in a sudden gust of wind. A bright light pinned us all, followed by an eruption of red and blue flashing lights as a DEI Shadowhawk decloaked above us.

"This is the Department of Extraordinary Investigations!" Philip's voice roared over the PA. "Officers stand down! APD officers stand down!"

"Boy, that was quick," I muttered under my breath.

The Shadowhawk set down in the middle of North Avenue, its whirling blades whipping over our heads as Philip leapt out, brandishing his badge and shouting, "D-E-I agent! Officers stand down, stand down! DEI agent! Stand down, stand down!"

"Holy . . . cow," the officer said, releasing me.

Philip ran up, holding his badge up like a shield, shades glowing red like night-vision goggles and carrying an enormous black combat shotgun carefully pointed away from the APD officers. "Special Agent Philip Davidson, DEI! Miss Frost, Miss Frost, are you all right?"

"I'm not hurt," I said, "but the tattoo killer tortured Cinnamon to get to me."

"Damnit!" Philip shouted, staring straight at me, then surveying Cinnamon, the officers, and the rest of the scene in one quick glance.

Then he threw the shotgun over his shoulder and scooped Cinnamon off the hood of the car. "Pilot! I need an emergency evac—"

"If you disappear her, I will *kill* you," I shouted after him.

Philip nodded, never looking back. "Emory Hospital—special emergencies unit, stat!"

Philip deposited Cinnamon in the back of the Shadowhawk and stepped back, motioning to another officer, who was already grabbing a first aid kit as Philip closed the door and whirled his hand for the black helicopter to lift off. It left the ground in a rising whine, and Philip bore down on us in a whirlwind of debris and rage.

"Half of Little Five Points is bleeding out in the Masquerade," I shouted. "Alex, Jinx, Wulf, Buck—and would someone get these cuffs off me!"

"Do it," Philip said. "What are we facing in there?"

"The killer was Christopher Valentine—*yes!*—but he's dead," I said, as the female officer freed my hands. "He was controlling Wulf through a magic tattoo. And guess who was helping him—our favorite poseur vampire!"

"Transomnia," Philip snarled. "Are they still in there?"

"Transomnia skipped, and Wulf is dying and Mirabilus is dead," I said, "but they had a buttload of guards. I took them out when I arrived—"

"*You* took them out?" the first cop said. "*How?*"

"Magic," I responded. "But all of the guards were gone when I came out. I don't know if they're gone or just regrouping—"

"Aw, *hell*," Philip said, looking off sharply—sirens started blaring out of City Hall East, and I heard more approaching rapidly from the distance. "And now we're about to get a swarm of badges descending on a sea of Edgeworlders. It can't ever be easy, can it?"

He stood there, just a moment; then he came to a decision.

"Ladies and gentlemen," Philip said, loudly, as if he was speaking to far more than just the two officers. "We have five victims, including one witch and one werewolf—yes!—at the mercy of the minions of a serial killer. I need you at my back, but be sharp! Don't plug anyone just because they look odd or furry! Let's move."

They ran. I realized he hadn't asked me where to go, what else to look for. He just ran for the Masquerade, and the two officers followed him without a second thought. I tried to follow, but the pebbles and glass that I had sailed over before brought me to a standstill when I was halfway there. The sirens and the lights grew louder and louder, but I kept walking, walking towards the Masquerade. I was shaking when an officer stepped up beside me, covered my shoulders in a blanket, and sat me in the open door of his police cruiser.

And the rising whine of the Shadowhawk returned—one, then two, then more, backed by a deeper thrum. I and the new officer looked up to see three Shadowhawks decloak around the Masquerade, disgorging black-suited officers that rappelled down to join the fray. Above them, the long cigar shape of a zeppelin was dimly visible, its black metal hide illuminated by the backwash of a huge spotlight.

"Holy . . . cow," the officer said, just like the first one had.

"You're telling me," I said.

∜ ● ∜

Most of Mirabilus's thugs were gone. Philip said they rounded up one minion holed up under the bar in Purgatory—Baldy, who turned out to be the same low-rent gun thug that had gone after me during the stage show but ended up plugging 'Mirabilus'. True to form, the former stage magician had used a plant to 'fake' (or at least keep control over) his own shooting. They also picked up a confused and astounded chauffeur who had been waiting for Mirabilus and company to return to his rented car, but Philip seemed to have already checked the guy's story out by the time he got back to me, two hot steaming coffees in his hands.

"Mirabilus is dead," he said, looking back at the Masquerade, "but you're right—no sign of Transomnia."

"Transomnia helped me at the end," I said. "Said Mirabilus was using him."

"He's an accessory to murder," Philip said. "You're not suggesting we let him go?"

I pulled back my right lip to expose my missing molars. "You won't hear that from me," I said, "but you won't see me going after him, even if I thought I could take him."

"Fair enough," Philip said. He sighed. "The medics did what they could to revive him but . . . we were too late to save Wulf."

"I know," I said. "I know."

256

He reached out and took me into his arms, kissed my forehead, held me while I cried. "I know," he said. "I know."

"He just wanted my help," I said. "Just wanted a normal life—"

"Hey," he said. "You saved a young girl today, and your friends. We lose some, but we win some."

"Fair enough," I said, wiping my cheek. "What about North Carolina?"

"Goose chase," he said. "We're holding the girl. She claims she was just trying to create trouble for her boyfriend, but she's got a relatively new magical tattoo—"

"Controlling charm," I said.

"Given what I saw of Mirabilus and Wulf," Philip said, "Oh yeah."

"I'm sorry I didn't call you sooner," I said.

"Kidnappings always make for tough calls," he said softly. "You did the right thing. Jinx's boy Doug *tried* to call it in—"

"Good for him," I said. "*Good* Doug!"

"Ha," Philip replied. "But he got routed to 911 hell, very hinky—"

"Mirabilus again," I said bitterly. "He was bragging about it."

Philip nodded. "By the time he'd given up and drove down to the police station, the shit had already hit the fan."

"At least he tried," I said. "More sense than the rest of us—"

"None of this is your fault," Philip said. "*None* of it."

"I know, I know," I said. But I had trouble believing it, looking over at the ambulances, at the one pulling away, and the one waiting on a body bag to be loaded. "But still . . . I just have one question."

"Shoot," Philip said.

"That damn box," I said. "Mirabilus didn't use it to take down Buck, and it didn't look like he was going to use it in the ceremony on me. He went on and on about the Children of this and the Inheritance of that, but never mentioned the box. But it was far too sophisticated a magic to imagine it was just a trophy. So . . . what the *fuck* was it for?"

"I have a better question," he replied. "Mirabilus *was* killing people and taking their tattoos to put on that damn box," Philip said. "But it wasn't *his* damn box."

I just stared at him.

"When we got the lid, we also got some of his notes," Philip said. "I've read them. From what I can tell . . . up until recently

Mirabilus *was* just eliminating the competition. The tattoo harvesting is something new, just a silver lining, so to speak, that turned his hobby into profitable work he could do for someone else. The box was a *commission*."

"So, if it wasn't his . . ." I said, horrified.

"Then *who* was it made for?" Philip said, touching his hand to his ear, "Yes, this is Special Agent Davidson. Yes, I'm with Frost. No, she—there's a problem with her *what?*"

"What is it?" I asked. Philip's eyes had bugged and he was looking at me strangely.

"No, I don't think she has a—yes, that was the—" His eyes narrowed and his face grew hard, stony. "We'll be there right away." He took his hand out of his ear and stood, motioning to me. "We gotta go. We'll take a Shadowhawk—it's faster."

"What's wrong?" I asked, standing as well. "Where are we going?"

"Emory," Philip said. "Cinnamon is dying."

45. Silver Shock

Cinnamon lay in the hospital bed, bedraggled and alone.

The rest of us recovered quickly. Buckhead healed on his own. Alex needed only minor patching. I ended up back in the hospital for one more day—mostly scrapes and bruises, but the real problem was my hands—the doctors said that if Transomnia had heated the pitch to boiling, my hands would have been scalded instantly, and the complications could have killed me. As it was, I escaped with minor burns, where goop had collected at the forks of my fingers.

Jinx was recovering as well. When Valentine opened her eyes, he dispersed the fungal opacity and let in far more light than her shrouded retinas were ready to handle—but not enough to cause damage. Her spooky geode eyes now have black snowflakes, letting her see a little. For now, she was stuck wearing darkened shades, but the doctors said that eventually, when her retinas finally adjusted, she might regain as much as ten percent of her vision. Who knew what that would do to her magic?

As for Cinnamon . . .

At first the doctors called it 'hyperargyria'—silver shock—a kind of blood poisoning peculiar to shapechangers that can be caused by just trace amounts of silver in the blood. With her massive dose, she slipped into a coma, face ashen gray and gums blue, heart palpitating every time they laid her on her back. When we got to the hospital she was in the middle of a seizure, and they came damn near close to losing her.

But they didn't. She survived the night, barely, and they called in specialists who knew how to handle silver shock—rolling her on her side to stop the shaking, clearing her blood of trace silver with something like dialysis, and feeding her intravenously to build up her strength.

But apparently silver poisoning *also* wreaks havoc on shapechangers' immune systems. Not a week into her treatment, just one day after she came out of her coma, her fever shot back up and she started hallucinating. An opportunistic pneumonia had settled in her lungs, sending her back into the ICU; and when the doctors fought that off with one cocktail of drugs, she picked up another kind of blood poisoning, a flesh eating bacteria called MRSA—same brand that had attacked Valentine's *projectia*—that they think she picked up from a bad IV administration. They moved her to a special ward of the hospital, and we all had to wipe our hands with sanitizer every time we left her room.

It took until damn near Thanksgiving for her to fight it off, but at long last, her fever broke and she finally started improving. I was there, every day, sometimes in the morning, sometimes on my break, sometimes in the evening—often, all three—talking with her, cheering her up, slipping her coffee or éclairs, bringing her teen magazines and audiobooks of Laurell Hamilton and gossip about the boys back at the werehouse.

So now it was the Saturday after Thanksgiving, and everyone was out of town or off at parties—Philip back in Virginia, Savannah with her vampire clan, the werekin with their mundane families, the collegiates back in their hometowns, even the hospital priest was gone, helping out with a benefit for the homeless.

And so it was just up to me to show up at the hospital, seeing Cinnamon, lying there like a bedraggled cat, suddenly brought back to life when I walked in the door; and then suddenly we began talking and joking and laughing at all the were-mistakes in *Underworld: Evolution* as it played on the hospital TV.

And it was only then that I noticed she was wearing on her wrist one of those snap-on hospital nametags, just like I wore when I was a patient, not a month ago. And for some reason, I noticed, really noticed the name on it: Cinnamon Frost. Dimly I remembered the doctors telling me the DEI officers had to guess at her name, and had just assumed that Cinnamon was my daughter. I had laughed, saying that no mother would just have left her daughter alone with the medics, but I didn't really object. And then, as I looked at the bracelet, I realized in the whole month that I'd been there I had *never* objected or corrected them—nor had she.

And around this point I realized: I'd decided to adopt Cinnamon.

"So, Cinnamon," I said, reaching out to pat her tufted little hand. "I was thinking, you know, about you not having a mom."

"What of it?" she said, suddenly sullen.

"Well, I don't have a daughter."

Cinnamon looked up at me in shock. Her eyes grew all shiny and large, though it was difficult for me to see it with all the water building in mine. Then she reached over and grabbed me and pulled me too her and held on tight, claws pricking me gently through my shirt.

"Mom?" She said the word so gently, it was like magic. And then she bawled. "Oh, Mom. Oh, my *Mooooom*."

"It's okay, Cinnamon," I said, patting her head. "I'm so glad I found you."

Yeah, yeah, I know: sappy as hell. Wake the fuck up. When people talk in real life, they don't make up all sorts of flowery phrases to say what they feel; they say the first thing that comes to mind and then sit there holding each other, glad to be alive.

And we did just sit there, for a long long time, her hugging me hard enough to squeeze the air from my lungs, me cradling her and stroking her soft, feline ears and cooing softly. Finally she said, "How is this going to work?"

"I don't know, Cinnamon," I said. "You're a bit big for me to tell you to clean your room."

"Oh, Mom," she sobbed. "Give me a room, and you can tell me to clean it anytime."

46. PAYOFF

The Valentine Foundation is going to pay out. I'm not joking. It's a big scandal. There are half a dozen investigations ongoing, but apparently Mirabilus was playing his cards *very* close to his chest, because the Foundation appears *completely* legit. In fact their board was *mortified* to find out that Valentine had been killing potential prizewinners. The money may be tied up for years in court until the investigations around Mirabilus are settled, but the hands of Alex's wristwatch tattoo are still turning, counting out one day for each turn of the Earth beneath the stars—and so they're going to pay out.

Even better, I didn't win just by default—there's a clause in the contract which stipulates that if one party in the challenge fails to even attempt the feat, the result is decided not by default, but by a panel of experts. They lined up a half dozen of them, but not one of them could explain through trickery or science how it I made a tattoo watch actually rotate. That only left magic as an explanation.

Footage of me putting the watch on Alex even made it into the promos for the next season of the Valentine Foundation's cable show—and so business at the shop has been booming. I've even managed to turn the loss of my tattoos into a benefit: I held public inkings for the butterfly and the snake, and plan to do the hawk next month. The Dragon, on the other hand, my masterwork . . . will take more time.

Cinnamon is going to be more than I can handle. She's *officially* taken over my storage room for her bedroom and *unofficially* taken over the rest of my flat besides. I'm sure there will be a thousand forms and pieces of paperwork we're going to need to sign to make this official, but I can deal with that. What I'm really dreading is the next step: she can barely read, so I'm planning to enroll her in school.

If you thought cats would scratch you if you put them in the shower, you ain't seen nothing yet. Send iodine this Christmas.

Savannah and Darkrose have been hunting for Transomnia. We think the little shit's left town. At this point I'd be inclined to let him go—without him, Cinnamon and I would be dead. Of course, without him I'd have all my natural teeth, but I've worked up a payment plan to do some tats for my dentist in case the money from the challenge gets tied up in red tape.

I'm still wearing Saffron's collar. I hate it, Darkrose offered to remove it, but Savannah overruled her. I think she's right—I almost died even *with* her protection—but I'd feel a lot more comfortable about it if I didn't know she was enjoying it.

The Masquerade will remain open, for now. The publicity was good for it—as was the death of Mirabilus. It turns out *he* was behind the land deal that had closed the Masquerade—one of a half-dozen other shady land deals uncovered when Jack Conway finally tracked down the mysterious server failures at APD. Mirabilus, or one of his pawns, had hacked the entire City Hall East network, enabling him to intercept 911 calls, create fake land-use permits, change the A/C settings and God knows what else. Until it's sorted out, the Masquerade stays open. Hooray.

I've made one call to Stratton, South Carolina, to make peace with my Dad. He was pleased to hear from me. I had expected him to give me shit about my tattoos, about never calling; but he had heard through the grapevine all the things that had happened, and just cried and told me again and again how happy he was that I was alive. Apparently he isn't *that* happy—he still won't get in a car and drive a hundred and fifty miles to Atlanta, to see me. I didn't tell him about Cinnamon yet. It didn't seem like the time to mention his new granddaughter, a weretiger.

Philip is gone, most of the time. He's on some kind of circuit over the Southeast. I never found out what the stealth shape was, that night outside the Masquerade—he just said, "Well, we can't always get the Shadowhawks where we need them quickly enough, it's not like we can haul them on the back of a flatbed." He's similarly tightlipped about who might have given Mirabilus the box as a commission. But when he *is* in town, once every month or so, I buy him coffee, and he takes me out to the gun range for target practice. We aren't calling it *dating* yet, but here's hoping we'll start.

Isn't all that *great?* Doesn't it sound so *wonderful?* Happy, happy, joy, joy.

But the truth is I still wake up almost every night, sometimes screaming, sometimes crying, always holding my right hand in my left, massaging my first two fingers, reassuring myself they're still there. Sometimes it's Transomnia in my dreams, red eyes gleaming as he snips my fingers off one by one; sometimes it's Mirabilus, blue chips of ice glinting as he strips the skin off my back; and sometimes, I just plain wake up screaming.

When I do, Cinnamon comes and curls up in the bed beside me to comfort me; but just as often she wakes up bawling, holding herself, shivering, and I have to comfort *her*. And that's when the worst feeling sets in: that I could have *done* something, that I could have *stopped* the trouble earlier. That I could have kept Cinnamon out of it. That I could have seen the trap Transomnia was in and helped him escape sooner. That I could have kept Wulf out of that damn body bag.

No, I'm not going to become a police officer, or a bounty hunter, or a detective, or anything like that. I like tattooing, and I'm not going to give it up.

But I *have* started karate, three times a week. Darren is amazing. He's working with my physical therapist to help design a program to get me up and running as fast as possible. In the meantime, I get to see him run up a wall at the end of every class.

And, in addition to the karate, I have two other new weekly appointments—one with Jinx to school me in graphomancy and help me master the power in my tattoos, and one with Canon Grace, to help me decide what I *should* do with my powers.

I will not hide. I will not run. I will *not* live in fear.

Because I'm not just a tattooist.

I'm Dakota Frost, and I'm a skindancer.

கை ● இ

The Dance Continues
Coming Next

SKINDANCER
Blood Rock
Excerpt

From the outside, my baby blue Prius looks as normal as can be: a streamlined bubble of a car with an aerodynamic rear-hitch bike rack, humming along on a hybrid gas/electric engine. She couldn't scream 'liberal soccer mom' louder if she was a Volvo plastered with NPR stickers. Peer inside, however, and you see something completely different.

In the driver's seat, yours truly: a six-foot-two woman with a purple-and-black Mohawk, short in front, *a la* Grace Jones, but lengthening in back until it becomes a long tail curling around my neck. Striking, yes, but what really draws your eyes are my tattoos.

A rainbow of tribal daggers curls under the perimeter of my Mohawk, starting at my temples, cascading down my neck, rippling out over my arms, and exploding in colorful braids of vines and jewels and butterflies. Beautiful, yes, but that's not why you can't look away—its because, out of the corner of your eye, you saw my tattoos *move*—there, they did it again! You swear, that leaf fluttered, that gem sparkled. It's like *magic!*

Why, yes, they did move, and yes, they are magic. Thanks for noticing. All inked at the Rogue Unicorn by yours truly, Dakota Frost, best magical tattooist in the Southeast.

Beside me sits a five-nothing teenaged girl, listening to a podcast on her iPod. Normally she's dressed in a vest and Capri pants, but today she's in a shockingly conservative schoolgirl's outfit that clashes with her orange hair and elaborate tiger-striped tattoos.

At first what you see is easy to interpret: an outsider trying to fit in, or a rebel forced to fit in. But then your eyes do another double take: are those . . . *cat ears* poking out from beneath her head scarf? Did they *move?* And is that a *tail?* My God, honey, could she be one of those . . . what are they called . . . "werecats"?

Why yes, her ears did move, and yes, she's a weretiger. But didn't your mom tell you it's rude to point? She has a name, Cinnamon Frost, and she's my adopted daughter.

Both the Prius and the weretiger in its passenger seat are relatively new to me. I met Cinnamon only two months ago visiting a local werehouse to research a werewolf tattoo, and ended up adopting her after rescuing her from a serial killer who had used her to get to me. I picked up the Prius shortly thereafter, a little splurge after winning a tattooing contest.

The adjustment was hard at first: Cinnamon took over my house and tried to take over my life. But my Mom had been a schoolteacher, and I'd learned a few tricks. In the first few weeks after she moved in I put the hammer down, never smiling, setting clear boundaries for *her* behavior and *my* sanity. Finally—when she got past the point of the tears, the "not-fairs," and the most egregious misbehaviors—I eased up, and we once again shared the easy "gee you're a square but I like you anyway" camaraderie we'd started with.

Now we were peas in a pod; whenever I went out she tagged along, riding shotgun, listening to her audiobooks while I jammed to Rush. The two of us look as different as can be, except for the identical stainless steel collars about our necks, but one minute seeing the two of us laughing together and you'd think I'd been her mother for her whole life.

But today my sunny bundle of fur was feeling quite sullen.

"Don't worry," I said, patting her knee softly. "*One* of them will accept you."

"Yeah, yeah," she said, pulling her leg away and tucking her knees under her chin. Cinnamon *claimed* she didn't want to go to school, but I'd learned her moods and knew that not only did she *want* to go to school, she'd had her heart set on *that* school, and was crushed to be rejected out of hand. She propped her head on her knees and stared out into the gentle leafy tunnel that was Ponce de Leon Avenue. "Just don't you be sorrying me about it."

"Who, *me*?" I said, grinning. "Do *I* say sorry? Oh, I'm *so* sorry—"

"Don't you be starting that," she said, putting her knuckles in her ears. Unlike a normal human, actually putting her long, clawed fingers into her huge cat ears could prove dangerous. Werekin could heal most normal damage pretty quick, unless it was dealt by something silver—but still, she tries to be careful. "Don't even be funning about it—"

My cell rang and I gave it a squeeze to pick up. I loved my new Bluetooth earpiece, even though our receptionist at the Rogue Unicorn Tattooing Studio told me it made me look like I'd been 'possessed by the Cybermen,' whatever that meant. "Dakota Frost," I said. "Best magical tattooist in the Southeast—"

"Dakota," Uncle Andy said. "It's Rand. Where are you?"

"Out school shopping with Cinnamon," I said. When I was a kid, "Uncle" Andy was my father's partner; now that I was an adult, *Detective* Andre Rand was my guardian angel in the Atlanta Police Department. Normally smooth, he sounded *very* stressed—and that scared the hell out of me. "What's wrong?"

"Whats happened?" Cinnamon said suddenly, staring at me. "Who died?"

Immediately when she said it, I felt she was right. Something catches in a person's voice when they report death. Listen for it, in those few horrible times in your life when someone around you gets the call: you can tell it from the grief in their voice, from the crumple in their reaction. Even a news announcer goes sad and sullen if they care one whit about who died.

"Andre," I said, more urgently this time. "What's wrong? Is someone hurt?"

"How quickly can you get over to the Oakland Cemetery?" he said.

I scowled; that was downtown, south of the last school. "Ten minutes."

"Whatever you do, hurry," he said. "Just—hurry."

The phone hung up and I cursed, punching the trip computer to find the fastest route.

"Don't be using that thing," Cinnamon said, snapping her head aside in a kind of a sneeze. "It will rots your maps right out of your brain—"

"Crap," I said. "It's not going to let me do this while we're moving—"

"Whip us round, takes Moreland to Memorial," Cinnamon said. She pointed at an upcoming street. "No. Hooks right here, then rights on Fairview, *then* Moreland."

I raised an eyebrow. "Not bad for someone new to downtown—"

"Don't be so shocked," she said. "I catches on fast."

We shot down a mile of old warehouses and new apartments on Memorial before reaching the brick ramparts of Oakland Cemetery at the cross street of Boulevard. The winter chill had long since stripped the leaves off the trees, leaving branches stretched to the cloudy sky like the claws of dying things pleading to Heaven.

When we hooked around to the entrance, we found an officer guarding the driveway. As we pulled up to the striped sawhorse, I steeled myself for a runaround. My dad was on the force, Rand was a friend, heck, I was even sort of dating a Fed—but somehow six-foot-two tattoos-and-Mohawk just doesn't mix well with cop.

But the officer's eyes lit up when he saw us. He didn't even check for ID—he just pulled the sawhorse out of the way and waved us forward. This was bad—they'd closed off the whole cemetery, and it was huge. I rolled down my window and asked, "Which way—"

"You Frost? Straight back," he said, eyes a little wild. "Straight back! And hurry!"

"This is bad," Cinnamon said, head craning back to look at the officer. "Rand's sweet on ya but we never gets special treatments from the piggies—"

"Don't call them 'piggies'," I said, swallowing, speeding down the tiny road.

"Why?" she asked, flicking an ear at me. "They can't hears us."

"And you knows that none of them are weres?" I asked, miming her broken diction. "You knows for sures?"

Her face fell. "No, I don't."

We bumped down a worn asphalt road through a canyon of elaborate Victorian markers and rows of Confederate graves. I grew more and more apprehensive as I saw officers spreading through the homes of the dead, searching. The road sunk down, the graves grew smaller, more sad, and we rolled to a halt in a forest of headstones at the bottom of the hill between the Jewish section and Potter's field.

What seemed like a thousand flashing lights waited for us: police cars, an ambulance, even a firetruck, surrounding a crowd of uniforms, paramedics and firemen gathered at the end of the road in front of the low brick wall that ringed the cemetery. Striding out of them was a sharply dressed black man, bald as Kojak and twice as handsome: Detective Andre Rand.

I opened the door, my boots crunched on gravel, and my vestcoat swished as I stepped out of the car, *fhwapping* behind me in the wind as I slammed the door shut. The eyes of the officers fell on me, narrowing; I became acutely conscious of my Mohawk, of my tattoos, of my leather pants and ankle-length faux-snakeskin vestcoat: they all felt conspicuously out of place in this land of grey tombs and black uniforms. I'd felt more comfortable talking to the buttoned-down principal of the school we'd just visited; now I just wanted to go and change.

"Hi, Rand," I said, forced cheerful, putting my hand on Cinnamon's shoulder as she materialized in front of me—though she had drawn so close it felt like she was hiding behind. "Whats you— ahem. What do you have for me?"

At my grammatical slip Rand glanced down at Cinnamon briefly, trying to smile. His neck was wrapped in a stylish turtleneck, not unlike mine, but the rest of him was in one of his GQ suits that never seemed to get dirty no matter what he'd gone through. Today, however . . . his suit was torn. There was blood on the back of his hand. And not even Cinnamon could spark a smile. Rand was off his game, and I was getting more and more worried.

He glanced up, scowling. "Dakota, thanks for rushing. We really need you but . . . this is bad. Really bad. Cinnamon can wait in—"

"I can takes whatever you gots," Cinnamon said indignantly.

He nodded sharply, turning back to the knot of officers. "Alright. Let me show you—"

"No-one thinks to ask me whether *I* can take it," I said, stepping round Cinnamon.

Rand grinned back at me, but just kept walking. "McGough," he said, "this is Dakota Frost. I think she can help us—"

"Well let's hope somebody can, we're outta options," said a small, wiry, wizardly looking man wrapped in a Columbo trench. Like Rand, his coat was torn, his hands bloodied, but where Rand was thrown off his game, McGough's movements were still crisp, his eyes sharp. A few nicks and cuts? *Bah.* Didn't even slow him down.

But when he saw me, his eyes lit up in surprise. "Jeez, you're tall."

"And a happy hello to you too," I said, followed slowly by, "Detective McGough."

He looked down at Cinnamon, scowling. "You really want a minor on the scene?" Rand and I just looked at him, and Cinnamon raised a clawed hand and mimed a swat. "Fine, fine," he said. "When DFACS comes calling, don't come crying to me."

"DEE-fax?" I muttered.

"Department of Family and—" Rand began.

"Alright, boys and girls," McGough cracked with authority, wading back into the officers. They all jumped; he was little taller than Cinnamon, but his presence dominated the scene. "Move aside and let's see if Rand's pet witch can figure out how to handle this."

Before I could even *try* to correct the 'pet witch' crack, the officers—all nervous, most worried, many nicked up like they'd been in a fight with a cat—parted so I could see the outer wall. My breath caught, and it took me a moment to realize what I was seeing.

The brick wall was sprayed with graffiti, a huge shock of exaggerated letters exploding out of a coiling nest of elaborately thorned vines. The graffiti "tag" was amazing work—even *I* had to admire the roses woven into the vines, and they're a specialty of mine—but it was just background. Dead in the center of the tag, a man was crucified in a web of barbed wire, half-standing, half-sprawling in a splash of his own blood.

The man moaned and raised his head—and with a shock I recognized him: Revenance, a friend we knew as a guard at the werehouse—and a vampire of the Oakdale Clan. *What was he doing out in the day?* Automatically I looked up for the sun. I relaxed when I saw it hidden by clouds—and then something clicked in my mind, and I looked back in growing horror.

Revenance wasn't crucified in the wires, but in the graffiti itself. The painted vines had erupted from the wall, fully dimensional, moving like they were alive, curling around him, hooking into his flesh, drawing blood and pulling outward—pulling as we watched.

The graffiti was tearing him apart.

Acknowledgements

It's been a long road from my first stories in grade school to that night in 2007 when Cinnamon burst her way into the werehouse, and it would be hard to thank all the friends, family, teachers and colleagues who have helped me along the way. So I'll thank instead all the people who helped me after I emerged from the haze of graduate school and began writing again in earnest.

First there are the Dragon Writers, the alumni of Ann Crispin's Writer's Workshop at DragonCon 2002 who have stuck together for all these years providing fellowship, critiques and moral support; then there's National Novel Writing Month, a November challenge which prompted me to start writing novels again. But it wasn't until I found the Writing Group at Barnes and Noble at Steven's Creek in San Jose that things really began to gel.

The Writing Group's facilitator, Keiko, set the tone with her innovative writing prompts and "we write, not critique" policy. Group regulars like Gayle, Liza, Carl, Mel, and Matthew have all worked together to create a wonderful environment for many writers to grow. Much of Frost Moon, including the first meeting of Cinnamon and Dakota, was written in 20 minute chunks at the Writing Group and then read aloud to the most supportive yet honest audience I could ask for. Thank you guys.

Frost Moon is deliberately set in a world next door, and I am indebted to my research staff: to David for info about the APD, to Vandybeth for background on vampires, to William for his descriptions of Atlanta, to Keiko for linguistic analysis, and to my wife Sandi for character backgrounds. And my apologies to the whole city of Atlanta, which I metaphysically abused to wedge Dakota and her world right into the middle of landmarks like City Hall East and Little Five Points.

Frost Moon benefited greatly from the invaluable critique of my beta readers: Keiko, Gayle, Mel, Liza and Betsy at the Writing Group, also my wife Sandi, father-in-law Wally, and stepmother-in-law Barb (who copyedited it and read it aloud as an audiobook); and my good friends in the "Edge" from whom Atlanta's Edgeworld got its name: the betas from the Edge included Fred, Diane, Gordon, and Dave.

Frost Moon would not be in your hands if it wasn't for Bell Bridge Books. Thanks to Nancy for noticing me typing away in the Dragon Con Writer's Track and recommending Bell Bridge Books to me, to Debra for taking a chance on me and for her detailed editorial feedback, and to Debs putting up with me endlessly tweaking the manuscript days before the deadline.

And finally, thanks go out to the Big G. You know who you are.

-the Centaur, February 10, 2010

About Anthony Francis

Dr. Anthony G. Francis, Jr. graduated from Georgia Tech in 2000 with a PhD in computer science and a certificate in Cognitive Science. In academia he applied principles of human memory to computer information retrieval; in industry he's worked on software for search engines, robot pets, the military, the police and the CDC. Anthony spent most of his adult life in Atlanta, Georgia but he and his wife moved to San Jose, California when he joined Google's search quality group. Perhaps surprisingly, Anthony has no tattoos, though he has spun fire and is a brown belt in the martial art Taido. Anthony is a science fiction author and a comic book artist and loves exploring the collision of hard science with pure fantasy. *Frost Moon* is the first in the *Skindancer* urban fantasy series, in which he has two books written, two trilogies planned, and has also started a YA spin-off featuring Dakota's adopted daughter, Cinnamon. You can visit him and learn more about the world of Dakota Frost at www.dakotafrost.com

Frost Moon